BLOOD
of the
DEMON

DIANA ROWLAND

BANTAM BOOKS

NEW YORK

A Bantam Books Mass Market Original

Copyright © 2010 by Diana Rowland

Published in the United States by Bantam,
an imprint of The Random House Publishing Group,
a division of Random House, Inc., New York.

BANTAM is a registered trademark of Random House, Inc.,
and the rooster colophon is a trademark of Random House, Inc.

978-0-553-59236-8

Cover design: Dreu Pennington-McNeil
Cover illustration: Juliana Kolesova

Printed in the United States of America

www.bantamdell.com

2 4 6 8 9 7 5 3 1

PRAISE FOR *MARK OF THE DEMON*

"*Mark of the Demon* is a nifty combination of police procedural and urban fantasy. Not too many detectives summon demons in their basement for the fun of it, but Kara Gillian is not your average law enforcement officer. In the course of Rowland's first book, Kara learns a lot about demons, her past, and above all, herself."

—CHARLAINE HARRIS, *New York Times* bestselling author of *From Dead to Worse*

"*Mark of the Demon* crosses police procedure with weird magic. Diana Rowland's background makes her an expert in the former, and her writing convinces me she's also an expert in the latter in this fast-paced story that ends with a bang."

—CARRIE VAUGHN, *New York Times* bestselling author of *Kitty Raises Hell*

"If Karen Chance and Kim Harrison's books had a baby and that baby was a ninja, it would be *Mark of the Demon*."

—ANN AGUIRRE, national bestselling author of *Blue Diablo*

"Rowland spins a tale that is riveting, suspenseful, and deliciously sexy. With a unique take on demons, and with one of the most terrifying serial killers ever, *Mark of the Demon* will keep you up late at night turning pages."

—JENNA BLACK, author of *Speak of the Devil*

"*Mark of the Demon* is a fascinating mixture of a hard-boiled police procedural and gritty yet otherworldly urban fantasy. Diana Rowland's professional background as both a street cop and forensic assistant not only shows through but gives the book a realism sadly lacking in all too many urban fantasy 'crime' novels."

—L. E. MODESITT JR., author of the *Saga of Recluce*

"A well-woven supernatural procedural that keeps the pages turning, hooking you on both the characters and the crime."

—LAURA ANNE GILMAN, author of *Free Fall*

"In a world full of paint-by-numbers urban fantasy, *Mark of the Demon* is a breath of fresh air. Diana Rowland brings a cop's cynical eye and gallows humor along with a great sense of storytelling to make this one of the standout books in the field. I'm looking forward to the next one."

—M. L. N. HANOVER, author of *Unclean Spirits*

"A highly polished supernatural crime thriller... From the forensic and police procedures to the descriptions and dialogue, every facet has the ring of authenticity.... A great part of the success of this novel is how well the supernatural elements are integrated and grounded into a real-world crime procedural.... If I had read this book as a 'blind test' I would have guessed it to be the author's seventh or eighth novel. It really is that good.... This is a very exciting urban fantasy debut."

—SciFiGuy

"Diana Rowland's *Mark of the Demon* is like an episode of *CSI*... only with more realistic science, better police procedural, and *demons*.... *Mark of the Demon* is fast-paced and fun. It's sour, bitter, sweet, salty, and sexy. It's science without technobabble, and gritty without being gross.... After gobbling up this debut, I'm really looking forward to what Diana Rowland offers us next!"

—*InterGalactic Medicine Show*

"*Mark of the Demon* floored me. Completely. I could NOT put this book down for a single minute.... Action, arcane witchcraft, demons, and dream travel—I can't rave about *Mark of the Demon* enough. Part urban fantasy, part romantic suspense, *Mark of the Demon* will grab you, keep you enthralled."

—*Wild on Books*

"*Mark of the Demon* is a great novel for those who enjoy a suspenseful crime-solving mystery.... This is one great mystery.... There are twists and turns and great chemistry between Kara and Ryan.... Not to be missed."

—*Babbling About Books*

"Utilizing her real-world experience as an ex-cop/forensic assistant, debut author Rowland pulls together an edgy new urban fantasy novel that's both a police procedural and a demonic thriller. The collision of heroine Kara's dual careers sets the stage for an engrossing and gritty tale that also possesses a dangerously sexy edge. Through Kara's eyes readers get a crash course on a serial killer case with an unholy twist. Brava to Rowland for creating a vivid heroine and several transfixing secondary players." —*Romantic Times*

"From the opening sequence to the very ending, *Mark of the Demon* never loses its pace and its atmospheric feel....A very solid debut and I can definitely see a bright future for both the author and the series. Recommended."

—*The Book Smugglers*

"One of those books that starts off with a nice bang and rarely let me down from then on....Welcome to the urban fantasy genre, Ms. Rowland. Here's to many more such engrossing reads." —*Lurv a la Mode*

"A delightful collaboration of genres including urban fantasy, suspense, romance and police procedural. Debut author Diana Rowland takes everything that I love in a book and puts it all together to write an outstanding novel. Take a dash of *Charmed* mixed with some *Dexter* and you have *Mark of the Demon*....A breathtaking, heart-stopping, white-knuckler thriller that grabbed me by the throat and didn't let go!" —*Enchanted by Books*

"Excellent...Diana Rowland has hit a home run, not only with urban fantasy fans, but I believe anyone who reads forensic science/police procedure books will enjoy *Mark of the Demon* as well." —*Preternatural Reviews*

"An imaginative new entry into paranormal fiction, filled with suspense, demonic lore and a touch of spice, and let's hope there will be more of the same."

—*The Daily Advertiser* (LA)

Also by Diana Rowland

MARK OF THE DEMON

To Mom,

for supporting the arts

Acknowledgments

My name might be the only one on the cover, but there's no way this book would have happened if not for a number of other people.

Therefore, heartfelt thanks go to:

Natasha Poe, Amanda Kleist, and the rest of the St. Tammany Coroner's Forensic Science Center, for their valiant attempts to help me understand the science behind DNA testing. Any DNA-related errors in this book are completely mine.

Dr. Michael DeFatta, for answering even *more* forensic pathology questions.

Dr. Peter Galvan, Judge Don Fendlason, Tara Zeller, and District Attorney Walter Reed and his staff, for answering numerous questions concerning campaign financing, public corruption, civil forfeiture, and other legal issues that made my head hurt.

Nicole Peeler, for being a kick-ass critique partner.

My fantastic agent, Matt Bialer, and his awesome and cool assistant, Lindsay Ribar, for *everything*.

Jamie S. Warren and Juliana Kolesova, for creating such incredibly wonderful covers for my books. I am a lucky, lucky author!

David Pomerico, for continuing to answer my many stupid questions.

My fabulous and gifted editor, Anne Groell, for helping me make this book far better than it was when I first sent it to her.

My sister, Sherry Rowland, for being my biggest non-nerd fan.

And finally, extra special thanks (and hugs and kisses!) to my husband and daughter for being so incredibly patient and supportive this past year. We're going to Disney World this year. I promise!

BLOOD

of the

DEMON

THE DEMON WAS LITTLE MORE THAN A MIST OF FOG and teeth, barely visible to normal sight. It coiled in slow undulations in the backseat of my Taurus as I drove through the night, the tires of the car humming on the asphalt in low rhythmic counterpoint to the movement of the demon. The nearly full moon draped my surroundings in silver and shadow, making even this deserted highway running through a rank swamp look beautiful. There were no other headlights along this stretch of road, but this was little surprise since there were no houses or businesses out here—nothing but swamp, marsh, and the occasional patch of dry ground that pretended to be woods.

I could hear the demon murmuring softly to itself in hunger, and I stilled it with a nudge of pressure on the arcane bindings. It would feed soon enough, but I needed it to complete the agreed-upon task first. I'd dealt with this type of demon many times before and knew that the creatures were far less useful after a feed—preferring to coil in sated comfort rather than hunt.

I continued to drive until I felt the change in the demon—a sudden tension as if it had perked up its nonexistent ears. I pulled over to the side of the highway, then walked around to the other side of the car and opened the back door. It felt a bit absurd to cart a demon around in the backseat of my car, but I couldn't exactly perform a summoning out in the middle of the swamp. I was limited to summoning demons in the prepared diagram in my basement.

Murmuring again, the demon slid out in eager anticipation of a hunt. The demon was an *ilius*—a third-level demon, about as intelligent as a dog but a thousand times better at tracking. It was little more than a shifting fog, visible in my *othersight* as a coil of smoke with teeth that flashed and disappeared like a teeming mass of vaporous piranhas. Without othersight—a sense beyond the senses that revealed more than the mundane world most people were able to see—it was essentially invisible, except for the deep feeling of unease it left in those it touched.

I opened the paper bag and pulled out the baseball cap, allowing the *ilius* to twine around it and fill itself with the scent, the feel of the one I sought. "Seek," I said, and reinforced the spoken command with mental pressure. The demon shimmered in my othersight, then sped away across the grass and through the trees like an arcane zephyr.

I let my breath out as soon as it was gone, then leaned back against the car to wait for the demon's return. That it would find the missing hunter I had no doubt. Whether that hunter was alive or dead would decide my next move. I only hoped the demon wouldn't take very long. Even at four in the morning, the south Louisiana heat in July was oppressive, and out here in the middle of the swamp, the humidity was easily near a hundred percent. Sweat beaded on my face and neck and I wiped it away with a sleeve, hoping I wasn't wiping away too much of the mosquito repellent that I'd doused myself in. Hundreds of the little bloodsuckers hummed around me, but so far the repellent was keeping them at bay. At least the *ilius* didn't have to worry about mosquitoes.

There were twelve levels of demon that could be summoned by those with the ability to open a portal between this world and the demon realm. The higher the level of demon, the more powerful—and the more difficult to summon. But I'd had no need for a high-level demon for this. This summoning had been more for practice, to get my feet wet again, than anything else—though finding the idiot who'd decided to go hunting in the swamp by himself was an added benefit. But this was the first demon I'd summoned in a couple of months, and I'd needed the reassurance that I still knew what I was doing.

White-blond hair like a river of silk cascaded over me as he bent to kiss me. "Do you miss my touch yet, dear one?" His ancient eyes were alight with crystalline amusement.

I looked up at him, narrow-eyed. "Yes and no."

He laughed and took me by the hand to lead me to a white marble balcony that overlooked a shining blue sea. "Is it such a difficult question?"

I watched the demons in flight above the water. "I miss your presence, but you also kinda scare the crap out of me, y'know?"

He stood behind me, sliding his arms about me in loose embrace. "I would never harm you, Kara. Summon me. You will be safe."

I leaned my head back against him as his embrace turned into a slow caress. He nuzzled my neck, sending goose bumps racing over my skin. "But your idea of 'safe' might not be the same as mine," I said, groaning as his teeth gently nipped at my earlobe.

"I will allow none to harm you, Kara," the demonic lord murmured. "Summon me. You need what I can give you."

I shuddered as if to throw off a chill, still unsettled by the remnants of last night's dream. That's all it had been—a dream. Nothing more.

Gooseflesh rose on my arms despite the warmth of the night. I wished I could really be that certain.

There was another type of demon above those twelve levels: the demonic lords. It was considered pretty much impossible to summon a demonic lord. Or rather, with enough power and preparation it was technically possible to summon one, but surviving the experience was another matter entirely. Yet I'd accidentally summoned Rhyzkahl, one of the highest of the demonic lords, and I'd even survived the experience.

In a manner of speaking.

Rhyzkahl had created a link to me after I'd unintentionally summoned him, and for a time he had come to me in dream-sendings, so vivid and real that it was impossible to tell whether I was awake or asleep. Plus, elements of these sendings could intrude into the waking world, as evidenced by one instance where he healed an injury I'd received when I was awake. But those had stopped after he'd saved my life. I'd had dreams of him since, but they never felt as visceral as the sendings.

I knew I should be pleased and relieved that the link had apparently been severed. But I wasn't sure how I felt about that. Or him. It didn't help that many of the dreams were filled with scorching erotic content—with me as an eager participant. I woke from them shuddering with a combination of pleasure and need—feelings that quickly shifted to confusion and uncertainty. Was he sending these dreams in order to remind me of what we'd shared and what he could offer? Or were the dreams merely messages from my screwed-up psyche, reminding me that I had no boyfriend, no sex life, and no prospects?

Either way, I could do without the reminders.

I felt the demon's return before I saw it. I pushed off the car and straightened as it swirled around me, illusory teeth grazing me. I suppressed a shiver. "Show," I commanded as I closed my eyes. Images flickered behind my eyelids, hazy and difficult to follow, but along with the images came scent and sound and a sense of distance, as if I'd walked the demon's path. I could have done without the scent. The hunter was quite dead, face bloated and swollen, and the rank stench of decomposition surrounded him. I had no idea how he'd died—whether from drowning or injury—but the important thing was that I knew the body was in this area.

I opened my eyes, then held the door open for the *ilius.* It swirled around me again and I could feel its rising hunger. It had completed its task and wanted to be fed. I tightened my mental grip on the arcane bindings, even as sweat prickled under my arms. "Not here. Soon."

The demon flashed red in my othersight, then slid into the backseat again. I got into the driver's seat as quickly as I could. I'd never heard of an *ilius* feeding on a human, but there was a lot I didn't know about demons. I didn't care to find out what would happen if it got hungry enough. Fortunately, the place I was headed was only a short distance down the highway. Once again I pulled the car over and released the demon. "Follow," I commanded, then set off at a light jog down a well-worn path, grateful for the moon that lit my way. I could feel the demon following me and had to shake the unnerving sensation that it was chasing me. A few hundred yards later I stopped at the edge of a bayou. I turned back to the *ilius* and held the image of a nutria in my mind—a large ratlike creature with nasty yellow teeth. Nutria were an invasive species that had quickly overrun south Louisiana and did terrible damage to marshlands—so much so that nutria-eradication programs had been created.

I had my own nutria-eradication program right here. "Feed," I said, continuing to hold the image in my mind and sending the mental emphasis that it was to feed *only* on the nutria.

It zoomed past me so quickly that I nearly lost my balance, and before I could even blink I heard an animal shriek; it was quickly silenced. I looked away from the sight of the demon winding itself around one of the creatures. I'd seen an *ilius* feed before. There was no blood or rending of flesh, or anything graphic and grotesque. To anyone without arcane ability, it merely looked as if the nutria seized up and convulsed, dying for no apparent reason. But othersight would show that the *ilius* was gently and painlessly slaying the creature with a near-surgical jab of arcane power, then drawing out and consuming its life force—or essence.

The demon dropped the empty husk of the nutria and dove on another. I kept my eyes fixed on the moon above the trees, ignoring the imagined mental screams of the ratlike creatures. After about half a dozen nutria, the demon slowly coiled its way back across the water to sleepily wind around me like a cat preparing to settle in for a nap. A demonic, life-eating, piranha-toothed, misty cat.

I stepped back from the demon and began the dismissal chant. Wind rose from nowhere, bringing the scent of rotting vegetation and nearly making me gag. But I kept my focus steady, and a few heartbeats later a bright slit opened in the universe—the portal between this world and the demon sphere. A ripping crack split the quiet of the swamp, and then the light—and the demon—were gone.

I gave myself a minute to catch my breath, then headed back up the trail to my car, not looking back at the scattered bodies of nutria along the bank of the bayou.

SUNRISE HAD BATHED the eastern sky in purple and gold by the time I made it back to St. Long Parish. I'd gone farther on my hunt with the *ilius* than I'd expected, nearly to the Mississippi–Louisiana border. The hunter had obviously managed to cover some distance in his little flatboat before running into trouble. On the way back I called an acquaintance who was a member of a local dog-search team and gave her the approximate GPS coordinates. She thanked me and didn't ask any further questions. I'd given her tips before that had—of course—panned out, with the admonition that I didn't want questions and that she was free to take all the credit for herself. She assumed I was clairvoyant. I wasn't about to correct her.

My phone buzzed when I was about half a mile from my house, and I grimaced. It had to be work if I was getting a call this early in the morning. I was a detective with the Beaulac Police Department, working violent crimes and homicides. I'd been back at work for only a week after being on medical/administrative leave for nearly a month, thanks to the serial killer known as the Symbol Man. I'd closed the case but had not escaped unscathed—even though I didn't have a single scar to prove it.

My caller ID showed that it was from my sergeant's cell phone. I hit the answer button. "I'm not on call and my shift doesn't start until ten today, Crawford. Leave me the fuck alone."

Cory Crawford laughed. He'd been promoted to sergeant a few weeks ago when my former captain was appointed chief of police. That appointment had left an opening, which created a reshuffling all the way down the line. I'd had a few issues with Crawford in the past, but, to my surprise and relief, he'd become a completely different person after his promotion.

"Nah, it's not work. I was just wondering if you could do me a favor since you live out in the middle of fucking nowhere."

I grinned. My house wasn't quite in the middle of nowhere, but it was far enough away from Beaulac—and most civilization—that I had a heaping portion of privacy. And since I summoned demons in my basement, privacy was pretty damn important to me. "What do you need?"

"I need you to swing by Brian Roth's place and wake him the fuck up. *His* shift started at six this morning. He still isn't in yet, and he has a meeting with a witness at eight."

I continued past my driveway. Brian lived in a gated subdivision just a few miles from where I lived, on a sprawling piece of land that was almost as wonderful as the ten acres I owned. "He's not answering his cell?"

"Would I be calling you if he was?" he said with asperity. "But the witness is a friend of the captain's, and if

Brian doesn't show I'm gonna have to write him up." I could hear the reluctance in his voice.

Brian and I had started in police work at about the same time and had even been teammates when we were road cops. Then we'd both been promoted to detective within months of each other, though he'd gone to Narcotics while I'd been put into Property Crimes. I glanced at my watch. Almost seven-thirty now. Brian would be pushing it to get to work in time to meet the witness. It took me nearly half an hour to make it in from my house.

"I'm almost there. I'll bang on his door and then call you back."

"Appreciate it."

The gates to his subdivision were closed, but they swung open obligingly after I punched the police access code into the little keypad. A few minutes later I pulled into the driveway to his house—two-story with white brick exterior, faux columns by the front door, a double garage, and decent landscaping. It was the kind of house that would be impossible to afford on a cop's salary, but his dad was a judge and his stepmother was a lawyer, and they'd supposedly purchased the house for him as a wedding present. I'd heard rumors that he tried to refuse it and had reluctantly accepted it only after his dad showed the house to Brian's new wife. It didn't surprise me that he might have refused it. Brian was a decent guy who worked hard, and I didn't see him as the type to be comfortable accepting such a large gift, even from family.

A red Ford F-150 was parked in the driveway next to a gold Ford Taurus with public plates—Brian's department-issued vehicle. That told me that he was most likely at home, since I knew the pickup was his personal vehicle. But a shiver went through me as I approached the house, and I paused, trying to capture the fleeting sense of unease that had drifted by me. My gaze fell on the door and my eyes narrowed. It was pulled mostly shut, but the latch hadn't caught and it was ajar approximately half an inch. I quickly retreated to my car and grabbed my gun and holster out of the glove box, then returned to the door, clipping the holster onto my belt and holding my gun at the ready position. I couldn't see any sign of forced entry. *Maybe he just didn't pull the door all the way shut?* I wanted to believe that, but the continued sense of unease nagged at me.

I nudged the door farther open with my foot, staying behind the jamb. "Brian?" I called. "It's Kara Gillian."

Silence. Not even the brush of movement on carpet. If he was in there, he was being awfully quiet. I gave the door a soft kick to push it open all the way, then took a quick peek in.

It took me several seconds to register what I was seeing. At first my mind insisted that he'd fallen asleep on the floor in front of the TV. Then it finally processed the thick pool of blood surrounding him. "Oh, shit," I breathed, even as grief and horror knotted my throat. I wanted to rush in to see if he was still alive, but I forced myself to use proper caution. There was no way to know what had happened, and I sure as hell didn't want to end up like Brian. I edged in cautiously, scanning and covering the area with my Glock as I fumbled my phone out of its holder with the other hand and dialed 911.

"This is Detective Gillian; I have an officer down. Brian Roth. I'm at his residence." I rattled off the address. I barely heard the dispatcher's acknowledgment as I got close enough to see that there was no way Brian was still alive. Not with the skull pieces and brain matter spattered across the floor and wall. "Fuck. Be advised that—fuck. It's a 29." A signal 29 was a death. It was easier to say, in more ways than one.

"Are you code 4?" She was asking if the scene was safe.

"Unknown. I'll need backup units to clear the house." I continued to scan the living room, doing my best not to disturb any possible evidence. A piece of paper in the middle of the coffee table drew my attention, and I glanced down at it. Then I read it again when I realized what it was, dismay and dread twisting at my gut.

I never meant to kill her. It was an accident. I loved her. We just liked to play. I'm so sorry.

I looked sharply back at the body and saw the Beretta by his hand. "Shit. Looks like a suicide," I said. "And I think he killed his wife."

The dispatcher said something to me, but I didn't hear it. My gaze stayed locked on Brian's body as a wave of nauseating horror slammed through me. Images of dead nutria swam through my head as I desperately shifted into othersight, praying that I was wrong about what I was sensing.

But I wasn't wrong. I could see the arcane fragments left behind, like sinew on a gnawed bone. Brian's essence had been consumed just as thoroughly as the nutrias' had been consumed by the demon.

THE ILIUS WAS MY FIRST PANICKED THOUGHT. THEN, *No. No. That's not possible. I dismissed it. Didn't I?* My gaze stayed locked on Brian's body as my mind whirled. It *wasn't* possible. I *had* dismissed it. I was sure of it.

Then what had consumed Brian's essence?

Doubt clawed at me as I pulled my eyes away from the gruesome sight of Brian's body. *The note. His wife.* Focus on that now, instead of the horror that I was faced with. I tried to remember his wife's name and failed. I'd met her a few times, but we'd never had more conversation than, *So nice to see you again.*

They liked to play . . . Shit. That implied some sort of accident during sex play.

It was risky, but I went ahead and did a quick sweep of the house. There was always a chance that she was still alive. I knew I wouldn't be able to live with myself if it turned out that I'd sat back and waited for backup while she slowly strangled or bled out or something. Maybe

Brian had been wrong. Maybe he'd only *thought* she was dead.

But I couldn't find any sign of her. I returned downstairs to Brian, unable to bring myself to look at the body again and see that ragged hole where his essence had been torn away. *Had the demon somehow escaped being pulled back through the portal? And would it have fed on a human?*

I shook my head sharply. None of that made any sense. Even if the demon had somehow slipped my control, the place where I'd dismissed it was an hour's drive from here. *But they're fast, and it could have beaten you here.*

But why? I asked myself again in a mental wail. *Why the fuck would it come here?*

I took a shaking breath as I forced myself to logically consider possibilities. Perhaps the *ilius* had been drawn by the feel of the violent death and had escaped my control to consume Brian's essence after death had loosened his body's hold on it. Or perhaps there was something about suicides that attracted them—the willingness to die somehow making the essence easier to consume. I had no idea if that could be true. There was much that I didn't know about the demonkind.

My mouth felt as dry as the Sahara as I tried to come up with something that made sense. Luckily, the sound of approaching sirens distracted me from further mental flailing.

I stepped outside just as two marked units and an unmarked came screaming up the driveway, and I felt a sudden spasm of guilt for worrying about the demon. It suddenly slammed home that a fellow officer was dead. Someone I'd worked with and joked with had decided to shove a gun against his head and pull the trigger. I scrubbed at my face as two officers rushed up, dimly surprised to see that my hand was trembling.

"I did a quick sweep to see if I could find his wife," I heard myself saying, "but the house hasn't been properly cleared." Good, the professional part of me was keeping it all together, doing what needed to be done. I could fall apart on the inside and no one would know it. I looked past them to see Crawford's stout form as he ran toward the house from his unmarked. I glanced back to the officers. "Please take care of it. I need to tell Sarge."

The two officers acknowledged me and entered, guns at the ready. Just because there was a suicide note didn't mean it was a suicide, and there was always that outside chance that a bad guy was hiding somewhere in the house.

I could see the anguish in Crawford's eyes as he came to a stop before me, breathing harshly. "Kara, is it . . . is he . . . ?"

My throat tightened up and I gave a jerky nod. His face crumpled into stark grief, and I could see that he was holding on to control just as hard as I was.

"Looks like he shot himself, Sarge," I said, my voice coming out in a ragged croak. "But that's not all."

His expression was a brittle mask. "Dispatcher said his wife might be dead too?"

"That's what the note says," I said, then I shook my head. "But I did a sweep and I couldn't find her."

We fell silent in shared grief and pain until the two officers came back out a few minutes later. "Anyone else inside?" Crawford demanded.

They both shook their heads, faces tight and eyes haunted. "No one else," one said. "House is clear."

Crawford blew out a gusty breath as he moved to the door. I stayed on the porch while he entered and moved to within about five feet of Brian's body. I watched him take in the sight of the blood and the gun. The hard professional mien was in place. He was doing the same thing I was—doing what needed to be done and promising himself that he could fall apart later. He peered down at the note, then came back outside and looked to the two officers. "All right. String tape up, please, and get a scene log going." After the two departed, he looked back at me. "I'm sorry I did this to you."

"Not your fault," I said with a shrug I didn't feel. "Someone had to be the first to find him." I glanced at my watch. It had been only ten minutes since I'd found him. It felt like an eternity. "I don't think he's going to make that meeting with the witness."

"Fucker," Crawford said, a ghost of a smile on his face. He knew I was trying to break the awful tension. "I'm gonna have to write him up after all." We both gave stupid little giggles, then in the next breath Crawford had me enveloped in a big man-hug. I returned the embrace, knowing he needed the comfort as much as I did. A heartbeat later we stepped back, neither one of us the slightest bit embarrassed about the display of emotion.

"I need to make some phone calls," he said with a sigh. "Crime lab's already on the way."

"And we need to find his wife. Does anyone know where she worked? Does she have family around here?"

"We'll find all of that out," he said, the growl in his voice a promise. Then he stepped away to make his calls.

I was saved from slipping back into agonized ponderings about Brian's missing essence by the sight of the crime-scene van pulling into the driveway. It parked behind Crawford's car, and Crime Scene Technician Jill Faciane hopped out—a petite woman with short red hair and an elfin face, dressed in blue fatigue pants and a

Beaulac PD T-shirt. She headed toward me, pausing only to scrawl her name on the crime-scene log before ducking under the tape that had been hastily strung.

"I hate to say it," I said when Jill reached me, "but I'm really glad you're the tech on call." We'd worked together extensively during the Symbol Man case and had become friends in the process. I'd grown up fairly lonely and isolated due to my penchant for summoning demons, so having a female friend was something new and rewarding.

She gave a sharp nod of understanding. "You okay?"

"I'll be fine."

She shook her head, blue eyes dark and angry. "I hate it when one of our own dies. Even when it's some sort of stupid accident at home."

I knew what she meant. Police were a family, a brotherhood—no matter what the gender.

Her scowl deepened. "But a suicide. God *damn* it."

"The note says that he killed his wife," I said, voice grim.

She jammed her fingers through her hair. "It's just so hard to believe. I'd heard they were having some problems, but shit. Everyone goes through rough patches."

I shook my head. "The way it's worded makes it sound like it was an accident, but I did a quick sweep and couldn't find her."

"And so he killed himself? How the fuck could he do this to us?" I could hear the anger in her voice, and I understood it.

I sighed. "It's been a long time since we've lost anyone." Then I winced. "I mean—"

"Other than you," Jill said quietly. "But at least you came back." She shivered and rubbed her arms. "Those two weeks were awful."

I didn't know how to respond. After the showdown with the Symbol Man, it had been assumed that I was dead. There'd been plenty of evidence to support that assumption, including eyewitness accounts of me being eviscerated and a few gallons of my blood on the scene—though no body. A cover story had later been spun to explain my disappearance and surprising reappearance, but there were only two people in this world who knew what had actually happened, who knew that I really *had* died. For two weeks, at least.

"But your funeral," she said, forcing a grin, "man, that was some shit! The procession was five miles long!"

I made myself return the grin. "Everyone just wanted to get out of work."

Jill snorted and thwapped me on the arm. "You are so stupid." Then she gave a sigh. "Well, lemme get my shit so I can start processing this scene."

Crawford walked back over to me as Jill trotted to her van. "The rank will be making their way out here in due course, and the search is on for Carol." He gave me a penetrating look. "How're you doing?"

"I'm doing fine." I lifted a shoulder in a shrug. "I'll let myself feel it all later."

His lips twisted. "I know what you mean, but that's not what I'm talking about. I mean, how are you doing? I know you've only been back at work for a week."

I wiped a trickle of sweat away from my temple. The heat was beginning to ramp up as the morning progressed. "I'm all right. There're a couple of people who are being weird about my, um, disappearance, but they'll get over it."

Crawford turned and stepped off the porch, motioning with his head to follow. He walked past the crime-scene tape to the meager shade offered by a scraggly oak tree, then took a pack of cigarettes and a lighter out of his jacket pocket. "I've been a cop a long time, Kara. I thought I'd seen it all." He pulled a cigarette out and lit it, took a heavy drag. He'd stopped using chewing tobacco and taken up smoking instead, which made no sense to me. He'd also shaved his mustache, which had really thrown me. On the other hand, he still dyed his hair brown and wore dull brown suits with wild and garish ties. So I guessed some things never changed.

"Anyway, I've seen enough weird shit to be willing to accept that there's a *lot* of weird shit out there," he continued. "I don't believe that story about you having to go so deep undercover that everyone had to believe you were dead, but I figure if there really is another story, it's probably best that no one knows it." He shrugged and blew out smoke. I resisted the urge to move so that I was more upwind of him. He was surprising me with this apparent willingness to accept the inexplicable. I still wasn't about to tell him what had actually happened during those two weeks, but I had the oddly comforting feeling that if I was to ever tell him, he'd be fairly accepting.

Crawford shrugged. "I guess I'm saying that if you need anything, let me know." He looked over at me. "Any change with your aunt?"

I shook my head stiffly. My aunt Tessa was in an extended-care facility—a place that catered specifically to neurological disorders. I knew that Tessa hadn't suffered any sort of brain injury, but I still needed to have her body cared for. She was missing her essence as well, though hers had not been consumed the way Brian's had. It was just . . . missing. Temporarily mislaid, I hoped. I'd hated to put her in a home, but at least I could console myself with the knowledge that she had no awareness of where she was.

"No," I answered. "No change. I've been trying to go through some of the stuff at her house, get it cleaned up a bit, just in case…" My voice broke, and I couldn't continue.

"In case she doesn't wake up," he said, more gently than I ever would have expected from him.

I nodded, even though that was only part of the reason I was trying to go through Tessa's things. It was her library that I was most interested in. Tessa's essence had been used to provide added potency for a massive arcane ritual, and I still clung to the hope that it could be reversed and she could come back to her body. Tessa's library contained hundreds of texts, scrolls, and documents related to the arcane, and I remained optimistic that one of them held some answers on how to help restore her essence.

Unfortunately, my research had come to a screeching halt before it even began when I discovered that my aunt had warded her library with layers upon layers of arcane protections—and that they had *not* been set to allow me passage. That fact bothered me on a number of levels—not the least of which was that, without access to the materials in that library, I might never see her alive and well again.

My gaze slid back to the open door of the house. I could see Jill moving around inside, taking pictures and measurements. I could also see the motionless lump that was Brian's body, but I was thankfully far enough away that I couldn't feel the gaping lack of essence. This was different from my aunt's situation. His essence had been consumed, not just pulled away whole. Even if his body weren't dead, there'd be no way to return his essence to him. There was no essence left to return.

And what could have possibly done that to him? I asked myself again, frustration and worry twining together in my gut. The only creature I knew of that could consume essence was an *ilius,* but that didn't mean much. There was a whole lot that I didn't know, and I still couldn't shake the sick feeling that I'd screwed something up in my dismissal of the demon. What if I was responsible for this? Had the demon sensed Brian's death and swooped down onto that essence just as it was beginning to shuffle free of its mortal coil? Was that even possible?

Damn it. There was too much that I didn't understand. Unfortunately, there were only two possible sources of information for anything to do with the arcane. The first—and what would normally have been the simplest—was my aunt's library.

The second source of answers to questions about the arcane were the demons. I had a feeling I was going to be summoning again tonight—especially since a higher demon might also be able to help me penetrate the arcane protections on the library that had so far stalled my progress.

I looked over at Crawford. "Sarge, I'd like this case."

He seemed to consider it for a couple of seconds. "Well, since you were first on the scene, I'll let you run with it for now."

"Thanks." That would give me some more time and opportunity to dig into the circumstances surrounding Brian's death and maybe shed some light on what could have eaten his essence.

And, if it *was* something I was somehow responsible for, hopefully I could make sure it wouldn't happen again.

3

By the time I was able to head home, I felt drained, emotionally and physically. The scene at Brian's house had taken only a couple of hours to wrap up, but we'd spent the next few hours trying to track down where Carol Roth might be. She'd been at work the day before but hadn't shown up this morning, and we couldn't find a single person who could state that they'd seen her since she left the office. I'd even requested copies of the surveillance video from the gate for the previous twenty-four hours, in the hopes that there might be some hint or clue there, but the camera system was brand-new—which apparently meant that the security company had no idea how to retrieve video from it and would have to call in a tech to download what I needed.

We'd run down every other possible lead, uncomfortably aware that her body could be anywhere—and in south Louisiana, there were a shitload of places to dump a body. *But why the hell would Brian dump her body someplace remote if it was an accident? And then why kill himself? He wasn't the type to panic.* Nothing made sense with this case, and it bugged the shit out of me.

Then, to add to the emotional beating, I'd stopped by the neuro center to see my aunt—or, rather, her empty shell. I hadn't stayed long, just enough to verify with my othersight that she didn't have the same "look" that Brian's body did. Still, it was depressing seeing her normally animated face so waxy and still, and the short visit had left me with a hollow ache of worry in my gut.

I made the turn into my long driveway, mood abruptly lifting as I rounded the last curve and saw the car parked in front of my house. I was quite familiar with that dark blue Crown Victoria—with the heavily tinted windows and more than the usual number of antennae on the back. Add the government plate and it practically shrieked *federal agent.*

I found myself smiling as I pulled up beside the Crown Vic. Leaning against the hood of the car with his arms crossed over his chest was a tall man with reddish-brown hair and a rugged face. He was wearing a polo-style shirt and blue jeans, which showed off his workout ethic nicely. It was the most casual I'd ever seen him attired. It didn't make a difference. His entire demeanor announced his profession even more than his car did.

I didn't give a crap about his profession at the moment. My day had started out shitty, but it definitely looked as if it was turning around now.

I climbed out of my car and slung my bag over my shoulder. He pushed off the hood of his car with a grin.

"Hello there, Special Agent Kristoff," I said.

He gave a mock sigh, but his green-gold eyes sparkled with amusement. "So formal."

I laughed. "Fine. Hi, Ryan." I'd met Ryan during my

investigation into the Symbol Man murders, when we were both assigned to the serial-killer task force. My first impression of him had not been a positive one—arrogant, condescending, and dismissive. Later I'd discovered that he could see the arcane, and I came to trust him enough to tell him that I was a summoner. Other than my aunt, he was probably the only person who knew that little fact about me.

After that initial trust had been established, we'd become friends—something that was both rewarding and baffling to me at the same time. Like my friendship with Jill, I treasured this connection with Ryan. Yet at the same time, I couldn't help but wonder if we would ever go beyond "just friends." Or if I even wanted that. Hell, I had no idea if *he* was remotely interested in anything beyond friendship.

And this is the last *thing I need to be worrying about,* I chided myself. *My life is complicated enough as it is right now.*

"Dare I ask why you're standing in my driveway?" I said instead.

"Because, while you were dead, someone fixed your door for you." He turned to glare at my pretty new door. He'd been the one to break it a couple of months ago, busting in when he heard me screaming. It had been only a bizarre demon-induced nightmare, but he'd thought something far worse was happening.

I had a strong suspicion that he was also the one who'd fixed the door, though he'd never admitted it. "Aw, poor you," I said. "You have to stalk me from outside."

"Actually, I was in the car with the AC cranked up until I heard you coming up the driveway. Did you know that it's insanely hot?"

I snorted and started up my front steps. "You'd think this was a subtropical climate. You're spoiled by your time at Quantico. Don't worry." I glanced up at the sky. "Give it a couple of hours and we'll have our usual afternoon thunderstorm. Then it'll be hot *and* humid."

Ryan made a strangled noise as he followed me into my house. I lived in a single story Acadian-style house, with peeling paint and a broad front porch, on enough of a hill to allow me to have a basement; it was located in the middle of ten acres at the end of a long, winding driveway. Very private. I loved it.

"I'm too used to living up north," he admitted. "I'm melting like a Nazi at the end of *Raiders of the Lost Ark*."

I dumped my bag on the desk by the door and then turned to him. "So what brings you back to these parts?" It had been more than a month since I'd last seen him. We'd exchanged a few emails, but since we were both understandably reluctant to mention anything related to the arcane in email, they'd been fairly terse and boring.

His mouth twitched. "Well, I think I'm going to have to get used to this insane heat and humidity. I'm on a temporary transfer down here."

My heart gave a mad thump of delight, and I had to fight to keep my face from showing anything more than a pleased smile. "Seriously? There are enough crimes related to the arcane in this area to warrant that?"

"There is a variety of reasons," he said, shrugging, "and I'm not privy to all of them, but the suits at the top apparently felt it was worth it to base our little task force in this region, at least for now."

"Well, I approve," I said, with as much of a sober nod as I could manage.

He laughed. "I'll be sure to pass that on to the powers that be."

"You do that!" I couldn't keep a straight face anymore and had to grin. "Okay, seriously? I have to admit that this is the best news I've had in quite some time."

He tilted his head. "I can't decide if that's incredibly flattering or seriously pathetic."

I rolled my eyes. "Pathetic, obviously, because I just realized that I'd forgotten what a smart-ass you are."

"You know me too well."

I wish! I thought, then hurriedly pushed the thought from my mind. "So, are you working anything right now?"

He made a face. "Nothing fun. I'm working a public corruption case—utterly mundane. Can't really talk about it."

I nodded and resisted the urge to pry. I'd been in law enforcement long enough to know that there were some things that had to remain confidential—if I wanted to remain friends with him, that is.

I gave a mental sigh. Ryan was seriously good-looking, though certainly not in any pretty-boy sort of way. He was about a head taller than me, with nice broad shoulders, a trim waist, and gorgeous eyes that I often felt were wasted on a guy. But I didn't have very many friends, and I was—okay, I admit it—too chicken to make any sort of move and risk blowing the friendship all to hell.

But, damn, there were times when I really wanted to jump his bones.

"So where's your partner?" I asked instead. During the Symbol Man investigation, Ryan had been partnered with Special Agent Zack Garner, who looked far more like a lifeguard than an agent specializing in arcane and supernatural incidents.

"That blond bastard is on vacation. California."

I laughed. "Surfing?"

"You nailed it. So how about you?" he asked as he looked through my fridge for something to drink. He snagged a Diet Barq's out of the bottom drawer and quirked an eyebrow at me. "Anything going on that you can talk about?"

I grimaced. "Yeah. I've had a pretty shitty day. Sarge called me this morning to go wake up one of our narcotics detectives, and I found him dead of an apparently self-inflicted gunshot wound."

"Damn," he said quietly. "I'm sorry to hear that. It doesn't get much shittier than that."

I scrubbed at my eyes and leaned back against the counter. "Actually it does."

He gave me a disbelieving look.

I took a deep breath. "Brian's essence was gone. Consumed."

He was silent for several heartbeats. "You mean, like your aunt?"

I shook my head. "Tessa's essence was drawn out to power an arcane ritual. It was intact—sort of like taking a battery out of a robot and using it in something else. Brian's essence was . . . eaten. There was nothing but shreds left."

Ryan sat down at the table and looked up at me, a frown playing across his face. "How can you tell? I mean, doesn't the essence leave the body after death anyway?"

"Yes, but not immediately, and it's more of a gentle release." I pulled out a chair on the other side of the table and plopped down. "Fuck, you're going to make me try to explain this? Um, it's like the body—the physical shell—has the essence in a firm grasp. When it dies, the grasp is loosened, which allows the essence to float away whole, so to speak. But when it's consumed, there are ragged edges still left behind, like meat torn from a bone."

He gave a shudder. "All right, that sounds pretty hideous. So, he . . . what, doesn't go to his afterlife or whatever now?"

I rubbed my temples. "It's a bit more complex than that. Everything I've been taught about essence and potency says that, while there's no such thing as actual from-one-body-to-the-next reincarnation, essence does get reused. Think of it like water being poured back into a pitcher. The next time a child is born, another glass is poured out. But if too much essence gets consumed, then there won't be enough to create new life, and we'll start seeing some nasty side effects."

"Such as?"

"Stillbirths," I said quietly. "Ill patients dying when they should have been able to recover. An empty 'pitcher' would almost have a vacuum effect as it pulled back any available essence."

He frowned. "What about population growth?"

"More essence can form, or grow from existing essence, but it takes time. Think of a tomato. Takes weeks to grow it but minutes to eat."

"I think it scares me that you know this," he said, a slight smile twisting the corner of his mouth.

I shifted uncomfortably in the chair and didn't smile back. "I think it might have been my fault."

He straightened. "Wait. What? Why on earth would you think that?"

I quickly explained about the *ilius* and my worry that somehow I'd failed to dismiss it properly. But by the end of my recitation he was already shaking his head.

"Nope, not buying it. I don't know that much about summonings and demons, but it doesn't make any sense that it would escape your control and then go swoop down on *this* guy. Even if he did commit suicide."

I sighed. "I know, but I can't think of a better explanation."

"Then you haven't figured it out yet," he said. "You will."

I gave him a small smile. His belief in me was probably misguided, but it was still reassuring. "Well, just for that, I'm going to let you come with me to my aunt's house while I try—yet again—to break in to her library so I can do some research."

He gave a bark of laughter. "Like Tom Sawyer 'let' his friends paint the fence?"

I grinned and stood. "Damn, I didn't know you could read."

"Yeah, well, it was an audiobook."

"Smart-ass. I'll meet you over there."

I STOOD IN the hallway of my aunt's house and scowled at the door to the library. I loved my aunt. I really truly did. She was the only family I had left after my parents died— my mother of cancer when I was eight and my father from a drunk driver three years later. She raised me and became my mentor after determining that I had the talent to become a summoner of demons. Aunt Tessa had the capacity to drive me crazy, and there were times I wanted to throttle her, but I did love her.

However, at the moment I was back to wanting to throttle her. She'd rigged her library so full of twisty-ugly wards and other arcane protections that I felt like a member of an arcane bomb-disposal unit. And though I'd known she had a zillion arcane protections on her house and library, I'd assumed—foolishly, as it turned out—that my aunt had allowed some sort of exception for me, her only living relative.

I couldn't even open the library door to see what kind of condition the room was in, because of the protections that writhed and pulsed in angry coils of purple and black—visible only to someone who could see the arcane. To the average person, it looked just like a regular door.

Actually, the average person wouldn't get close enough, since part of the protections on the library—and on the house itself—involved a complicated aversion effect that made anyone trying to get into the house suddenly think of something that urgently needed doing elsewhere.

The aversions hadn't been hard for me to get around, but the rest of the protections were another matter entirely. Working with arcane wards was not my forte. It required skill and potency—much like a summoning. I needed more experience to gain the skill, and potency was difficult to come by except during the full moon. The reason that summonings were usually done when the moon was at or near its fullest was because natural potency was rich and calm at that time. During waning and waxing of the moon, potency was scattered and hard to control. It was low and weak during the dark moon, but it was even, which was safer. Fluctuations in potency could be devastating when summoning a demon. I'd summoned the *ilius* the night before the full moon—safe enough to do with a third-level demon—but a summoning of anything higher than eighth or ninth level was best left to the night of the full. The restrictions of the phases of the moon were a pain in the ass, but the only method of storing potency that I knew of was the one the Symbol Man had used—torture and murder. Needless to say, I didn't want to go there.

Ryan let out a low whistle. "That looks seriously ugly."

"It's ridiculous," I complained. "Why the hell did she need all of this?"

"I dunno, but she was apparently not kidding about keeping people out."

"I'm her only fucking relative. I should be able to get in."

He peered at the winding wards. Ryan was able to sense the arcane, though not to the degree I could. "Fucking shit. Where would you even start?"

"That's the problem. I've been poking at the edges for the past couple of weeks, because it doesn't look so bad there. But every time I get that part undone, it re-forms." I scowled at the door and the writhing wards. I'd been spending almost as much time at Tessa's house as at my own—to the point where I'd begun to keep clothing and toiletries in her spare room. "I'm just going to have to dive into that big knot in the middle." I *thought* I could see where to begin to unravel the damn things; all I needed to do was work up the nerve to touch them arcanely. *You're being chicken*, I berated myself. *If you're wrong, you'll get a big zap. Get over it!*

"Well, here goes nothing," I muttered as I began to mentally reach out. "It's not like my aunt would try to—"

I threw myself backward as I saw the protection ward flash red in my othersight. . . . *kill me! Shit!* The edge of the arcane lightning bolt crackled over me, sending a stinging pain sparkling through my extremities as I landed heavily on my back on the hard wooden floor.

"Shit! Kara!" I heard Ryan shout. "Are you all right?"

I blinked away the stars crowding my vision to see him crouched over me, his face a mask of horror and concern. "Okay, that hurt," I croaked.

He reached out and pushed my hair back from my face. "Are you all right?" he repeated.

"Yeah," I wheezed, more than a little surprised by his gesture. "Just let me lie here and gasp for a while."

He must have seen it in my eyes, for he abruptly jerked his hand back and shoved it through his hair instead. "That was insane," he said, blowing out his breath. "A fucking lightning bolt?"

I finally progressed to rolling over onto my side, and from there I managed to shove up to a sitting position against the opposite wall. My limbs still twitched, and the stinging pain was only just beginning to fade.

"Damn it," I said, frustrated. "I guess I'm going to have to summon a demon to get through these wards."

Ryan reached down a hand to help me up. I was grateful for the assistance. My knees still felt wobbly, but at least the pain was pretty much gone. I'd been lucky. Landing on that floor had hurt like crazy, but it was better than being fried. I'd caught just the edge of it, and that was more than enough. "Your aunt has a summoning chamber here, doesn't she?" he asked.

I gave him a thin smile. "She sure does. And she has that all warded up as well." I sighed and tugged my T-shirt back into place, rolling my head on my neck to try to get everything back into proper alignment. "I'm going to have to summon in my own chamber and bring the demon over here."

He crossed his arms over his chest. "Why do I get the feeling that you're not talking about summoning some nice little dog-size creature?"

"Because you're annoyingly perceptive. I need oodles of answers, and there's a *reyza* that owes me a favor." A *reyza* was a twelfth-level demon—the highest level of demon that could be summoned by normal means. Demonic lords could be summoned as well, but the rituals involved were so insanely complex and required so much power that it was damn near impossible unless the lord was willing, which was pretty much never.

He raised an eyebrow at me. "And how the fuck are you going to get an eight-foot-tall demon with giant wings, horns, and a tail from your basement to here? In the trunk of your Taurus?" Ryan had good reason to be familiar with the appearance of a *reyza*—he'd been closer to one than he'd ever wanted to be when he was captured by Sehkeril, the demon who'd allied with the Symbol Man.

"You just leave that to me," I said with a smug smile. I headed toward the door, with Ryan following.

"So, uh, do you think you'll need any help transporting your demon?" He managed to keep his tone light and nonchalant, but I knew how badly he wanted to see a summoning.

Of course, he *had* seen a summoning before, but from a vantage that he probably had not desired—on the inside of the circle, as one of the intended sacrifices.

I gave a dramatic sigh. "Oh, well, I suppose I could use some help. Yes, you can come to the summoning." Then I lowered my head and glared at him. "And the *only* reason I'm even considering allowing you to attend this summoning is because this particular *reyza* owes me a debt, so I feel fairly secure that he won't immediately try to rip us both to pieces."

He grinned.

I rolled my eyes, but I couldn't help smiling. There were

times when the federal-agent attitude dropped away completely and he was like a teenager. I loved seeing these other facets to his personality—and that he was willing to reveal them to me almost made me feel like a trusted insider.

I closed and locked the front door and walked down the steps to where our cars were parked in the driveway. I turned back to speak to him, then paused, looking at Tessa's front yard, squinting in the late-afternoon sun that bounced off the lake.

He noticed my puzzled expression and glanced at the yard, then back to me. "What's wrong?"

"Someone mowed her lawn." And fairly recently too. Perhaps the day before? And the flower beds out front had been weeded and tended. I gave myself a mental *thwack* for not noticing this earlier.

Ryan gave the yard another sweeping glance, then shrugged. "Probably one of her neighbors doing her a favor."

I chewed my lower lip as I scanned up and down the street. "Maybe," I said, not totally convinced. Aunt Tessa's house was on the lakefront, a neighborhood made exclusive by the price and quality of the houses. The houses here were old and lovely and had been either exquisitely maintained or carefully restored; most were now tourist attractions. Every yard on the street was in exquisite condition. An unkempt lawn was not the sort of thing that would be tolerated in this area, and it was perfectly reasonable to assume that one of her neighbors had taken up the task. "But how did they get past the aversions?"

Ryan frowned. "Are the aversions strong enough to keep someone from mowing the lawn?"

"Well, they're placed on the house itself, but their effect certainly extends past the flower beds." Then I gave a shrug. "On the other hand, I have a hard time being upset about it, since, if the tending had been left to me, there'd be nothing but dead flowers and tall grass." Proof in point was the fact that it had taken me this long to even notice the lawn. But the question of *who* and *how* definitely had me baffled. Maybe the aversions were beginning to fade? It was tough for me to tell, since I was used to ignoring them.

Unfortunately, I didn't have time to worry about that now, but I made a mental note to look into it as soon as I had the chance. It was just her yard, anyway. If I thought someone had been in her house, then that would be a completely different thing.

I turned back to Ryan. "Okay, I've been awake since about nine last night, and I need to make preparations for the summoning and then take a nap, so you have to go away for a while. Come to my house at ten tonight."

He grinned with wicked deviousness. "Aww, can't I come over and nap with you?"

"What? No!" I blurted before my brain could engage. Shock flickered briefly in his eyes, and then his grin slipped, to be replaced by his neutral fed smile. *Fuck, Kara. Overreact much?* I thought with a mental groan. "I mean, I really need to rest, so I intend to sleep. . . . Unless you are offering to bore me into somnolence?" I added, struggling to bring back the teasing tone of the conversation.

"Ouch!" He laughed, but I could detect a forced edge to it. "All right, I'll see you at ten." And he turned and sauntered off to his car.

I watched him go, mentally thrashing myself for reacting like such an idiot. What the hell was wrong with me? I teased and joked with my coworkers all the time. So why the freak-out when Ryan did the same? He was teasing too. Right?

I exhaled as he backed out of the driveway and drove off. I had to face facts: I was no good at dealing with men. I couldn't even tell if he had any real interest in me. How pitiful was that? Still, it wasn't like I knew him all that well. We'd been thrown together for a month on the Symbol Man case, and that had pretty much been it. It was sad that my best friend was someone I barely knew, but even if I did know him, did I want to get involved with him?

Not sure. That was the best answer I could give myself. Not only did I not want to chance losing him as a friend, but I also didn't know enough about him. The demonic lord Rhyzkahl had implied that Ryan was more than he seemed. Unfortunately, I'd had no chance to pursue that, as I'd been more consumed with finding a way to help my aunt. Hell, Rhyzkahl could have merely meant that Ryan had more arcane ability than he was letting on, or maybe even that he colored his hair. But the comment still bothered me, if only because it cast doubts I didn't want to contemplate. I *liked* Ryan.

But enough about that. I had a demon to summon. And a U-Haul to rent.

4

MY HOUSE WAS STILL PRETTY CLEAN FROM MY SUM-
moning the night before, which meant that all I had to do
was scoop the dirty clothes off the floor and run the vacuum around. Clutter and messes could harbor pockets of
unwanted energy, or so my aunt had always said—even
though I was fairly sure that was merely a line of bullshit
she used to make me clean my house occasionally. But I
wasn't going to tempt the fates by forgoing it.

Fortunately, the cleaning didn't take much time at all,
and once I'd made the necessary changes to my diagram
for summoning a *reyza* instead of an *ilius,* I went to bed
and slept for a solid four hours. I woke up at nine p.m.,
then took my shower and tried to convince myself I wasn't
being stupid for allowing Ryan to attend the summoning.

My stomach gave a nervous flip-flop, and I scowled.
Fear had its place during a summoning—caution was always prudent, and a summoner had to maintain his or her
guard in expectation of the worst. But fear that made for

uncertainty or shaking hands was the sort that would get a summoner killed.

Of course, thinking about it that way didn't exactly help control the fear. *Don't be afraid, because if you are, well, you know, you could die a miserable, bloody death.*

"Been there, done that," I muttered. Then I couldn't help but smile. I *had* pretty much been through the worst that a summoning could offer, so what the hell was I worried about?

Fortunately, I didn't have long to fret. At ten on the nose, the doorbell rang.

I pulled the belt on my robe tight and opened the door, gesturing Ryan in. He had a smile on his face.

"You're going to transport a demon in a U-Haul truck?"

"Well, as you pointed out, it's not like I can stuff him into the trunk of my car. Are you ready?"

He gave a shrug and a nod. "Ready as I can possibly be, I guess."

I walked to the door that led to the basement, then stopped and turned to him. When I spoke, I kept my voice deathly serious, because this *was* deathly serious.

"Ground rules," I said, holding up a hand. "Do exactly as I say. Stay exactly where I tell you. Keep your mouth shut unless I specifically tell you that you can speak, and then only say what I say you can say. And," I took a deep breath, "do *not* mentally extend to feel anything arcane."

His expression turned puzzled. "I . . . don't know how to do that anyway."

I scowled at him. "You think you don't. And you probably don't. But just in case you do and you feel something that you would like to feel more of—*don't!*"

He nodded gravely. "I understand."

I hoped he did. "All right." I pulled the basement door open. "There are two circles down there. One's big and complicated and has candles around it and is chalked out in all sorts of nifty colors. The other's a lot smaller— chalked in blue and green by the wall opposite the fire-place. You get the small one. Go down the stairs and step into that circle without touching the chalk, then face the wall and close your eyes."

He gave me another grave nod, then walked down the stairs and to the circle. To my intense relief, he didn't waver at all from my directions and turned to face the wall.

I let out a breath. Yes, I was being a total chickenshit, but I preferred to change into my summoning garb down-stairs in the summoning chamber. It might have been complete superstition on my part, but every time I'd tried to change upstairs, something had gone wrong with the ritual. And I wasn't about to take a chance while summon-ing a *reyza*. I quickly slipped my robe off and folded it, then walked downstairs and tugged on my summoning garb—a simple gray silk shirt and pants, buttery soft and easy to move in.

You are such a weenie, I scolded myself. But I wasn't about to let him see me naked. Though I'd briefly had the insanely wicked thought of telling Ryan that *he* had to be naked to be a part of the ritual . . .

Probably a good thing I'd chickened out on that as well. Distractions during summonings were bad. *And, oh, how I would have been distracted!*

I moved to the circle I had created for him and took a deep breath to settle myself. "You can turn around now and open your eyes," I said. He did so, and even though his expression didn't flicker, I was fairly certain that I caught an amused glint to his eye.

Yeah, I deserved that much. "Okay, you can stand or sit within the circle, but decide now, because once I get started I don't want any movement from you. Also, no matter what happens, do *not* move from this circle." He gave me another grave nod.

"All right, do you have any questions?"

He shook his head. "None for now."

I smiled, working to control the nervous fluttering in my stomach. "I'll get started, then."

I pulled potency and activated the wards that I'd placed around his circle earlier, satisfied as they flared into life in shimmering blue and green that matched the chalked colors. Ryan could see the runes, I knew, which I hoped would make it easier for him to remember to stay put. I then turned and walked over to the main diagram, doing my best to put Ryan's presence out of my mind. He was doing as I'd commanded—staying perfectly still and not making a sound.

I set the bindings and wardings on the main diagram carefully, not daring to skimp even though I—supposedly—had been promised a payment of honor debt from this particular demon. I'd summoned him right before being assigned to the Symbol Man case and then never had the chance to summon him again.

I took a deep breath and began the chant, sensing as much as seeing the protections and bindings flare into life in coruscating colors. I could feel the arcane shudder as the portal connecting the two spheres began to form—a light-filled slit in the fabric of the world, bringing with it a wind and a potency that fought my control. I held my focus with tenacity as I lifted the knife and made a shallow slice on my forearm—spilling the drops of blood that the higher-level summonings required onto the diagram. It felt odd to mar my skin—smooth and scarless since my return from the dead. The cut was never deep—not enough to require stitches, and just enough to leave a hairline scar. I usually made the cut through the same scar, to avoid looking like I compulsively cut myself. But now my skin had become a clean slate again—at least for a short time.

I watched with satisfaction as the runes flared and the portal widened in perfect accord with my will.

"*Kehlirik.*" The name of the demon filled the basement, the naming merely the last step in a summoning where my will was just as vital as my spoken words. The wind died and the light-filled portal snapped closed, leaving me blinking in the sudden dark. I could feel the movement of the demon in the circle, and I drew the bindings in close as I prepared to deal.

"I am Kara Gillian. I have summoned you, Kehlirik, to serve me under terms that honor us both." I held the bindings carefully, braced for him to fight me. Would he remember his debt?

"I am honored to serve one who has received such favor from Lord Rhyzkahl," the rumbling voice said from the circle.

I blinked at the motionless form of the demon for several heartbeats, nonplussed. Favor? Well, Rhyzkahl had saved my life, so I guessed that counted as a pretty big favor. I'd worry later about what it all meant.

"Kehlirik, when last I summoned you, you stated that you would teach me arcane methods in payment of a debt of honor."

"I did." He sank into a crouch, folding his wings and

resting his clawed hands on his knees as the tip of his tail twitched by his feet. My eyes had adjusted and I could see his face—level with mine, now that he was crouched. Eyes rich with keen intelligence offset the bestial look of his face—flat nose above a wide mouth set off by curved fangs. A thick ridge crest swept back over his head, with curved black horns on either side. "I will repay that debt if such is your desire." Then his gaze shifted to Ryan's circle, and to my shock his lips curled back from his teeth and he hissed.

I reflexively tightened my grip on the bindings. "Honored *reyza*," I said quickly, "this man is under my protection."

The demon snapped his gaze back to me, a growl rumbling in his throat, then to my utter relief he lowered his head in acquiescence. "I will abide by your desire, summoner, and will not harm the *kiraknikahl* while he is under your protection."

The what? I glanced at Ryan with a questioning look, and he gave me a baffled shrug in response. I had no idea what the word meant, but there was only so much I could bargain for in this summoning, and demons—especially *reyza*—tended to be pretty stingy about imparting information. Everything had its price, and I had other questions that were far more pressing at this time. *Such as, did I screw up in my dismissal of the* ilius, *and could it have attacked Brian's essence?*

But, more than anything, I needed to get into Tessa's library, and that alone was going to take every bit of negotiating I had, debt or not.

I mentally filed the word away for later research. Maybe once I got into the library I could find out for sure.

"Kehlirik, I have need of your aid this night—specifically, your skill with wardings and protections."

The demon tilted his head. "I am quite skilled in such."

I smiled. Flattery would get you everywhere. "I know. Tessa Pazhel is my aunt, and I have need to enter and access all portions of her library and the contents therein, as well as her summoning chamber."

He stood, the tips of his horns nearly brushing the ceiling of the basement. "I accept the task and terms as payment of the debt."

I exhaled and released the bindings, then closed and grounded the portal energy. Kehlirik ascended the basement stairs with a speed and grace at odds with his size. As soon as he was out of sight, I turned to Ryan's circle and lowered the protections, then looked up at him.

"Okay, possibly stupid question here, but have you ever encountered Kehlirik before? And what the hell is a *kiraknikahl*?"

He gave me an exasperated shrug as he stepped out of the circle. "How the fuck should I know?" Then his eyes widened. "Holy shit, I do know that demon!"

"You do?"

"Yeah, he was over at my house to watch the Super Bowl," he said, not bothering to hide his grin. "We shared a coupla brewskies. He's like my best bro!"

I rolled my eyes and headed up the stairs, though I couldn't help but smile. "Never mind," I said over my shoulder. "*Kiraknikahl* obviously means *asshole*."

5

The cab of the U-Haul reeked of cigarette smoke, but since the air conditioner was nonfunctional it meant we had to drive with the windows down anyway. Fortunately, it was a warm night, and the open windows made for an almost pleasant ride.

Kehlirik had been surprisingly willing to be toted like cargo in the back of the truck, apparently looking upon the whole thing as one more unusual experience that he could relate to his demonkind buddies. I knew that experience in other realms helped demons gain status, so I had to guess that riding in a truck counted. In fact, he'd almost looked excited, which for a twelfth-level demon was utterly unheard-of.

Unfortunately, the U-Haul had been the best idea I could come up with for transporting the demon, since, as Ryan had pointed out so cleverly, there was no way in creation that he would fit into my Taurus. I wasn't even sure he'd fit into an SUV, which I could have probably rented as well. He would have been cramped—especially with his wings—but, more important than that, I really didn't want to risk anyone seeing that I had a big horking *demon* riding in the back of my car.

Not that the *reyza* was a demon-from-hell kind of demon. The creatures I summoned had been named thousands of years ago, long before any of the world's religions had designated "demons" as agents of evil and residents of hell. I wasn't enough of a theologian to know how that had all come about, but *my* demons resided in a different sphere of existence that converged with this one, and they were no more evil than a gun was. Powerful, dangerous, and deadly, yes. Evil incarnate, no.

It was a thirty-minute drive from my secluded house in the sticks to my aunt's house on the lakefront. St. Long Parish was small and quiet, mostly rural, in comfortable driving distance of New Orleans. Beaulac, the parish seat, was barely big enough to be defined as a city, and the only reason Beaulac had as large a population as it did was because of Lake Pearl. The city curved around the lake as if hugging it possessively, and Beaulac took great pains to make sure that the lake and its environs were clean and attractive. Tourism, hunting, and fishing were the main attractions of Beaulac, but there was also a cadre of *über-rich* who lived in the area, mostly on the lakefront. These were people who had no need to commute anywhere— either retired from lucrative careers or independently wealthy.

My aunt Tessa had been fortunate enough to inherit her house from a distant great-aunt shortly after my mother died. The inside of her house was beautifully decorated and maintained, and aside from a few modifications that she'd made, it would have fit right in with any of the other museum-quality houses in the area.

Only, very few people ever got the chance to see the inside.

I turned onto the two-lane highway that paralleled the more sedate drive that bordered the lake, then frowned and took my foot off the accelerator as I saw the flashing lights of marked units up ahead. "Shit."

Ryan flicked a glance at me. "What?"

I grimaced, glancing at my rearview mirror. There was no way to turn around, and even if there was, it would look insanely suspicious. "It's state police. They must be doing a DWI checkpoint."

His face etched into a frown as he looked at the distant flashing lights. "Are you sure it's not some of your guys?"

I continued to slow. "Nope. State police have all blue lights. We have red and blue, as does the sheriff's office. Shit." I wiped my hands on my jeans. There was no reason for them to want to look in the back of the truck, but there was also no way to warn Kehlirik to remain quiet and still. This U-Haul didn't have a window between the cab and the truck. I was just going to have to hope that Kehlirik would wait until I opened the back door to emerge. I didn't want to think about what would happen if he came out in the middle of about a dozen state troopers.

A wicked grin crossed Ryan's face. "I dare ya to sic the demon on them."

I tried not to laugh, but I wasn't very successful. "Stop that."

"I double-dog-dare you. I'd love to see them scatter, screaming like little girls."

"Shut up! I knew it was a mistake to bring you along," I said, thwacking him on the arm. But the mental image was there, and I couldn't help but snicker. "Okay, that would be pretty damn funny." I glanced at him, matching his grin with one of my own and allowing myself to enjoy the brief moment of shared silliness. Then I forced my face into an overly serious expression. "Now, behave yourself," I ordered, as I slowed to a crawl and joined the short queue of cars going through the checkpoint.

"Yes, ma'am!" he replied, drawing such a dour and stern face that I almost burst out laughing again.

"Why do I put up with you?" I asked in mock despair.

He sighed tragically. "You're obviously madly in love with me."

I let out a snort of amusement, even as a silly thrill ran through me. "And you're obviously on drugs!"

Then we were at the roadblock and I had to school my expression into a less giddy one. I didn't recognize the trooper who waved me to a stop, but I didn't have much cause to deal with troopers either. The road we were on was a state highway, which made it the troop's jurisdiction, though usually the only time anyone gave a crap about that was when there was an accident and we had to decide who would write the report.

"License, registration, proof of insurance," he recited, tilting his head back to look up at me, which I could tell bugged the crap out of him. I'd worked plenty of checkpoints, and I knew that I liked to be able to see into the person's car and smell their breath.

I gave him a friendly smile and handed him the rental paperwork, then pulled my license out of my wallet, positioning it to be sure that he caught sight of my badge. I expected him to say something about that, but he didn't, which only made me more nervous. Not that I was a staunch believer in "badging" one's way out of tickets or DWIs, but this was one time when it would be seriously nice to just be waved on through. I kept my ears trained on the back of the truck while the trooper looked over my paperwork. Ahead of the truck and to the right, I could see another trooper administering a field sobriety test to a dark-haired young man beside a yellow Mustang. My lips twitched as I watched the man stagger and nearly fall on his face during the walk-and-turn. Yeah, he'd be taking a ride in the back of a car real soon.

I returned my attention to the trooper as he lifted his eyes from the paperwork. He glanced over the truck, mouth drawing down in a slight frown. "Why are you driving a rental truck at midnight?"

I shrugged and smiled. "I worked late today, and this was the only chance I had to get over to my aunt's house to clean some of the crap out of there."

The frown stayed on his face. "Have you been drinking tonight?"

"No, I've been working a case."

I heard the sound of claws on metal from within the truck, and it took every ounce of control I had to keep from reacting. I had a brief frisson of hope that it hadn't been all that loud, that I was aware of it only because I'd been listening for a sound, but I wasn't that lucky. The trooper's gaze snapped toward the back, and his frown deepened. "What's in the truck?"

I gave a sigh. "I think one of my boxes fell over. Look, I'm not trying to be a pain, but I don't want to be up all night moving this stuff."

His eyes narrowed. "Do you mind if I take a look?"

I could feel Ryan tense beside me. For all of his joking, I knew that he was aware of how disastrous it would be if anyone caught sight of the demon, and I was suddenly thrilled that I was a cop. Not because I was able to badge my way out of situations—which obviously wasn't going to work here—but because I knew my rights.

I kept my tone even and polite as I met the trooper's eyes. "I don't think there's any need for you to look in the truck. I really don't have time for that, and unless you have probable cause"—I stressed the two words very lightly—"to believe that I'm involved in something illegal, I'd appreciate it if you could let me get on my way." Because this was what too many people didn't realize: Just because an officer asks to look in your vehicle doesn't mean you have to say yes.

His expression hardened, but I could tell that he knew he was stuck. He could still make my life difficult by asking me to take a field sobriety test or finding other ways to delay me. It was even possible that he would call for a drug dog to come out to the scene—and I didn't want to think about what the dog's reaction would be. But to my intense relief, he handed the paperwork back without a nod or smile. "Have a nice night."

I could tell he didn't mean it.

I took the paperwork and my license, keeping the smile plastered on my face. "Thanks. You too!"

I didn't mean it either.

He stepped back and I eased the truck forward, my pulse finally slowing to normal once we were past the roadblock.

"Well, he was a tight-ass," Ryan said, as if remarking about the weather.

I laughed. "He *definitely* would have screamed like a little girl at the sight of a demon."

The rest of the drive was blessedly uneventful, and it was with deep relief that I made it to Tessa's house. I backed into her driveway, as close to the garage as I could get and still be able to open it. I shut the truck off and hit the remote for the garage door, then hopped out, moved to the rear. I tugged the back door of the truck up.

Kehlirik crouched in the center of the truck, holding on to the straps that I'd provided for him. He peered at me as I opened the door. "Did you have any problems in here?" I asked him.

He blew his breath out in a snort. I'd never seen a *reyza* smile, but the expression on his face was one that I could have sworn was delight. "A unique experience. I am appreciative of the opportunity."

I had to bite back the laugh. I didn't want to offend him, so I kept my expression sober and merely inclined my head in acknowledgment. "I am pleased that it suited you." I stepped aside and gestured into the garage. "If you would follow me, honored one?"

He released the straps and made a graceful leap into the garage. He apparently understood the need for secrecy. Which was good, because the last thing I needed was a neighbor seeing a ginormous winged beast going into my aunt's house.

"C'mon, Fed Boy," I said to Ryan as he climbed down from the truck. "Get your ass inside so I can close the door."

He shut the door of the U-Haul and quickly moved inside the garage, while I punched the inside button to shut the garage door. As soon as it was closed, I flipped on the lights and led the way into the house, with the demon following.

Even though Tessa's house was more than one hundred years old and in the tourist section of town, it was clear—to me, at least—that she was accustomed to having visitors of the demonic variety. The most telling feature was the broad staircase that led to the attic. At least twice as wide as normal and sturdily built, those stairs had been designed to make it easier for the demons she summoned in her attic to come down to her library. In fact, after I got the library wards cleared, I needed to get into that summoning chamber. Those wards didn't appear to be quite as nasty, however, after my experience with the library wards, I wasn't quite ready to take the chance.

I adored my own summoning chamber, but I wanted to have the option to use hers. After all, it had cost me close to a hundred dollars to rent the truck for one night, which only added to my annoyance. I was a cop. I wasn't rich.

I entered the hallway, stopping a few yards away from the door to the library. I looked back at Kehlirik and gestured to the door. "I need to get into that room and have free access to everything within. I also need the wards restricting access to the summoning chamber in the attic cleared. Can you do that?"

Kehlirik narrowed his eyes as he moved slowly closer. He crouched, his gaze traveling over the frame, the door, and even the wall. I knew what he was looking at. To anyone without skill in the arcane, it was just a pretty white door set in a wall that was papered in an elegant flowered design in muted tones of rose and gold. However, to anyone with any skill in the arcane, the door and wall crackled and hissed with power, crawling with blue and purple wards that writhed and coiled malevolently. I grimaced. It hadn't been so bad before I'd started dinking with the damn protections. Apparently I'd unwittingly triggered something nasty earlier, and now it looked like the level of protection had quintupled—like cutting off one head of a hydra.

Ryan let out a low whistle. "It looks worse now."

The *reyza* pulled his attention away from the sinister

energies to peer at me. "You have attempted to get through."

It wasn't a question, and I twitched a shoulder self-consciously. "Yes. Quite unsuccessfully, as you can see."

"And you survived." His nostrils flared. "I am surprised."

My gut tightened. "It was . . . close." I said, my mouth a bit dry at the memory. "I really didn't think my aunt would put something so lethal in place."

"*She* did not," he replied, returning his focus to the door. Hands on knees, wings tucked along his back, he fell silent again.

My gaze traveled over the roiling potencies on the door. "Then who did?"

The *reyza* rumbled softly deep in his chest before speaking. "She summoned another to do so. This looks like Zhergalet's work. He is merely a *faas*, but his skill with wards is unique and admired."

"Oh, so my aunt subcontracted her alarm system," I said with a relieved laugh. Kehlirik turned his head and blinked at me. "Sorry. I thought she'd done all of this work herself, and I was feeling pretty inadequate since I couldn't even dream of doing anything this intricate. But now that I know she summoned someone to do it for her, I don't feel so bad."

Kehlirik looked back at the door, then stood, shifting his wings on his back and folding his arms across his chest. "It is an impressive piece of work. There is an underlayer of protections here that seems to be fairly standard. It would prevent the average human from entering and would prevent most from even recognizing that the door exists. Aversions," he gestured with a clawed hand to a coil of purple energy, "to make one reluctant to be here."

But then he shook his head. "But those have been in place for years. Zhergalet placed deep protections on this door recently—perhaps three turnings of this world's moon."

Something my aunt had been working on three months ago? Then I went still. That was about the time that the Symbol Man murders had started again. Right about the time that I first encountered Rhyzkahl. Could that be why she wanted to close her library off? To keep me out? Or to keep out Rhyzkahl? Surely she trusted me more than that. I felt hollow but also incredibly confused. The wards in place were extreme and deadly. Why the fuck had she become so protective of this room three months ago?

I scrubbed at my face, disturbed on innumerable levels. "All right, can you get in?"

He was silent for several heartbeats, then gave a grave nod. "It will not be swift. It will take me until tomorrow night." Then his gaze locked on mine, and his lips curled back from his wickedly sharp teeth. "Usually I would request renegotiation of terms or demand an admission of debt, but as you are the favored one of Rhyzkahl, I will grant this service as my gift to you."

I quickly controlled the shocked expression that was surely on my face and produced a weak smile instead, thinking furiously. I didn't know which lord Kehlirik served. I assumed he served one, since that was one of the best and easiest ways for demons to gain status—to serve a high-standing lord. And from what I knew of the demon realm, and from what my aunt had told me, Rhyzkahl was one of the highest of the lot.

But did Kehlirik serve Rhyzkahl, or was he trying to curry favor with him? Either way, I had no idea how risky it could be to accept such a gift. Few things were truly *gifts* among the demonkind. On the other hand, refusing a gift could definitely be construed as a major insult.

Shit. I *needed* that library available to me. I looked back at the *reyza*. "Honored Kehlirik, your gift is precious to me, and it will not be forgotten." He inclined his head gravely as I controlled the urge to sigh. I had no idea if I'd just screwed up colossally by accepting it, but rejecting it seemed like a quick ticket to an insulted retaliation.

Whatever. I didn't feel like worrying about it at that moment. I had plenty to worry about already. And normally I would have loved to stay and watch the demon work and perhaps learn some new techniques and skills, but, despite my earlier nap, fatigue dragged at me. Summonings of *reyza* were exhausting affairs. "Kehlirik, do you need me to stay here with you while you work?"

The demon shook his head, already beginning to tease layers of arcane energy apart. "No, summoner. But you will need to adjust the anchors holding me in this realm to permit me to stay through the day."

Now I felt like an idiot. I hadn't even considered the possibility that the task I'd set him might take more than a few hours. I'd summoned him and bound him to this sphere with lunar potency. When day came, those bindings would unravel and he'd be drawn back to his own sphere. Moreover, since being drawn back like that wasn't a proper dismissal, it was supposedly quite painful for the demon.

I had only one problem. I'd never had any need to adjust anchors and had absolutely zero clue how to do it—and I highly doubted that he was going to teach me for free. I cleared my throat. "Honored one, I do not know this skill. I will be in your debt if you would teach me."

Kehlirik peered down at me, silent for long enough that

I had to fight the urge to hang my head in shame. Then he turned to me fully, spreading his wings, or at least as far as he could spread them in the width of the hallway. He folded his heavily muscled arms across his chest. "I accept your admission of debt, Kara Gillian. We will negotiate the terms on your next summoning of me."

My neck was getting a crick in it from looking up at him. "Yes, honored one."

"I would also speak with you at length"—his gaze flicked to Ryan and then back to me—"in private, before you dismiss me back to my own world."

Hunh. Did he want to tell me something about Ryan? Or did he just not want Ryan hearing whatever it was he had to tell me? Either way, the comment left an unpleasant churning in my gut. "Agreed," I said, doing my best not to show how much the request unnerved me.

Kehlirik rumbled, looking again at Ryan. I thought the demon was going to hiss and growl, since the expression on his face was certainly malevolent enough, but he did neither. He snorted, nostrils flaring, then unfolded his arms and returned his attention to me. I saw Ryan roll his eyes and flip the demon off behind his back—something that would have made me laugh out loud a few minutes ago, but now I had too much uncertainty roiling through me. For a brief instant I hated the demon for stealing away the companionable ease I'd felt with Ryan, but I knew I couldn't put all that on Kehlirik. Rhyzkahl had seeded doubts already with his insinuations that I didn't know all there was to know about Ryan. Kehlirik had merely brought all of that out into the open with his obvious antipathy. *And why the fuck would any of the demons know who Ryan is anyway?*

"Abide closely, then," the demon said, yanking me out

of my tortured musings, "and I will show you how to re-anchor."

The lesson was a quick one, though it still left me sweating. It wasn't a difficult procedure, but it was oddly complex. Still, Kehlirik seemed pleased enough with my grasp of it and carefully walked me through the procedure.

I stepped back when I finished and looked at the revised bindings. Now when the night turned to day and the potencies shifted from lunar to solar, the anchors would re-form around us both. It was an interesting piece of work, and I thought I could see something else about it, but, again, I was tired and on edge and didn't have the energy to delve too deeply into it.

But another thought occurred to me during the lesson. If it *had* been my *ilius* that had consumed Brian's essence, then I was looking at an isolated event, since the demon would have been drawn back to its own sphere at sunrise. I despised the thought that I could be at fault, but it was better than thinking that there was some other essence-eating creature on the loose.

The demon gave an approving nod. "You grasp the concepts quickly. Very well, I will remain here and work."

"I'll secure the house and close all the curtains and stuff," I said. "If anyone comes to the house...just stay away from the door."

The *reyza* rumbled again. I figured this time it was the demon version of *No shit, Sherlock.* "I will place an aversion on the door after you depart," he said instead. "And I should be able to sense anyone approaching in sufficient time to hide my presence."

How the hell an eight-foot-tall demon with wings and horns and a tail would hide himself was beyond me, but I decided it was best not to worry about it. I quickly went through the house and locked all the doors and windows, making sure the curtains were all drawn, then gave Kehlirik quick instructions on how to use the phone in the kitchen in case he needed to contact me. Again, he seemed utterly delighted, and I could see he was restraining himself from trying it out at that instant.

"All right, I'll check on you during the day, then," I said. The demon merely snorted softly, already engrossed in untangling the wards. I jerked my head at Ryan and headed toward the door to the garage. I half-expected him to give the demon the finger again, but he managed to control himself and followed me out.

"I've changed my mind," he said, after we'd shut the garage door and were in the truck.

"About what?"

"That demon. I don't think he's my best bro anymore. He is *so* not getting an invite to my next Super Bowl party."

I shook my head and started the truck. "And people say *I'm* weird."

6

"YOU ARE WORRIED."

I nestled against Rhyzkahl's chest, the weight of his arm around me a comfort. The sun pierced the broad canopy of the tree we sat beneath, casting a shifting lace of light across us. I could feel the warmth of his breath on the top of my head and I closed my eyes, relishing the exquisite peace of the moment. I didn't want to respond to him, and besides, it didn't feel like a question.

But he straightened, ignoring my little whine of protest as he pulled his arm away from me, and stood. I scowled up at him. "I was comfortable."

"Comfort is a trap," he responded.

I stood and brushed leaves from my dress. It was a lovely creation of dark-blue brocaded silk, with a scattering of jewels sewn onto a plunging bodice. I felt as if it was a favorite, though there was a faint part of me that knew I'd never seen it before. "Of course I'm worried. I miss my aunt, and something's eating essence."

"And I would be pleased to give you such aid as to ease your worry."

I gave him a sour look. "Give? You don't just give anything. You're a demon."

"Not all prices are onerous." As if to prove his point, he moved to me, pushing me back against the tree and capturing my mouth in a kiss. His hands braceleted my wrists over my head as his lips shifted from my mouth to my throat. I dropped my head back, groaning as heat flushed through me.

"I do not ask for more than you can give, dear one," he murmured against my skin. He continued to hold my wrists, tightening very slightly when I tried to shift his hold. His teeth grazed my neck, and a shiver raced through me. "I can show you what you are truly capable of."

"Yes," I whispered. "Show me."

He lifted his head, triumph flashing in his eyes, then abruptly released me and straightened. "The sun is rising," he said, which made no sense, since the sun was high in the sky. He frowned. "This will not be comfortable for you, but it will get easier."

I came awake with a shuddering gasp as nausea twisted through my body. I sucked in my breath, hands tightening in the sheets as a sensation like the worst hangover I'd ever had rolled over me, literally feeling as if it started at my head and rolled down throughout my body to my toes. Nausea and headache and weakness, and then it was gone, leaving me sweating and shaking, even though it had lasted perhaps only half a dozen heartbeats.

I took an uneasy breath and slowly sat up, images and sensations from the dream shimmering through my head and already beginning to fade like fog under a rising sun. Had that really been just a dream? He'd seemed to know that I was about to feel like shit. But, then again, I could think of countless times when my alarm clock had been incorporated into my dream right before I'd woken, so maybe that was the same kind of thing.

Through my bedroom window I could see that dawn was turning the eastern sky orange and purple, and I abruptly realized what had happened. The potencies had shifted from lunar to solar, and my link with Kehlirik had to re-form. I took another deep breath, nausea all but gone now. *Okay, that sucked major ass. Did Kehlirik feel that too?*

I glanced at my clock and sighed. It was barely past six a.m., which meant that I'd managed to get only about four hours of sleep.

Complete with a dream about Rhyzkahl. *I'm dreaming about him only because Kehlirik mentioned him. That's all. He was just on my mind.*

Suuuure.

I thought about sticking my head under the pillow and trying for more sleep, but the beeping of the pager on my nightstand derailed that line of thought.

I sighed and scrolled through the message: *Signal 29, Ruby Est.* A death—but at least not a murder, since the signal for that was a 30. So it was someone who had died from either an accident or illness. Hopefully that meant it would be a nice and simple open-and-shut case, but even as I thought it, I knew I was probably jinxing myself.

THE ADDRESS WAS for a section of Beaulac that I very seldom had cause to go into. Ruby Estates was *the* elite neighborhood for people who had more money than they knew what to do with. It was a gated community with its own security service—though, like any other security service, it was mostly staffed by the kind of people who could be hired for eight dollars an hour. All of the lots were on or near the lakefront, at least an acre in size, and the neighborhood in general was lovely, wooded, and quiet. I had no doubt that there was a fair measure of drug use and domestic violence within the walls in this subdivision, but it was kept quiet enough that we seldom got called out to deal with it.

The address wasn't hard to find. It was the one with several police cars and an ambulance in front of it—far more attention than any regular person would ever get for a slip and fall. But this was the house of Parish Councilman Davis Sharp and a stunning example of what shit-loads of money could do for you. Davis Sharp had cleared the majority of the trees off his land so that everyone driving by could see his three-story mansion—complete with an absurdly broad staircase that swept up to the second level like some plantation gone mad. Personally, I thought it was a hideous waste of what was surely a few million dollars. But, then again, I lived in a house with peeling paint in the middle of nowhere, so who was I to judge?

In addition to being a parish councilman, Davis Sharp was a prominent restaurateur and had been making noises about running for the open congressional seat in the district. He was charismatic and well connected, and his restaurant, Sharp's, was where people went to be seen in St. Long Parish.

It wasn't technically a crime scene, but the front yard had been cordoned off anyway, yellow crime-scene tape flapping sluggishly in the dull breeze that drifted off the lake. I had to admit it was a lovely view, though the serenity of the lake stood in sharp contrast to the police vehicles lined up along the driveway. I also couldn't help wishing that the breeze would pick up a bit. I'd thrown on my standard detective garb of dress slacks and tailored short-sleeved blouse, accessorized with gun and badge. No jacket. Not in this heat. It was barely eight a.m., and already I could feel sweat prickling under my arms.

I ducked under the tape, eager to get inside the house—more for the promise of air-conditioning than from a desire to get started on the investigation. A uniformed officer stood by the door with his arms crossed over his chest and an intensely bored expression on his tanned face. Allen Demma had close to twenty years with the department—a corporal who would probably never be promoted any higher. In fact, he'd been a corporal when I first started on the road. He was great at following orders and abiding by the rules, but he just didn't have the drive to be a leader of others. Personally I didn't think he'd be with the department much longer. I knew he was approaching burnout and was frustrated at being repeatedly passed over for promotion. On the other hand, he wasn't old enough to draw retirement yet, and I had no idea what someone like him—who'd been a cop his entire life—would do for a living if he left law enforcement.

I didn't like thinking about what I would do if I ever decided to stop being a cop. It was so much a part of who I was that I had a hard time imagining doing anything else.

"Hey, Allen," I said. "Whatcha got?"

Allen gave me a small nod of greeting as he pulled his notebook out of the pocket in his shirt. "Davis Sharp was last seen alive by the maid, Auri Cordova, last night. She cooked dinner, then left at about six p.m.," he recited, tone flat and clipped. "At approximately five this morning, she returned and let herself in and found Sharp on the floor of the shower in the master bathroom, the water still running. She shut the water off and realized that he was dead, at which time she called 911."

I made notes of my own on my pad. "Thanks, Allen. Is there a Mrs. Sharp?"

He glanced at his notebook again. "The maid said that Mr. Sharp informed her that Elena Sharp left the day before yesterday to spend some time at their condo in Mandeville. The coroner's office has already been in touch with Mrs. Sharp and made notification."

I frowned. "Do you know if Mrs. Sharp is on her way back?"

"No idea. Sorry."

"All right. Well, I appreciate it. You've been a big help."

He gave a short nod of response. *I bet he was recently passed over for promotion again.* I couldn't think of anything I could say to him, so I took the easy way out and said nothing as I continued on into the house.

There were a couple of uniformed officers inside, who directed me upstairs to the master bedroom, then returned to their deep discussion of LSU football. The house was even more impressive on the inside. Wallpaper that looked like expensive fabric, marble floors, dark-wood molding, and all of the lovely decorative pieces that were perfectly placed to draw the eye to the next lovely decorative piece. The stairs were grand and sweeping— the sort you see in movies where the beautiful woman comes slowly down while being admired by everyone below. I made my way up the stairs, feeling oddly conspicuous and out of place—grimacing at the way I clumped and certain that everyone was watching me. I even glanced back when I reached the top and was stupidly relieved to see that no one had paid the slightest bit of attention.

The second floor was more of the same as the first, with window dressings that matched the bedding in the master bedroom, and a bathroom that seemed to take up one entire side of the house. It was to that bathroom that I was directed now.

I'd never met Davis Sharp in person and had never been flush enough to be willing to drop the cash that an evening at his restaurant would cost me, but I'd seen enough pictures of him in the society section of the newspaper to know that he'd been a well-styled man with a very professional appearance, as one would expect of an aspiring politician. Which, of course, made his current situation all the more jarring and definitely snicker-inducing, though everyone on the scene was being exceedingly careful not to let their amusement show, at the risk of being slammed for it later.

It took me a few seconds of puzzled staring to figure out what had happened. I finally decided that Councilman Sharp had either slipped and hit his head or passed out in the shower, managing to fall so that he was face-down, wedged into the corner, with his chin nearly touching his chest and his ass sticking nearly straight up in the air. I'd seen a couple of cases of positional asphyxiation before, and this one pretty much fit the bill.

But I saw those details only peripherally. My gut dropped and a chill swept through me as I felt the discordant wrongness. I shifted quickly into othersight to verify, seeing the tattered remnants of essence clinging to the body. *Another one,* I thought in numb horror. What the hell could be doing this? I knew that it couldn't be my *ilius,* since it wasn't possible for a demon to stay in this sphere without some sort of binding. But whatever it was, it wasn't an isolated event anymore.

Could it possibly be another summoner? But summoners were rare, and the chances of another one being in this area *and* summoning a demon that could eat essence seemed too high to even comprehend.

So was it something else entirely? Frustration gnawed at me, briefly chasing away the horror. There was far too much that I didn't know.

And whatever it is, what if there's more than one?

I mentally shied away from thinking about how disastrous that could be and forced myself to concentrate on the mundane aspects of the investigation. I stepped back and pulled my notebook out so that I could jot down the notes I needed to make about the scene. The bathroom and bedroom were neat and tidy, and when I opened a closet I saw orderly rows of shirts and slacks, with shoes lined up precisely along the floor. A second closet was empty save for a few wooden hangers—the kind I told myself I would someday buy to replace the cheap metal ones I got for free from the cleaners. I went back into the bathroom and peered through drawers, finding nothing unusual except for the lack of anything feminine.

His wife went to their condo in Mandeville? I mused. *Apparently it wasn't just a weekend getaway.* That was an interesting—and important—detail. I gave the bedroom area one final scan, then went down the hall to a smaller bedroom to speak to the maid.

She was shaken but coherent. I asked her a few quick identification questions, ignoring my near certainty that she was an illegal immigrant and instead being grateful that she spoke damn good English. Auri had worked for the Sharps for the past two years—coming in to cook and clean on Mondays, Thursdays, and Saturdays. Except that this week she'd come Friday as well, at Davis Sharp's request. She seemed terribly nervous, which I wrote off as concern that I would make an issue of her status, but when I gave her my standard "I'm far more interested in working this case than dealing with immigration issues" speech, she surprised me by shaking her head firmly.

"No. I no worry about that. It Mr. Sharp," she said, gesturing with a fluttering hand toward the bedroom. "He bad upset yesterday."

"Because of his wife?"

"*Sí.* Miss Elena go Thursday morning and take all her things. But that not all."

"What else was there?"

"Another lady come over Thursday after Miss Elena go. I hear her talk to Mr. Sharp, then they go upstairs." She pursed her lips in clear disapproval. "A few minute later he come down and tell me I can go, ask me to come back Friday because Miss Elena not coming back and he need laundry and cooking."

I blinked. "Hold on. Have you ever seen this woman here before?"

She shook her head slowly. "No . . . I no think so. I come most time in morning and see Miss Elena go out for walks with ladies from neighborhood, but I no think this lady one of those. But yesterday I come here again. I clean house and cook dinner like Mr. Sharp want, but he no look happy. He stay upstairs most of day. This other lady come and let herself in back door, then she go upstairs like she live here." Auri scowled and shook her head. "Mr. Sharp, he lean out bedroom door and shout down to me, tell me I can go early." She spread her hands and shrugged. "I leave dinner in fridge and go." Her lower lip trembled. "I come today, I see dinner still in fridge. Then I go to bedroom to pick up laundry. I hear water, so I think he in shower. I clean, start laundry, and water *still* running. It been almost hour, so I call for him, then I look...I think he hurt real bad. I see him in shower, on floor, and he no breathing." Tears welled up in her eyes. "I turn off water and call police."

I pressed her for any further details or a description of the woman, but Auri apparently had caught only a fleeting glimpse of the woman as she went upstairs. Light hair, slender figure, dressed in what looked like expensive clothes. *And that describes half the female population of this subdivision,* I thought in mild annoyance. I finally got as much contact information as I could from her and let her leave.

So, was Sharp getting some action on the side? If so, how long had it been going on? And was that why his wife left? And had this other woman come back later?

I returned to the bathroom, drawn back to the body despite the wrongness of it. I had to clench my hands to keep them from shaking. *Could it just be me? Is it my judgment that's out of whack?*

I let out an unsteady breath as I took a mental step back, looking around the bathroom and the adjoining bedroom for any similarity at all to Brian Roth's death. But nothing leaped out at me. Different neighborhoods, different class of victim.

Maybe a similar cause of death? Brian's was an apparent suicide, but there were still a lot of questions, and until we found Carol we wouldn't know anything for certain. And, on the surface, the Davis Sharp case looked as if it was going to be a garden-variety accident or possibly a heart attack, but the fact that his wife had apparently left him certainly added a twist. I had to keep in mind the possibility that this was a murder staged to look like an accident. I'd check with Jill later to see if Crime Scene found anything suspicious, and I'd also check the maid out as much as I could.

I heard Crawford come up behind me, making a noise in the back of his throat at the sight of Sharp's still-damp rear end.

"Nice view. Got anything yet, Kara?" he asked as he took in the scene.

"Just some basics so far." I gave him a quick rundown, then closed my notebook, my gaze inexorably drawn back to the body. The emptiness seemed to mock me, and now I couldn't help but wonder if maybe I was seeing wrongness in something that wasn't wrong. Maybe something had changed in the way essence was released after death? Changed in the universe in general? Maybe this was happening to all bodies, not just the ones I'd seen yesterday and today. I hadn't been on any death calls—natural or homicide—since my own "death." Maybe crossing through the spheres had changed something in my perception?

No, that didn't make any sense. The essence had obviously been ripped away as soon as death had loosened its grip. I could see the trailing threads, and I couldn't imagine any possible way for that to occur naturally.

"Kara?" Crawford's voice jerked me out of my thoughts. "Are you with me?" he said, a mixture of annoyance and worry in his voice.

I flushed and gave a sharp nod. "Yeah, Sarge. Sorry. Well, this looks like an accident, but his wife left him, and he might have been getting some action on the side, so it's possible that there was something hinky going on. I'll check the wife's alibi and see if I can find out who this other woman was."

"Sounds good." He snorted. "Well, this is a prominent local businessman and parish councilman, so we jump through all of the damn hoops to figure out exactly how this guy ended ass end up in the fucking shower."

I gave him the amused smile he expected, but I didn't feel amused. I felt shaken. Shit, I needed to figure out if this essence loss was happening all over or just to a few people. And, once again, just like in the Symbol Man case, I couldn't tell my supervisors what was really going on. *Yeah, Sarge, I'm looking for a link between these two utterly unrelated cases because someone has eaten their souls.* Yeesh.

Crawford sighed gustily. "All right, Kara. I know you already have Brian's case to work, but that should be only paperwork. And with luck you'll be able to wash your hands of this one pretty soon." Then he snickered. "No pun intended." He looked at me with a crooked grin. "Get it? Shower . . . wash . . ."

I lowered my head and gave him a look. "Go. Away."

He grinned. "Okay. This one is hopefully a dumb accident with a rich fuck who slipped on some soap." His eyes slid to Sharp's naked ass. "And I'll be *behind* you the entire way."

I groaned. "Somebody shoot me, please."

IT WAS WELL past mid-morning by the time the scene was completely processed and the body carted away by the coroner's office. The heat had risen to the point where I was damp with sweat from the short walk from the house to my car. I climbed in, deeply grateful that, by pure happenstance, I'd parked under a tree. Still, I cranked the AC to arctic levels and allowed the vents to blast me with air that was nowhere near arctic but was a damn sight cooler than the air outside.

I was just about to put the car into drive when I saw Crawford jogging up, a grim look on his face. I rolled the window down as he approached.

He stooped to look in at me. "Brian's wife has been found."

I could tell by his expression that she hadn't been found alive. "Where?"

"City Hotel." An expression of distaste crossed his face. "What the fuck was she doing *there*?"

He exhaled. "That's what you're going to find out. I have to finish up a couple of things here, and then I'll meet you over there."

"You got it, Sarge."

7

Somehow the temperature managed to rise at least twenty degrees during the ten-minute drive to the Beaulac City Hotel. At least it felt like it. It didn't help that the cheap asphalt of the parking lot soaked up the heat and radiated it back in concentrated waves, designed to wring as much sweat as possible from anyone silly enough to be outside.

The Beaulac City Hotel—where rooms could be rented by the hour or the week—hadn't seen a fresh coat of paint in decades. Several windows had been replaced by plywood, piles of old trash lurked in corners, and an ashtray by the door to the office had reached its capacity a few hundred cigarette butts ago. A sour smell of sweat and piss mixed unpleasantly with the heat rising from the asphalt, enveloping me as I approached. Crime-scene tape had been strung around the rusted metal poles that supported the second-story balcony, and I could see the officer manning the sign-in log standing in the meager shade offered by the second floor. After a hard look at the battered poles, I wasn't so sure it was a better option to be in the shade.

I signed the log, then ducked under the tape. Another uniformed officer leaned against the outside wall by an open hotel-room door, his usually bald head covered with about a millimeter's length of hair. I'd known Scott Glassman for years and had worked on the same team with him when I was on the road. He was a solid cop with no desire to ever go into Investigations—a "good ole boy" who was perfectly happy being perpetually assigned to patrol. He had a troubled expression on his face that shifted to a sad smile when he saw me, and I abruptly remembered that Scott and Brian Roth had been good friends and hunting buddies outside work. This whole situation had to be pretty hard on him.

"Hey, Scott," I said. "Are we sure that it's Brian's wife? Who made the ID?"

His expression was grim. "I did. I thought I recognized her, but I verified it with the driver's license in her purse. And the blue Prius in the parking lot is hers."

"Damn," I said. "I was really hoping that Brian had just been using a figure of speech." I swept my gaze around the nasty hotel. "Any clue yet on why she was *here*?"

"Well, I spoke to the manager. He says she checked in night before last, alone—under the name 'Jane Smythe'— but apparently she was something of a regular."

"At a dump like this?" I had a hard time wrapping my mind around that.

He scrubbed a hand over the stubble on his head. "I guess it was a game they played more than once. I dunno. But the manager says he doesn't know shit about anyone else coming to the room." He scowled. "Manager doesn't know shit about a lot, but I'm about to run his ass to see if he has any warrants, because he's being a pain in *my* ass."

"If you could lean on him, that would be a big help. Why'd it take so long for her to be found?" My gaze swept the exterior of the building. "Place like this probably turns the rooms over pretty quickly, I would think."

He scowled. "Manager said that she would always be out in a few hours, so he didn't bother checking in the morning." I made a face, and he sighed and nodded in agreement. "And the chick who cleans the rooms called in sick yesterday, and obviously he's too much of a lazy fuck to do it himself."

"At least she was finally found." I grimaced and swiped at the sweat that snaked down my forehead. "Maybe now we can figure out what the hell happened. I guess there's no such thing as surveillance cameras around here?"

He shook his head. "Not that work. I already checked."

I gave his arm a companionable squeeze. "I appreciate the effort."

"Yeah," he said with a sigh. "I just wish the whole situation wasn't so fucked up."

I merely nodded in response, suddenly very glad that no one knew the other horrific detail about Brian's death. It was hard enough on everyone to lose a member of the force, especially under these circumstances, and it wouldn't help to know that, on top of all that, his essence had been eaten.

A shiver walked down my back, and I turned to step into the gloomy hotel room, steeling myself against the knowledge that this body might be like the others, with nothing but tattered remains of essence fluttering in an ethereal wind.

Jill was inside, taking measurements. She looked up

and gave me a small nod of greeting as I entered. "Hell of a way to spend a day, huh?" she said with a shake of her head. "Anyway, I'm finished here. She's all yours." She gestured to the floor on the other side of the bed.

I stepped around and was rewarded by the sight of a woman's body, nude except for a red silk scarf that hung loosely around her throat like an accessory. She lay on her side as if sleeping, eyes half closed with the flat, dull look of death in them. Her hair, auburn and artfully highlighted, snaked across her face, plastered in spots with dried sweat and saliva. She was young—late twenties perhaps—and she had the kind of slender figure I could never hope to attain, no matter how much I exercised. The portion of her body nearest the floor was mottled in red, and a naïve observer might first believe that she was heavily bruised, but I'd seen lividity—or livor mortis—on enough corpses to know that the redness was due to the settling of the blood in the body once the heart ceased pumping.

I crouched by the body, placing my feet cautiously even though the scene had already been photographed and processed. I was still learning the ropes when it came to homicide investigations, but I'd been a cop long enough to know that you had to watch where you stepped on a scene.

I couldn't tell how long she'd been dead—that determination would have to come from the coroner's office—but even my limited experience told me that she obviously hadn't died in the last few hours. But that was a minor concern for me right at the moment.

I was far more focused on her essence, or what might remain of it. I shifted into othersight, nearly swaying in relief when I saw nothing more than a faint shimmering glow. Yes, this was what it was *supposed* to look like. No tattered threads, no torn edges. Just a soft residue from an essence that departed its shell the normal and natural way instead of being ripped free. This residual glow would linger for a day or two more, then naturally dissipate.

I pulled myself out of othersight and let my gaze travel over her, taking in the whole scene. There were articles of clothing scattered on the floor, but I didn't see any suitcases or bags.

I glanced back at Jill. "She had a purse?"

"It's on the table."

I glanced over. It was a small clutch-size thing—not one of those career-woman monstrosities that could have held a week's worth of clothes and toiletries. It didn't look as if she'd planned an extended stay. Or even an overnight one. "Any trace evidence? Fingerprints?"

Jill grimaced. "Sure. Tons. Which is the problem."

I echoed her grimace. "A few hundred people have been through here, and it all becomes one noisy mess."

"You nailed it, chick. I'll do my best, but I think you're gonna get your best evidence off the body."

I nodded in understanding, and she stepped away to write dates and times on her evidence bags. I looked again at the strewn garments. I murmured under my breath, "We just liked to play...." That's what Brian's suicide note had said. Damn.

"You find something, Kara?"

I looked up to see that Crawford had come in behind me. "It's more what I'm not finding, unfortunately."

He crouched beside me. "What do you mean?" His gaze swept over the body, taking in the details. I could see his eyes flick quickly from the clothing to the rumpled bed to the scarf, tallying it up, no doubt coming to the same conclusion that I'd come to.

"I'm not finding signs of struggle, defensive wounds, anything like that," I said.

An expression of regret passed over his face. "Keep going."

I sighed. "I think that our first theory was right, Sarge—this is sex play gone bad." I gave a nod toward the silk scarf. "It wasn't a robbery, because she's still wearing her earrings and her wedding ring." I pointed to the diamond studs in her earlobes and then to the fair-size diamond cluster on her left hand. "I can't see anyone leaving those behind. I'm willing to bet she and Brian were engaging in some autoerotic asphyxia play, and it went a touch too far. I think he was slowly choking her and releasing, giving her that hypoxia rush—" I broke off with a curse. "What a fucking waste. Brian should have known better than to play with dangerous shit like that."

"Yeah," he said, voice quiet and hoarse. "I would never have figured him for something like this. Guess you never know people."

I took a deep breath and made myself continue. "I think he was playing this game with her, and then one time when he let it go she didn't start breathing again. He tried CPR—there's even bruising in the middle of her chest—and when she still didn't come back, I guess he panicked and bailed out." I shook my head. "I dunno. It doesn't make sense. He's not the sort to panic. I can't believe he wouldn't have called 911 and at least *tried* to get help."

"This whole situation is fucked from top to bottom," Crawford said, and when I looked at him sharply, he winced and shook his head. "No pun intended there. I swear." But even unintended, the horrific pun had broken some of the dark mood, which was a relief to both of us.

He inclined his head at me, a thin smile playing on his face. "How do you know about asphyxia play?"

"Back when I was a property detective, I worked a fraud case at the adult video shop downtown. It was a pretty complicated case, and I ended up learning more than I *ever* wanted to know simply by being around the place so much."

Crawford nodded, eyes dancing. "I remember that." He stood and walked to the door, and I followed suit. "What's your plan now?"

I made a face at the wall of heat that enveloped us as we stepped outside. "Wait for Doc to do the autopsies. Anything else will depend on what he says."

He peered into my face. "You look fried. As soon as you're finished here, you should go home and get some sleep."

I snorted but couldn't help but smile. "I intend to. You just make sure no one else decides to die today."

8

UNFORTUNATELY, MY DEEP DESIRE FOR A NAP WAS foiled by the coroner's office, though I had to grudgingly admit that it wasn't their fault. A nasty—and fatal—traffic accident on one of the highways at the north end of the parish meant that we had to wait for them to collect those victims before coming to get Carol Roth.

I took refuge in my car as the heat rose—keeping the AC cranked up as I pecked out my initial reports on my laptop. But by two p.m. there was still no sign of the coroner's office, and I was uncomfortably aware that I'd promised Kehlirik to check on him during the day. And one did *not* blithely break promises to the demonkind.

Then again, I never promised to check on him in person. I grinned at the realization, pulled out my cell phone, and hit the speed dial for my aunt's house.

By the fourth ring I was coming to the reluctant conclusion that Kehlirik had either forgotten how to answer the phone or was too busy with the wards to break away.

But on the fifth ring I heard it pick up with a rumble on the other end that could only be from a *reyza*.

"Kehlirik, this is Kara Gillian."

"Greetings to you, summoner." The powerful bass of his voice seemed to vibrate the phone against my ear.

"And to you. Is everything going all right? Do you need anything?"

"All is well," he replied. "The wards on the summoning chamber are cleared. The library will take more time, but a mere *faas* cannot create a ward that can defeat me." I could hear him snort in derision at the thought.

"I have the utmost faith in you, honored one," I said, keeping my voice grave, though I wanted to laugh. "It's probably going to be a few more hours before I can get back over there."

"That is acceptable. I will use this device to contact you should I require anything else." I could hear the eager edge to his voice, and I grinned. How long would it take for him to find a reason to use the phone again?

I hung up after assuring him that it was quite all right to call me if he needed anything, relieved that I'd taken care of that responsibility. I leaned my head back against the headrest and watched the shimmer of heat come off the pavement. Everyone else had taken refuge in their own cars, except for one officer who stood in the doorway of the hotel room. He'd cranked the AC in the room up to get some relief from the heat and had spent the last hour on his cell phone.

My thoughts drifted back to the sense of responsibility I had toward Kehlirik. I'd thought that it was just honor that drove me to check on him, but I realized there was more to it than that. I summoned these creatures from an alternate plane of existence, and *I* was the one responsible for their safety and well-being. Even though technically they couldn't be killed here, since a mortal injury would merely send them back to their own sphere, I knew too well that it wasn't comfortable or pleasant to go through that.

The relationship between summoner and demons was a strange and complex one, and I was still learning some of the nuances of it. When I'd first started my training as a summoner, I was mildly horrified at the entire idea—the fact that summoners basically yanked demons from their home world and brought them here to serve them. But as I learned more, I saw that it wasn't as simple—or crude—as that at all. True, the demons did not care to be summoned, and their honor demanded that they put up a struggle and demand a sacrifice or offering in return. Yet, at the same time, they gained great status among their own kind by being summoned, and I couldn't shake the feeling that the demons benefited in other ways from sojourns in this sphere.

I finished up my reports, then gave the officer at the door a break for a while. It was too miserably hot to make one person suffer alone, so the few of us remaining there rotated the duty. It was early evening before the coroner's black van pulled into the parking lot of the hotel, to our huge relief. The investigator and her assistant both looked frayed and were in little mood to engage in conversation. I couldn't blame them—they'd been baking on the side of a highway while the fire department had surgically ripped vehicles apart to extract victims, both living and dead. I was also more than eager to finish up at this scene, so once we all made sure that there were no previously unseen injuries on Carol's body, she was bagged, tagged, loaded into the van, and taken to the morgue.

I released the scene as soon as they were out of the parking lot and was in my own car less than a minute later. I was tired and cranky and wanted nothing more than to go home and crawl under the covers and hide from the world, but I had no choice. I *had* to go back to my aunt's house and dismiss Kehlirik.

I turned the radio in the car to the country music station, singing along loudly to Carrie Underwood and fighting the fatigue that dragged at me. When I finally turned onto Tessa's street, I felt as if I'd run a gauntlet of street signs and other drivers. The sun glowed ruddy orange across Lake Pearl as it began to dip below the horizon. I parked in Tessa's driveway, pulling myself out of the car just as a shudder of arcane nausea rippled over me. I staggered, putting a hand on the hood of my car to get my bearings back, taking deep breaths until it passed. *And here we go from solar back to lunar. Ugh.*

Now I understood why summoners seldom maintained a summoning for more than a few hours, though at least this transition didn't seem as intense as the one this morning. I took a settling breath as the feeling faded, then pushed off the car and headed up the porch, disabling the protections and aversion wards twining around the door as I entered.

The hallway was empty and the library door open, which I took as a positive sign. At least the *reyza* had made it that far.

But I still peered around the doorway with more than a bit of caution. I let my breath out at the sight of Kehlirik crouched in the center of the library, arms folded across his knees and wings tucked along his back. His skin had a vaguely greenish cast, and I thought I detected the barest tremor in his wings. *Well, that answers the question of whether or not Kehlirik had felt it too.*

I extended cautiously but couldn't feel any of the nasty-ugly wards that had been there earlier. I looked to the demon with worry. "Are you all right? You were successful?"

He nodded once. "I was." His nostrils flared. "I . . . have hunger. Forgive me, but it was more difficult than I had expected."

"No need for apology, honored one. I can prepare food for you." The *reyza* looked like shit. I'd never seen one so pale and still before. That must have been one doozy of a battle with the wards. "Um, can you eat our food?"

He shifted his wings. "I can, though I prefer not to eat flesh."

I blinked. A vegetarian demon. "Right. Wait here. I'll return in a moment." I turned and hurried off to my aunt's kitchen, grimacing. I wasn't even sure if there was anything to eat in the house. Nothing perishable, that was for certain. I rummaged through the pantry, frowning. I'd cleaned her refrigerator out weeks ago, and there wasn't a hell of a lot in her pantry either. A box of microwave popcorn, a bag of pretzels. Saltines. A can of Blue Runner red beans and a box of Minute rice.

"Poor man's red beans and rice it is," I muttered to myself. Beans were vegetarian, right? Hopefully he wasn't vegan, because I had no idea if Blue Runner beans qualified. But at this point there wasn't much choice. I opened the beans and dumped them into a pot, then set water boiling in another pot. I also grabbed a bag of popcorn and jammed it into the microwave. Kehlirik looked like he needed food *now*.

I stirred the beans as the popcorn popped in the microwave, my mind wandering as I looked out at the sunset settling across the lake in streaks of pink and blue. A view like this would be the only way I could get used to living in the middle of town. I adored my privacy, but the view from Tessa's kitchen window was absolutely exquisite.

The microwave dinged and I removed the bag. I was just pouring it into a bowl when I heard a scream and a shout from the hallway. That was *not* Kehlirik.

Then a resonating growl. That *was*.

I dashed out of the kitchen, still clutching the bowl of popcorn. Jill was in the hallway, staring at Kehlirik, who stood in the doorway to the library. I could see what was happening—one of those damn slow-motion things as I watched Jill pull her gun. *Shit!*

"*No!*" I shouted to both of them. I didn't have much fear that Jill would be able to hit him; I knew how fast and powerful a *reyza* was. I was far more afraid that his retaliation would be fatal for her. "Kehlirik, no! Jill, stop!"

Jill snapped her head around to look at me, eyes wide in shock, her gun still pointed at the demon. Kehlirik stood motionless, but I could feel the coiled tension in him, and I knew that if he decided to react, it would be faster than I would be able to see, even exhausted as he was.

"Jill, it's not what you think." Then I grimaced. "Okay, maybe it is what you think. But he won't hurt you, I swear it." I looked back at Kehlirik. Still not moving, he glowered down at the diminutive tech. I moved forward and thrust the bowl of popcorn at him. His gaze slowly dropped to the bowl, then lifted to me. A low rumble emanated from him, and I wasn't quite sure if it was meant to be a growl.

"I'm cooking more food for you," I told him, "but until

it's done, here's some popcorn." I pushed the bowl at him again.

He huffed and took the bowl in both hands, then sank into a crouch, gaze returning to Jill, eyes now almost level with hers. "My thanks, Kara Gillian," he said, his deep voice resounding in the hallway. He picked up a single kernel between two clawed fingers, examined it with a frown, then carefully crunched it between his wicked fangs.

"Kara?" Jill's voice was shaky, but, to give the woman credit, she hadn't run screaming. "Mind sharing with me what the fuck is going on?"

I sighed. "It's . . . hard to explain. But I promise I will." I was still trying to figure out how the hell she'd gotten in here. "But you should probably put the gun away. It won't do you much good against him anyway, and besides, he won't hurt you."

Jill stared at me for another several heartbeats, then looked back at the demon, who was now eating the popcorn by massive handfuls. Finally she lowered her gun and holstered it.

I let my breath out in relief. "How did you get in here?"

She gave me an exasperated look. "I walked in the goddamn front door. I live on the next street over, and I drive past here every day. I saw your car out front and thought I'd pop in and see how you were holding up after today. I rang the bell, but there was no answer."

I couldn't keep the laugh contained. "Well, the bell's broken, and you weren't supposed to be able to walk in the goddamn front door." Then I winced. "Crap, I took down the wards when I came in." *Nice, Kara.* Good thing it was only Jill.

She scowled and put her hands on her hips. "Kara, who the fuck is that? Or *what* the fuck?" She flung her arm out to gesture at the demon—who I would have sworn was staring mournfully into the depths of the empty popcorn bowl.

I jammed my fingers through my hair. "Okay, come into the kitchen while I stir the beans and I'll explain. Or at least I'll try to." I glanced at Kehlirik. "If you come too, I'll make more popcorn."

The demon stood quickly. "That would please me, summoner. I find this *pahpcahn* quite appealing."

Too fucking weird. I turned and headed to the kitchen and stirred the beans, which were about to burn. I turned the heat down, then threw the Minute rice into the water. I'd never claimed to be a gourmet cook. If it wasn't for the invention of the microwave, I'd have starved a long time ago.

Jill followed me in, slowly pulling herself onto one of the stools on the other side of the counter, her eyes staying on the demon as he stood by the kitchen door. I didn't miss the fact that he had effectively blocked the one exit. I pulled another popcorn bag out of the pantry and stuffed it into the microwave. After I had it going, I turned back to Jill.

"Okay, long story short, I have the ability to summon creatures from another plane of existence. They're called demons, but they're not the 'demons from hell' that you were taught about in Sunday school."

Jill gave me a withering look. "I'm Jewish."

I blinked. "With a last name like Faciane?"

She gave a funny little shrug. "It was my late husband's name. I didn't feel like changing it back after he died."

Jill was a widow? "Oh. I'm sorry, I—"

She waved her hand impatiently. "It was a very short

marriage. Very. But it's also a very long story. So please get back to the subject at hand? Hmmm?"

"Sure. Sorry. Anyway, the demons are arcane creatures from a different plane of existence. I can create a portal between our two spheres. And . . . um . . . I summon them."

Jill's eyes were narrowed. The microwave dinged, and I tore my attention from her long enough to pull the bag out and pour more popcorn into the bowl that the demon still clutched. I turned away and busied myself with pouring the rice into a bowl, then dumping the beans on top. I stirred it up quickly, then passed it over to the demon, who had already finished off the popcorn.

Jill groaned. "Blue Runners and Minute rice? Dear God, my mama would be having a stroke if she saw that."

Jill was from New Orleans, with a mama who probably cooked red beans and rice every Monday, according to New Orleans tradition. With real red beans that had been soaked overnight and real rice.

"What, you thought my aunt was going to teach me how to cook?" I snorted, then looked at Kehlirik. He was carefully scraping the last dregs from the bowl with the side of the spoon. My mouth twitched. "That was acceptable, honored one?"

The demon rumbled. "Most acceptable. I have never had reason to sample the food of this realm. I find it quite interesting."

"Great. Put him on the Food Channel," Jill said sourly. "Can we please get back to this whole business of you summoning demons?"

"Look, they're not evil. *Demon* is just the term that they've had for centuries, and it was sorta co-opted by various religions and turned into an evil-creature definition. They're really more like aliens, except that they're from a different plane of existence instead of from a different planet."

Jill regarded me, a sour look still on her face, blue eyes fixed on me. I suddenly realized I was scared to death that she was going to walk out and never speak to me again. And I wasn't sure if I could handle it if she bailed.

"Jill," I said, doing my best to keep my voice steady, "I'm still me. I'm not a bad person."

She blinked. "I know you're not bad," she replied, as if shocked at the idea. She fell silent for several heartbeats, then threw up her hands. "What the fuck. As dark secrets go, this is a doozy, but you're still the coolest chick in Investigations." She smiled at me, and I returned the smile in weak relief, literally gripping the counter behind my back to support myself.

Kehlirik daintily wiped the corner of his mouth with one claw as he handed the bowl to me. "My thanks, summoner. The wards laid by Zhergalet throughout the house have been removed." He flared his nostrils. "You will need to restore these yourself or summon another to renew them for you." He huffed softly. "You should attempt to do it yourself, even if you must summon guidance. You have the strength for it, if not the experience."

I felt like I was being counseled by a professor. "Do you know anything more about why those wards were placed on the library?"

His heavy brow drew down. "I have formed some theories, but I would need to gather more information before I would be willing to give voice to them." He settled his wings and folded his arms across his chest. "Lord Rhyzkahl has a message for you. He desires you to summon him, and he has given his word that there will be no reprisals for doing so."

I felt rooted to the spot. I had certainly not expected anything like that. The *no reprisals* thing was pretty damn important, but my mouth still went dry at the thought of summoning him. Demonic lords considered a summoning of their person to be an affront and an insult of the highest order, which meant they had an annoying tendency to slaughter any summoner who actually managed to bring them through successfully. But if Rhyzkahl had truly promised that there would be no reprisals, that meant I could do a far less rigorous summoning ritual, since I wouldn't have to maintain ten jillion levels of protections to keep from being torn to shreds. Also, if he *wanted* to be summoned, that meant the pull through the portal would not be as difficult. It would be damn near as simple as a first-level summoning.

So, now I was torn. In the past few weeks I'd come to accept that I'd seen the last of the angelically beautiful and deathly powerful demonic lord. I'd had no reason to believe that I would ever see him in the flesh again. Not when such summonings were so dangerous. I still dreamed of him, but those dreams were nothing like the utterly realistic sendings of before, which had been possible due to a link he'd placed on me when I accidentally summoned him. I'd come to the conclusion that the link had been broken when I passed through the spheres and re-formed on earth, but there was a part of me that wasn't so sure. *Could* he still be touching me through the link? Or was I dreaming of him because my subconscious couldn't control itself?

Then again, if he wished me to summon him, my questions surrounding the dreams seemed rather irrelevant now.

"Did he say—" I cleared my throat and tried again. "Did he say *why* he wanted me to summon him?"

"He did not advise me of such, merely bade me give you the message." He lowered his head and looked at me with his ruddy eyes. "The moon is still full enough tonight."

I controlled the urge to rub the gooseflesh on my arms. "You may tell him that you have delivered the message." I had no idea whether I would comply or not. But I did miss Rhyzkahl, in a weird way. I was well aware that he wanted to use me, but he *had* given me a chance to live, and he'd been under no duress whatsoever to do that. And then he'd informed me that he'd taken the payment for it already, telling me in not so many words that I didn't owe an honor debt to him. That was important, since honor was pivotal in the demon realm. Oaths were law, and you impugned the honor of a demon at your own peril. "Kehlirik, was there something else you wanted to speak to me about?" *Something about Ryan?* I added silently.

The demon seemed to hesitate for a breath before shaking his head. "I did, but it is no longer of any import."

Maybe it had nothing to do with Ryan after all, I thought, but Kehlirik spoke before I could do more than wonder.

"Summoner, I have been here overly long."

Suddenly I could feel it too, though I hadn't realized it until he said something about it. I felt stretched and on edge, like the feeling you get when you're positive that something hideous is about to happen. But now that he'd identified the cause of it, I relaxed. It wasn't a premonition—merely the arcane bindings that were connected to me stretching and warping from long use that they weren't designed for.

"Yes, of course. Kehlirik, I thank you for your aid, and for your gift."

He inclined his head. "And I thank you for the meal." He crouched before me. I hesitated, not certain if I wanted to do a dismissal in front of Jill. But, hell, might as well give her the full initiation now. I lifted my arms and started the dismissal chant, using the words to shape my will. A cold wind swirled through the kitchen, and I heard Jill's surprised yelp. A slit of blinding light appeared behind the demon like a rent in the cosmos—which it basically was. Kehlirik threw his head back and let out a loud bellow as the light swallowed him, and an instant later both light and demon disappeared with a loud crack like a breaking glacier.

I pushed my hands through my hair, then slid a cautious look at Jill. She was staring at the place where the demon had been, lips pressed together, frowning. Then she took a deep breath and looked at me.

"Okay," she said in a shockingly calm voice. "That pretty much takes care of the possibility that you were playing some sort of elaborate practical joke on me with someone in a *really* good costume."

I gave a breathless laugh as I pulled myself onto a stool. Dismissals were tiring, and I'd already started out exhausted. "Sorry, chick. That was the real thing." I looked at her warily. "Are you ... I mean, is this going to be ..." My words trailed away. I didn't know how to ask what I wanted to know.

"Oh, hell, Kara. I've always known that you were more than a little off. Now I know *why*. If anything, the knowing makes you a lot easier to understand."

I smiled, woozy with relief and gratitude. I could feel

tears forming and I sniffled. She gave me a mock glare. "Don't you fucking cry on me, bitch."

I laughed, scrubbing away the beginnings of the tears. "Not a chance."

"If I wasn't on call, I'd suggest seeing if that crazy-as-shit aunt of yours has any booze in this house, because I think that we both need to get stinking fucking drunk."

"I think you're absolutely right."

"But," she said with a wicked gleam in her eyes, "I have something almost as good out in the car. Good thing I was on my way home from the grocery!" With that she turned and dashed out the door. Less than a minute later she returned, proudly holding a gallon of double-chocolate-fudge ice cream. "Well, what are you waiting for? It's melting. Get the damn spoons!"

I did.

9

WE DIDN'T POLISH OFF THE ENTIRE GALLON—THOUGH
not for lack of trying—but it was enough for us to get past
the weirdness of the evening.

I'd never had a close friend. Ryan was the closest I had,
but I'd known him for only a few weeks. *And the demons
hate him,* I had to remind myself. *Or at least Kehlirik does.
Why?* And how the fuck did any of the demons even know
him well enough to hate him? I liked Ryan. I really did, but
I couldn't ignore my doubts any longer. And there was
also an insecure part of me that wondered if we were
friends only because he knew about me being a summoner and he could sense the arcane too.

But now Jill knew about the arcane and the summoning and was cool about it. Or maybe she wasn't cool about
it, but she was going to pretend to be cool about it for my
sake, and that was all I could hope for. I trusted her.

And how much do I trust Ryan? the quiet voice whispered at the back of my head.

I'd ended up telling Jill everything about the Symbol

Man case—all of the details that had been conveniently left out of my written reports. I even told her about Rhyzkahl, and, more important, I told her what had happened the first time I summoned him. And this was something that I'd never told Ryan. *Hey, I summoned a demonic lord and then we had crazy fantastic sex on the rug in front of the fireplace.* Ryan was a *guy,* and guys—even ones you were just friends with—could be funny about hearing details of your sex life when it didn't include them. Or maybe that was only me being a total chickenshit again. That was more likely, considering my dearth of experience in dealing with guys.

But Jill got it. And when I told her how Rhyzkahl had saved my life, her response was a slow nod and "That is so totally cool."

I replaced the wards with my own crappy ones, then made it back to my own house, doing my best to avoid thinking about summoning Rhyzkahl. I sat at my kitchen table and tried to distract myself by focusing on the notes from my cases, but the broad door to my basement beckoned me and my thoughts kept going back to the demonic lord. There was a pretty damn big part of me that *wanted* to see him again, wanted to know where I stood with him. Then there was another fairly major part that was fully aware of how self-serving he was. He was a demon, not human, with an alien moral code. Demons were not good or evil in any sense that we as humans understood. To them, honor was paramount, yet at the same time they never did anything without cause.

So I knew he wanted something from me—wanted my aid, or skills, or wanted some opportunity I could provide for him. He wasn't asking me to summon him because he missed me, or because he desired me, or because he was fond of me.

That also raised the question of why he had saved my life, but unfortunately I had a feeling I'd already answered that one. *He wants something from me.* Altruism simply did not exist in the demon ethic.

But that could work both ways. There were things that he could do for me. I certainly had some pressing questions about essences and other arcane matters that I hoped he could answer.

I tugged my notebook out of my bag and tore a clean page out. I had too many questions, and I wasn't sure if I had time to dig through the maelstrom of disorder that was Tessa's library. *Or maybe you're just looking for an excuse to summon Rhyzkahl?*

I dug the tip of my pen into the paper as my annoyance with myself rose. There was no getting around it. I'd already essentially made up my mind to summon him. And tonight was the last night that the moon would be full enough to do it until next month.

According to Kehlirik, Rhyzkahl had given his oath that I could safely summon him. And the chances of Kehlirik lying about that were somewhere between none and none. Not with the demonic sense of honor in play. The demonkind could be vicious and dangerous and devious, but they did not lie. Instead, they were deeply skilled at telling truth in a way that would have you believe what they wished.

Screw it. If I was going to do this thing, I might as well make it worth my while. As long as I had a demonic lord at my disposal, I would see what information I could wring out of him.

I had two bodies stripped of essence. I'd start with that. I pulled the paper closer and began to write.

 1) *Could another summoner be using an* ilius *to consume essences? And why?*

 2) *And if not an* ilius, *then what the hell is doing it?*

 3) *Whatever is doing it, how can I stop it from happening again?*

I paused, pen on the paper, throat suddenly tight. My next question had nothing to do with the two bodies.

 4) *Is there any way to recover essence?*

This one was all about my aunt. If there wasn't a way to recover an essence that had been pulled away, then there was no point in keeping my aunt's body alive any longer.

That wasn't something I wanted to dwell on at the moment. I took a steadying breath and kept writing. I had some questions that I was fairly certain Rhyzkahl knew the answers to. I wasn't sure if I would have the nerve to ask him, but I went ahead and wrote them anyway.

 5) *What the* fuck *is a* kiraknikahl?

 6) *Why did Kehlirik react with such hostility toward Ryan?*

I looked down at the list, then folded it carefully.

I was going to summon the demonic lord.

I was usually nervous before summonings. There was a considerable amount of danger involved—especially in higher-level summonings—and so it was prudent to be overly cautious and meticulous.

The last time I'd prepared to summon a demonic lord, I'd been scared out of my mind—pretty damn certain that my chances of surviving the ritual were slim. But this time

I had his word, albeit via Kehlirik, that there would be no reprisals upon me for summoning him.

A demon's word was inviolate.

But I was scared shitless anyway. There were plenty of dangers other than the demon itself. I stood at the edge of the diagram, suddenly wishing that I'd had more to eat at lunch and had taken the opportunity to nap earlier. The moon was a day past full, which wouldn't be an issue with any summoning below eighth or ninth level, but this was a *demonic lord*. Yet Kehlirik had stated that the moon would be full enough, so I could only hope that Rhyzkahl's willingness to be summoned would offset the slight reduction in potency.

I took a deep breath, forcing my thoughts into the proper mind-set, and began to chant, shaping my will. The portal wouldn't open at first and I sought to focus harder, but it was like trying *not* to think of a pink elephant. The crack formed and began to widen, but I felt sluggish, as if I were swimming through tar. I took another deep breath, seeking that point of my will that would shape the portal to my desire. Slowly, agonizingly, it widened farther, an arcane wind picking up and swirling throughout the room as I sucked air harshly between my teeth. My muscles trembled with the unexpected difficulty I was having with this portal. I hadn't even named the demon yet, but I wondered if the difficulty was because of who I intended to summon, *what* I intended to summon. The words and the chants were minor aspects of the ritual, and I had shaped the portal from the beginning with Rhyzkahl in my mind. *I'm psyching myself out. That's a sure way to get killed.*

The wind swirled higher as unexpected pain wrapped

through me. I bit back a whimper, then gritted my teeth and forced the name out.

"*Rhyzkahl.*"

The wind died down and the light-filled portal snapped closed. I wanted to sag and drop to my knees, but I didn't dare show the weakness. My vision cleared and, to my aching relief, I could see the crouched figure in front of me. I held the bindings, trembling, though I knew that if I'd actually brought Rhyzkahl through, they'd be useless. At this point I was hoping and praying to any gods who would pay attention to me that it *was* Rhyzkahl. He'd given his word not to harm me, but if another demon had somehow come through, I was dead meat. I'd been tired to begin with, and this ritual had been far more draining than I'd expected. *Stupid,* I railed at myself. *Stupid and complacent. Nice way to end up dead.*

I heard a soft hiss from the center of the diagram—a susurration that could have been either pleasure or menace. Then he stood, straightening slowly as if settling each vertebra in place, shaking his hair gracefully to ripple in a white-blond fall down his back. It had been weeks since I'd last seen him—tall and muscled and radiating the familiar aura of power and sexiness and unspeakable danger. He wore a white shirt tucked into black breeches that fit closely to his incredibly well-formed ass and legs, and if anything he was more gorgeous and perfect and angelic than before.

"That...was not a pleasant experience," he snarled, crystal-blue eyes flashing as his gaze rested on me. A frisson of terror shot through me, jerking me out of my appreciation for his physique. I'd been fairly cavalier about summoning him, failing to keep in mind just how powerful an entity he was. I'd done a lousy job of opening the portal, and it had probably been quite painful for him.

I still gripped the bindings even though I knew they were useless against him. He'd brushed them aside like dust the last time. "Lord Rhyzkahl," I said, fighting to keep my voice steady. "The *reyza* Kehlirik told me that you wished me to summon you and . . . and that you gave your oath that I would not be harmed if I did so."

He lowered his head and regarded me silently for several nerve-racking heartbeats. Then he smiled, menace disappearing as if it had never existed. "I will keep my oath. Release the bindings, Kara. You know they are useless anyway."

I gave a shuddering exhalation, releasing my hold on the arcane bindings. They'd been more of a security blanket than anything. Rhyzkahl stepped out of the diagram to approach me. "You are looking far better than the last time I laid eyes on you, dear one."

The last time he'd laid eyes on me, my bowels were spread out on the floor before me. "I cannot thank you enough for saving me," I said, inclining my head.

He waved his hand as if brushing the mere idea away. Then he put a finger under my chin and tipped my head up, forcing me to meet his gaze. He looked down at me, deep and ancient eyes searching. I tried to suppress the shudder but wasn't completely successful. I felt stripped bare.

He released me, frowning now. "Kehlirik warned me of your fatigue. He was not mistaken."

"I'm fine," I said, a muscle in my jaw twitching.

He lifted a silky eyebrow. "I gave you a chance to live and now you will throw that gift away? Most insulting."

Great, now he was starting in on me too. I scowled. "No

insult is intended. I haven't slept much lately, and I have a lot going on at work." I took a deep breath and tried to regain a measure of control. "You bade me summon you. I have done so. What is it you want of me?"

"Direct as always. I admire that. So different from the demon realm, with its endless scheming and intrigue."

"There's plenty of that here too. I can't stand it. So what do you want?" My tone was more sour than I'd intended, but he just smiled again and turned away. He stepped to the cold and unlit fireplace. I sure as hell wasn't going to light a fire in the middle of summer in south Louisiana. He trailed a hand over the back of the armchair, then looked back at me.

"I wish you to be mine," he said.

I stared at him, skin tingling as the memory of the last time he'd been in the basement rushed through me. *Best sex ever—no doubt. And he wants me to be his...? He wants me?* I tried to remain rational. He wanted me, but as what? Wife? Girlfriend? What the hell kind of relationship did one have with a demonic lord? And was that something *I* wanted?

I took another couple of seconds to work some moisture back into my mouth. "Yours? Like, how? Marriage? Adoption? Lease with option to buy?"

His smile widened. "I wish you to be my summoner."

Well, that was a bucket of ice water. *Not wife. Not girlfriend. You moron.* "Your ... summoner."

"Yes."

I pushed down the absurd sting that he didn't want me as some sort of consort. Yes, it was completely irrational. I knew that. I should be pleased that he was more attracted to my arcane abilities. But I'd never claimed to be free of insecurities. "And what would being your summoner entail?" I asked, wary. I was grateful for the rude wake-up. I'd almost forgotten what he was.

He sat down in the armchair, slouching just enough to make it sexy instead of sloppy. "You would summon me periodically, thus granting me greater access to this sphere while still under the restraints of the summoning protocols." He slid a look to me. "Do not fear, dear one. I would not be unrestrained. My time would be limited, as any demon's is."

I slowly walked over to the fireplace, hitching myself up to sit on the table, oddly pleased that it had the added effect of allowing me to look down at him. Not that it made me feel superior in any way at all. He still radiated stunning power and potency. And why did he have to be so damn *hot*? I bit back a groan as my body eagerly reminded me that it had once enjoyed his hotness quite a bit. "So what's in it for me?"

His eyes sparkled with uninhibited delight. "Your brief time in the demon realm has done wonders for you. For starters, you would have access to me." He waved a hand in a grand gesture that encompassed his entire person.

I lifted my chin defiantly. "Well, what if I don't want to sleep with you again?"

He tipped his head back and laughed, as close to a full belly laugh as I thought I would ever hear come out of a demon. I scowled at him, and then, in a movement that was damn near too fast for me to follow, he was standing in front of me, holding my face in his hands. "That is not what I was referring to, dear one, but obviously it has been on your mind a great deal if that is the first thing that occurred to you."

I flushed at the truth of his words, heat rising in my

face, then abruptly his mouth was on mine and a different heat began to rise. I didn't resist as his tongue sought mine and his hands slid around to my back. A small moan escaped me as his body molded against mine. I wrapped my legs around his waist without even thinking about it, and he pressed against me, showing me that he was more than willing to pursue that line of thinking. Damn, but I'd missed this. Missed feeling sexy... desirable. *But he's only doing this to sway my decision...*

His hand slipped beneath the silk of my shirt, skimming over my breast. Gooseflesh rippled over my body, and I could feel my nipple harden beneath his palm. My legs tightened around him, and he obligingly ground against me, forcing a gasp from me. I tugged at his shirt without thinking, wanting to feel the exquisite perfection of his skin. It was as incredible as I'd remembered—satin over rippled iron. *But it's just sex.* Really great sex, yeah, but... I could get sex anywhere, right?

Like maybe with Ryan?

I shuddered and broke the kiss with a small gasp, pulling back from him. I couldn't do this, couldn't make the kind of decision he wanted when I was overwhelmed and confused. He straightened, the smile still playing on his face.

"Not as delightful as you remembered?"

I let out a shaking breath and scooted back a few inches on the table—far enough that the evidence of his arousal wasn't pressed right up against the evidence of my arousal. "It was... delightful, Lord Rhyzkahl, I cannot deny that. But I need to be able to think clearly." I took a deep breath. "What do you mean, 'access to you'?"

"My knowledge, my power, my skills." He folded his

arms across his chest. "Do you deny that you desire greater knowledge of the arcane?"

Shit. I couldn't deny that, not when I had a list of things that I needed to know more about upstairs on my kitchen table. "Okay, there is a lot I need to learn. But I'm not sure I'm ready to . . . er, commit to you like that."

"Ah, so I must woo you." His eyes glinted. "I have never had need to do so." He leaned close to me, sliding fingers across my cheek. "I must remember how it is done."

I snorted and lightly batted his fingers away. "*Not* like that."

I felt a brief shimmer of potency, then he withdrew his hand and straightened, dark power smoldering in his eyes. "Yes," he said softly. "Your brief sojourn in the demon realm did you well."

Another sliver of fear began to spread through me, but before I could berate myself too harshly—*I batted his hand away? Holy crap, what was I thinking?*—he turned away, clasping his hands lightly behind his back. "Very well. I will woo you. I will answer three questions without debt."

I blinked. "Are you serious? Three questions with no debt of honor incurred?" Then I cringed. *Nice going, moron. That was two questions right there.*

"Three questions. No debt. A courting gift, if you will."

I hopped off the table, relieved that he wasn't going to be a stickler about when the questioning would start. But if he was trying to "woo" me, then being a jerk about the questions certainly wouldn't endear him to me. "I'll be right back," I said, as I took off up the basement stairs, then raced down the hall to the kitchen, bare feet slapping against the wood floor. I grabbed the paper off the table and spun to race back to the basement.

And careened right into him. I would have fallen back on my ass, but he seized me by the arms, steadying me, then continued to grip my arms. His body was firm and warm against mine, and I nearly expected him to lower his head to kiss me. I even tipped my head back without thinking, then felt slightly foolish when I realized that he wasn't looking down at me at all.

Instead, his gaze slowly traveled around my small kitchen, and it abruptly occurred to me that he was looking around like someone who had never seen anything like a modern kitchen before. *And most likely he hasn't.* Demonic lords were rarely if ever summoned. It was the others—the twelve levels of demon, *reyza, syraza, zhurn, mehnta,* and so forth—who were usually summoned and who had the opportunity to come to this sphere. But even they had little chance to "see the world," so to speak. I knew that when I summoned, it was a stark rarity for any demon to leave the summoning chamber. Far too much risk of discovery by the outside world. Tessa occasionally brought demons down from her attic summoning chamber, but just to her library. I'd brought the *ilius* out only because it was practically invisible. And, of course, the lords were almost never summoned by anyone who wanted to continue living. No wonder Kehlirik had been so elated at the opportunity to ride in the back of a U-Haul truck.

"Have you been to this sphere before?" I asked, almost hesitantly. "I mean, other than the time I called you. And, um, the time that the Symbol Man called you. I mean, have you ever been outside a summoning chamber?"

He continued to take in his surroundings. "Centuries ago. It was quite different, as I recall."

I gave a breathless laugh. "I would imagine so." I pulled

very lightly against his grip on my arms and he released me, almost as if he was barely aware of me anymore. I stepped back as he moved to the back door and opened it. It briefly flashed through me that I shouldn't allow him outside in case anyone came over, but then I remembered that not only did he not look like a demon, no one ever visited my house anyway. And I would hardly be embarrassed to be seen in public with *him*.

He walked down the stairs and out into my backyard. He stopped about ten paces from my house, then looked up at the moon. He inhaled—not deeply or dramatically, just the deep breath of someone who wanted to take in the scent of his surroundings. I slowly followed him, stopping at the bottom of the steps. After several minutes he turned back to me, face inscrutable. He walked to me and stopped, looking down at me.

"Three questions."

I gulped softly and nodded, remembering the crumpled paper in my hand. I peered down at it, but the light was too dim for me to read it well. "I . . . uh, need to go back inside."

He gestured toward the house. I returned inside and he followed behind me, closing the door as I looked down at my list. Shit, just three questions? I ran my fingers through my hair as I tried to figure out which ones were the most important.

I gripped my hair, then released it and looked at the demonic lord, experiencing a brief moment of disorientation as the reality struck me that *Lord Rhyzkahl* was in my kitchen.

"Okay. Is it possible that an *ilius* has been summoned here and is consuming human essences?"

"No," he said, folding his arms over his chest. I waited a

beat, then silently cursed myself for phrasing the question so poorly. "An *ilius* would never consume human essence," he continued after several seconds, apparently realizing that being too much of an asshole about the questions was not the best way to impress me. "Not only is it forbidden—for too much of such would upset the balance of potency in this sphere—but they have no taste for humans." A slight smile played on his face.

I bit back my desire to blurt out something stupid like *Really? They don't?* He'd been magnanimous about giving me a more thorough answer to my first question, and I didn't want to push my luck. Okay, so it wasn't an *ilius*. What the hell else could it be, then? But I needed to consider how to word it so that I would get an answer that was useful to me.

I thought for a minute, then decided to skip to a different question. This one was vitally important to me, and I wanted to be certain that it got asked. I carefully phrased the query in my head. "How can I restore to my aunt the essence that was stripped from her during the ritual to summon you by the Symbol Man?" It wasn't the smoothest sentence structure in the world, but it asked the question I wanted answered.

He acted as if he hadn't heard me as he slowly walked around my kitchen, opening drawers and cabinets, looking inside the fridge, face completely expressionless. I was about to repeat my question when he spoke.

"It is a series of rituals—each similar to a summoning, but you would be calling to her essence. Gather aspects of her—blood, hair, as well as items dear to her heart." He went on to describe the ward structure as he walked toward the front of the house. I trailed in his wake, scrawling notes furiously on the back of the piece of paper. Then he paused and looked back at me. "But it is not a fast process. It may take some time, and you will need to take care with each step."

I caught myself before asking, *How much time?* That could have counted as question number three. Instead, I nodded. "Thank you."

He continued on through my house, stopping when he reached my living room. "I have seen this only through the touch I had in your dreams. It is quite fascinating to see and sense it in the flesh." He brushed fingers across my desk and the computer, then moved to the fireplace, gazing at the photos on the mantel. There were only two pictures. One was of my aunt and me, which had been taken during Mardi Gras several years ago. We were both dressed in purple jumpsuits—the purple people from the "Purple People Eaters" song.

The other was a picture of my parents, taken just a year or so before my mother got sick. In the picture, they were sitting next to each other on a low oak tree branch at City Park in New Orleans, with my mother leaning against my dad, his arms around her. Her hands were clasped around one knee and her head was tipped back against him, her blond hair teased by a breeze.

This was one memory that was fixed forever in my essence. I'd taken that photo when I was six years old, having begged and whined and pleaded to be allowed to use my dad's 35 mm. I'd used up nearly the whole roll of film, and this had been the best picture of the small handful that came out.

Rhyzkahl's gaze lingered on the photo for long enough that I had an unnerving desire to snatch it away from him. For some reason I didn't like the thought of him looking at it, whether through my dreams or in reality. "Do you still have a link to my dreams?" I demanded.

This time true delight lit his eyes. "You miss my presence in your bed?"

I glared at him, refusing to rise to his bait. It was beside the fact that there was a measure of truth in his words.

He came to me, sliding a hand through my hair. He cupped the back of my neck, then pulled me close and kissed me again—a powerful kiss, and one that showed just how much he was in control. Then he released me, leaving me to stagger to regain my balance, skin aflame with heat.

"The dream link I had to you was destroyed when you died in my realm," he said, inclining his head to me as I struggled to control the mad thrum of my pulse. "And that was your third question. A pity. Now you will need to summon me again to seek answers to more questions."

Then, before I could respond or react, he stepped back and was gone in a flash of white light.

10

I WASN'T SURE I'D EVER GET TO SLEEP, AS ANNOYED AS I was at both Rhyzkahl and myself. But three glasses of wine helped chill me out, and that, combined with my overall exhaustion level, allowed me to sleep until nearly seven a.m., which was good since I knew it was going to be a long day. Although it was a Sunday, Dr. Lanza was performing the autopsies on Brian and Carol Roth this morning, and once that was finished I needed to pay a visit to Tessa.

"Three questions," I grumbled. I glared at myself in the mirror and tugged a brush through my hair. "You couldn't handle three simple questions." I'd even been lucky enough to have questions already written out, and I'd still screwed it up. And now it would be another month before I could summon him again.

He was sneakier than I'd expected. That, or I was stupider.

I scowled as I put on mascara. "Stupider. Definitely stupider."

* * *

THE DOOR TO the morgue was propped open with a chunk of concrete when I arrived. Doc wasn't at his desk in the outer office, so I stepped in and peered into the cutting room, wrinkling my nose at the odor. It wasn't a dead body smell. This morgue never smelled like that. The morgue tech, Carl, was obsessive-compulsive about cleaning, and the stench of bleach and other cleaning products was nearly overwhelming.

The door to the cooler on the opposite side of the room swung open and Carl exited, pushing a stretcher with a black body bag on it into the room. Carl was Doc's right-hand man in the morgue and often helped out with body collections—or "body-snatching," as it was gruesomely termed. I'd never seen him ruffled, even at the grossest or strangest of death scenes. He did his work with a silent efficiency that would have been dour if dour wasn't too much of an emotion for him to display.

He saw me and gave me a barely visible nod. "Morning."

"Morning, Carl. Helluva way to spend a Sunday."

"Busy week. The fridge is full." The way he said it made it sound like he'd just gone grocery shopping.

"Where's Doc?"

"Traffic. On his way." He pushed the stretcher up against the metal table that was locked into place at the sink. "Gonna cut the Roths today," he continued as he smoothly unzipped the bag. "The councilman will probably be tomorrow."

I felt almost overwhelmed by what was the equivalent of a verbal barrage from the normally silent and seemingly emotionless morgue tech. I also couldn't help but feel a twinge of disappointment that Doc wouldn't be doing all three while I was here, though I knew that I was being selfishly unrealistic, especially since it was a Sunday. But I really wanted to find some connection between Brian Roth and Davis Sharp, anything that could point me to an answer as to why both had no essence left. Doc had a shitload of experience, having worked in Las Vegas and Houston before taking the job with St. Long Parish, and I had a lot of faith in his opinion.

Oh, well. Nothing to do but be patient. "You, uh, need any help?" I asked Carl.

He lifted his head to look at me as if he'd never really seen me before. I couldn't decide if his direct gaze was creepy or not.

The faintest whisper of what might have been a smile shimmered on his face, then he nodded toward a side table. "Gloves and smocks there."

I turned to the table, forcing myself not to grimace. I'd offered to help more out of courtesy than a desire to handle bodies, but I couldn't back out now. I found a smock and pulled the blue plastic over my head, tying it at the waist the way I'd seen Doc and Carl do it, then snagged gloves out of the box marked *Small* and tugged them on.

Carl had folded the flap of the bag back, revealing the body of Carol Roth. The scarf was still wound around her throat, damp and limp from the moisture of being in the cooler, the dark-red fabric stark against the waxy pallor of her skin. Now that the blood had settled and lividity was fixed, I could see faint ligature marks on her wrists and ankles. A little bondage play before the asphyxia, or was there more to it? And, to my relief, I could still feel the faintest hum of essence about her. I knew it wouldn't be there for much longer. I surreptitiously touched her arm with a gloved finger, confirming for myself that she felt "normal."

"Stupid way to die," Carl murmured.

He kept surprising me with the conversation. Or maybe I'd formed an opinion of him as emotionless and dour because I'd never really had a chance to talk to him. "I agree," I replied. I couldn't see how the risk of death could be worth the erotic thrill.

He moved to the other side of the metal table, then reached across and grabbed the body by the arm and knee, giving a sharp tug to slide her into position. "She was an easy one," he said, straightening her limbs on the table.

I frowned, Jill's comment about Brian and Carol having marital problems suddenly coming back to me. "You mean she slept around?"

He paused, his hands stilling on her legs, and looked up at me. "Actually, I was referring to her weight and how simple it was to get her onto the table. It's not as pretty when it's someone weighing four hundred pounds."

"Ah. Right. Sorry."

He kept looking at me, hands still motionless on the woman's thighs. "But it's funny you should say that."

"What, that she slept around?"

He made a small motion with his head that I was fairly certain was a nod. "She had a reputation."

Now, that added a new dimension. "Was she cheating on Brian?"

"I don't know that. She'd been married before, to a lawyer in Mandeville. Supposedly he caught her with one of the other lawyers who worked in his firm. Divorced her."

So maybe it *hadn't* been Brian after all. A frisson of

relief surged through me at the thought. I knew that I was basing a lot of hope on what was—at the moment—merely gossip about Carol, but I also knew there'd be plenty of other people in the department who'd feel the same way if Brian's name could be cleared.

I tilted my head, regarding Carl in an entirely new light. "How do you know all this?"

The faint smile flickered on his face again. "Most people don't like the work I do, so they dismiss me from their minds as soon as possible. They forget I'm there, and I hear things."

I couldn't help but laugh. "You must have dirt on everyone."

The smile was almost real now. "I know a lot of things about a lot of people."

It made me wonder what he knew about me.

The outer door banged shut and we both looked up as Dr. Jonathan Lanza walked in. He dumped his keys and phone on the desk in the outer office and then continued in to the cutting room, grabbing gloves and smock without breaking stride.

"Morning, Kara, Carl," Dr. Lanza said, yanking protective gear on as he moved to the table. He peered at one of Carol's wrists, then shook his head as his gaze traveled over the rest of the body. "God knows I've seen stupider ways to die, but this sure isn't a way I'd want to go." He shook his head. "It's definitely a *homicide*," he continued, stressing the word, "but I'm inclined to agree with the sex-play-gone-bad scenario. The ligature marks are fairly light, and I'm not seeing any signs of struggle, though I'll run a full tox screen to make sure she wasn't drugged up first. Negligent homicide, perhaps? I'm not the one who decides how the charges go. I just tell you guys how she died." Then he gave a small sigh. "Not that it matters if Brian did this."

"I'm keeping an open mind as far as that goes," I said.

Doc nodded, then his gaze shifted to me, taking in my attire. "I see Carl conned you into helping out. Keep this up and I might hire you away from the PD."

I wrinkled my nose. "No thanks, Doc. This one's fine, but if this had been a week-old decomp, you and Carl would be on your own."

He laughed. "Oh, so that's how it is?"

"Yup. That's how it is."

He grinned and picked up his clipboard, beginning his examination of the body.

Carl took a hypodermic syringe and held it out to me. "You said you wanted to help," he said calmly. "Do you want to get the vitreous?"

"Ugh! No. Way." I shuddered as Doc laughed, and even Carl cracked a smile. Getting the vitreous involved sticking a needle into the eyeball and drawing the fluid out. At the first autopsy I'd attended, Carl had made a point to show me how the needle could be seen through the pupil after it was inserted. I could handle a lot of things, but the needle in the eye always squicked me out.

Carl gave a soft sigh and shook his head as he swiftly and expertly slid the needle into the side of each eye to extract the clear fluid. "I have to do everything myself," he teased.

How had I ever thought this man to be dour and humorless?

He squirted the fluid into a tube, then dropped the syringe into a Sharps container. Meanwhile, Doc set his clipboard aside, and pulled a black case out from beneath a cabinet. He popped it open and pulled out three pairs of colored goggles and a device that looked like a complicated flashlight. I recognized it as an ALS, an alternate light source. "Kill the lights, please, Kara."

I obligingly flicked the lights off, then put the yellow-tinted glasses on as Doc began to shine the ALS carefully over Carol's body.

"Look at that," Doc said, as the bruising on her neck stood out in stark contrast to the rest of her skin. "There may not have been much showing, but here you can see where the scarf dug in." He scanned it over her torso and thighs next. "And there ya go." Several bite marks stood out clearly. "Just a few love nips. Nothing too hard or too deep."

I bent closer, frowning at the marks. "Wait," I said, and pointed to a mark on her right breast. "Shine the light on this one."

Doc complied. "See something?"

A flutter of excitement wound through my belly. "Would you say that the teeth that left those marks are in good shape? All of them there?"

He shrugged. "I'm no dentist, but it looks like there are impressions from all the front teeth, at least."

I straightened. "Brian was missing a tooth in the front. Got it knocked out during a pickup basketball game last week and hadn't had it fixed yet."

Carl let out a low whistle. "And if Brian didn't kill her, why would he kill himself?"

"Exactly. If he didn't kill her, then I rather doubt he pulled the trigger." The thought of a fellow officer being murdered was hideous, but it was a damn sight more bearable than the thought that he'd *been* a murderer. I peered again at the bites as Doc bent his head for a closer look. Unfortunately, the marks weren't nice and clear, and

I couldn't tell for certain if there was a gap in the bruising or not.

After a few seconds Doc sighed, shaking his head. "I can't tell. They're not hard bites. We'd have to consult a forensic odontologist. Or we can find out for sure another way. Kara, can you get me a swab, please?"

I handed him the swabs and the vial of sterile water. Doc dampened the swab with the sterile water and then carefully wiped across the bite marks. "Whoever bit her left saliva behind," he explained. He repeated the process in several more locations on her body, then finally switched off the ALS and pulled off his goggles while I turned the room lights on.

Doc packaged the swabs up in an evidence envelope. "Fortunately, it doesn't matter if whoever it was wore a condom. Saliva's just as good." He put the envelope aside, then picked up a syringe with a wickedly long needle and jabbed it into her groin area, working it around until he was able to get into the femoral artery to draw blood. Then another syringe went into the area just above her pubic bone, drawing out urine. "I'm running a full tox screen on her," he said, glancing at me as he filled various vials. "It still looks like an accidental asphyx, but we want to be sure she wasn't drugged."

I started to run my fingers through my hair, then stopped when I remembered that I was wearing gloves that had *dead person* on them. I sighed as my nose suddenly started itching fiercely. Never failed: As soon as I knew I couldn't touch my face, I was overwhelmed with the need to.

If it's not Brian's DNA, then he probably wasn't the one who killed her, and his murder was merely staged to look like a suicide. Which led to the question: *If that's the case, were Brian and Carol killed by the same person?*

I shook my head. I was getting ahead of myself. First I needed to find out if it was Brian's DNA. "This will tell us for sure if it's Brian, right?"

"I'll call down to the lab in Slidell to tell them I need a rush on a comparison," Doc said. "I'll *casually* drop that this is the son of a judge, but it'll still be at least a week or two. Convenient that we have access to Brian's DNA." He nodded his head toward the cooler.

I watched as Doc completed the rest of the rape kit, including the vaginal, rectal, and oral swabs, the nail scrapings and clippings, blood and hair samples.

The rest of the autopsy went quickly. Carl took the completed rape kit and disappeared into the office to get it sealed and ready to take to the lab. Doc worked quietly and efficiently, opening her up and removing the organs, weighing and slicing samples, then peeling back the skin and muscles of the throat. "The hyoid bone isn't broken, so it wasn't a forcible strangulation—not like your Symbol Man cases." He straightened from his close examination. "Asphyxiation held just a bit too long." He shrugged. "Y'know, Carol had a rep for being pretty indiscriminate about who she fooled around with. I think most of the PD and half the DA's office had slept with her."

"I can't believe I'm so out of the gossip loop," I said with a laugh.

"It's better that way, trust me. Besides, you've been a little preoccupied lately." He glanced at me. "How's your aunt doing?"

My throat tightened. "No change."

He gave me a sympathetic smile. "It's been only, what,

six, seven weeks? There's no trauma, so she has every chance of coming out of this."

I sighed, and once again had to resist the urge to run my fingers through my hair. "Yeah. Sure." I wished it was as easy as that.

"Doc's right," Carl said from behind me, thoroughly startling me. "She'll come out of this. But you're too stressed out. You need to eat more. You look better with some meat on your bones." He extended a saw to me. "Wanna cut a head open?"

I groaned. "No. And thank you for going straight from eating to cutting heads."

He shrugged and plugged the saw in as I escaped to the viewing room.

I ALMOST DIDN'T come back out for Brian's autopsy. Even on the other side of the wall, I could feel that there was something wrong about the body. I'd maintained a fleeting hope that I was wrong on the scene, both with Brian Roth and Davis Sharp, but the gaping void and tattered remains were still there.

I forced myself to return to the cutting room once Brian's body was on the table. His body was a lot messier, mostly because of all the blood that had seeped out into the bag from the big holes in his head. His head had been wrapped in a sheet to try to control some of the blood, but it was still a nasty mess when Carl opened up the bag.

Doc pulled Brian's lips back and looked down at his teeth, eyes narrowed. "Missing right front incisor. You're right, Kara."

I allowed myself a pleased smile. "All right, Doc," I said. "Did he pull the trigger himself or was he murdered?"

"No fucking idea," he said, narrowing his eyes as he picked up a scalpel and began to shave around the holes in the scalp and skull. "But I'm hoping to have an answer for you soon." He peered at the wounds, lifting sections of skull that had been in the body bag and fitting them to the still-intact part of the skull. He put his hand out and Carl placed a long plastic rod in it without being asked—a sign of how long the two had worked together.

Doc poked the rod into the hole at Brian's right temple, working it carefully until it protruded through the other side. Despite the morbid look of the thing, there was no better way to get a solid idea of what the trajectory of the bullet had been.

Doc peered at the rod, then shrugged and glanced back at me. "Well, the angle's consistent. . . ." He frowned, then shook his head. "And he was definitely shot at close range, though I'm not seeing signs that the gun was flush against his head."

"What do you mean?"

He pointed to the shaved area of scalp. "There's plenty of stippling from gunpowder, but there aren't any burns or blackening of the edges, and"—he peeled the scalp back to show the skull—"on a contact wound, you'd have a stellate-shaped entrance wound, and you'd see blackening on the skull as well."

"So . . . he didn't kill himself?"

He merely gave an infuriating shrug. "I can't say that either. He could have held the gun a few inches away."

"You're no help," I said sourly. "What about gunshot residue on his hands?"

"There could be GSR on his hands just from being in the same room when the gun was fired," he pointed out.

"Oh, yeah."

"Don't give up hope yet," he reassured me with a gesture toward the bagged hands. "I'll check to see if there's any blowback on his hands, plus I'll ask the lab to swab the gun for contact DNA. It was his duty weapon?"

"Yeah."

"Then if someone else's DNA is found, that's fairly telling." He unbagged Brian's hands, then lifted them for me to see and for Carl to photograph. "This isn't much help either."

I scowled. "Covered in blood."

"Yep. He had his hands in a pool of his own blood."

"So for now it's undetermined?" I asked, knowing the answer already.

Doc nodded. "For now. Sorry."

I stripped off my gloves and other protective gear. "All right. I guess I have to make some phone calls." And continue to try to figure out what was eating essence. "You'll call me if you find anything interesting on Davis Sharp?"

"You'll be the first to know," he replied.

Well, I wanted to bury myself in work, I reminded myself as I left the morgue. *At this rate I won't have time to worry about anything else.*

II

A VISIT TO TESSA WAS NEXT ON MY TO-DO LIST, AND I
pulled into the parking lot of the Nord du Lac Neurological Rehabilitation Center shortly before noon. Nord
Neuro, as everyone called it, was a three-story facility situated across the street from St. Long Parish Hospital. The
owners did their best to make the place look warm and
inviting—nice landscaping, clean exterior, fresh paint—
but there really was no way to make that kind of place
look *nice*. Still, I appreciated that it didn't look like a total
hellhole. I'd tapped heavily into my own savings as well as
Tessa's to pay for her care—grateful that I had the power
of attorney to do so. Nord Neuro was a private facility,
which meant that it was fucking expensive, even with
Tessa's insurance. But I knew that, one way or another, I
would be paying the bills for only a couple of months.

I shut the car off but stayed where I was, gripping the
steering wheel and listening to the tick of the engine as it
cooled. I hated coming here, but more than that, I hated
having my aunt here. Hated it with my entire being—and

the only reason I could stand it at all was because I knew that she was completely unaware of her surroundings. *Or is she?* Rhyzkahl had said that an essence could return—sometimes on its own, but with more surety if coaxed along. That's why I was here today—to collect what I needed for the ritual that would hopefully do that coaxing.

I got out of my car, hefting my backpack onto my shoulder. *Don't get your hopes up,* I chided myself. It was all well and good to hope, but the seemingly inevitable disappointment was bitter. *And if more essence gets consumed, how will that affect my aunt?* Her essence was floating free at the moment, but if the balance were to shift too far, her essence would be sucked back into the "pool" instead of returning to her body.

I didn't like thinking about that.

The glass doors slid open, and I mentally braced myself against the feel of the place. It didn't have the sour food and urine smell of most nursing homes, but it held enough of the over-antiseptic hospital smell that I had to shiver.

Tessa was in a "no vent" section, which simply meant that she didn't need a ventilator—at least not yet. She shared a room with another coma patient, a middle-aged woman who'd been there for several months. Her husband was sitting next to the bed when I entered. He spoke in a low voice with a woman who I figured was either an attorney or a doctor, judging solely by her professional appearance—dressed in a stylish dark-blue suit, brown hair accented with honey-blond highlights coiled up into an elegant twist, and understated yet elegant jewelry.

He looked up and gave me a smile as I entered—the kind of smile that was exchanged between people who shared a difficult circumstance. I returned the smile and then felt guilty. He was there every time I visited, reading to his comatose wife from a wide variety of books. I could count on one hand the number of times I'd been to see Tessa.

"Good to see you, Kara," he said. "This is our lawyer, Rachel Roth."

The woman turned to me and gave me a neutral but pleasant smile. "It's nice to meet you. I hope it won't disturb your time with your aunt if we talk in here. If so, it's no trouble at all for us to go down the hall."

"No, that's quite all right," I said, suddenly realizing that this was Brian's mother. *No, his stepmother.* I remembered Brian saying something about his birth mother passing away quite some time ago. I hesitated, then added, "I'm sorry for your loss. I worked with Brian."

She gave a soft sigh. "Thank you. It's been a hard few days. You're with the PD?"

"Yes, ma'am."

"Kara's a homicide detective," Mr. Roommate said. "She's the one who tracked down the Symbol Man."

Ms. Roth's eyebrows lifted as she looked at me with renewed interest. "You must have some fascinating stories."

"Too many," I replied with a small shrug. "Excuse me. I'll leave you two to your conversation. It was nice meeting you, Ms. Roth." I quickly retreated out of the conversation and over to my aunt's side of the room. I wasn't about to tell Ms. Roth that I'd been the one to find Brian's body or that I was in charge of the investigation.

The two resumed their low conversation, and I caught snatches about negligence, accident, and insurance. I'd gathered that Tessa's roommate—whose name I kept forgetting—had been involved in some sort of motor vehicle accident. Apparently, Rachel Roth was handling a related lawsuit.

I set my backpack on the floor on the far side of the bed. There was a difference between Tessa and her roommate, though. The other woman was in a coma because of injuries from her accident. Tessa's *body* was fine. She was just missing her essence.

I shifted into othersight to take a quick peek at the other woman. Yes, she was there, still in the body, waiting only for her body to heal and recover. I had no way to tell if that would ever happen, but I knew that it *could* happen. I sighed and switched back to normal sight, then sat in the chair beside Tessa and looked her over with worry. She looked paler, her cheekbones more pronounced. Her breathing seemed shallower as well, and I had to wonder how long it would be before she ended up on a ventilator. Her body was definitely declining. *How much time do I have?*

I swallowed back the knot of fear in my throat and pulled out a book. I started to read to her softly, trying not to disturb Mr. Roommate's conversation with his attorney while hoping that they weren't paying attention to me. I'd grabbed a book at random off the rack in the drugstore, a lurid and intentionally comedic romance about sex-starved vampires that had me stifling giggles by page three.

Finally what I was waiting for happened—the two finished their conversation and Mr. Roommate left to walk Ms. Roth out. I quickly pulled the curtain between the beds. It had seemed rude to do so earlier, but now it would give me time to hide what I was doing in case anyone came into the room.

Because they would definitely freak, I thought grimly as

I pulled the syringe out of my backpack. I wasn't medically qualified by any stretch of the imagination, but I needed some of her blood, and getting it in the traditional method for a summoner—a shallow slice on the forearm—would cause far too many questions. I figured a poke from a needle would go unnoticed, especially with all of the other needle sticks she was getting.

I managed to find a vein on the third try, exceedingly glad that my aunt wasn't awake to berate me on my total lack of skill. I breathed a sigh of relief as I drew the syringe full of blood, then carefully dropped the whole thing into an evidence tube, capped it, and put it into my backpack. Then I went after her hair and pulled about fifty strands, complete with root. These I dropped into an envelope, folded it, and stashed it in the backpack. I pulled the two cotton swabs out next and quickly swiped inside her cheeks. *Just like doing a rape kit,* I thought.

I finally opened the curtain, then took nail clippers out of the backpack and started trimming her nails, though they really didn't need it. One of the staff must have recently clipped them, but even the slivers I was able to gather were sufficient for what I needed. Mr. Roommate came back during that process and gave me an approving smile. I gave a small smile and nod back, and hid the fact that I was saving all the nail clippings in another small envelope.

I had just stuffed the little envelope with the clippings into my backpack when a young, slender redhead in a nurse's smock bustled in. She gave Mr. Roommate a smile that could only be described as perky, but when her gaze shifted to me she blinked in what was obviously surprise.

"Oh, hi! I don't think I know you," she said with a bright smile. "Are you family?"

"I'm her niece," I said, prepared to be defensive about how seldom I visited. "I'm Kara Gillian."

"Oh, of course!" she chirped. "You're the one listed on her chart." As if to prove her point, she picked up the chart from the end of the bed, eyes flicking over it. "Well, Miss Kara, I'm Melanie." She grinned and proudly pointed to the name badge pinned on her chest. It made me wonder if she sometimes forgot her name and had to look down and check. "And you can be assured that I'm doing everything I can to make sure that Miss Tessa is as comfy as she can possibly be!"

"I . . . uh, appreciate that," I replied, feeling almost cowed by her exuberance.

"Well, I used to go to Miss Tessa's store for lunch darn near every day," she continued. "She would always put extra sprouts on my turkey sandwich, just the way I liked it, and never *ever* charged me a single dime extra. So I feel like it's fate that she's here for me to take care of now!" Melanie beamed at me while I struggled to think of some sort of coherent response. Behind her, I could see Mr. Roommate hiding a broad grin behind his hand. I gave him a despairing look, but he merely gave me a helpless shrug as if to say, *She's a nut, but she's harmless.*

I suppressed a sigh. "Well, Melanie, I'm sure she's much happier knowing that she's in such caring hands."

Her smile grew even wider, if that was possible. "Oh, thank you for saying that! And I sure am glad to see y'all coming in. Maybe it's my imagination, but she sure seems perkier after each visit."

I blinked. "Wait. Is someone else visiting besides me?"

"Sure is! There's a man who's been stopping by late in the evenings. I figured it must be another family member, since visitors are restricted to immediate family only at that hour."

What the fuck? "Can you describe him?"

She bit her lip. "Wow. Um . . . well, he's older than me. And he's kinda tall, I guess." She shook her head and gave me a bewildered look. "I'm sorry. I tried to talk to him and introduce myself, but he just kinda looked at me and didn't say much. I assumed it was her husband or brother or something."

"She doesn't have either," I said with a frown.

Melanie's eyes grew wide. "Oh, no. He must have lied about being family!" Then her face brightened. "Maybe it's a boyfriend, and he lied so that he could be near her! Y'know, out of *love*. And he was so subdued and quiet and eerie and all because he was so sad she was here." She put her hand on her chest and gave a tragic sigh.

I stared at her as Mr. Roommate was overcome with an inexplicable coughing fit that sounded suspiciously like laughter. There was a part of me that wanted to shake her and demand to know how anyone could be that naïve, but a slightly more rational part of me pointed out that there was a dearth of innocent exuberance in the world, so physical violence probably wasn't the best option here.

I cleared my throat. "Melanie. Is there anything at all that you can tell me about this other visitor? Can you describe him?"

She chewed her lower lip. "Hmm . . . he was tall, thin, super quiet. Didn't smile. Just sat by her bed for a while, then got up and left." She heaved another dramatic sigh. "I guess he was pining for her. The poor thing."

I could feel a headache forming between my eyes. "Hair? Eyes? Anything?"

She gave a firm nod. "Yes, he definitely had hair. And

his eyes were kinda light. I think maybe they were green. Or blue. Or they mighta been like a light hazel." She beamed at me, clearly thrilled to have been such help.

I couldn't make my mouth form words at first. "Your powers of recall are ... amazing," I finally managed.

She actually gave a small squeal of delight. "Oh! I'm so glad I could help!" She hung the chart back on the end of Tessa's bed. "Well, let me get back to my rounds. Nice to meet you!" And with that she bustled right on out the door.

I stared after her for several seconds, then turned to look at Mr. Roommate, who had tears of laughter running down his face.

"Oh, God," he gasped. "I'm sorry I laughed. But isn't she a complete goofball?"

I grinned despite myself. "Hard to believe she's for real. So, have you seen this mystery visitor?"

He shook his head as he wiped his eyes. "I'm sorry. I can't stay too late, so whoever it is, he must come in after I've gone. But maybe you can look for a name on the sign-in log at the front desk?"

"Good idea," I said. "You'd make a good detective."

"I'm a wimp," he said with a smile. "I'll stick to watching the fictional ones on TV."

"Don't tell anyone," I said as I collected my things, "but I'm a total wimp too."

UNFORTUNATELY, MR. ROOMMATE'S good idea was a bust. There was no record of anyone signing in to visit Tessa.

I got into my searing-hot car and jammed the AC on, then pulled out of the parking lot. *Was* someone else visiting Tessa? Melanie seemed like a dingbat, so perhaps she had Tessa mixed up with another patient. Or maybe it was just someone Tessa had known from her store or her neighborhood. But if that was the case, then why wouldn't there be a record of it on the sign-in log?

I pulled into my driveway and did my best to push the worry about Tessa's visitor out of my head. I needed my focus for the first stage of the ritual that Rhyzkahl had described to me. *At least I was able to pry that information out of him before wasting my questions on my stupid concerns about the dreams,* I thought with a mental scowl.

I headed down to the basement, then swept and cleaned the floor to prepare it for the new diagram. I'd forced myself into the habit of erasing my diagram and putting all my implements away after each summoning, but I didn't want to take a chance on any stray marks messing up what I was about to do. Especially since I didn't really know what I was doing.

Sketching with tedious precision, I laid out the diagram for the call to Tessa's essence according to the parameters that Rhyzkahl had detailed for me, quite glad that I'd taken notes. Because this shit was *confusing.* It didn't look at all like the sort of summoning diagram I normally used. But then again, I wasn't doing a summoning; I was doing something else entirely. According to Rhyzkahl, this diagram, once completed and with the right amount of potency channeled into it, would send out a call to Tessa's essence and hopefully draw it back to this plane.

I finished chalking the diagram, then opened my backpack and pulled out the stuff I'd taken from Tessa at the neuro center. I mixed it all together in a silver bowl—blood, hair, swabs, fingernails—to form a disgusting gloppy soup, then painted it around the edge of the diagram. Once I finished, I set the bowl aside and sat back on my heels to examine my work. It looked as if I'd done everything right, but this was so new to me that I had no idea if I'd even be able to see if I'd screwed something obvious up. I sighed and rubbed my eyes. Nothing to do now but keep going and hope for the best.

I stood and pulled potency. It came into my control sluggishly and unevenly, but since I wasn't going to try to create a portal, it didn't matter that it pulsed erratically. Or at least I hoped it didn't. Rhyzkahl had said that the phase of the moon wouldn't matter—which was a good thing, since there were a number of stages to this ritual that would need to be completed over the next several days.

I channeled the power down into the diagram as Rhyzkahl had explained, watching carefully as it settled into the runes. I released my hold on the potency, relieved as the diagram began to emit a soft resonance, yet at the same time feeling that the whole thing was pretty damn anticlimactic. *But it's not finished,* I reminded myself. There was still a lot more work to be done. My problem was that I was too used to summonings—where complicated rituals and diagrams had the impressive result of wind and light and, of course, a demon. This was little more than a *buzz.*

Seriously unimpressive.

I could only hope that Rhyzkahl knew what the fuck he was talking about.

12

As soon as I made it in to the station the next morning, I went to my sergeant's office to give him a rundown of what Doc had found during the autopsies of Brian and Carol Roth.

Crawford nodded slowly after I finished. "Okay," he said, turning his pen end over end. "So, Carol Roth might have been killed by someone other than Brian, which then casts a great deal of doubt on his death being a suicide."

"Right. And if we wait for test results, any trail could be too cold to follow."

"God, it would feel good to clear him of this shit." Crawford tapped the pen on his blotter, a flicker of a grimace passing over his face. "I hate to do this, but...I'm going to give these two cases to Pellini."

I stared at him, certain that I had misheard him. "Sarge," I said, trying not to stutter in outrage. "Pellini has a backlog of cases. He can't write a coherent report to save his life. He's marking time until he can retire. The only other case I have is Davis Sharp. I can do this!"

Crawford shook his head. "I know you can, Kara, but... I was told to reassign these cases." He looked pissed, which made me feel slightly better. At least this wasn't because he thought I couldn't handle the caseload.

"I guess the theory is that there'll be too many ill feelings if you start getting all the juicy cases," he continued. "We don't have that many murders around here, and the other detectives want their share." He pulled a sour face, and I knew that he didn't really give a shit about hurt feelings.

I still didn't bother to hide my scowl. Unfortunately, there was a measure of truth to what he'd said. There was already some resentment and ill will toward me over the resolution of the Symbol Man case and my strange disappearance, and Sarge was only doing what he'd been told to do.

But *Pellini*? I'd counted myself lucky that I'd never had to work directly with the dour, overweight detective. He'd been with Beaulac PD for only four years, after fifteen with NOPD, and so far the best impression I had of him was that he was lazy, sloppy, and generally unpleasant to be around. He seemed miserable, and I had the feeling that the only joy he had in life was when he was making other people miserable as well. But would cases be reassigned just because of his whining? He whined about *everything*. Usually everyone simply ignored it.

"Go get him up to speed on what you have so far, Kara." Then Crawford paused. "Give him a chance. He does have a lot of experience." But I could see the doubt in his eyes.

I nodded and muttered something about typing my notes up, then left Crawford's office to return to my own. It took me only about twenty minutes to type what I had so far on the two deaths, but I was as detailed and thorough as possible so that no one could point any fingers at the quality of the work I turned over to Pellini. I wanted to dither and put off handing the cases over to him, but unfortunately I had too much else I needed to do. As soon as I finished typing, I printed the reports out, then made my way to Pellini's office.

His door stood open and I could see him leaning back in his chair, looking at something on his computer. The screen was faced away from me, so I couldn't tell what it was. But when he saw me in the doorway, he clicked on something else, making me suspect that it hadn't exactly been work-related—not that I had any room to judge, since I did my own share of Internet surfing on taxpayer dollars. Pellini's office was about half again the size of mine, which meant that it was the size of a *large* closet. Pellini was as well, or darn near. He was big and blustery, with greasy black hair and a thick mustache that looked like it belonged on a seventies-era porn star. The rest of him was far from porn-star quality, though. He'd given up on maintaining any sort of physical standard well over a decade ago, and his belly hung so far over his belt that I had a hard time imagining how he put his pants on. Not that I tended toward mental exercises related to Pellini and his pants . . .

I extended the small sheaf of printed pages. He looked at them, then reluctantly straightened in his chair and leaned forward to take them in something just short of a snatch, blowing his breath out as if that small effort had winded him. Which it probably had. I made a mental note to get my own out-of-shape ass to the gym. I was nowhere near as bad as Pellini; I could still run two miles without puking, though it sure wasn't pretty. But I knew I owed it to the cops I worked with to stay in something resembling good condition. I couldn't even imagine how Pellini would handle backing someone up in a fight or a foot pursuit.

I kept the professional smile glued into place as he glanced over what I had so far—even when he gave a snort that sounded suspiciously derisive. "I'll have to teach you how to do a follow-up," he said, his tone pompous. He looked up at me, a slight sneer curving his mouth. "You got fucking lucky with the serial killer. Now it's time for you to learn how to do a proper investigation."

I clenched my jaw tightly enough to feel my teeth squeak to keep from saying something that would no doubt be career-destroying. "I don't think I got *lucky*," I said stiffly. "I put in a lot of time—"

"You got lucky," he said, cutting me off. "But don't take offense," he continued, as I tried to control my seething. "Most cops make great careers out of being lucky." Then he gave me an arrogant smirk. "I'll teach you how to solve a case by actually working it, though."

I forced myself to nod. "Sure thing, Pellini. Maybe we can go out for a beer and you can tell me about some of the big murder cases you worked in the city."

His face reddened, and I knew I'd struck at least a glancing blow. Pellini had worked in patrol and then courtroom security. He'd worked in Investigations in NOPD for only a year before coming over here, and that had been in Property Crimes. Not that there was anything shameful about Property Crimes—I'd worked them for two years before taking on the Symbol Man case—but by that measure I had more experience than he did. And I had a feeling that, if we were to compare stats, I'd still have him beat—even with the fact that he'd been in a metro area and I'd been in sleepy rural Beaulac. I still wasn't sure how he'd managed to talk his way into being a homicide detective over here, but I also knew that wondering about that sort of thing was a waste of energy.

He huffed and stood, tugging at his pants to get them positioned properly beneath the great shelf of his belly. "I'm gonna go talk to Brian's dad. I'd ask you to come with me, but me and the judge go back a ways from our NOPD days. I'm sure he's going through a rough spot right now, and he'll feel better knowing that a senior detective is handling the case. Plus, it's gonna be a lot of guy talk, and it'd probably be over your head."

I resisted the urge to be offended by any of the myriad of insults implied in that statement and instead forced myself to be relieved that I didn't need to spend any more time with Pellini. "No problem," I said brightly. "Let me know when you need any help." *As long as it's not with finding your dick under that roll of fat,* I thought silently as I left and returned to my own office.

I closed my door, allowing myself to fume for a few minutes, followed by some wallowing in self-pity. *Is Pellini's connection to Judge Roth how he got the cases reassigned to him? He pulled strings?* And if so, did the judge know what he was letting himself in for? I briefly debated throwing something heavy and breakable, but about the only thing that fell into that category in my office was my computer, and I wasn't quite brave enough to go there.

I finally had to settle for wadding up the contents of my printer tray and chucking the paper balls across the room. Nowhere near as satisfying, but by the time I cleaned up the resulting mess, I had pretty much burned through the majority of my ire.

My cell phone rang, yanking me out of my funk. "Kara Gillian," I answered.

"Hey, Kara, it's Doc. Got some bad news for you about your councilman."

"Now what?"

"Well, it wasn't an accident."

My stomach tightened. "Are you sure?"

"Yeah, unless he fell down and hit his head twice. The impact and positioning's all wrong for it to be just from falling in the shower. There's not enough trauma to be life-threatening, but I'm pretty sure he got whacked a couple of times with something heavy—enough to knock him out or stun him—and then he was stuffed into the corner of the shower so that he'd asphyxiate."

"I hate you," I said automatically, since that was the reaction he was surely expecting, but my mind was racing a thousand miles an hour.

He laughed. "Sorry. I'll get back to you later about specifics."

I hung up the phone, feeling a strange combination of dread and relief. *Two homicides.* Suddenly I had the possibility of a common thread between Brian Roth and Davis Sharp. But what other connection could Brian Roth have had with Davis Sharp? They were probably at least acquainted with each other, due to Sharp's restaurant, but that would also apply to half the population of Beaulac.

I waggled my mouse to turn off my screen saver, and started typing in online searches for *essence, souls,* and anything I could think of that could give me a bit of a clue as to what besides an *ilius* could consume essence. Brian's death might not have been my case anymore, but I had every intention of figuring out why the hell both of their essences had been consumed. This wasn't a waste of tax-payer dollars, I told myself, since technically it did relate to police work, even though it wasn't anything that would ever go into a written report.

Doing online searches was always a toss of the dice as far as what came back, but I'd been shocked and pleased before at some obscure discoveries, so I always figured it was worth a try. I knew that there were other arcane prac-titioners in the world—not just summoners—and it made sense that someone somewhere might have men-tioned something. In fact, I occasionally found obscure information in the guise of fiction—sort of like how I'd found information on the Symbol Man in a comic book.

But I didn't have the same kind of luck this time. I spent a fruitless hour surfing the Internet, finding plenty on vampires, some Japanese *manga,* even some out-landish erotic fiction about unicorn-riding soul-eating succubi zombies, but nothing I could put a finger on and say, "That's it!"

I wiped my browser history and cleared the cache. Then I sighed and settled in for an afternoon of incredibly mundane but necessary paperwork. Ah, the exciting life of a detective.

13

I PULLED INTO THE PARKING LOT OF ST. LUKE'S Catholic church shortly after noon the next day. As the investigating detective into Davis Sharp's murder, it was reasonable—and practically expected—for me to attend his funeral, though not for the reasons that were usually put forth in crime fiction, where the detective attended the victim's funeral in order to corner and question suspects.

In my world, if a detective tried to question suspects at a funeral, he or she would be suspended or fired before they could say, *But that's how it's done on TV!*

This was essentially little more than good PR—show the grieving family and the public that the police department *cares* and intends to take the case very seriously and personally.

I pulled my jacket on right before I reached the door, noting with mild amusement that I wasn't the only attendee avoiding wearing a jacket out in the sweltering heat. I'd dressed in my one good-quality suit—the one I wore for court and funerals—and even worn low heels and tasteful jewelry for the occasion. I didn't have a problem with the PR aspect of attending funerals—after all, most of our funding came from tax dollars, and murmuring polite regrets wasn't terribly onerous. But at the same time I *was* interested in seeing who would attend, even if interrogations weren't on the schedule. And, given Auri's testimony, I was especially interested to see if any slender blondes showed up.

I held the door for an approaching couple, then entered after them, echoing their sigh of relief as the air-conditioning enveloped us. Then I had to bite back a snort of annoyance. *You have got to be fucking kidding me.*

Damn near every woman in the place had blond hair. And was slender. And was dressed to the nines.

I continued in, suddenly feeling much less confidence in the "niceness" of my suit. I could feel assessing gazes, and I was glad that at least I'd worn my badge. Maybe these taxpayers would now be inclined to vote for new taxes out of pity, since the city's detectives were obviously so underpaid that they had to buy their clothing *off the rack.* The horror.

I fixed a pleasant and subdued smile onto my face, dutifully signed the guest log, then found an out-of-the-way space near the back where I could people-watch. I managed to pick out Davis Sharp's widow fairly easily, aided by the fact that I'd downloaded her driver's license photo before coming to the funeral. Elena Sharp was a strikingly lovely woman, with almond-shaped eyes, light-olive-toned skin, and dark-brown hair highlighted with auburn that fell in a skillfully layered cut down her back. In fact, she was damn near the only woman in the church who *wasn't* a blonde.

And she's a suspect.

Crawford had been less than thrilled when I finally touched base with him to inform him that Councilman Sharp's death had been no accident. "What a pain in the ass," he'd grumbled. "Last thing we needed was a homicide of someone rich and connected."

I knew what he meant. There would be a ridiculous amount of pressure to find suspects, get confessions, and close the case quickly—preferably by the end of the day.

Elena Sharp had left for Mandeville the day before her husband's death, but that didn't rule her out as a suspect. And, yes, she had a semblance of an alibi—the testimony of a security guard at her complex who stated that her car had been there the entire night. But she could have easily used a different vehicle, and it wasn't that long a drive back to Beaulac.

I'd called Ms. Sharp on Monday and asked her to come in for an interview. While she was quite cordial with me, she also made it clear that, if I wanted to talk to her, I would need to come to Mandeville, since she had no plans to remain in Beaulac once the funeral was over. I knew that I could put pressure on her to come in, yet there was always the chance that she would "lawyer up" if I did. I didn't have enough probable cause to get a warrant, but I also didn't have any problem making the hour-plus drive to Mandeville.

So for now I merely watched and waited.

"Lousy week, huh?"

I looked over at the speaker. He seemed vaguely familiar—a fairly good-looking man in his forties or so, with a Hispanic cast to his features. He was dressed in an appropriately dark suit, but it didn't look to be anywhere near the outrageous quality of those worn by some of the other men.

"I beg your pardon?" I said.

"A lot of deaths in the past week," he explained. "Seems that way, at least." He sighed and shook his head. "First the Roth couple and now Davis. I guess bad things really do happen in threes."

"Perhaps so," I answered noncommittally. I was far more used to bad things happening in sweeping tsunamis of dozens, or at least it seemed that way to me. "Did you know Brian and Carol Roth?"

"Yes, I did. I'm Adam Aquilo. I work with Brian's father. I'm Judge Roth's law clerk." He extended his hand and I shook it politely.

"I'm Kara Gillian," I replied. "I think I've seen you at the courthouse before."

He nodded. "I recognized you. Of course, it helps that you're dressed like a cop. Made it easy to place why you looked familiar."

I glanced down at my suit and rolled my eyes. "Yeah, I don't quite fit in with the fashion parade."

He gave a low laugh. "Why do you think I staked out a spot against the wall too? My suits come from JCPenney."

"Oh, law clerks make enough to shop at the *expensive* stores?"

He grinned. "Yeah, I'm rolling in it."

"So you were friends with the Sharps?"

"I know Elena. . . . Well, I knew Davis as well, I suppose, through his restaurant, but I'm really here more as Judge Roth's representative. The social and political scenes tend to run together, you know."

I gave a nod of understanding. I doubted that anyone expected Judge Roth to be in attendance—not when Brian's funeral was set for the next day.

I glanced toward the front of the church. Elena Sharp stood by her husband's casket, graciously accepting the sympathy and polite embraces of mourners as they filed by. "She's a very beautiful woman," I remarked. "Davis was a lucky man."

Adam pursed his lips. "Just between you and me, she was the lucky one. She was trailer trash before he married her."

I raised an eyebrow. "Really?" This was good. No need for interrogations when people were more than willing to gossip.

"Really. That's why everyone was so baffled when they found out she'd left him. And apparently she filed for divorce the same day."

That was news to me. "Well, she probably still gets a decent settlement, right?"

He shrugged. "I suppose, but the money was only part of it. She loved being Mrs. Davis Sharp—society wife." He gave a soft snort of what might have been derision. "She loved all the trappings—the parties, the events. Loved being seen and noticed. Like her car. Davis bought the two of them matching red Mercedes convertibles as a wedding present. She wanted hers to be bright yellow, so everyone would know it was her when she drove it. But they don't come in yellow, and Davis—thank God—refused to let her have it painted." He shook his head and straightened. "Well, I'd best go do my duty. It was nice talking to you."

"And you too," I replied with a smile. *And thanks for the gossip,* I added silently.

* * *

I DIDN'T STAY much longer. There was no reason for me to pay my respects to the widow and plenty of reason not to, since she was a suspect.

A low rumble of thunder greeted me as I exited the church. By the time I pulled out of the parking lot, it was a full downpour and I had to flick the wipers to high to be able to see anything.

My phone pinged to tell me I had a text message, but since I was already driving white-knuckled, I waited until I was stopped at a red light to look at it.

It was from Ryan.

This weather sucks ass. Why the fuck am I moving here? Surfer Boy says Hi.

I grinned and quickly thumbed in a reply.

Wimp. This is just light drizzle. Ur moving here cuz we are only ones who can tolerate you. Everyone else hates you. Sad but true. Say hi to surfer boy.

The light turned just as my phone pinged again. The next three lights were green, so I finally gave up and pulled into a parking lot to read his reply.

I knew it. Those fuckers. Explains why no one comes to my Star Trek themed xmas parties. But you still love me forever and ever?

I couldn't help grinning like an idiot as I read it, even though I knew he was joking around.

Only out of pity. And only when you bring me
donuts.

I replied. I waited, and half a minute later it pinged.

Donut love. I'm cool with that. If you're not busy,
come by our office. Zack is pining for you.

"What a dork," I muttered as I pulled back onto the
road. But I was smiling.

14

I'D NEVER BEEN TO THE LOCAL FBI OFFICE BEFORE, AND upon entering I realized that I hadn't been missing much. There was no reception area, or secretary, or phones—in fact, it was pretty much just a white room about the size of my kitchen, with two metal desks, a black filing cabinet, and some chairs that looked like they'd been purchased at a thrift store. And I had the distinct feeling that Ryan and Zack had been forced to beg, borrow, and bribe to get what little they had.

An older couple stood inside near the door, but there was no sign of Zack or Ryan.

"They're in the back," the woman said before I could ask, jerking a thumb toward the opposite wall. I looked where she'd indicated and saw the outline of a door that I'd missed seeing at first. "Agent Kristoff is looking for an umbrella." She looked out sourly at the sky. The rain had slacked off considerably on my way over here, and I personally didn't think an umbrella was necessary for the twenty-foot walk to what I assumed was their car—the only car in the lot that wasn't obviously some sort of official vehicle. But since I wasn't the one who had to go hunting up an umbrella, I kept my opinion to myself.

"Thanks," I said instead. The sour look remained on her face, though the man with her gave me a gentle smile. I figured them both to be in their late fifties or so, but there was a pallor about the man that made me suspect he was sick—and not with something that would soon pass.

The door in the back wall opened and Ryan emerged, carrying a large black umbrella. "Here you go, Mr. and Mrs. Galloway. I'll walk you out to your car." He gave me a smile and a slight nod of acknowledgment, then held the door open and the umbrella ready for the couple. He escorted them to their car, carefully shielding them from the few drops of rain that still fell, then jogged back to the office as they pulled out of the small parking lot.

He wasn't smiling when he returned.

"Everything okay?" I asked.

He made a rude noise in the back of his throat. "Would be better if I had victims who could understand that if they aren't willing to testify, then there's not much I can do for them."

I gave a sympathetic grimace. "Who are they? Or can't you tell me?"

"Sam and Sara Galloway. They used to own a popular—and profitable—restaurant on the lakefront called Sam and Sara's."

I had a vague recollection of a restaurant by that name. I didn't eat out much, so I wasn't exactly up on the local cuisine. "They went out of business some time ago, right?"

"About ten years ago. They were forced out of business, but I can't really go into more detail right now."

I shook my head. "Then don't. Where's Zack?"

Ryan nodded toward the back door just as Zack emerged. Blond and tan, Agent Zachary Garner resembled a lifeguard more than a federal agent. It didn't help that he looked like he was barely twenty, though I knew he surely had to be older to be a federal agent.

"Good to see you again, Detective Gillian," he said with a broad smile.

"Likewise, Agent Garner," I replied, then grinned as he came forward and gave me a hug. "Good grief, Zack, what did you do to your hair? Did you try to highlight it?"

He ran a hand over his head and gave me a sheepish smile. "Yeah. I was trying for blond tips, but it didn't quite work out."

I eyed him. "Your hair was already blond. Now you have . . ."

"Orange," Ryan stated. "You can dance around it all you want, but the truth is that his hair is Oompa Loompa orange."

"Well, just the tips," I said, "but, yeah. Wow. You need to get someone to fix that."

"I've already made the appointment," Zack assured me with a smile. "You look quite dressed up. Court?"

"Funeral." I made a face. "Victim from a case I had over the weekend—parish councilman who was ass end up in the shower. At first we thought it was an accidental positional asphyxiation, but now it's looking like a homicide." I took a deep breath and looked over at Ryan. "He was like Brian Roth. I mean, he had no essence left either."

Ryan frowned. "Missing? Or consumed?"

I fought the urge to shiver. "Consumed. So it definitely wasn't an isolated event with Brian."

"Can you fill me in?" Zack asked. I did so, quickly outlining the pertinent details. Special Agent Zack Garner was also well informed about the arcane, though I had no idea if he had any particular talent for anything of that ilk.

He looked intensely troubled after I finished. "Only those two so far?"

"Yeah, but that's two more than I'm comfortable with." I paused. "I shouldn't even be using the word *comfortable* at all. Frankly, it worries the shit out of me."

"I can understand that," Zack said, brow creased. "What was the councilman's name?"

"Davis Sharp. He owned Sharp's restaurant, among others."

The frown deepened on Zack's face, and he and Ryan exchanged a look. "Is there any connection between him and the other one?" Zack asked me.

"I don't know that yet. I still have a lot of digging to do. Brian probably ate at Sharp's every now and then, but other than that I got nothin'." I frowned at the two of them. "Do y'all know something about this?"

Zack leaned back against one of the metal desks. "Davis Sharp's name came up in the case we're working on. I don't see how it could have a connection to what you're working, but I'll see if we can get clearance to share what we have with you, in case it does."

"I appreciate that," I said. "You never know what'll turn out to be important."

"Are you sure it's not some sort of naturally occurring thing?" Ryan asked. "Maybe it's not something sinister at all."

"No, I'm not sure," I replied honestly, "but I find it hard

to believe." I looked back to Zack. "Kinda like I find it hard to believe that you actually go out in public with that hair."

"You never used to be so cruel, Kara." Zack made a comically tragic face. "You've obviously been spending too much time with Ryan."

"No fair!" Ryan said with a laugh. "She summons demons, yet I'm the bad guy?"

"Hey, at least the demons don't hate *me*," I teased in retort.

Zack seemed to tense. "What do you mean by that, Kara?"

I hesitated, for some reason feeling that I'd be tattling on Ryan if I spoke about what happened during the summoning. But Ryan didn't seem to care. "She let me watch a summoning of a *reyza*," he explained. "Big fucker by the name of Kehlirik—who seemed to pretty much hate me on sight. Called me a *krakkahl* or some shit like that."

"*Kiraknikahl,*" I corrected, but my eyes were on Zack. He hadn't moved or twitched or reacted at all to what Ryan said—remaining so still and expressionless that I had the eerie impression that he was fighting *not* to react.

Then Zack grinned and it was gone. "See? It's true, Ryan. Everyone hates you. Even the demons."

Ryan gave a dramatic sigh. "And here I was planning to treat you two to dinner."

"That's a good start," I said with an approving smile. "But I'm not sitting at the same table with *him*." I jerked my chin toward Zack and his orange-tipped hair. "That is, not unless he wears a hat."

"So very cruel," Zack moaned. But he opened the bottom drawer of the filing cabinet and pulled out a baseball cap that had *FBI* in large gold letters across the front. He tugged it on and looked to me for approval. "Better?"

"Much. Now, let's go before Ryan changes his mind about paying."

I exited the small building with the two agents following. "Where are we going? We should probably take separate cars since I—" I broke off, going still as an odd nauseating sensation shimmered past me.

"Did you feel that?" I said after a few seconds. I hadn't missed that the two agents had gone still and silent as well.

"I did," Ryan replied, as Zack nodded agreement. "What was it?"

"Dunno. It's arcane, but—" I stopped again, feeling as if something had slithered by. There was a strange hint of menace to it, but nothing I could put a finger on. I shifted into othersight, slowly scanning the parking lot, but the enhanced perception merely intensified the feel of nasty. "It's dangerous," I whispered, shifting back to normal sight.

"We should go," Zack murmured, hand on his gun. "Kara, get in your car. We'll wait until you're in. Get on the road and we'll call you to arrange where we're going."

I didn't need any convincing. I walked quickly to my car and slid in, locking the doors immediately. I pulled out of the parking lot, glancing back to see that Ryan and Zack were getting into their car with similar dispatch. About a minute later, my cell phone rang.

"Any idea what that was?" Ryan asked.

"Not a clue," I admitted. "I couldn't pinpoint anything, so it might have been some sort of random wash of potency. But it was skeeving me out, so I'm totally cool with running away."

"Same here. Look, I'll have to give you a rain check on

the free meal. Zack got a call about this Galloway case and needs to take care of some things."

"Not a problem," I said. "But, please, do one thing for me?"

"Yes?"

"Take Zack to a hairdresser *first*."

15

I SCOWLED AT MY REFLECTION IN THE FULL-LENGTH mirror in my bedroom. Brian Roth's funeral was in an hour, and my dress blue uniform hung on me like an oversize sack. My choice of attire for the funeral yesterday had been easy—dress like a detective. But this was a funeral for a fellow officer, which meant that everyone—from the chief on down—would be dusting off the dress blues. Until this moment, though, I hadn't realized quite how much weight I'd lost, thanks to the too-stressed-to-eat diet that I'd been on for the last few months. On the one hand, I was elated that the insistent little pudge at my belly was gone. Flat stomach! Hooray! However, the idea of buying a whole new wardrobe was nowhere near as pleasant. Not on a cop's salary.

I sighed and cinched my belt a notch tighter in an effort to keep my pants from falling down. The extra fabric wrinkled uncomfortably at my waist, but it was better than giving the entire community a free show. I scowled down at my clown-sized pants, glad that I didn't have to wear a fully rigged duty belt, with holster and handcuffs and baton. My pants would definitely end up around my ankles then.

I fiddled with the positioning of my name tag and tried to remember when I'd last put the damn uniform on. Two years ago, I decided, at the annual departmental awards ceremony when I'd dutifully accepted my five-year service pin. I wrinkled my nose and leaned closer to the mirror, repositioning said pin on my right breast pocket. Since making detective, I hadn't had any other need to wear the uniform. I rarely worked off-duty details like so many of the other detectives did. And, fortunately, the department hadn't lost a cop in the line of duty since I'd been there.

My fingers paused on the pin. *Except for me.* There was a part of me that still felt guilty for subjecting everyone to the agony of thinking I'd died, even though it wasn't my fault and the only other option would have been for me to actually die permanently. But funerals were horrible, wrenching affairs, and the brotherhood of police officers was a tight one. The loss of a cop was the loss of a family member, and I knew I wasn't the only one dreading going to this funeral.

And Brian's is guaranteed to be a ridiculously overblown affair. Since he'd been the son of Judge Harris Roth, that meant that every attorney, politician, and kiss-ass would be there.

I winced and gave myself a mental smack for the uncharitable thoughts. Brian had been a cop, and as such he would get the honor due a cop, even though he hadn't died in the line of duty, and even though his death had numerous questions still surrounding it. However, apparently word had leaked out that there were questions as to whether Brian had killed Carol. I suspected that Pellini had probably let something slip, but on this occasion I couldn't find it in myself to be annoyed with him for sharing information about an ongoing investigation. Everyone's morale had lifted immeasurably, just knowing that there was a chance Brian had been innocent.

But this service would be a far cry from Carol Roth's funeral. Her parents had insisted on a very private, very personal service, which had been performed with an extreme minimum of fuss the day before. I wasn't sure if her former father-in-law, Judge Roth, had attended—or been invited. I couldn't blame Carol's family for that. Since it had been assumed that Brian killed her, I could see why they didn't want any of his family there. Plus, Judge Roth was likely having a hard enough time as it was.

Sighing, I stepped back and regarded myself in the mirror again. I looked like shit. Even I could recognize that. I had dark circles permanently embedded under my eyes, my face was sallow, and my uniform was about three sizes too big for me now. *Yeah, well, maybe averaging only three hours sleep a night isn't helping much either. And that's only with the help of a few glasses of wine.*

A hard knock on the door interrupted my self-loathing. I stuck my tongue out at my reflection, then went to the door and peeked out through the peephole.

I pulled the door open and frowned at Ryan. "You look sharp," I said. And he did too, which made me feel ten times as sloppy. He looked one hundred percent Fed, in a well-tailored dark-blue suit, crisp white shirt, and gray tie. "Why?"

"I figured I'd come with you to the funeral."

My knees nearly wobbled in relief, and I realized how nervous I'd been about facing the rest of the department. I knew I was being stupid, but since the last funeral had been mine, I couldn't help but feel an odd sense of *awkward*. "Thanks," I said fervently. I didn't need to say any more. He got it.

"You need a new uniform," he said, narrow-eyed gaze traveling over me.

I snorted and grabbed my keys. "I wear the damn thing barely once a year, and we don't get our annual uniform allowance until next January. By then I'll probably have gained all the weight back." I headed out the door, locking it behind me.

"Good," he said as he followed me down the stairs. "You're all angles and elbows right now."

I gave him a sour look. "You certainly know how to make a girl feel sexy."

He grinned. "Well, how about: If anyone can make an oversize polyester uniform look hot, it's you."

I had to fight to keep from revealing how tickled I was at the thought that he might consider me hot. Not that he did. He'd already said I was all angles and elbows. Instead, I made a point of looking down at my attire and then rolling my eyes. "You are obviously incredibly desperate for female company."

He shrugged. "Maybe I have a thing for smart chicks in uniform?"

This time I did laugh. "And apparently the heat is affecting your perception. Just get in the damn car."

I'D BEEN MORE than right about the expected turnout. The location of the funeral had been changed at the last minute to the municipal auditorium, since none of the churches in the area had anywhere near sufficient capacity to handle the number of people who wished to pay their respects—even with Brian a suspect in Carol's death. I found a spot against the wall and did my best to blend in and stay unnoticed, though I wasn't having too much success with Special Agent Ryan Kristoff standing beside me in full-fledged FBI mode.

The line for the viewing snaked throughout the auditorium, and I couldn't help but think that the place would have been best served by having a setup with ropes and poles like the ones for the rides at Disney. I didn't join the queue. I'd never had a desire to look at the carefully waxed and made-up faces of the dead, and I also felt no desire or need to offer my regrets to the grieving parents. I didn't know them, they didn't know me, and there was no need to make the line even longer, in my opinion.

I casually scanned the crowd. About every third person was a police officer—either from Beaulac PD or from neighboring agencies. Brian had been fairly well-known and had also worked with the sheriff's office for a time, so I could understand why so many officers were here. But I had to force myself not to roll my eyes at the insane number of political hangers-on that streamed in. This place was a local lobbyist's wet dream. I mentally tagged every parish and city councilman, darn near every courthouse employee, the entire DA's office, the mayor, constables, judges, justices of the peace . . .

I finally gave up trying to track who was attending. *Face it, everyone is here.* But at least that gave me more of a crowd to hide in.

Unfortunately, though, not enough of one. I stiffened when I heard the loud whisper off to my side, clearly meant to be heard.

"Too bad the last funeral was complete bullshit."

I clenched my jaw, refusing to give the speaker the

satisfaction of looking over to see who he was. Besides, I didn't have to look. Detective Boudreaux's redneck twang was distinctive even in a stage whisper. *Dickhead,* I thought murderously, and shoved my hands into my pockets to hide the fact that they had tightened into fists.

My tension must have been palpable. Ryan turned his head and gave me a questioning look.

"It's nothing," I said softly. "It's only a couple of people being idiots. It'll blow over." I still couldn't fathom why *anyone* would think I had faked my death to get attention, but I knew there was no accounting for the stupidity of some people.

His eyes narrowed and then his gaze lifted toward Boudreaux—or so I assumed, because I still wouldn't look over.

"Who's the fat fuck standing next to the pimple-faced fuck?" he asked in a low calm voice, as if he were asking what time lunch would be.

I flicked the quickest of glances toward Boudreaux. "The fat fuck is Pellini. The pimple-faced fuck is Boudreaux." I shook my head. "It doesn't matter. Ignore them."

Ryan made no response, his gaze sweeping the rest of the room. "I'm sorry, Kara," he said after a moment.

"About what?"

A flicker of annoyance and regret passed over his face. "I didn't realize that anyone honestly thought you'd faked your death. I thought it was only a couple of idiots."

I forced myself to shrug. "It *is* only a couple of idiots. Don't sweat it. It'll blow over. Eventually something else will happen that they can sink their teeth into and they'll forget all about it."

His mouth tightened. "Right. They'll forget all about it." I could feel the tension coming off him.

I sighed softly, exceedingly grateful when the service started. I was even more grateful when Jill came up to me, reaching for my hand and giving it a squeeze. I smiled at her, suddenly aware of how lucky I was. It was too damn easy to fall into a cycle of oh-poor-me.

The service was long and tedious, with every possible political figure making his or her weeping way to the podium to extol Brian's virtues—which was surreal and strange, considering the ongoing investigation. As I'd expected, the funeral was turning into the ultimate suck-up for everyone who wanted to get in or stay in Judge Harris Roth's good graces. The air-conditioning in the auditorium wasn't dealing with the enormous crowd very well, and by the time the service finally wrapped up, everyone was sweaty, edgy, and bored.

I hung back while people filed out. I watched Harris Roth walk by, dressed in a perfectly tailored black suit that I suspected was not from a department store. I'd seen him only in photographs before, but I had to admit that they didn't do him justice. He was tall and imposing, handsome in a way that had nothing to do with the set of his features and everything to do with his air of confidence and authority. He was far from ugly, though, with a strong jaw, black hair heavily touched with gray at the temples, and dark eyes that looked straight ahead without seeming to see anyone. Though his eyes were dry, I had no doubt about the depth of his grief. It was etched into his face and seemed to surround him like a cloud. I couldn't imagine what it must be like to lose a child—especially in such a way.

I recognized the woman on his arm as Rachel Roth. She

was the second Mrs. Roth—but I didn't know a lot more than that. I was hideously uninformed when it came to the social scene. Where Harris was strong-featured and handsome, Rachel Roth was strong-featured and ... well, handsome really was the best word. She was by no means unattractive, but she definitely had to work hard to make the most of what she had. To give her credit, she did so, and did it well. She carried herself with confidence and ease, her figure was toned and fit, her hair was exquisitely highlighted, her makeup was flawless, and her clothing was impeccably styled. Even her crying was perfect, as she dabbed very carefully at her eyes with an actual cloth handkerchief, looking poised and dignified doing so— which was personally annoying. When I cried I looked like the Elephant Man, and I was in the habit of taking the back door out of tearjerker movies so the rest of the people in the theater wouldn't see my puffy eyes and swollen nose.

But even her delicate crying seemed to be too much for Harris to handle. I saw him glance at her, then look quickly away—pain rippling across his face as if her tears were a brutal reminder of what he'd lost. For an instant it looked as if he wanted to pull away from her, but she kept hold of his arm. Apparently she needed his support more than he wanted to distance himself from her grief.

"She and Brian were really close," Jill murmured from beside me. I glanced at her with a raised eyebrow, and she shook her head. "No, not the icky kind of close," she said, nose wrinkling. "She was his stepmother, but from everything I heard she was more of a mother to him than his natural mother."

"What happened to his real mother?"

"The first Mrs. Roth? Oh, she passed away a little over a decade ago. Some sort of cancer, I think."

I gave the appropriate grimace.

"The judge married Rachel less than a year later," Jill continued. "I think that most people thought it wouldn't last, that it was just a reaction to his grief, but it's been almost ten years now." She shrugged. "Proved them all wrong. And she's a pretty hotshot attorney on her own. Does a lot of pro bono work too, especially at nursing homes and neuro centers like the one your aunt's in. Victims' assistance, abuse and neglect, that sort of thing." Her eyes followed Harris as the pair exited the front door. "Ya gotta admit, he's not bad-looking at all, and there are puh-lenty of women who would have loved to have a chance to be the next Mrs. Judge Harris Roth."

I glanced at Ryan to see his reaction to Jill's assessment, but he was scanning the crowd and not paying attention to our conversation. I looked back to Jill. "He's good-looking, sure, but he's only a local judge."

"He still has a fair amount of influence. Any judge does. He just won his third term too, since no one qualified to run against him last month."

Ryan flicked a glance our way. "Well, Judge Roth got lucky when Ron Burnside broke his leg the day before qualifying opened," he said. Obviously he'd been paying more attention than I'd given him credit for.

I blinked stupidly at him while Jill let out a low whistle. "Oh, man," she breathed. "I didn't know he was planning to run against Roth."

Ryan gave a stiff nod. "He hadn't started campaigning, but there was some talk around the parish about it."

"Why would a broken leg stop him?" I asked.

His face clouded. "Because he died the next day during

surgery to put a pin in. He had a history of atrial fibrilla-tion, and it was concluded that the accident triggered an attack."

"Ah." I felt a small pang of regret. I hadn't known Ron Burnside well at all, but I'd been in court with him nu-merous times. He was a public defender—genial and good-natured, with a quick smile and a firm handshake—who did what he could for the crap clients that he had. Unlike a lot of cops, I didn't view all defense attorneys as evil incarnate, and most certainly not public defenders. They had an essential place in the system. It wasn't a per-fect justice system, but it was what we had, and I knew that if I was ever arrested I'd want the chance to have someone defending me.

I fisted my hands in my pockets and frowned. "I re-member him being a nice guy. But I don't think he would have had a chance of beating Roth. I mean, I don't know much about politics, but it seems as if it would be point-less to run against a sitting judge unless there's some big scandal or something."

"You're right," Ryan agreed. "But Roth would still have had to mount a campaign."

"Which would have cost him major bucks," Jill fin-ished, nodding knowingly.

I couldn't help but feel a little stupid as I looked back and forth between them. "How do you two know so much about politics? And how much money are we talking about?"

Jill grinned. "My dad used to be a councilman down in New Orleans. And I'd be willing to bet that a campaign against even a crap opponent in this little parish would cost, oh, maybe a hundred grand or so." She gave Ryan a questioning look. "You agree?"

He folded his arms across his chest, gaze skimming the crowd again. "That sounds about right."

I closed my dropped jaw. "A hundred grand? Are you kidding? For a piddling parish election?"

"A judge has a lot of power," Ryan reminded me. "And costs add up in a campaign. If you add in television, it gets even more expensive."

"Right," Jill said. "Now, that's not all out of his own pocket—a majority of that is from campaign contributions—but anyone who runs for public office has to be prepared to shell out a fair chunk of change. Of course, a sitting judge is going to have an easier time getting contributions."

I caught movement from the corner of my eye, and I stiffened. I almost didn't look at the pair approaching me, then changed my mind. No, I was *not* going to let those two moronic detectives intimidate me. I took a deep breath, then turned to look straight at Pellini and Boudreaux as they came up to me, steeling myself for another of their obnoxious comments about my funeral. *At least I have Ryan and Jill beside me.*

But instead of making a snide crack, Boudreaux stopped in front of me and stuck his hand out. I looked down at his hand for a heartbeat, then looked up at his face, perplexed. What the fuck was he up to now?

"Kara," he said, voice quiet and earnest, "I wanted to let you know that I'm glad everything worked out for you with the Symbol Man case. You did the department real proud, and I'm glad you came through it safely."

I continued to stare at him. *Who are you, and what the fuck have you done with Boudreaux?* I wrenched my gaze over to Pellini, but his expression was as open and earnest as Boudreaux's. Boudreaux still stood there with his hand extended, and after another few heartbeats I was able to lift my own hand to his. He smiled and shook it, then stepped back. Pellini shook my hand next, and for an instant I thought he was going to pull me into a man-hug, but instead he merely gave me a smile that was amazingly close to being nice. Good thing, too, because I was pretty sure that if he'd tried to hug me, I might have kneed him in the crotch out of pure reflexive instinct.

They walked out, leaving me to stare after them in absolute shock. I turned to look at Jill and was relieved to see a similarly stunned expression on her face.

"What the fuck happened to those two?" she asked. "Did we slip into an alternate universe?"

I gave a baffled shrug. "That's the most reasonable explanation I can think of." I shook my head. "Too fucking weird. Hell, it's probably a setup for some nasty joke. Oh, well, I'm ready to get out of here."

Jill glanced at her watch, grimacing. "I need to dig out too. Shitload of work to catch up on." She gave me a quick hug, then headed out the door.

"C'mon, Fed Boy," I said to Ryan, then saw that he was staring off into the distance again. I snapped my fingers in front of his face. "Yo, Ryan. Time to go."

He pushed off the wall, then winced and put a hand up to his head.

I seized his arm as he swayed. "Are you all right?"

Straightening, he brushed his hand over his face and gave me a shaky smile. "I'm all right. I think I have a migraine coming on. Must be the heat in here."

His voice was steady, but his eyes were like hollow pits in his face. "Do you want me to bring the car around?"

"I can make it to the car. I'm all right. I just need to

close my eyes for a few minutes." He shrugged and smiled, but I could see it was forced.

I walked with him to the car, trying not to look like I was hovering over him. To anyone else it probably looked like he was merely walking slowly, but I had the unnerving impression that he was struggling to stay upright. I'd never had a migraine, but I couldn't imagine that the bright sun and south Louisiana heat were helping matters any.

Ryan climbed into the car and practically collapsed into the seat, pulling the door closed and then leaning back against the headrest. I started to slide into the driver's seat, then paused, narrowing my eyes at a car on the other side of the parking lot. *How many bright red Mercedes convertibles can there possibly be in Beaulac? And I doubt that Davis Sharp is driving his.* I hadn't seen Elena Sharp inside the auditorium, and I was fairly certain that I would have noticed had she been in attendance. So why would she be out in the parking lot now?

As I watched, the red Mercedes thrummed to life and then sped off in a roar of quality German engineering. I caught a quick glimpse of the driver—she was wearing sunglasses, but I was still fairly convinced that it was Elena Sharp.

I shrugged it off for now and got into the car, cranking the engine to get the AC going. "Put your seat belt on. Are you all right?" I asked again.

He complied with my command. "I'll be fine. Just need to close my eyes for a bit," he repeated.

"You look like shit," I said, as I pulled out into traffic.

"You're one to talk," he replied. I glanced at him sharply. It hadn't been delivered with any tone of joking, but I bit back my reply. He obviously didn't feel well, and there was no point in me overreacting.

I maintained my silence as I drove back to my house, and when I pulled into my driveway I saw that he was asleep. At least I hoped he was asleep. I felt a quick stab of fear that something awful had happened, but his chest still rose and fell in a nicely reassuring manner.

I parked the car in front of the house and gently nudged his shoulder, really hoping I could wake him up, since I didn't want to think about carrying him into the house. But his eyes snapped open as soon as I touched him.

"We're at my house. Do you want to crash here for a bit?"

He rubbed at his face, then nodded. "Yeah. Yeah, that sounds good."

He seemed steadier on his feet as he walked to the house and up the stairs. The twenty-minute nap he'd taken in the car had obviously helped a lot. "Are you hungry?" I asked as I headed to the kitchen.

He hesitated, then nodded again. "I should probably eat something."

I searched through my fridge for something quick and easy. I finally settled on a microwaved mini-pizza. I half-expected him to make a crack about my cooking, but he didn't even bat an eyelash, merely wolfed it down in about three bites. I was relieved to see some color come back to his face after he ate, though he still had dark circles under his eyes as if he hadn't slept for a week. I thought I had the monopoly on those.

I stuck another pizza in the microwave, and when I turned back around he had an empty wine bottle in his hand, looking at it with narrowed eyes and pursed lips. I groaned inwardly.

"Don't worry," I said. "I don't have a drinking problem. I was trying to relax enough to get some sleep last night. And for the record, that was emptied over the course of about a week."

His eyes lifted to mine. "I never said you had a drinking problem."

"You didn't have to." I took the bottle out of his hand and dumped it in the trash, wincing as it clanked harshly against the two other bottles in there already.

"My, aren't we touchy."

I took a deep breath to calm myself. "You're right, I am." I busied myself with getting the second pizza out of the microwave and putting it on his plate. "Sorry."

He lifted the pizza and blew on it to cool it. "Did you summon again Saturday night?"

I blinked at the non sequitur. "Yeah."

"That's cool." An oddly strained silence fell for another minute or so while he ate. At least he was looking better. I expected him to ask me more about my summoning, but if he wasn't going to ask, I wasn't going to offer.

Finally he leaned back in the chair and pushed his empty plate away. "Okay, much better," he said, giving me a more normal smile. "So, what did you summon that wears boots?"

I stared at him, then twisted to look at the floor by the back door. Great. A damn near perfect boot print. *Shit. Teach me to mop my floors more often.* "I . . . uh, I summoned Rhyzkahl."

He frowned at me. Or, rather, he gave me a facial expression that was about ten times as frowny as a frown. "How the fuck? *Why* the fuck?"

I forced a laugh, trying not to look guilty, which was how I felt for some reason. "I know, I know. But he wanted me to summon him, and I was given his oath that I would not be harmed."

He lowered his head and looked at me, gaze penetrating. "What did he want?"

"He, uh . . . wants me to be 'his' summoner."

His expression didn't change. "And how does *that* work?"

I briefly explained what I knew, especially pointing out the bit about how he would still be constrained by the summoning protocols. "I don't think he's been to this sphere for centuries, except for the botched summonings and the time I called him, and he didn't exactly get to see the sights then," I said.

Ryan snorted. "I'm trying to picture him walking through a mall."

I laughed. "That would turn some heads."

"He'd probably get scooped up by a model talent scout."

"Right! I can see him on the cover of *GQ*."

"Yeah, pulling the head off someone like a fly."

The comment, delivered so evenly, shocked me to silence.

"Don't forget what he is, Kara," Ryan said in a low voice, gaze steady on me and all trace of humor gone.

Annoyance surged through me. "I know what he is, Ryan," I replied, more calmly than I expected. "I'm the summoner, remember?" I couldn't believe that he was trying to warn me about demons. I'd been summoning for ten years, and he'd never even *seen* a demon before a couple of months ago.

"I remember. And that's why I worry about you." He

stood, chair scraping on the tile floor. "Yes, he saved your life, and I'm deeply grateful for that. But you were the one who told me that the demons never do anything for the sake of being nice. I just don't want to see you putting yourself in a position of being bound to him."

I could feel myself scowling, even though I wanted to show myself as calm and cool. "Look, I'm being careful. I'm considering everything."

The troubled expression on his face etched a bit deeper. "Just...shit, don't let him get too...*close* to you, all right?"

It was getting harder to keep my expression neutral. "Too close to me how?" I wasn't so sure I was as successful in keeping my voice even.

He scowled. "Fucking shit, Kara. Do I have to spell it out? I'm worried that you're going to fall for that gorgeous face and body and forget what he is, and that you'll succumb to him and end up in his thrall and forget—" He bit off whatever it was he was about to say and looked away, an expression of pain flashing across his features so quickly that I wasn't even sure that's what it was. He took a shuddering breath. "And forget...who you are," he finished.

I worked moisture back into my mouth. "I find that a bit insulting," I said carefully, measuring each word as it came out. "I know who I am."

He growled something under his breath and jammed his hands down into his pockets. "Shit, you know what I mean."

"I'm not sure I do," I said. "You think that I'll fall into his arms and then forget that he's a demon and rush to do his bidding and lose all self-control. End up in his thrall, right?"

His eyes flashed with anger and something else I couldn't interpret. "No. Yes. Shit. Kara, come on. I'm sorry, but the thought of you and that creature together..." He gave his head a shake, as if to rid it of an unpleasant image. "It makes me want to throw up."

I couldn't help it. I laughed. "Holy shit! Are you *jealous*?"

He shot me a look of such pure menace that I took a step back. In the next heartbeat it was gone, replaced by an expression of frustration, making me doubt what I'd seen. "I'm not *jealous*," he spat. "Don't be stupid."

I stared at him for about ten seconds. Then I turned away and busied myself pointlessly with cleaning up the counter. "Yeah, wouldn't want to be stupid. Wouldn't want you to hang out with someone who might lose every ounce of brain they have if they look at a gorgeous guy." *And why can't you be jealous?* I added silently, throat tight. *Just a little?*

"Ah, fuck, Kara." He sighed. "You know I didn't mean it like that."

I industriously wiped the counter down. I didn't want to turn around. Didn't want him to see that I was blinking furiously to keep the damn tears back. When had I become so fucking weak?

After several seconds of silence, I heard him sigh again. "I need to take care of some stuff. Are you going to be all right?"

"I'm fine," I said, rinsing the sponge out in the sink, twisting it harder than necessary to wring it out. "Are you feeling better?"

There was a brief pause, then, "Yeah. I'm fine. I'm good to drive."

"Okay," I said. "I guess I'll see you later."

He was silent again for several seconds. "Yeah, okay," he said finally. "See you later."

I didn't look back until I heard the front door close. Then I stopped blinking and allowed the tears to come.

16

AFTER RYAN LEFT, I ALLOWED MYSELF A HALF HOUR OF sniveling, then washed my face, changed clothes, and buried myself in work—my tried and true way to avoid thinking about things that upset me. Or, rather, I *tried* to bury myself in work. Unfortunately there really wasn't much work that needed doing. I was already caught up on my paperwork, and I didn't feel like driving over to my aunt's house to get started on the arcane research I needed to do.

I finally went down to the basement and set up the next stage of the ritual to call Tessa's essence back. This stage required more than an hour of channeling potency into the diagram, which ended up having the welcome benefit of tiring me out. I needed only *two* glasses of wine to fall asleep.

Yet, even exhausted, I still had chaotic and unsettling dreams of Ryan and Rhyzkahl. I couldn't remember much beyond a few snatches of scenes—images of the two facing each other in arcane conflict, surrounded by demons.

I woke late, mood not improved when my coffeemaker refused to turn on. I tried a variety of methods to make the damn thing work—including yelling, crying, and cursing—but it still stubbornly refused to produce coffee.

I finally gave up and headed to the coffee shop and its overpriced product. Without coffee, the day had a good chance of sucking, and I really didn't need any more suck in my life at the moment.

I FUMBLED IN the glove box of the Taurus for sunglasses, jamming them onto my face with one hand while trying to adjust the sun visor with the other. The mid-morning sun speared relentlessly through the windshield at the absolute perfect height to evade the sun-blocking powers of the visor. I had the air conditioner cranked all the way up, but the air it produced was only slightly below tepid and I could feel sweat trickling down my back. I'd briefly experimented with driving with the windows down, but even at ten in the morning the outside air was hot enough to make that pointless. At least the minimal air-conditioning wouldn't turn my hair into a tangled mess the way open windows would. And since the day's agenda involved driving down to Mandeville to interview Elena Sharp, I figured it would be best if I avoided arriving with bride-of-Frankenstein hair.

Sure, she can pop on up to Beaulac to lurk outside Brian Roth's funeral, I thought sourly, *but she's still going to make me drive to Mandeville to interview her?* And I was willing to bet that the AC in her car worked pretty damn well. On the other hand, the trip to Mandeville would conveniently keep me out of the office for the rest of the day. That was a win.

The drive to Mandeville was uneventful, and it didn't take me long to find the complex where she lived. I pulled in and realized quickly that even though it wasn't a three-story house on the shore of Lake Pearl, Elena Sharp's new residence was by no means a mere apartment. From the gated entrance—complete with a security guard who actually checked my credentials—to the lushly landscaped surroundings, the entire complex screamed wealth.

I spied Elena Sharp's distinctive red Mercedes, parked between a Lexus and a BMW. I stuffed my grungy Taurus into a spot next to an Audi, then walked down a path shaded with flowering crape myrtles to her unit. I rang the doorbell and heard the deep, sonorous tones vibrate beyond the oak and glass door, followed by the sound of heels on marble. A few seconds later the door was opened by Elena Sharp.

She was a few inches taller than me and wearing heels as well, which gave her enough of a height advantage that she was most definitely looking down at me. She wore a strapless mid-calf-length formfitting dress that molded over a flat stomach, narrow hips, and generous tits that I had a feeling were not factory originals. On her the dress looked elegant and expensive. On me it would have looked tawdry and pathetic. Actually, on me it would have looked stolen as well, since I figured it probably cost several hundred dollars. Not that I knew that much about fashion, but I could tell what was way out of my price range.

"Ms. Sharp, I'm Detective Kara Gillian with the Beaulac Police Department," I said as I extended my hand. "As I stated on the phone, I'm investigating the circumstances surrounding your husband's death."

Her eyes flicked over me, taking in my clothing, my gun

and badge, even my hairstyle—or lack thereof. I had a fleeting sensation of being cataloged, and I had to wonder if she could tell that I shopped mostly at stores that ended in *Mart*. Her eyes went back to mine, and she reached out and clasped my hand in a brief shake. Her manicure was perfect, her hand cool and smooth in mine. "Detective Gillian," she said, polite smile curving her lips. "Please come in." She stepped back and motioned me in. I obliged, then followed her as she turned and led the way to a sitting room.

The sitting room was about the same size as the one in my house, except that in my house it was called a living room and definitely looked lived in. This was a room where one was expected to sit and perhaps sip tea and speak of lovely things in soft and cultured tones. Everything here looked expensive and elegant, with sleek furniture that exuded an aura of quality, fresh flowers on the coffee table, and a rolltop desk beneath a window that offered a stunning view of Lake Pontchartrain. It was beautiful, but I had a hard time imagining anyone spending much time in the room.

She sat smoothly on a sleek couch that I figured cost more than every stick of furniture in my house. The only other place to sit in the room was a large wingback chair that I knew without a doubt would swallow me whole, but I didn't really want to sit on the couch with her if I was going to be questioning her. I gave a mental sigh and sat carefully on the forward edge of the wingback, telling myself I didn't really look ridiculous. "I appreciate you taking the time to talk to me," I began, setting my notebook on my lap.

Elena Sharp crossed her legs and laced her fingers over

her knee. "And I appreciate you making the drive to Mandeville, Detective Gillian," she said, with a slight nod as if to say, *There now, we have the pleasantries out of the way.*

"So, Davis was murdered," she continued, mouth quirked in a humorless smile. "I take it I'm a suspect?"

Oh, yeah, she wasn't stupid by any stretch. "You understand that I can't rule you out."

"Oh, I know." She closed her eyes briefly, then shook her head and sighed. "One more way for Davis to screw me."

"You moved out and filed for divorce the day before his death," I said, glancing at my notes. "How long were you two having marital difficulties?"

She gave a breathless laugh. "Oh, no. *We* were not having marital difficulties at all. *I* was. I . . . didn't want to be with him anymore." An odd mixture of pain and fear flickered across her face, quickly smoothed away into a polite smile—though the echo of it lingered in her eyes.

Interesting. Had she been afraid of her late husband? Enough to leave him? Or have him killed? "Yes, ma'am," I said, glancing again at my notes. "You called the police twice in the last three years for domestic violence complaints." I watched her face, keeping my expression friendly and neutral.

"Yes," she said. "So I did."

"You never pursued charges."

She stood and walked to the window, folding her arms across her chest and almost hugging herself as she gazed out at the lake. "I know that everyone thought I was just a stupid trophy wife. And you know what? I was—the trophy part, that is." She ran her hands unconsciously over her dress, smoothing out nonexistent wrinkles. "But I'm not stupid. I grew up in a trailer, went to the public high school, and learned pretty early on that what money and influence couldn't get, a blow job and a fake orgasm could." She shrugged and gave a self-conscious laugh.

I suddenly felt better about my own financial situation. "So you married Davis for his money."

She gave me an *oh, please* look. "Well, duh. He was almost twenty years older than me. But I'm not a total mercenary. We actually had a lot of fun together, and I never really expected him to ask me to marry him." A faint smile flickered across her face. "Shocked the shit out of me, to be honest."

"So, now that he's dead, you're pretty well set, right?"

Elena shook her head. "I'm all right, but if you're thinking that I inherited the massive Sharp fortune, then you're sadly mistaken. I signed a rock-solid prenuptial agreement with that man." She lowered her head and looked at me. "I had my own lawyer look it over damn carefully too, and a few changes were made, but we managed to come to some agreeable terms and went ahead and hitched on up."

"It sounds like a corporate merger," I said before I could censor myself.

She gave a small bark of laughter. "It was, in a way. Like I said, we had fun, but I also looked out for myself. And Davis was the same way. Who knows; maybe that's what he liked about me. I'm attracted to powerful men. I guess that's my downfall." A look of regret crossed her face, then she shrugged her bare shoulders and it was gone. She moved to the desk and opened a drawer, removing a manila envelope. "Anyway, in a divorce, this is what I would get," she said, as she pulled a sheet of paper out of the envelope and passed it to me.

I skimmed the page from her prenuptial agreement

quickly. "That's . . . a pretty decent sum of money," I pointed out, trying not to look as boggled as I was.

She gave me a wry smile. "Yeah, I know. Trust me, I remember where I came from. Unlike a lot of the rich bitches that I've hung around with, I can appreciate how rare this sort of lifestyle is. I'd have been able to live the rest of my life in pretty decent comfort."

"And what do you get now that he died before your divorce was final?"

A ghost of a smile curved her lips. "Well, he has two kids from his first wife, and they get most of his estate." She pulled another sheet of paper from the envelope and handed it to me. "I get a lump sum, plus a monthly stipend for the rest of my life."

I glanced over the numbers. Pretty much the same that she would have received in a divorce. I doubted that she'd faked the documents. It was far too easy for me to check— and I would—and she wasn't that stupid.

But there were plenty of other possible motives for murder besides greed. "Can you tell me more about the 911 calls?"

She looked at me, green eyes bright in the sunlight that streamed in through the high window. "We had arguments sometimes—when he wanted me to do something or go somewhere, and I'd made other plans or that sort of thing. He told me that it was my *job* to be with him and look good, 24/7. And . . . he got jealous too. He wanted me to be beautiful and charming, but he also didn't want me to pay too much attention to other men. Even his close friends." She sighed. "Davis would occasionally get physical. I got scared the first time." She shook her head. "Don't get me wrong, I've been smacked before, but I just didn't expect it from him. It wasn't even *hard*. My pride was bruised more than anything. Anyway, I locked myself in the bedroom and called the cops." She brushed her hair back from her shoulders, an expression that might have been embarrassment coloring her features. "They came, took statements, told him to leave for the night." She gave me a rueful smile. "He came back the next day with an armload of presents."

"That's a pretty standard pattern for an abuser," I said evenly.

"Oh, I know," she said, with an unapologetic shrug. "And if he'd been slapping me around on a daily basis, I'd have been out of there in just my underwear, if necessary. I'm a mercenary, but, as I told you, I'm not stupid. In the five years we were together, he slapped me only twice." The look she gave me was challenging. "That's hardly a standard pattern for an abuser."

It was two more slaps than I would ever put up with. "So why did you leave him?" I countered.

There it was again—the pain and fear. Her gaze flicked around the room, refusing to light anywhere. She swallowed and smoothed her hands over her dress again, then sat back down on the couch and clasped her hands together in her lap. She took a breath to settle herself and looked up at me, a smile that was clearly artificial sculpted onto her face by sheer will. "I found out he was cheating on me."

With the mystery blonde? Or was there someone else? "That's the only reason?" I said, then realized how it sounded.

Elena lifted a perfect eyebrow. "That's not enough?"

It certainly was for someone like me, but would she really be willing to leave the lifestyle because her husband had screwed around? It didn't ring true. "Sorry. So you found out he was cheating on you and you filed for divorce?"

Her nod was stiff, and an expression of regret crossed her face. *She didn't want to leave him.* I'd have bet money on it. So why did she? There was still fear. It showed in the way her hand clenched on the arm of the couch, the jiggle of her foot, and I didn't think it was just nerves at being questioned by the police.

"Can you tell me who he was having an affair with?" *Maybe someone with more reason to want him dead?*

I saw her knuckles go white briefly, then she gave a stilted shake of her head. "I ... never knew her name. I only knew about her."

Bullshit. Why divorce him and leave that cushy nest without solid proof? "I find that hard to believe," I said instead, leaning forward slightly.

Her makeup stood out in harsh contrast to her skin as she paled, but she shook her head again. "I didn't know. I didn't want to know. I just got out."

Again, bullshit. Elena Sharp did not strike me as the kind of woman who would leave her nice luxurious nest without even trying to fight off a usurper. I narrowed my eyes. "Why did you really leave your husband, Mrs. Sharp?"

She gave a deep exhalation, as if trying to appear exasperated. "Look, does it matter anymore? He's dead, and I'm a widow instead of a divorcée."

"It matters a great deal, Mrs. Sharp," I said, hardening my voice. "Your husband was murdered. You understand that, right? If he was involved with someone else, then you need to tell me everything you know."

Her hands trembled. "I can't tell you!"

Now it was *I can't tell* instead of *I don't know.* I stood and gave her my best tough-bitch-cop look. "You *can* tell me. Do you think this is all going to go away? That the police will get tired of looking into your husband's murder? If you think you need protection, I can arrange it, but you have to be honest with me!"

"It's not like that...I mean—"

"Then tell me!" I demanded. "Tell me why you left your husband. Tell me who he was screwing around with. The only person who's going to take a fall here is you!"

She shook her head, eyes wide. "No. I've lost too much already. I won't go to jail for...for something I didn't do!"

I sat down and gentled my voice. "Then be honest with me. It's the only way out of this."

She looked at me, green eyes on mine. Then she closed them and took a deep breath. *Yes,* I thought with a touch of triumph. *She's ready to spill...*

"I think I need to speak to my lawyer."

Fuck.

She opened her eyes and looked at me steadily. *She's not stupid. And she's stronger than she gives herself credit for. Fuck.*

I closed my notebook and stood. "Mrs. Sharp, thank you for talking to me," I said formally. "If you can think of anything that might help in the investigation of your husband's murder, please call me." I handed her my business card.

She stood as well. "I didn't kill my husband, Detective," she said, taking the card from me. "And I didn't pay to have him killed either."

"Then you have nothing to worry about," I assured her. "Have a good afternoon, Mrs. Sharp. I'm sure I'll be in touch again."

I left the apartment and returned to my car. I cranked

the engine, then rolled the windows down and turned the AC on full blast to push the overheated air out, drumming my fingers absently on the steering wheel as I waited for the air to cool from roasting to tepid. She'd enjoyed that lifestyle, the money. Why leave it without a fight? Was she being blackmailed? Threatened? And what about Sharp's essence? Was she somehow responsible for that?

I drove away from the apartment complex, returning to Beaulac with more questions than when I'd left.

BY THE TIME I made it back, it was late enough that I didn't feel a need to go to the office. I stopped and bought a new coffeemaker, then swung by my aunt's house. I had enough of her *person*, but now I needed some items that were personal to *her*—something that would resonate with emotional ties to this plane. I parked in Tessa's drive-way and ran up the steps to the front door. *Her favorite teacup, and her hairbrush. And maybe that scarf that I—*

I stopped with my hand a millimeter from the door-knob, thoughts derailed by the faint prickling sensation in the wards that I'd placed after Kehlirik had removed the others. I slowly pulled my hand back, heart beginning to beat just a bit faster as I shifted into othersight and looked at the wards. I couldn't see anything amiss with them, and I frowned. Something felt *not right* on the door, but for the life of me I couldn't see anything at all out of place in the aversions. As far as I could tell they were exactly the same as I'd left them. Had something passed through them? And would I even know if something had?

I turned and looked out over her yard. Mowed. Trimmed. Weeded. I could almost explain that away—especially now that the wards were mostly disabled. I wasn't strong enough to have aversions that would keep someone out of the yard. Okay, so someone was taking care of her lawn. Not a reason for huge worry. *But someone's also visiting her in the neuro center...*

I gingerly reached my hand out and took hold of the doorknob, letting out a soft breath as the prickle faded away to nothing. Overactive imagination? I entered and closed the door quietly behind me, then stood stock-still in the hallway, listening and sensing as hard as I could.

The only sound was the ticking of the clock in the kitchen, but I still couldn't shake the incredibly nebulous sense of *not right*. I walked down the hall to the library, trying to move silently, which was a joke on the creaky wooden floors.

I stopped in front of the library, chewing my bottom lip as I looked at the closed door. Had I left it open or closed? For the life of me I couldn't remember. I extended mentally, testing to make certain that the wards on the library had all been disabled. And had *stayed* disabled.

To my relief, there were no wards visible in my othersight. I entered cautiously, letting my breath out when I didn't feel the beaded-curtain sensation that I was used to—the ripple of arcane sensing that would have told me that there were still active protections. I also didn't feel any bolts of lightning strike me down, which I definitely took as a good sign. I gingerly peered in.

The room was so quiet I could hear the rush of my own pulse, but I couldn't shake the feeling that there was something off. I stood in the doorway for at least a hundred heartbeats, but nothing stirred or jumped out at me.

I finally stepped out of the library, firmly closing the door. I continued on to Tessa's room and gathered up a few personal items, then left the house, locking the door behind me and making sure that the wards were still active.

I drove back to my own house, unnerved. There was absolutely no sign, physical or arcane, that anything had been disturbed, but there was a visceral part of me that *knew* that someone—or something—had been in that house in the last day.

17

I DUMPED MY BAG BY THE FRONT DOOR AND IMMEDI-
ately headed down to my basement. An uncomfortable
sense of urgency nagged at me—heightened now by the
oddities of Tessa's house and her possible mystery visitor.
*And screw Kehlirik and his suggestion that I replace the
wards on my own. Next full moon I'm summoning someone
to do it for me.* My wards sucked ass. I had no problem ad-
mitting that.

I carefully sketched out the next section of the diagram, resisting the desire to rush through it in order to get
the damn thing working sooner. It would take only one
incorrect sigil to render the entire thing useless, and I was
fairly sure that I didn't have the luxury of time to try this
again if the first attempt failed.

I opened my backpack and arranged the items carefully
within the diagram. The teacup, the comb, the scarf. I also
added the picture of the two of us dressed like Purple People. The glop of blood, hair, and fingernails had dried into
a nasty dark-brown crust around the inner circle, and I

had to be very careful not to touch any of it in case a crucial aspect of it flaked away.

Inhaling, I pulled potency, weaving it into the runes in a careful progression. The power came in uncomfortable sputters thanks to the waning moon, and after just a few minutes I was sweating with the effort of feeding it into the diagram.

I finally released the potency and stepped back, eyeing the diagram nervously. It remained quiescent, and dismay began to knot my throat as seconds ticked by. *I made a mistake somewhere. Shit. I'm going to have to start over from the beginning.* But where the hell had I screwed up? Starting over wouldn't do me any good if I repeated the mistake.

Then the diagram gave a sudden *pop*, which I felt more than heard, and began to resonate. Relief washed through me, and I had to bend over and put my hands on my knees for a few seconds. *Okay, crisis averted. I hope.*

I made my way upstairs, legs shaking from exhaustion. I collapsed into bed, but, despite my fatigue, I slept badly—worry about my aunt and her house crowding my dreams and waking me repeatedly.

I was also apparently still angsting pretty heavily over my argument with Ryan, judging by the number of unsettling dreams that featured him. I woke with a headache a few minutes before my alarm went off, then stared morosely at my bedroom ceiling as the sun speared annoying fingers of light through my blinds.

It bugged the shit out of me that we'd had a fight—a strange and stupid one at that—and the thought that we might not still be friends left me with a dull ache in my chest. Okay, so he might never be interested in me beyond friendship, but that was better than nothing at all.

Right?

I was in no mood to go in to work, but I still possessed enough shreds of pride that I didn't want to waste a sick day on wallowing in self-pity. Not that I wasn't unspeakably tempted to do so as I huddled under my covers. But I suspected that I was turning into one of those horribly needy people who cling far too hard to people who are nice to them. I liked Ryan. Quite a bit. But how much of that was simply because we shared knowledge of the arcane? I wanted very much to think that there was more to our friendship than that, but maybe I'd misread the signs out of my deep desire for there to be more.

I groaned and stuffed my head under the pillow. It was true. I *did* want there to be more. "I am so pathetic," I mumbled into my pillow.

On the other hand, why would he be so overly protective of me—even if it was rather insulting—if he didn't consider me to be a good friend? And how much of my reaction to him the other night had been fueled by a fair amount of guilt that he was right—at least partially? I'd certainly jumped right into Rhyzkahl's arms on our first encounter, though the reasons for that were far too layered for me to begin to peel apart. But, in my own defense, I hadn't succumbed to his thrall, or whatever Ryan was afraid of. I was still me.

Right?

And for that matter, who are you, *Ryan Kristoff?* I thought, feeling suddenly defensive. *How the fuck do demons know who you are?*

I threw off the covers and practiced a few choice curse words. This entire line of thought was a sure way to drive myself nuttier than I already was.

It was barely six a.m. After a moment's thought, I

pulled on workout clothes, packed a gym bag, grabbed some work-quality clothes, then headed to the gym. I was the kind of member the gym loved: My dues were automatically debited from my checking account once a month, and I showed up about half as often as that. But I felt a deep need to sweat some annoyance and frustration out, and this was a better option than cleaning my house.

To my surprise, the gym was fairly crowded, and I realized belatedly that everyone else was also trying to squeeze a workout in before work. I saw a number of familiar faces, though after a few minutes of racking my brain for names, I realized that they were familiar because I'd seen them recently, at Brian Roth's funeral. Elected officials, or people in the social scene. No one I actually *knew*.

I didn't have much of a workout plan in mind, which was probably a good thing since most of the equipment was occupied. I finally settled for a workout that consisted of: *Wander around until you see an open machine and then do that exercise.* Amazingly, at the end of twenty minutes I felt like I'd accomplished something. I put in another twenty minutes on the elliptical trainer, and then showered, changed, and made it in to work barely on time.

I didn't see Boudreaux or Pellini in their offices as I headed to mine, but somehow I doubted that they were out tracking down leads in the deaths of Carol and Brian. More likely, they were conducting a thorough investigation of the breakfast menu at Lake o' Butter Pancake House.

I allowed myself to feel virtuous as I settled in at my desk, pleased when my lieutenant walked by my office and gave me a nod in passing, and doubly pleased when I heard him inquire a few seconds later as to the whereabouts of everyone else.

Now that I'd successfully established to the rank that I looked like I was working, it was time to actually *do* the work that would hopefully give me some results. It was, unfortunately, boring, but after three hours I had managed to type up subpoenas for the Sharps' financials, so I could verify for myself everything Elena Sharp had told me.

Definitely action-movie material.

The courthouse was only a block away from the station, but it was already hot enough that my blouse clung to me after just that short walk. I breathed a sigh of relief as the air-conditioned climate of the courthouse enveloped me, not even caring that in about a minute I'd be covered in goose bumps as the sweat dried.

I gave a nod to the officers working courthouse security, giving an extra smile to Latif—the tall dark-skinned woman holding the metal-detector wand. She was an amazon, with hair cut so short she might as well have shaved her head, but on her it totally worked and made her look like a gorgeous badass. We'd been in the same class at the academy, finishing one-two in the academic portion. She was number one. She'd have been a terrific road cop, in my opinion, but she was a single mom and had told me that not only did she need the more normal hours of courthouse work, but she also couldn't put herself in a position to leave her daughter without a mother. I could totally respect that.

Latif gave me a wide smile as I passed through the security area. "Hey, woman. Whatcha got going on?"

I lifted the manila folder with my subpoenas. "The exciting side of investigations. The paperwork."

She chuckled. "Warrants?"

"Subpoenas."

"Woo. The really fun stuff!" she said, as she peered at a piece of paper on the desk by the X-ray machine. "Well, Judge Roth is supposed to be the duty judge today, but he's not in."

"I'm not surprised. The funeral was only the day before yesterday."

Latif grimaced. "Yeah. He's been out since it happened. That whole thing sucks. Oh, here we go. Judge Laurent is taking duty today."

I'd had warrants signed by Judge Laurent before, so I knew where his chambers were. I made my good-byes to Latif, then headed up to the second floor.

His secretary sat behind the desk out front—a curvy brunette who managed to look lush instead of pudgy. I envied this ability. She gave me a smile as I closed the door behind me. "You need something signed?"

I lifted the folder containing the subpoenas. "If he's not too busy?"

She took the folder from me. "Well, he's always *busy*," she said, "but I'm sure he has time to take care of this. Let me run this back to him."

She exited through a side door and returned about a minute later, motioning me to go on back. I gave her a smile of thanks as I went through the door and walked down the short hallway to the judge's chambers.

I'd been in Judge Laurent's courtroom several times, testifying in various cases. He'd been on the bench for at least twenty years and would probably be retiring in a few more. He looked like a crotchety wizard, and every time I saw him I couldn't help but think that he needed only a pointed hat and a staff to go with his judicial robes.

So far I'd managed to refrain from offering that suggestion.

He gave me a crinkled little smile as I entered, then went back to perusing the subpoenas. "Financial stuff, eh?"

"Yes, your honor. I want to verify some information given to me during an interview."

His lips twitched as he glanced up at me. "What, you don't believe everything that a suspect tells you?"

"I guess I'm the suspicious sort, sir," I said, smiling.

He chuckled as he began to page through the documents. "This is for the Davis Sharp death? I didn't realize it had been ruled a homicide."

"The final ruling isn't in, but there's some evidence of blunt force trauma that's inconsistent with a simple fall in the shower." I wasn't telling him anything that a press release wouldn't contain.

"Hunh. His wife is a suspect?"

"Well, she hasn't been completely ruled out, but there are other possible suspects as well." It was beside the fact that I had no idea who those other possible suspects might be.

He snorted in derision. "Sharp was too used to having his fingers in every political pie. Just because he knew everyone from that damn restaurant of his, he thought that meant he could get away with anything." He scowled as he scanned the papers. "And unfortunately, he usually did."

Now, this was interesting. "What sort of things?"

Judge Laurent glanced up at me, then leaned back in his chair. "Well, like his two kids. Both complete pieces of shit. Both have been nailed for misdemeanor drug charges or simple battery several times. And I can't count the number of times Sharp has called me up, wanting me to pull some strings to 'fix' things." The scowl etched itself deeper onto his face. "I've taken only one campaign contribution from him." He chuckled. "Actually, he only ever gave me one. After I finally told him to fuck off, he never contributed again. Go figure." Then he shrugged. "Not that it made much difference in the end. He found other people to clean up his shit." He gave me a telling look. "Campaign contributions are a matter of public record. You can look it all up online."

I couldn't help but grin. "That's very good to know, sir."

He gave me a grave nod, but his eyes were twinkling. He carefully read through the documents, then finally picked up his pen and signed his name to each subpoena. "Good luck with your investigation, Detective Gillian," he said, as he handed the papers back to me.

"Thank you, your honor." Well, that had turned out to be more productive than expected. I exited his chambers, giving a wave and smile to his secretary.

My cell phone rang as I neared the courthouse doors. It was Ryan's number. I looked at the blinking display, trying to decide whether to be mature and answer it or pleasantly childish and hit the ignore button.

Maybe he's calling to apologize. I sighed and hit the answer button. "Hi, Ryan."

"Where are you?"

My finger twitched toward the disconnect button, but I managed to restrain myself. "I'm doing just peachy, and thank you for asking," I replied. "I was getting subpoenas signed. I'm just leaving the courthouse."

"You hungry?" His tone was clipped and stiff.

I was, but did I want to be subjected to more of the same judgmental crap? I screwed my face into a grimace. "Yeah, sure, what the hell." I was such an optimistic idiot.

"Okay, meet me at the Ice House in fifteen." Then he

hung up. I stared down at the phone, debating whether I should call him back and tell him to fuck off. *But maybe he's the type who's lousy with apologies.* I sighed and clipped the phone back onto my belt. Yes, I was definitely an optimistic idiot. But the alternative was to write him off completely, and I couldn't bring myself to do that.

I walked back to the station and to my car, jamming the air-conditioner control to the max as soon as I had it started and rolling down the windows to allow the broiled air within to escape.

The Ice House was only a few miles from the station, along the street that ran parallel to the railroad tracks. I'd been to this restaurant only a couple of times before, but I remembered it as being a quiet, dark place with deep booths. It had been an actual icehouse a few decades ago, and then it was converted into a family-style restaurant a few years after the real facility had shut down. They'd converted the vats into large round booths and left all the piping visible. It was a pretty neat interior, but the food hadn't measured up, and the Ice House restaurant closed a few years later. Since then it had been a Chinese restaurant, a seafood buffet, another family-style restaurant, a barbecue house, and still another family-style restaurant, all maintaining the same interior look. It had suffered through a variety of names, but everyone always just called it the Ice House.

Ryan was waiting for me right inside the door. He looked a bit haggard, but he flashed me a quick smile when I entered, then allowed the hostess to lead us to one of the vat/booths in the back. I scooched into the booth and took the menu from the waitress while Ryan got settled in.

I looked across the table at him, more relieved than I

could say aloud that he was here, that he'd called me. I was still angry and hurt, but his friendship was important to me. *Too important?* a small voice inside worried at me, and I pushed it down as best I could.

"I was a dick," Ryan said without looking at me as soon as the waitress walked away. "Sorry."

Well, it was better than no apology at all. "It's all right. Are you feeling better?"

"Yes, I am. I slept about ten hours and woke up feeling human again." His eyes met mine briefly, then dropped down to the menu, flicking over the offerings. "What's good here?"

I raised an eyebrow at him. "You're the one who picked it. I figured you'd been here before."

He shook his head. "Nope. I just heard it was a cool place."

I gave him a sharp look, but his attention was on the menu, so I decided that the pun was unintended and unnoticed. I'd let that one slide.

"I don't go to restaurants very often," I admitted. "I'm a microwave girl."

"Yeah, well, you need to start eating more," he said with a slight scowl as he looked up again, eyes raking me.

"Fine. Then you can pay."

"Deal," he said, a smile lighting his eyes.

I laughed. "Hey, that was easy." The knot of tension in my shoulders began to unwind. *Apology offered and accepted.*

The waitress came to take our drink orders, and since the menu wasn't complex—or all that interesting—we went ahead and ordered burgers. After she walked away, I looked back at Ryan. "So is this an apology thing, a make-Kara-eat thing, or one of these we-need-to-talk things?"

He lifted a shoulder in a shrug. "All of the above, but don't make it sound so damn ominous. I was a dick. You do need to eat. And we do need to talk. But not a we-need-to-talk kind of needing to talk."

"Uh-huh." I picked a pink packet of sweetener out of the container on the table and started to toy with it. "So what do we need to talk about?" Good, I'd managed to make that sound casual and not as angsty as I actually felt.

"Jesus Christ, Kara," he said with a scowl. "Not *that* kind of we need to talk, just a we need to talk to each other more because we're friends. Plus, as far as knowing shit about the arcane, neither of us has too many people we can be open with."

I made myself smile, but old doubts churned within me. "Yeah. Friends," I said. "And we can talk about the arcane." *Would we even be friends if not for that?* "Though Jill knows now. About the arcane and the summoning."

His eyebrows lifted. "How the hell did that happen?"

I gave him a quick rundown of Jill's encounter with Kehlirik. "And she was okay with it," I said, still feeling the relief that she hadn't run screaming. "Or at least okay enough with me to accept it."

He leaned back in the booth. "I like Jill, what little I know of her. Haven't seen much of her since the Symbol Man case, of course, other than at the funeral. And my present case isn't the kind that has me working with any local agencies. But she seemed pretty cool."

A stupid spike of jealousy jabbed at me, and I fought the juvenile urge to scowl. *What am I, in third grade? It's just Jill.* "Yeah, she's cool," I said, deliberately bright.

"Any progress on finding your essence-eater?"

I made a face. "No. I'm pretty much fumbling around blindly right now." I paused while our food and drinks were delivered. "I still need to do a lot of research," I said as soon as the waitress left. I picked up my burger and took a bite, then grimaced. Now I knew why this place was deserted on a Friday afternoon. It wasn't horrible, but it certainly wasn't great.

Ryan's expression mirrored my own as he swallowed his first bite. "I'm not sure I want to know what kind of animal was put into this burger."

I took a long swig of my diet soda to wash it down, then tried the fries to see if they were any better. Overly greasy, with too much salt. I sighed and blotted at them with my napkin. "Anyway, the *reyza* was able to remove the wards, so now I can get into my aunt's library." I made a face that had nothing to do with the quality of the food or lack thereof. "Now my only challenge is finding the right book or paper or scroll. If she has a system in there, it's way beyond me."

He was quiet for a moment as he continued to work on his burger. "Have you been to see her?"

"My aunt?" I sighed and shrugged. "I've been a few times. But it's not *her*. I mean, she's not there, and it feels really weird sitting in a room visiting the empty shell. It's like visiting a chair." I toyed with a limp fry, dragging it through the ketchup. "But I know it's expected of me, so I go every now and then, enough to keep people from saying I'm a lousy niece."

He surprised me then by reaching across the table and gripping my hand. I looked down at his hand on mine and then up at him. "Not everyone's against you," he said. "Give it time. Like you said, stuff blows over."

I forced a smile. "I know. It's cool." A busboy entered through the back door, and I had to breathe shallowly as the smell of rotting garbage from the alley wafted in with him. "Okay, I'm officially blaming you for choosing this place."

"It's pretty vile," Ryan agreed.

I looked up as the busboy came over to the table, and I pushed the barely eaten burger away from me. "You can take that," I said, gesturing to the plate. "I'm finished."

The busboy scooped up the plate but nearly dropped it again as a din of barking and snarling erupted from beyond the back door.

The waitress looked up from her lethargic table-wiping. "Tommy, go chase those damn dogs away. I told you to stop feeding them scraps."

Tommy dumped my plate into a plastic bin, then set the bin on a table near our booth, casting a black glare at the oblivious waitress as he slumped out the back door.

"Next time you can take me to someplace *really* classy," I murmured to Ryan. "Like maybe the fried-chicken stand at the gas station."

Ryan laughed and opened his mouth to respond, but a sudden nauseating roil of potency swept past us, momentarily robbing us both of breath before it was gone, leaving what felt like a taint of sewage in the arcane. "What the fuck was that?" Ryan gasped, gripping the edge of the table.

"The parking lot...by your office," I managed to say, fighting back the taste of bile. "Feels the same." A heartbeat later, a shrill scream of pain and terror came from the alley.

"That's the kid," Ryan said, already out of the booth and moving to the door. I wasn't as fast but managed to stumble after him, only a few steps behind. It was hard to move quickly when you were trying hard not to throw up.

Obviously Ryan hadn't felt that awful surge of *yuck* as intensely as I had.

Ryan yanked the door open—not bursting through like an idiot but taking an instant to assess the situation in the back alley.

Not that it made a difference. In the split second that it took Ryan to finish pulling the door open, a sleek black shape hurtled through the door, striking Ryan square in the chest and knocking him flat. I caught a flash of teeth and claws as Ryan twisted as he landed, throwing off the . . . dog? That was the closest analogy I could come up with in those rushed seconds. Caninelike head and snout, lots of teeth, four legs, but with a slick, reptilian way of moving.

I yanked my gun from its holster as the thing launched itself at Ryan again. But Ryan reacted with a speed that impressed me, getting his legs up in time to catch the creature in the chest, shoving it away.

"Shoot it!" he yelled over the shrieking of the waitress. I didn't need the encouragement. I squeezed off three quick rounds, the sound of the shots slamming through the restaurant, setting my ears ringing. The dog-thing jerked and shrieked as at least two of the shots found their mark, but a heartbeat later it was back on its feet, snarling at the two of us. Now I could get a better look at it, but it didn't help. It was still vaguely doglike and really fucking scary-looking.

Ryan was breathing hard. "Did you hit it?"

"Yes! Shoot it some more!"

We both lifted our guns and started shooting, but this time the demon dog was ready, twisting to evade with unnatural speed that allowed only a few of the rounds to find their mark.

"Sonofabitch! Is it a demon?" Ryan demanded, as it appeared to shake off the effects of being shot as easily as shaking off a mosquito bite.

"Not one of the kinds I know," I shouted, probably louder than necessary, but my ears were ringing from the shooting. "But it's definitely other-planar." I could see the telltale light instead of blood streaming from the wounds. I tried to remember how many rounds I'd fired. I didn't have a spare magazine on me. I'd been going to lunch, damn it!

It launched itself at us again, in a blur of red eyes and white teeth. We both dove in opposite directions, as if we'd rehearsed it, but the dog-thing had apparently missed that particular rehearsal and twisted in midair to rake its claws at Ryan.

Ryan let out an explosive curse, then, in an act that was either incredibly courageous or incredibly stupid, grabbed the dog by its lower jaw and jammed his gun into the creature's side, angling down and squeezing the trigger repeatedly until the slide of his gun locked back on his empty magazine. The dog-thing let out a howl of pain and rage, but a gut full of lead still didn't seem to slow it down much. It snarled and twisted its head free of Ryan's grasp, and I could see it poised to snap those deadly jaws onto something vital. I let out a yell and copied Ryan's technique, jamming my gun against the creature and firing until the gun was empty. It had the desired result—at least partially. It screamed and lost interest in Ryan, turning that crimson gaze on me.

Okay, this is bad, the thought flashed through my head. I was out of bullets, and even with what had to be more than a dozen rounds in it, the thing wasn't dead. Or, rather, it wasn't dead *enough*. White light streamed from it in several places, but it didn't look as if it would be discorporeating in the less than a second I probably had before the jaws clamped down on me. Given more time, I could possibly dismiss it back to whatever sphere it was from. But, then again, I didn't think I'd be able to open a portal in the very short amount of time I had to work with.

Before I had a chance to enjoy the last split second of life as a whole person, another shot slammed through the room. The dog-thing's head exploded in a burst of blue light, and then the body dropped heavily to the floor. I crabbed back, struggling to catch my breath as sparkles began to crawl over the body. A few seconds later the sparkles had completely consumed it, leaving behind nothing but a foul-smelling stain on the floor.

I looked up, past the arcane stain, then smiled weakly in relief.

"Good to see you, Agent Garner," I said, voice only a little shaky. "That was some mighty fine shootin', Tex."

Zack grinned and gave me a mock salute as he lowered his gun. "Why, thankee, ma'am."

I managed a wheezing chuckle, then got to my feet and looked to Ryan. "Are you all right?"

Ryan scowled and lifted his shirt, revealing a set of rippled abs that would have been incredibly nice to gaze at for a while if not for the four parallel scores across them that were just beginning to ooze blood.

"Barely got me," he said, tugging the shirt back down. "I'll be fine."

I gave him a small smile of relief, then stepped over to crouch by the stain on the floor. I stayed there for a few heartbeats, absorbing the feel of the lingering residue, then straightened.

"That's what we felt the other day by your office," I said to both of them.

"So it's been stalking us for a few days," Ryan said, expression grim.

"I think so," I said, then looked back to Zack. "Don't take this the wrong way, because your timing was fantastic, but what are you doing here?"

A slight smile touched his lips. "I, uh, get 'feelings' sometimes. I've learned to listen to them. And I had a feeling I needed to see what Ryan was up to."

So Zack had a touch of clairvoyance? I had a hard time being surprised, especially since I knew that he was sensitive to the arcane. "Well, I'm quite grateful to your *feelings* right now." My gaze shifted higher. "And even more grateful that your hair is no longer orange."

He laughed and ran a hand over his head. "Yep, surfer blond again."

Ryan's gaze swept the restaurant, taking in the waitress cowering under a table. "We have bigger problems right now." He jerked his head toward the back door. "Zack, check the back. There's a busboy out there, possibly hurt."

Zack met his eyes, a strange expression on his face. "You'll take care of the rest?"

Ryan's face went stony and bleak, and he gave a stiff nod. Zack slipped out the back door.

What the hell was that about?

Ryan stepped over to the table the waitress was hiding under and crouched in front of her. He placed a hand on hers and I thought he was going to help her out from under the table, but instead she went very still and quiet when her eyes met his. I watched the bizarre tableau, perplexed, as Ryan continued to hold the woman's hand, eyes fixed on hers while a strange and terrible smile curved his lips.

After perhaps half a minute, he took a breath and looked away. The waitress blinked, then gave Ryan a smile as he gripped her hand more firmly and helped her out from under the table.

"Here you go, ma'am," Ryan said. "The dogs are all gone now."

The woman let out a normal chuckle that completely unnerved me, considering what she'd just witnessed. "Oh, I knew they'd get in here someday, the way Tommy likes to feed those darn strays! Thank you for chasing them off, darlin'."

"It was no trouble," Ryan replied, giving her a charming smile. His eyes flicked to me and he gave a slight motion of his head toward the door. I glanced over to see Zack coming back inside.

"Ryan, the boy was bitten, but he'll be all right." He gave Ryan the strange look again. "You'll see to him?"

Ryan's face could have been carved from iron. He didn't nod, just stepped past Zack and walked outside, returning less than a minute later supporting a limping Tommy. "Ya gotta be careful of those feral dogs, kid. You never know when one might take a snap at you." He eased the boy down to a chair. "You gonna be all right?"

The boy bit his lip, clearly doing everything he could to be manly and not cry about the wound in his leg. It wasn't gaping or anything, but it was *big*, and I knew that the kid was going to need some serious stitching. How anyone could think that a stray dog with a normal-size jaw had made that injury was beyond me.

But at the moment there were many things that I felt I wasn't quite grasping.

"Ryan—" I began.

He jerked his hand up in a *keep quiet* gesture, eyes unfocused. I wanted to shriek, but I forced myself to hold it in. About a dozen heartbeats later, he blinked and looked back at Zack.

"Okay, the cook is the only other one in the place, and he wears an iPod turned up loud enough to drown out a nuclear explosion." He scrubbed at his face, hand shaking slightly, then his eyes met mine. "Some stray dogs got in the back door and caused a big mess. That's . . . that's what they remember."

I could only stare at him for several heartbeats. "What did you just do?" It came out much more calmly than I had expected.

An expression of true pain flickered across his face, then was gone. He gave me a smile that looked terribly sad, then gripped me by the shoulders, eyes quickly scanning me up and down. "You're not hurt, are you?"

"No," I said, voice strangled. "What about you?"

"I'll be fine." He squeezed my shoulders and then released me. "Okay, go now. Go back to work." He turned and walked to the front door of the restaurant. I watched him through the front window as he climbed into his car and drove off, then I turned to Zack, who was carefully picking up casings.

He didn't give me a chance to speak. "Kara, don't. Please." His eyes were troubled as he straightened. "There's a lot about Ryan that's . . . complicated."

"*Complicated?*" The word nearly exploded from me. "Those people just forgot about everything that happened! How often does he do this? *How* does he do this?"

"He doesn't do it often at all." Zack looked miserable, but I wasn't feeling very sympathetic at the moment. "No one else knows he can do this. Not even the FBI." He paused. "Especially not the FBI." He shook his head. "I know only because I've seen him do it before...when there was no other choice."

I had to tighten my hands into fists to keep them from shaking. "How much do you know about him?"

"Not enough. Please, Kara. If we cause a scene here, it will undo everything he did. Please. Just go back to work."

He turned away from me and started walking toward the front door.

I did the only thing I could think to do, and let him go.

18

I DROVE AWAY FROM THE RESTAURANT, HANDS TIGHT-
ening on the steering wheel at every crackle of the radio,
knowing that at any second there would be an alert tone
and a dispatch reporting shots fired at the old Ice House
restaurant, but the radio traffic remained stubbornly boring. A complaint about a barking dog. A report of a car
break-in. Nothing about a few dozen shots fired in a public place.

A chill ran over my skin. The waitress had gone from
hysterical to calm in the span of a heartbeat, seeming to
forget everything that had happened. My stomach
churned unpleasantly, and I wasn't sure if it was from the
poor meal or from what I'd witnessed. Was it something
Ryan was conscious of or just some sort of effect that surrounded him? *And has it ever been used on me?*

There was no way I was going to return to the office. If
anyone asked me, I'd plead some sort of work in the field.
Boudreaux and Pellini get away with it all the time, right?

Besides, it was Friday. Most of the rank would be gone anyway.

A shiver ran through me. Boudreaux and Pellini. Ryan had done something at the funeral to make them stop being dicks. I didn't even have to wonder about that. There was no way that their change of heart had occurred naturally.

So had he ever done something like that to me?

I drove to my aunt's house, passing through the wards and parking in the garage. It was a tight squeeze, but I didn't want to advertise the fact that I was skipping out on work. After I shut the engine off and punched the button on the remote to close the garage door, I stayed in the car and leaned my forehead on the steering wheel, listening to the muted creak of the cooling engine.

My mood swung wildly between confusion and terror. I wanted badly to give Ryan the benefit of the doubt, but it wasn't easy. The incident at the restaurant suddenly threw a dozen other things into a new and disturbing light. He'd obviously done something at the funeral. And Kehlirik had called him a *kiraknikahl*. Too bad I had no fucking idea what that was, but I had to wonder if it had something to do with this ability of his to make people forget things.

And Rhyzkahl said that Ryan wasn't completely aware of himself. If Ryan can fuck with people's memories as he is now, what would he be capable of if he knew what he was doing?

I finally got out of the car and went into the silent house, thoughts still tumbling. I had no idea which of us the dog-thing had been after. Maybe it was connected to the consumed essences. Or perhaps it had something to do with Rhyzkahl's interest in me. Or maybe it was unrelated to any of that.

I took a deep breath. Enough thinking about what had happened; I had plenty else to worry about. I fingered the folded piece of paper in my pocket with my list of questions. There was still plenty more I needed to know.

Like what the fuck happened today?

I gave myself a mental smackdown. *Forget that for now.* First I wanted to focus on finding anything to do with creatures that could consume essence. I needed to figure out what I was up against, then work out how to stop it. And after that, I wanted to find out as much as I could about summoners allying with demons. The Symbol Man had formed some sort of alliance with a *reyza,* but I had the feeling that had been more of an arrangement where the *reyza* was able to stay longer or did not require negotiations for each summoning—perhaps something like the adjustment of the anchor points that Kehlirik had shown me how to do.

But Rhyzkahl was asking for something else entirely. He wanted me to basically guarantee that I would summon him on a regular basis, with the payoff being that I wouldn't have to risk being slaughtered. Yeah, nice bonus.

I couldn't deny that having access to his knowledge and abilities was extraordinarily tempting, but having Rhyzkahl around was by no means the same as having a *reyza* on the string. Rhyzkahl wanted everything I could give him and more. And I wasn't sure just how much I'd be able to control him.

Okay, *not at all* was probably the answer to that. Plus, what would I be risking—to both myself and this sphere—by granting him increased access?

I walked down the hall to Tessa's library, reminding

myself that I needed to put some of the library wards back—something that would hopefully suffice until the full moon, when I could summon a demon to do it properly. But first I was going to try to find what I needed, and that wasn't going to be easy. Tessa's library was a nightmare of disorganization—at least to me. Shelves covered every inch of the walls, even above the door, and every one was crammed full of books, papers, scrolls, and other odds and ends that defied description. The floor was a maelstrom of tumbled books, and the large oak table in the center of the room was stacked so high that the books were nearly touching the large chandelier that hung in the middle of the room—a crystal monstrosity that looked like it should be in a ballroom.

I sighed. I had no idea how Kehlirik had managed to maneuver in here at all. I set my notebook down on top of a pile of papers on the table and pulled a book off a shelf at random, praying that there was some sort of system to my aunt's madness.

I woke up with a cramp in my neck and a dry mouth. Blinking to get my bearings, I realized that I'd fallen asleep in one of the chairs, and a glance at my watch showed me that it was five a.m. It was a tribute to my level of exhaustion that I'd passed out so thoroughly. I'd probably managed about four hours of reading and research before falling asleep, and in that time I'd barely scratched the surface of the books and papers in the room, coming to the conclusion that there was no discernible system whatsoever in this library.

After a quick shower and clothing change from the stash I had here, I dug my MP3 player out of my car, stuffed the buds into my ears, then jammed to the Dixie Chicks and Faith Hill while I puttered around the kitchen in a nearly fruitless attempt to locate food. I finally found and consumed some granola bars of indeterminate age, then felt ready to return to the library to make an assessment of what progress I'd made.

Not much was the best answer. I'd set aside a few books for later reading, but I hadn't found anything that came right out and told me what I wanted to know. *Kind of like Aunt Tessa,* I thought with a glower.

I couldn't call it wasted time, though. I'd always loved libraries, and while Tessa's collection was quite specialized, I still adored sitting on the floor and poring through the musty books and leather-clad tomes. When I was a kid, my parents had owned an old set of encyclopedias— the printed kind with a different volume for each letter of the alphabet. I would spend hours curled up on the couch leafing through the pages, not looking up anything in particular but just absorbing what there was to know. I hadn't seen printed encyclopedias in years. Such things now came in complete sets on CD. But I always told myself that if I ever had kids, I'd find a set of the printed volumes, because you couldn't leaf through on a CD in the same way.

I felt the same in Tessa's library, reading through random volumes and finding all sorts of fascinating nuggets of information. It was almost painful to have to close a book once I knew that it didn't have the information I needed, and I found myself making a personal promise to come back and browse when I didn't have such an urgent agenda.

Unfortunately, several more hours of browsing failed to turn up anything concrete, and I'd churned through Reba McEntire, Taylor Swift, Kellie Pickler, and Carrie

Underwood on my MP3 player. I found plenty on essences and souls but nothing specific on how to remove or restore an essence. And since there was no rhyme or reason that I could discern to Tessa's library cataloging system—if there was one at all—I was basically looking for everything on my list in every book I opened. It wasn't exactly an efficient system. I couldn't find anything on what could suck out an essence, no more than a stray sentence or two about the relationship between summoner and demon, and nothing at all on what a *kiraknikahl* was.

I heard an odd sound in the space between songs, and I pulled the earbuds off to locate the source of it, discovering to my chagrin that it was my cell phone, vibrating and ringing on the oak table. I turned the player off, an unfamiliar frisson of nervousness tightening my chest when I saw Ryan's number on the caller ID. I hesitated, a tiny part of me wanting to let it roll to voice mail. *Don't be an idiot,* I berated myself as I pressed the talk button. *He wouldn't hurt me.* No matter what else I was unsure of, I felt certain of that.

"Hi, Ryan," I said in as neutral a tone as I could manage. *Pretend nothing happened. Everything is normal. Denial is so lovely.*

"Kara, would you please unlock the door and let me in?" He sounded aggrieved. "I've been knocking."

"Sorry. I had my tunes on loud. I'll be right there." I closed my phone and stood up, brushing dust off my pants, then froze, looking down at a book that was open on the floor. I didn't remember getting the book off the shelf, and I glanced up, wondering whether it had fallen. It was certainly possible, considering the haphazard way that Tessa had the books stuffed onto the shelves, but what were the chances that a random book would fall in front of me and open to *that* page?

A wave of goose bumps crawled over my skin as I crouched and picked up the book. For there on the page was a full treatise on summoners forming alliances with demons. I cradled the volume almost tenderly as I quickly scanned the page. It didn't specifically mention alliances with demonic lords, but it sure seemed to be referring to the same sort of thing. Ryan would *shit* if he caught sight of this.

Ryan! I marked my place in the book and shoved it into my bag, then hurried to the door. I yanked it open to see Ryan standing on the walk, the troubled expression on his face clearing when he saw me.

"Sorry," I said. "I suddenly found something I was looking for and didn't want to lose my place. Come on in."

The tension on his face faded as he came up the steps, and I realized that he'd probably been apprehensive that I wouldn't speak to him again after what had happened at the restaurant. "What were you looking for?"

"Oh, I have a laundry list," I said, evading the question. "But going through Tessa's library is an adventure in disorganization. How did you know I was here?"

"You weren't at your house or at the station, so I figured you'd be here."

My car was in the garage, but he'd known I was here. When he called he hadn't asked where I was; he said that he'd been knocking. *He would never hurt me,* I reminded myself, somewhat surprised at how certain I was of this. I turned and headed down the hall, hoping I wasn't being hopelessly naïve. Just because I felt safe with him didn't mean it was actually safe to be with him—either physically or emotionally.

"I'm finally able to get into her library," I said over my shoulder, "so I figured I'd do as much research as I could."

An awkward silence settled around us as I gathered my stuff up. It seemed like both of us wanted to pretend that the weirdness of yesterday hadn't happened, which was fine with me, but now it felt like we were in a strange conversational limbo.

I cleared my throat, seeking to fill the void with any noise. "I never thanked you for coming to the funeral with me the other day. I'm ... not sure I could have handled it alone."

He shook his head, looking briefly haggard. "You're stronger than you give yourself credit for."

I shrugged, picking up the stack of books that I wanted to read more carefully. "So what are you up to now?" I wanted to ask him why he was here, why he'd wanted to track me down so badly, but I was a bit afraid of the answer. Or, rather, I wasn't sure I was ready for the answer. *Chickenshit.*

"Oh, well ..." I could see him hurriedly thinking of a response. "I was thinking of raising my cholesterol level at Lake o' Lard and was wondering if you wanted to get something too. Part of my Kara-needs-to-eat plan." He flashed a grin, but I could sense the faint edge to it.

I gave him the smile he was expecting. "Can we have a devil-dog-free meal this time?"

He laughed. "What, you didn't like the entertainment?"

I suddenly didn't want to play games anymore. I met his eyes. "Are you going to tell me why that thing attacked us?"

His smile faded. "I can't ... truly can't."

"Can't or won't?" I challenged.

"Can't. I promise! I honestly don't know."

I exhaled and nodded, but a knock out front stopped me from asking my next question, which would have been something on the order of *How the fuck are you able to change memories?*

"Hi, guys!" Jill's perky voice chirped from the porch. Ryan stepped out into the hallway with me following, as Jill walked in through the open front door. "There's a party and no one invited me?"

Ryan gave her a grin. "My God, what were we thinking?"

"Ryan thinks I'm too skinny," I told her. "We're going to forage for food. Wanna come?"

Her eyes flashed mischievously. "I don't want to intrude on y'all's date."

"It's not a date," we both said simultaneously, then turned to scowl at each other. I looked hastily away, absurdly put out that he'd been so quick to deny the possibility that lunch with me could be considered a date. It was beside the point that I'd leaped to deny it as well.

Jill let out a snort. "Oooookay, I can see that now. Sure, I'm up for food."

I set my stack of books down on the porch and dug in my pocket for the key, oddly conflicted that Jill would be joining us. There was still a strange tension between Ryan and me, and I couldn't decide if having Jill there would get us past what had happened in the past couple of days or if I would continue to react like a jealous third-grader every time Ryan looked her way. *How about if I stop being an insecure idiot? If he decides he likes her more than he likes me, then . . . more power to them. They're both my friends. I can be a grown-up about this.*

I just wished my stomach didn't hurt at the thought.

I pulled the front door closed, then jumped at the sudden loud bang from inside the house. I slowly opened the door again. "That came from the library," I said. I started to say that it was probably another book falling off a shelf, but an odd ripple of the arcane brushed me, sending a wave of goose bumps crawling along the back of my neck and reminding me unpleasantly of the encounter in the restaurant. I glanced back at Ryan, not surprised to see his gun in his hand. "You felt that?" I asked.

He nodded, brows lowered and gaze on the hallway. I looked back at Jill, with the intent to tell her to stay on the porch, but was shocked to see that she had her gun in her hand too and an utterly calm expression on her face.

"You felt it?"

She gave a small shake of her head. "No," she whispered. "But I got your back anyway."

I couldn't help but grin, even as another bang sounded, this time accompanied by a harsh clatter and the sound of several objects striking the floor. I gave myself a mental smack. *My* gun was in my car, in the garage. I hadn't expected to need it inside Tessa's house. And the only way into the garage was either through the house—down the hallway that ran past the library—or with the garage-door opener. Which was in the car.

I scanned the hallway in search of anything that could be used as a weapon, but the only possible candidate was a flowered umbrella in the corner by the door. *No way.* But maybe I did have a weapon. I had the ability to shape arcane energy, right? And I'd once seen Rhyzkahl use potency as a weapon. Of course, that was in a dream, but dreams of Rhyzkahl had strong ties to reality. It was at least worth a try.

I took a deep breath and focused on pulling potency to me, concentrating, visualizing it flowing into my control. I cupped my hands before me, sensing scattered energies slowly coalescing, becoming visible as a quivering blue glow in my othersight.

Holy shit. I was doing it. I was controlling arcane power. I felt a triumphant laugh bubbling up.

Then the arcane glow sputtered out. I frowned at my cupped hands, my triumphant laugh dying out as thoroughly as the power.

"Um, Kara?" Ryan said. "What was that?"

Feeling like an idiot, I sighed and dropped my hands, then stepped over to the corner and hoisted the umbrella. "Let's just say that I'm not going to be flinging arcane fireballs at anyone."

I could see the deep amusement in his eyes, but thankfully he didn't laugh outright. Good thing too, because I had an umbrella covered in giant pink flowers in my hand, and I wasn't afraid to use it.

"You two are seriously weird," Jill murmured.

"And yet you choose to hang out with us," I countered, starting down the hall, holding the stupid umbrella like a sword. Ryan fell in beside me, covering the area with the mundane protection of his gun, while Jill hung back and covered our collective rears.

I cautiously peeked around the door to the library in time to catch a movement that was almost too fast to follow with human vision. Something small and rat-size zinged across the room from one shelf to behind a book on the opposite shelf. In fact, I probably would have suspected that it was a bird or squirrel, except for the fact that I could clearly see—even without shifting into othersight—a trail like arcane dust in the thing's wake.

"I don't think your gun's going to be much good," I said softly as I stepped inside the library, trying to track where the creature had gone.

"Yes, your umbrella will protect us all," Ryan replied tartly, not holstering his gun. "What the hell is it? All I saw was a streak of light."

"Dunno." Maybe the umbrella would be more useful opened? Then I could use it as a shield. A very thin, wobbly shield. "I don't know if it's dangerous either, but it's definitely something arcane."

The thing came whizzing out from behind the book, straight at me. I yelped and swiped at it with the umbrella, missing it thoroughly and feeling like I was back in fifth grade softball. I'd sucked at sports back then, and I hadn't improved in the intervening years. I got a better look at it this time, though, and caught a flash of teeth and wings in a tiny humanoid form. *Like Tinker Bell on crack.* But Tinker Bell never had such sharp teeth and sure as shit didn't have a stinger coming out of her ass.

I heard the whiz of wings again and jammed the button on the handle of the umbrella, snapping it open just in time for the creature to glance off. It wobbled away, letting out a thin shriek that was high enough to be barely audible.

"Holy shit," Jill breathed.

"Jill, stay back," I warned. "I have no idea what this is or what it can do." *Or how it got in here, for that matter.*

She made a grumbling noise but obligingly stepped back. I shifted fully into othersight, hoping to find where the little bugger had gone to, but I shifted right back out, scowling blackly. There was so much arcane energy scattered about the room from all the books and scrolls, it was like putting on night-vision goggles in broad daylight.

A nearly sub-audible thrum warned me in time to duck under the umbrella as it dove at me. I had a much clearer vision of a stinger aimed for me, but I didn't even have a chance to swipe at it this time. I was far more concerned with not getting stung. I heard Ryan give a shout as he threw himself backward, into the hall.

I couldn't let whatever it was escape out into the real world. It was obviously arcane, but I didn't know if it was something native to this sphere or something that had been brought through from another. But I had a strong enough feeling that it was dangerous.

"You two guard the door!" I shouted. "Don't let it out of the room."

"Guard it with what?" Ryan shouted back. "My charming personality?"

"No, I don't want to kill it just yet!"

Jill appeared in the doorway with an umbrella in each hand, holding them like a samurai with a pair of katana. She thrust one at Ryan. "Here, I found them in the hall closet. It's been working for Kara."

Ryan jammed his gun into his holster, muttering something that sounded vile as he took the umbrella. "Oh, sure. Give me the one with the purple ducks on it."

Jill merely smiled and crouched, opening the umbrella. Hers was orange and yellow with a giraffe head on it. "You go high, I'll cover low."

Ryan opened his umbrella. "What are you going to do, Kara?"

"I need to trap this thing!"

"Fuck," he growled. "And I suppose you have to be in there *with* it?"

Yes. Out there would have been preferable, but that wasn't really an option. I quickly shoved a pile of books off the table, cringing as they landed in ugly heaps with the sound of tearing paper. I grabbed a pen off the floor and inscribed a quick and crude circle into the surface of the wooden table, still holding the umbrella over me. Tessa would be livid at the damage to her table, but I didn't give a shit at this point. I'd refinish the damn thing later. I stepped back and began to slowly pull power again, but this time into the circle. I was going to try a dismissal, but since I didn't have the faintest clue as to what this creature was and didn't know its name, the standard dismissal that I used for demons wasn't going to work. Instead, I was going to open a generic portal and try to keep it small enough so the arcane creature would get sucked through and returned to wherever it came from, but nothing else would.

There were only two things that could screw this up. First, if the thing was actually a resident of *this* sphere, I'd be spending arcane energy to make a portal for no reason at all. Second, if the thing had been summoned by another and was somehow bound to this sphere, I would need to do a far more specific dismissal.

I kept my attention divided as carefully as I could while I created my mini-portal, fighting to keep the power under control as it began to form and also paying attention to the shelf where I'd last seen the creature go. I'd never tried to create a portal of a specific size before, so I was going strictly on barely remembered theory. It also didn't help that it was hard as shit to draw power when it was daytime during a waning moon. But I didn't need a lot for what I was hoping to make.

Pain suddenly seared the middle of my back, and my control of the forming portal faltered badly as fatigue slammed into me. I fell to my knees and scrabbled at my back as I mentally grabbed for the portal. My fingers closed on something that wiggled and clawed alarmingly, sending a deep shock through me. *A third way for this to fail: There's more than one creature!*

I'd maintained my hold on the portal though, which had widened to a bright slit in the universe a few inches wide. I chucked the squiggling thing in my hand at the portal, grimly pleased when it was drawn in with a sharp *pop*, like a roach into a vacuum. I could hear Ryan shouting something to Jill, but I couldn't spare the focus to make it out. The pain had spiraled up, and the strange fatigue had increased to the point where it was taking everything I had just to maintain the portal. I heard a high-pitched whine from the shelf that I'd been watching, and then the other one shot out from behind the book. It grabbed on to the heavy chandelier, wrapping claws around a dangling crystal and resisting the pull of the portal as it bared its teeth at me. I knew that all I had to do was swat at it and it would fall into the vortex, but the pain in my back had increased to breath-stealing proportions, and even the thought of standing made my eyes water with the agony.

"Come here, ya little fucker!" I heard Jill cry out. I watched through pain-slitted eyes as she bounded into the room with a garbage bag in one hand and a pair of tongs in the other. Her lips pulled back from her teeth in a fierce grin as she snapped the creature up into her tongs and yanked it off the chandelier, crystal and all, then stuffed everything into the bag.

"What now?" she shouted over the strange whine of the vortex.

"Into the portal," Ryan and I shouted at the same time. Or, rather, Ryan shouted and I wheezed. Jill wound up and winged it right at the slit in a beautiful underhand throw that would have made any fast-pitch softball player proud. I had a split second of panic that it would be too large to go in with the garbage bag and tongs—then it shifted and disappeared.

"Kara, close the portal down!"

I shuddered, then yanked the power free of the circle, sending it down to ground into the earth. The sudden quiet seemed deafening, broken only by our collective harsh breathing.

I tried to stand up and whimpered. Ryan snapped his head to look at me. "Ah, shit."

The pain in my back was well on its way to excruciating now. He grabbed me and pushed me to lie facedown on the floor, ignoring my breathless scream at the motion.

"Jill, get hot water, a knife, and matches or a lighter," Ryan commanded. "Also, any salt you can find."

Jill dashed to the kitchen again. I couldn't help but think that she was enjoying this introduction to the arcane far too much.

"Just stay still," Ryan said, voice unnervingly calm as he pulled my shirt up. He didn't have to tell me that, though. Moving hurt too much, and the pain was spreading.

"How bad is it?" I managed to get out between clenched teeth.

"Bad enough," he replied honestly. I was grateful for that, because if he'd told me that it wasn't bad I wouldn't have believed him.

"It's not going to be easy, but I think I can get you through the worst of this," he continued. Jill careened back into the room, holding the items out for Ryan.

He took the knife from her hand. "Okay, Kara, this is going to really fucking hurt."

Maybe honesty wasn't such a good thing, because he was right. I heard someone scream, then realized that it was me. My vision went dark and I fought it briefly, then decided that maybe going with my instincts to pass out was a good idea right now.

So I did.

19

I WOKE UP TO THE SAME AMOUNT OF PAIN IN MY BACK, or so I thought at first. But after a couple of cautious breaths, I was forced to admit that it was nowhere near as excruciating as it had been before I passed out. Now it was merely on the level of *hurts like shit*.

I was lying facedown on my aunt's bed, the yarn of her afghan tickling my nose. I shifted to get a tuft out of my nostril, grimacing at the dull spear of pain that accompanied the movement. I heard a chair scrape, then Ryan bent down, crouching beside the bed. Behind him I could see Zack leaning against the wall, his arms folded over his chest and his brows drawn down.

"How do you feel?" Ryan said, voice soft and thick.

"Like someone decided to shove an ice pick into the small of my back. Otherwise, peachy." I moved carefully, relieved when I was able to roll onto my side without the pain becoming overwhelming. I gingerly reached to feel my back and discovered a wad of gauze and tape. There was a thick smell of garlic as well, so I had to assume that it had been used somehow in the treatment of the sting. Though I had no idea where they'd found garlic. Certainly not in Tessa's pantry. I'd tossed out anything perishable some time ago.

"Okay, so what was that thing?" I looked at him, eyes narrowed. "You sure knew what to do with it."

He glanced at Zack and a shadow passed over his face. He lifted a hand and scrubbed at his eyes, as if to brush the troubled expression away as well. "It . . . it's like dreams I had," Ryan said, looking back at me. "I mean, I sit here and rack my brains and I know—just *know*—that I've never in my life encountered anything like that." His eyes were shadowed, green and gold like the middle of a forest on a summer day. The light from the window caught his face just right to make him look like a rugged statue with marbles for eyes. Then he sighed and shook his head, and the image was gone. "I did what felt right, then called Zack. He knew how to deal with the sting and brought some supplies over." Zack gave a small nod of acknowledgment.

"And how did you know?" I challenged, looking at Zack.

"Dealt with something similar on a case several years back," he replied. His expression was pleasant, but I got the distinct impression that he was not going to be forthcoming with any further information.

I was silent for nearly a full minute, then cautiously pushed up to a sitting position. My back throbbed, but it was already starting to fade to a manageable level. "How long was I out?"

"Two days."

"What!" I straightened in shock, which sent a fresh throb of pain through my back. I groaned as Ryan smiled.

"Just kidding," he said, eyes twinkling. "Two hours."

I groaned again. Two hours was still pretty impressive.

"Jill went to get food," Zack said. "There isn't a damn thing to eat in this place except for some red beans that she turned her nose up at."

I laughed weakly. "Yeah, she doesn't think much of the instant stuff." I carefully levered myself to stand, taking slow breaths until the wave of dizziness passed. "All right. So did we manage to get all of those things out of the library before I lost it?"

Ryan nodded, expression sobering. "Looks like it."

"Then the next questions are: What were they, and how did they get in there?"

His face clouded again, then he gave a small shudder, as if throwing off a chill. "Zack said that they're some sort of very nasty pest but . . . not from here."

"From where?" I didn't look at Zack. I wanted to see how much *Ryan* knew.

"From an alternate plane. The demon plane, I think. Like that dog." Ryan's frown deepened, and I could feel a chill walk over my skin. His eyes were shadowed pits as they lifted to mine. "Don't ask me how I know this, Kara. I don't know."

There was so much I wanted to ask him. No, there was so much I wanted to shake out of him, like, *Who the fuck are you?*

"Okay," I said instead. "So it didn't kill me. That's a good thing. Then I guess I need to figure out how it got into my aunt's library."

"That I think I can help you with. There's a section of the library that feels really wacky."

I raised an eyebrow at him. "Wacky?"

Ryan laughed, only slightly forced. "Yeah, that's a technical term."

"How can you even tell in that library? There's arcane crap everywhere!"

He thrust his hands into his pockets, smiling sheepishly. "Um, we kinda moved a bunch of stuff around while we made sure that all of those things were gone."

"Ooooh, you are gonna be in so much trouble when my aunt comes back. For all we know she had a *system* in place."

He made a sour noise. "Well, it's a system of a big pile on the floor now. And there's a place that looks wacky. Are you feeling well enough to take a look at it?"

I started to respond, but the banging of the front door caught my attention. I heard pounding footsteps, then Jill came careening around the doorway, bags of fast food in each hand. The intense and worried expression on her face cleared instantly at the sight of me standing.

"Well, it's about time you got over your little mosquito bite," she said, flouncing into the room and plopping the bags on the desk. She crossed her arms over her chest, eyeing me. I grinned and hugged her.

"Get off me, you crazy bitch," she grumbled, but I could hear the relieved laugh in there as well. "Here— Ryan and Zack said you needed to eat. And I need to as well. I've been spending the last couple of hours perched in the damn disaster area your aunt called a library with a fucking fishing net, waiting for another one of those psycho pixie things to pop out, while Ryan and Zack moved books around and muttered to each other."

I had to laugh at the mental image. "Okay, food first, then fun with fishing nets."

*   *   *

Two Aleve and a hamburger and fries later, I was ready to deal with my aunt's library again. The ache in my back had settled to merely sore, and I managed to make my way down the hall with only one or two muttered invectives.

I brushed my hands over the library door frame. It felt odd without any wards on it. As I stepped in, I felt a crawl of sensation—not the usual beaded-curtain sensation of going through wards but more the feeling of approaching a source of wrongness. I now knew exactly what Ryan was talking about when he said "wacky." There was a section of the floor in front of the bookcase on the east wall, an area almost two feet across, that was *wrong*. I forced myself to step closer, certain that I had to be stepping near a diagram or circle, because every sense I had was screaming at me that this was a portal.

What I couldn't tell was if it was open. I frowned as I crouched. It wasn't open in the sense that I was familiar with—the slit of light making a doorway from one sphere to another—but it sure wasn't closed either. It was... *mushy* was the best word I could come up with. Stuff could get through but not easily.

I looked sharply back at the doorway. Ryan and Jill stood just outside the door, watching me warily, but it wasn't them I was interested in. "The wards," I said, unintentionally hissing softly on the last *s*.

Ryan frowned. "What about them?"

"I think they were twofold." Damn it.

"Why? What is that?"

"It's... a portal. Sort of. A weak spot."

"Oh, shit," he breathed. "The wards kept stuff in as well as keeping things out."

"Yeah," I said with a groan. "There were wards all throughout the library, which I couldn't understand. And when I had Kehlirik take down all the wards, that left that portal wide open, so to speak."

Jill leaned against the wall, thumbs hooked into her jeans. "So why didn't Kehlirik see that portal thingy?"

An unpleasant feeling settled in my stomach as I looked back at it. "I'm not sure. He was exhausted after clearing the wards, and with the books and other stuff piled all over, I guess he could have missed it." I rubbed my arms. "Heck, it wasn't until you moved all the stuff that we knew it was here." But surely a demon of Kehlirik's level would have been able to feel it. So why didn't he say anything about it? Maybe because he had more reason not to? *He'd wanted to speak to me—about Ryan. But after he cleared the library wards, suddenly it wasn't as important.* Because he'd found the portal? Now that I was close to it, I could feel a sickeningly familiar resonance about it. *It's probably big enough for that dog to have come through.*

Could this portal also have something to do with the consumed essences? I considered it but then dismissed the idea. The portal had still been warded when Brian's essence was eaten, so whatever was doing it couldn't have come from this.

Ryan voiced the question that we were all thinking. "Can it be closed?"

I sighed. "I have no idea. I don't even know if it *should* be closed."

Ryan frowned, but Jill angled her head to the side. "Oh, like maybe this is a pressure valve or something?"

"Yeah. And that's putting it a lot more clearly than I ever could have." I eased my back into a more comfortable position. "I . . . have to see if my aunt comes back, and ask her."

Jill shifted uncomfortably.

"And if she doesn't come back," I continued, throat tightening, "I'm going to have to ask, um, someone else."

I swore I could hear Ryan's teeth grind together. He muttered something under his breath and then spun away and strode down the hall. I clenched my hands and counted slowly to ten, then counted another ten for good measure.

Jill leaned her head out of the doorway to watch the retreating Ryan, then looked back at me, eyebrow raised questioningly.

"He and I had a bit of a discussion the other night wherein he stated that he was worried about me throwing myself at Rhyzkahl and falling for that pretty face and forgetting he's a demon."

She pursed her lips. "Hmm. And he doesn't know that you and ole demon lord have already bumped uglies?"

"No, he does *not*," I said. "And it's going to stay that way, now that I know he considers it akin to selling my soul."

A flicker of doubt passed over her face, and I sighed. "It's not," I assured her. "He's not a 'demon from hell' kind of demon."

"Then why are they called demons?" she asked, crossing her arms over her chest.

"The same reason that midwives were called witches a few centuries ago. Fear of what is not understood." I could hear the defensive tone in my voice, and it made me take a mental step back. I *did* fear Rhyzkahl. And I sure as hell didn't understand him.

She pondered this for several heartbeats, then shrugged and lowered herself to sit cross-legged on the floor. "Okay, so you can summon demons. And can work magic or whatever—"

"I can shape arcane energy," I explained.

"Uh-huh. Magic to me," she said, nose wrinkling as she smiled. "But then again, electricity is magic to me too. Flip switch, light comes on. So what about other supernatural stuff?"

"Like what?"

"Like vampires and werewolves and witches and that sort of thing."

I had to shrug. "I've never met any of those, as far as I know." I shook my head. "I take that back. I've met witches, but they're not the ride-the-broom, cast-spells kind of witches. But vampires and werewolves?" I shrugged again, but I thought instantly of the missing essences. Was that some form of vampirism? And what about that dog-thing? "I'm not going to say that they don't exist, because who am I to say that, but I've never met a werewolf or vampire that I know of."

She laughed. "Well, I don't know much about your magic woowoo stuff, but, *man*, Ryan sure has a raging case of the jealous going on over your demon lord, doesn't he?"

I made a sour face. "He's *not* jealous, trust me. He just thinks I'll forget who I am if I even look at Rhyzkahl."

Jill gave me a measuring look, then sighed and rolled her eyes. "Y'know, for a smart chick, you can be seriously fucking clueless."

I resisted the urge to roll my eyes right back at her. She was the clueless one if she thought Ryan's grouchiness meant anything.

Fortunately, she didn't seem to feel like arguing her point. "So do you think your aunt knew about that being there?" she asked, lifting her chin toward the corner of the library.

I blew my breath out. "She had to know. It doesn't feel

new. And I think I screwed up colossally by having all the wards taken down." But I felt a renewed flare of annoyance at my aunt. Why couldn't she have fucking told me about this? Surely a weakness in the fabric between the spheres was something that I needed to know about.

"Why didn't your aunt tell you about this?" Jill asked in an echo of my thoughts.

I gripped my hair, then shook my head. "Probably the same reason that so many people don't have wills. They don't want to consciously think that they won't have time to put things in order. Nobody wants to think about how sudden and unfair death can be. Everyone thinks that they'll have those last few minutes to gasp out their final instructions." I sighed. "Now I need to redo the wards as best I can and then summon a demon who can put them back as soon as possible." I scowled. It was nowhere near a full moon, which meant that it would be a bitch to summon anything decent. And more dangerous.

"Well, let me get this crap over with," I said. "Hopefully I can do enough to keep anything else from coming out." Jill stepped back, and I focused on pulling enough potency to weave the protections I needed. It came to my control slowly, like taffy on a cold day, reminding me that I wasn't exactly at my strongest. I hissed through my teeth as I shaped the sluggish energy, cautiously probing at the weak spot. I wasn't sure I wanted any of my wards to actually touch the weakness, just in case it could be warped or shifted, so I compromised and made a little dome of energy over it. After finishing that, I backed out of the library and set another level of wards—both keep-out and keep-in wards.

I sighed as I looked them over. I sucked at crafting wards, but I had a shred of confidence that they would hold until I could summon something that could place some more-robust protections. I pulled my phone out of my pocket and looked at my moon-phase calendar, even though I knew that it was only a week past the full. Another week until there was no moon. I'd have to give it a try then.

"Let's get out of here," I said to Jill, as I replaced the aversion on the front door. "I think we've done enough damage for one day."

20

It didn't feel like a Sunday. I was used to my weekends flying by, over before I could even blink, but so much had happened in the past two days that I kept thinking it should be Wednesday at least. Or September.

But now time had slowed back down to a non-frenetic pace, and I had a list of crap that I needed to get done, plus some stuff that I merely wanted to get done. I was pleasantly sore from my trip to the gym the other day—just enough achiness to remind me that I liked having a few muscles—and I really didn't want to gain back the pudge. So before I could talk myself out of it, I headed to the gym, taking the risk that I'd be shocking the people who worked there by showing up twice in one week.

At eight a.m. on a Sunday morning, the gym was practically deserted, unlike last time. With only a handful of people in the weights area, I was able to throw myself into my workout, welcoming the burn and the sweat as I attempted to drive away all of my uncertainties and insecurities.

At this rate, I was going to end up with six-pack abs.

"You're making the rest of us look bad," I heard from behind me as I waited for my pulse to slow between sets. I turned, reaching for my towel to wipe my sweaty face. A good-looking man gave me a friendly smile. I knew him, but my oxygen-starved brain refused to supply me with the information. "It's a Sunday," he said, smile widening. "Here we are talking about football and avoiding yard work, and you're working up enough sweat for all of us."

I grinned, flattered at the mild flirtation, just as the lightbulb went off over my head: *Holy shit, this is Judge Roth.* I'd seen him only in court or at the funeral, and he looked far different—and far more approachable—in simple shorts and a T-shirt.

"Sorry," I said, still smiling. "But if y'all can't keep up with me, that's not my fault."

He laughed. "I should know better than to tangle with strong women. There's no way to win!" Then he gave me a more appraising look. "I don't think I've ever seen you in here before. I'm Harris Roth," he said, extending his hand. "Are you new here?"

I shook his hand. He had a nice, warm grip. "Kara Gillian." I briefly debated mentioning that we'd met in passing in court, but then decided that would bring up too much other unpleasantness. "I've been a member here for a while, but my attendance is sporadic."

He gave my hand a squeeze and then released it. "Good to meet you, Kara. I won't keep you from your workout any longer, but I do hope to see you here again." With that, he gave me another charming smile and turned away. I finished the rest of my workout quickly, bemused and more than a little stunned that I'd been seen as someone worth flirting with. Especially since I didn't dress in the

Cardio Barbie spandex attire that most of the other women here favored. My workout clothing consisted of running shorts, a Jogbra, and a T-shirt. Sexy.

I headed to the locker room and retrieved my gym bag. I'd just turned to head toward the shower area when a blond woman in perfect makeup sidled up to me— dressed in exactly the kind of spandex getup that I wouldn't be caught dead in. To give the woman credit, though, it was obvious that she put in a lot of time and effort—and perhaps some surgical enhancement—to have the kind of body that looked damn good in spandex.

"I know you don't know me," she said in a low voice, "but I wanted to give you a bit of warning about Harris Roth."

I looked at her expectantly. The expression on her face seemed sincere enough. "It's none of my business, I know," she continued, "but I've seen him charm his way into the pants of a lot of pretty girls. And he really doesn't care what may happen to them afterward."

It took me a couple of seconds to find my voice. "Um, thanks. But I have no intention of sleeping with him."

She gave me a wry smile. "I'm glad you think so. But, trust me, he's a charmer. Anyway, you seem sweet and I didn't want to see someone else get screwed by Harris."

My cop sense lit up like a Christmas tree. "Who else has been screwed by him?"

She hesitated, then shrugged. "Well, she's not around anymore, so I guess it's not too terrible to gossip." The woman did a quick glance-around, then lowered her voice even further. "He had an affair with Elena Sharp, and then her husband kicked her out!"

I blinked. This was a far cry from the story that Elena had spun for me. "Wow." Now it was my turn to do the furtive glance around. "And didn't Harris's son kill his wife and then himself?"

She sighed. "Yeah, that was awful. I mean, Harris is a bit of a sleazeball 'playa,' but that was a horrible thing to have happen." I heard a bustle of women's voices coming into the locker room, and the blonde stepped back. "Anyway," she said, "I just wanted to make sure you knew what you were getting into."

I gave her a grave nod, hiding my bemusement. "I appreciate that. I'm sorry, what was your name again?"

"Becky. Becky Prejean." She gave me a wink and then scuttled off in a flash of spandex and artificial breasts.

I took my shower and dressed, thankfully unaccosted, but my mind kept turning over the tidbits of information. *Elena and Harris, huh?* Well, she did say she was attracted to powerful men. Yet another interesting twist.

But was it true? I headed out to my car and cranked the AC up, then called the dispatcher and asked for a local address for a Becky or Rebecca Prejean, white female, approximately mid-thirties.

A few minutes later I thanked the dispatcher and hung up. Becky Prejean lived in Ruby Estates. Davis Sharp's maid had said that a blonde came to see him after Elena left.

Coincidence? Probably. But Becky Prejean had raised my suspicions about a number of things, and I had a feeling I'd be driving to Mandeville again before all this was over.

THE REST OF my afternoon was an ambitious—and hideously necessary—combination of doing laundry, cleaning my kitchen, and scrubbing my bathroom. Usually, housework had a relaxing effect on me, but a simmering guilt plagued me throughout the day—railing at me that I wasn't making any progress on finding what was consuming essence, and reminding me that time was running out for Tessa. I'd hoped for a relaxing Sunday and a desperately needed recharge of my mental resources, but the various worries continued to pick at me.

Four times I picked up my phone to call Ryan—twice even going so far as to start dialing his number before I stabbed at the disconnect button in frustration. I had no idea what the hell I would say. *Wanna hang out? Wanna see a movie? I'm stressed out and need someone to vent to?*

Right. Like Ryan needed any more proof that I was completely neurotic.

I gave up and fired up my computer. *Bury myself in work...* As long as I had some free time, I could check one other thing that I'd almost forgotten about—Judge Laurent had mentioned campaign contributions, with a strong implication that there was something significant to be seen there.

Campaign contributions were public record and, thanks to the marvels of modern technology, were also available online. It took me a few tries to find the right website, but once I did I was rewarded with more information than I knew what to do with on every election and every candidate.

Narrowing my search to only the contributions made by Davis Sharp was far more enlightening. Stunning, in fact. Davis Sharp had contributed significantly to Judge Roth's campaign fund—giving the maximum allowed by law, going at least ten years back. I quickly scanned through the rest of Sharp's contributions. He'd supported various other candidates in other elections but none as much as Harris Roth.

I shifted my search parameters to look at all of Roth's contributors. That list was impressively long, but Sharp's name clearly stood out as Roth's biggest contributor.

I bookmarked the page and shut my computer down. I had an extensive financial connection between Davis Sharp and Judge Roth now. But what did it mean? Judge Laurent had implied that Sharp wanted favors in return for contributions, so I could only assume that he'd expected—and received—the same from Roth. Especially considering how much money he'd given to his campaign fund.

I was out of ideas, and it was with a nearly visceral relief that I watched the sun slip below the trees. Now I could at least assuage the part of the guilt that nagged at me about Tessa, even if the rest of my psyche remained in hopeless shambles.

I showered and changed, then headed down to my basement. This was the last stage of the call to her essence—the "arcane transponder" that would hopefully draw her back to this plane and to her body. I knew that a great deal depended on to what extent her essence had been drained during the summoning, and I knew that at some point I would have to accept the possibility that I might never get her back.

But now isn't the time to think like that, I told myself sternly. Now was the time for confidence in the ritual, total faith that it would be simply a matter of time before Tessa was back to normal. *And then get her to explain about the damn portal. And get her to give me some damn guidance.*

I sketched the final portion, cautiously crabbing around

the complex diagram. I winced as I stood up, and it wasn't all from the creak of my knees from crouching for so long. Was I depending too much on my aunt? But where else was I going to get the training I still needed?

Rhyzkahl, my thoughts whispered to me, sending an odd ripple of gooseflesh across my skin. I shuddered, rubbing my arms at the thought of being tied to him any more than I already was. I didn't—*couldn't* trust him. He was ancient and powerful and well skilled at lying without ever saying an untrue word.

Worry about that shit later, I railed at my psyche. *Focus!*

I took a deep breath and began to channel potency. After what was probably half an hour, I finally released the power, feeling it slide away into the diagram. I watched the diagram, nearly weeping in relief as it began to resonate. A heartbeat later, the resonance abruptly shifted into a hum—inaudible and powerful at the same time. I held my breath as the hum settled into a soft pulse, a sensation tickling over me that reminded me of everything that was Tessa.

It's calling and reminding her who she is. Reminding her where she belongs.

I made my way over to the cold fireplace and collapsed into the chair. There was nothing more I could do now. Rhyzkahl had warned me that it could take a long time, but I had no idea how much time Tessa had. She was already declining. A knot of grief threatened to twist my insides. It was doubtful that her body would last more than a few weeks longer.

I tipped my head back, staring up at the rafters of the basement. It was only slightly more than a week ago that I'd summoned Rhyzkahl—but it felt like a year. I still had no idea whether I would summon him again. I turned my head with a sigh and looked over at the little circle with the remnants of my aunt's items. I knew what she would say—that I'd be a complete fool to even consider it. But I had almost three weeks to make up my mind—and that was only if I decided to call him this next full moon.

The access to knowledge was unspeakably tempting, though I could well guess that there'd be limits on it. He would dole out his information as he saw fit in order to keep me wanting more.

I pushed up from the chair. At this point, anything was better than nothing. I had a feeling I'd be needing answers for a long time.

I looked over at the diagram containing the "beacon" for Tessa's essence, feeling and seeing the thrum of power even without shifting fully into othersight. My eyes traveled over the twined wards. Now that they were active and complete, it wasn't as confusing, and I could begin to see how they worked. I had basically channeled potency into the first diagram, and now the wards were slowly releasing it into the other circle to create this beacon.

My heart skipped a beat as I looked at the diagram, an odd new thought skimming through my head. If this diagram was actually storing potency, could that be done at other times as well? I could feel my breath quicken as I considered the implications of that possibility. *Holy shit. This would mean that it's possible to store potency without resorting to death magic.* The Symbol Man had tortured and murdered his victims in order to amass enormous amounts of power—enough to summon and bind a demonic lord. The restrictions of the phase of the moon had always chafed at me but never enough to be willing to resort to such hideous methods. Summonings required a smooth and consistent flow of potency, and fluctuations or hiccups could prove disastrous when opening a portal. But if there was a way to gradually bleed power off into a diagram and then pull it back out for use ... I reached for the back of the chair, the unspeakable elation nearly overwhelming.

"Holy shit," I whispered. Could it really work without the blood of innocent victims? I wouldn't have to worry about the phase of the moon at all. I could store potency in dribs and drabs throughout the month and then use that stored power at any time. Day, night, half-moon, no moon. Not only that, but it would be easier to summon the higher-level demons. Summonings were exhausting. The creation of the diagram was taxing enough, plus the effort of forming the wards, and then adding summoning on top required a huge amount of effort and concentration. The main reason higher-level demons were summoned only by very experienced summoners was that you had to be highly skilled in the forming of the portal to have strength left over to control the demon.

I scrubbed at my face, trying to keep everything in perspective. There would still be drawbacks. The convergence of the spheres was always a limiting factor, and I'd still have to negotiate terms in any summoning I performed, which in itself would limit how often I could summon.

I dug a piece of chalk out of the box where I kept my implements, then I moved to an open space on the basement floor, well away from Tessa's diagram. I didn't want to do anything that could interfere with that one. I crouched and began slowly sketching, thinking carefully about how to adjust the ward structure of Tessa's diagram for what I wanted.

It took well over an hour, and my back and knees were aching when I finally closed the diagram. I set the chalk down and brushed my hands off, then stood stiffly. I'd had to redo parts of it several times, going by pure I-think-this-makes-sense instinct. I could only hope that my instinct was on track. I scrutinized the diagram meticulously, looking for any remaining flaws.

Now to test it. A small test—just to see if I had any clue at all or if I was trying to do something that couldn't be done.

I took a deep breath and pulled potency to me. The power dribbled into my control in small erratic bursts, exactly as it had with Tessa's beacon. For a summoning, it would have been disastrous, but I didn't need it to be steady and strong since I wasn't relying on it to hold protections or bindings or anything else. I only needed it to go into the warded diagram. Focusing, I slowly released the potency down into the diagram, watching as it filled the structure, settling into the wards like a blend of light and water, visible as a shimmering brilliance to othersight.

I finally released the diagram from my control. I hadn't pulled much power—there wasn't much to be pulled— but as far as I could tell it was staying in the diagram, exactly where I'd channeled it.

"Holy shit," I said, giddy. *I made an arcane battery! And without all that messy murder and torture business!*

I watched the diagram obsessively for nearly half an hour, then decided that it seemed to be holding the power. The next question was, how much would it hold? Enough for a summoning? And could I then draw that potency out steadily enough to use it effectively?

I focused and channeled another small surge of potency into the diagram, deeply pleased when it settled in, like honey poured into a half-full bowl.

This was too fucking cool. I scrutinized my "arcane

battery" again, finally feeling a measure of confidence that the diagram was holding steady. It was tempting to see just how much this diagram could hold, but I forced myself to hold back, at least for now. I could sense that there was more potency after the second time I'd channeled the power and that there was room for some more, but there was no point in testing the storage capacity at this time. The big test would be whether I could *use* that potency.

I glanced over at Tessa's beacon, satisfied that it was still sending out its arcane call, then climbed the stairs and locked the basement door behind me. The worst that could happen if the diagram could *not* hold the power overnight would be that it would trickle away, back into the normal power structure of this sphere.

And if it was still there, and usable, by morning, then this whole summoning gig would suddenly be about a thousand times easier.

21

As soon as I woke up the next morning, I ran downstairs to check my storage diagram. Even before coffee—which for me was a major deal. The basement was stuffy and hot, but I barely noticed. The potency still lay pooled in the diagram, thrumming softly to senses beyond hearing. "Hot damn, I am *good,*" I murmured, grinning like an idiot.

Now, could I use it? I rubbed my hands together gleefully in my best mad scientist impression and ignored my body's demand for coffee and food. I took a deep breath to focus and pulled the potency from the diagram—slowly at first, then with more certainty, until I could feel the power coiling and crackling around me. I laughed as I felt the potency respond in shimmering undulations. It was only a couple of hours after dawn, at a time of the month when potency was erratic and hard to pull, and here I was with smooth and solid power at my disposal.

I toyed with the power for a while, practiced sending it back into the diagram and pulling it out again, my understanding of the wards deepening as I watched how the power flowed. I could see ways that the structure could be adjusted to hold power more efficiently or altered to allow for different uses.

I could also see why it was very likely that no one had figured this trick out before. Without that crucial component of the ward that was used in the beacon, this wouldn't work. *And how often does a summoner get the chance to glean knowledge from a demonic lord?* My skill at warding was novice at best, but I could still see that this ward was the sort of thing that only someone who was a "twelfth dan grandmaster" would be able to figure out. And Rhyzkahl had given it to me. Did he know the other ways it could be used?

I reluctantly released the power back into the diagram one more time, then broke contact with it, exhaling as the power settled into the shining wards. The next true test would be to attempt a summoning using stored power. *And a dangerous test as well,* I reminded myself. If I screwed up with a summoning, I wouldn't lose only the stored power, I'd lose body parts. *I'll be sticking to a lower-level demon, that's for sure.* Just like when I was beginning to learn how to summon.

But now wasn't the time for that. Now was the time for coffee. I hauled myself upstairs, suddenly feeling the fatigue hit me. Sure, the power was there at my disposal and it was far easier to draw it out of the diagram than out of this sphere, but I'd still been exerting effort to hold the potency, and I felt as if I'd summoned three *reyza* at once. *Note to self: Don't forget that this takes it out of you.*

I finished getting ready for work, then poured a cup of coffee and brought it out to the back porch. It wasn't even seven a.m. yet, but I could already feel the promise of the crushing humidity in the air. Ah, summer in south Louisiana. A season to be endured. But even the prospect of unbearably frizzy hair couldn't dim my mood. I knew that I was on to something huge with this power-storage diagram.

I heard my cell phone ring from inside the house but felt no great compulsion to leap up and answer it. I wasn't on call, and I wanted to enjoy my peace. I knew it wasn't from the neuro center—I'd set that number to a distinct ring as soon as I'd had Tessa admitted there. Eventually the ringing stopped, and about half a minute later I heard the chime that told me I had voice mail.

It will wait, I thought stubbornly. I felt as if I hadn't had a peaceful moment to myself in months. There was always something that had to be done, somewhere I needed to go. I *needed* to get into Tessa's library, I *needed* to learn more about wards and arcane and essence, I *needed* to solve these murders.

I *needed* to relax and take time for myself. Even if it was for only a few minutes.

My phone rang again, followed by another voice-mail chime. I tightened my grip on the coffee mug, feeling my shoulders hunch up and my lip curl into a pout. Not fair. This was *my* time. I wasn't on call.

Then I sighed. There were very few people who would call me for even boring mundane matters. And what if it was someone calling about Tessa from a different number?

I unfolded my legs and made my way back inside, oddly annoyed to see that the calls were from Ryan. Nothing to do with Tessa, after all. Not that I was annoyed to have Ryan calling me, but I realized that my worry about my aunt was increasing daily. I knew that I was pinning too many hopes on this ritual that Rhyzkahl gave me. I knew that I needed to face the reality that it might not work. Rhyzkahl had even said that the chances were slim. *So I'm stubborn. Screw it.*

I dialed my voice mail as I dumped the rest of my coffee out and rinsed my mug.

"Kara, call me."

I rolled my eyes and pressed the delete button. *Thanks for the details, Ryan.*

The second message was even more informative. *"Kara. Call me. It's important."*

Great. I started to dial his number but was interrupted as the phone rang, with the caller ID showing—surprise, surprise—Ryan.

"I was calling you," I said as I answered.

"I need you to come to North Highland Street in Gallardo," he said without any preamble. "Murder–suicide. Supposedly."

Gallardo was a small town just east of Beaulac, not large enough to have its own police force, which meant that the sheriff's office handled any issues. "That's outside my jurisdiction," I informed him.

"I'm not asking you to do any work. But you need to come look at something. You know where North Highland is?"

"No, but that's why I have GPS. Is this related to what I've been working on?"

"I don't know yet. That's why I want you to come out here," he retorted, a touch of asperity in his voice.

"Smart-ass. Fine. I'm on my way."

I was tempted to dawdle to get back at him for his unwillingness to part with information, but my curiosity won out. About forty-five minutes later I pulled onto a road running through a neighborhood that could only be described as "seedy." Or perhaps "every other house a crack house," if you wanted to get specific. There were a number of sheriff's-office vehicles there, marked and unmarked. I parked my Taurus behind Ryan's dark-blue Crown Victoria, then walked up to where the most sheriff's deputies were clustered. I could see now why Ryan hadn't bothered to give me a specific address. There was only one house on the street that bothered to have a house number displayed—and it was simply spray-painted on the black tarpaper that comprised the exterior. I gave nods and smiles to the deputies and detectives I recognized, then picked Ryan out of the crowd near the street and made my way over to him.

"So? What's the deal?" I asked.

He jerked his head toward the house we stood in front of. It wasn't the one with the spray-painted number on it, but that was about the only difference. The exterior was tarpaper, the roof was patched with a faded and tattered blue plastic tarp, and more than half the windows were broken. "Come and see." He ducked under the crime-scene tape and I followed, after scrawling my name onto the scene log. He led me up to a porch of dubious stability, then we entered a gloomy interior. Ryan flicked on a halogen lamp that had been set up in the corner, giving me my first look at what he wanted me to see.

My first reaction was, *Okay, two bodies shot in the head, both white, man and a woman, on the far side of middle age.* Then recognition hit me. *Shit—it's the Galloways.* Dismay filled me as I looked down at the couple.

The sense of *wrongness* slammed into me without

warning. I pressed my hand to my stomach before realizing I'd done so, coffee in my belly abruptly feeling like roiling acid.

"They're gone...but worse than the others," I said as soon as I could work moisture back into my mouth.

Ryan nodded gravely. "Zack thought it felt...off. I'm not as sensitive as you, but even I can feel that there's something bad going on here."

Probably *anyone* with arcane sensitivity would be able to feel it. They wouldn't know specifically what was wrong, but they'd have a lingering sense of unease about the two bodies. I made myself move closer, cautious of where I was stepping, not only to avoid contaminating evidence—though I was fairly confident that the scene had been recorded and swept already—but also because I didn't trust the floor to support my weight.

I crouched beside Sam Galloway. He'd been shot in the side of the head, and I could see stippling and scorch marks near his temple. I glanced over at Sara. "What's the explanation? That he shot her and then himself?"

Ryan nodded. "Gun's already been recovered. In his hand."

"I can't say that's *not* what happened," I said slowly as I shifted into othersight to deepen my assessment, "but I don't think that's the truth." I stood, shifting back to normal vision, unable to keep the shudder from crawling over my skin. "I...think that someone else killed them by pulling their essence away, and then made it look like a murder–suicide. They might have still been breathing when they were shot, but they weren't *alive* anymore." I put a hand to my stomach, sick. "Ryan, this means that some person, either with the ability to consume essence or controlling a creature with the ability, is using it as a weapon."

"Fucking shit," Ryan said, nearly growling the words. "You said this was worse than the others. What did you mean?"

I swallowed harshly. "The essence was...ripped out, before they died." An icy shiver rippled down my back. "I don't know much about what could be doing this, but I can't help but think it had to be insanely powerful to be able to rip it out before death, before the body had loosened its hold." I shuddered, then looked at him. "What were they doing here?"

He scowled, jamming his hand through his hair. "I told you that they used to be restaurant owners, right? Well, that was before a significant stash of meth was found in their freezer during a raid several years ago."

I frowned. The Galloways hadn't struck me as the meth-dealing type at all.

"The restaurant was seized," Ryan continued, "and they didn't contest it, most likely to keep their son—who *was* known to be the occasional meth user—from spending the next umpteen years in jail for production and distribution." His scowl deepened. "Even though there was nothing to point to a lab or any way to make that much meth."

I waited for a few seconds more, then threw up my hands. "Ryan, you've completely lost me. What does this have to do with why they were killed? I thought you were trying to convince them to testify in your corruption investigation."

He exhaled. "I can't talk about it here. Let's go back to your aunt's place and I'll explain."

22

MY STOMACH WAS DOING QUEASY FLIP-FLOPS AS I pulled into my aunt's driveway, a combination of shock and no food other than my morning coffee. And, since I took my coffee thick and sweet, I now faced a serious comedown off the caffeine and sugar high.

A headache indicated that it wanted to take up residence behind my eyes, and I squinted against the noonday sun as I walked up the stairs to the porch. I heard a low rumble from the west and I glanced up, seeing the dark mass of clouds on the horizon that promised afternoon thunderstorms. *About time.* The harsh weather could be a shock to people who weren't from this area, but the near-daily thunderstorms were about the only thing that made the summers bearable. The temperature would drop about ten degrees, and even though the humidity would climb up into the sodden figures, it was still better than the relentless heat. And I could handle the humidity just fine. I'd dry up and flake away in a desert climate.

Another low rumble accompanied me as I unwound

the aversion on the door. As if answering the thunder, my impending headache gave a warning throb as I slid my key into the lock. *Painkillers,* I thought. *And food.* I heard the sound of a car pulling into the driveway, and I glanced back to verify that it was Ryan. It was. And, even better, I saw that he had bags in his hand—the kind of bags that fast-food establishments packaged their wares in.

Finally, something was going right with my day.

I turned the key and stopped dead, hand still holding the key as my heart did a little jump. The door had already been unlocked. I released the breath I was holding and let go of the key, backing away from the door and pulling my gun from my holster. How much noise had I made coming up the stairs? I could hear movement within. As I slid to the side to get better cover, I could see a figure moving around, but it was impossible to see who—or what—it was through the sheer curtains. *But the ward had still been up,* I thought. I knew that much.

I turned to signal to Ryan but discovered that I didn't need to. He was sharp and must have seen me back away from the door. The bags of food had been abandoned on the hood of his car, and he stood at the base of the steps, his own gun drawn.

"Someone's in there," I mouthed silently. He gave me a small nod in response, waiting for me to take the lead.

With the door unlocked, it was an easy entry. I pushed the door open with one hand, quickly moving to avoid being framed in the doorway. "Beaulac Police," I shouted, covering the hallway and entry to the kitchen with my Glock. "Come out where I can see you!" In my peripheral vision I could see Ryan entering smoothly and shifting to a position where he could cover the areas I couldn't.

"Oh, shit!" I heard a male voice from the kitchen. "Kara, it's just me."

I couldn't place the voice, though it was familiar. "Come out where I can see you, and keep your hands in plain sight!"

I don't think I could have possibly been more surprised if the pope had exited the kitchen. Instead, it was Carl, Dr. Lanza's gangly morgue tech, stepping cautiously through the doorway, his eyes wide and his hands raised. "Kara, it's just me."

I struggled for words for a couple of seconds as I tried to process why the fuck the morgue tech would be here. *Could he be the one who's been screwing around with the wards?* If he was a summoner, I'd eat my left shoe. "What are you doing here?" I finally managed to ask, not yet lowering my gun.

"I've been keeping an eye on the place ever since Tess has been in the hospital."

A piece of the puzzle clicked into place. "*You've* been mowing the lawn?" And Carl was tall, thin, with light-hazel eyes. Melanie-the-dingbat's description hadn't been far from the truth after all.

He smiled faintly. "Yes, and doing the edging, and weeding her gardens. And I fixed a busted window, and her roses needed some pruning too, so I—"

"Why?" Ryan interrupted, voice sounding oddly harsh in the hallway. "Why do you give a shit about Tessa's roses?"

Carl blinked. "Well, she's my girlfriend," he said, as if it was the most obvious thing in the world. His eyes flicked from Ryan and then to me. "You didn't know?"

"No!" The word came out somewhat strangled. I holstered my gun and roughly shoved my hand through my hair. "No, she never saw fit to inform me that she had a ... social life." Not that it was all that shocking ... Okay, it *was* all that shocking. This was Tessa. Weird, strange, quirky Tessa, who summoned demons in her house. I frowned. "Look, don't take this the wrong way, but my aunt is kinda ... strange. And has some, er, secrets." Gah. This was starting to sound like she was some sort of spy. An insane one.

Carl lowered his hands, a small smile curving his mouth. "I know. She summons"—his gaze flicked quickly to Ryan, and I could see Carl censor himself—"strange creatures," he finished instead of what he was obviously going to say.

"Demons," Ryan growled.

Carl nodded once. "Yes, she's a summoner of demons."

I took a careful breath. I really didn't want to eat my left shoe. "Are *you*?"

"No. I just like her. A lot."

Ryan had holstered his gun as well and regarded Carl with a frown. "It's easy to say you're someone's boyfriend if they're not here to support the story."

Carl inclined his head in understanding. "Yes, I know what you're saying." He thought for a few seconds, then looked at me. "She told me that when you were fourteen, you had to be taken to the hospital for a drug overdose."

I flushed hotly. Trust Tessa to share that bit of wonderfulness. My teen years—before I began training to be a summoner—had been an unpleasant foray into drugs, rebellion, and general acting-out. If not for the summoning and the focus that helped me get my life back on track, I'd probably be dead by now. "All right, you two know each other pretty well, I guess." Then I frowned. "So you're not a summoner, but you must know how to shape wards. I had to take them down to come in."

He shook his head. "Actually, they don't affect me."

"'Scuse me?"

He shrugged. "I don't really know why or how. Honestly, I know that there *are* wards only because Tessa showed me their effect on others. But they don't affect me. I can walk right through them."

"That's...interesting," I said, unable to put anything more coherent into words. But at least some things were starting to make sense. "You've been visiting my aunt at the neuro center?"

"Yes. I don't know if it helps, but it makes me feel better. Look, if you're convinced that I'm not robbing the place, I really need to get going. I'm on call today."

"Um, sure." *Tessa has a boyfriend.* It would take some time for me to wrap my mind around that one. "Thanks for taking care of the lawn."

He inclined his head slightly, then gave more of a nod to Ryan. "I'll be seeing you around, then." And with that he slipped out the door. I watched him as he walked off down the street.

"He must live in the area?" Ryan said as much as asked.

"I'll check," I said, grimacing. "I'll check it all out. But I need to eat first."

"I'll go get your gourmet repast," Ryan said.

"I'm going to look through the rest of the house." I believed Carl, which was odd, considering how shocked I'd been to hear that he and Tessa were an item, but it was the kind of thing that was utterly believable even if I never would have thought of it on my own. Still, I felt a fairly compulsive need to search and secure the house and the library. I could believe they were dating, but that didn't mean that he wasn't also out to find something. *Like an open portal that my darling aunt failed to tell me about.*

I sighed and scrubbed at my face as I entered the library and flicked on the lights. Tessa could be erratic, impulsive, and even annoying at times, but I could never say that she didn't always have my best interests at heart. *Plus, she's mine,* I thought fiercely.

I quickly examined the wards in the library, especially the ones over and around the portal, finding nothing amiss. *But would I even know?* It was shameful, really, that my skills were so weak. I clearly had the ability and the affinity to handle and see the wards. And the more I came to know about my aunt and the wardings in her house, the more my suspicion grew that Tessa's ability to ward was also minimal at best. She had enough skill to shape the protections needed for summonings, but beyond that it looked as if she'd relied on others to do the work for her.

I squared my shoulders and returned to the kitchen, replacing the wards as I left the library. Ryan came in and sat on a stool on the opposite side of the counter from me, setting two bags from Taco House and a pad of paper in front of him.

"Let's start figuring out what we know," he said as he pulled about a dozen wrapped tacos out of the bag.

"Okay. We'll just list everything to start," I said. "Carol and Brian Roth are dead. Davis Sharp is dead. Brian and Sharp both had their essence eaten. A demon dog-thing attacked us. And the Galloways had their essence ripped away and are dead."

He nodded, jotting quick notes in a crabbed script. "And your aunt has an open portal in her library, and you were attacked by a—a psycho pixie-thing."

I unwrapped a taco, dribbling cheese onto the black

granite of the countertop. "The big question I have is whether there's really a connection between any of this shit."

"I'm not finished," Ryan said, still writing. "We should include the fact that I'm investigating Judge Harris Roth for misconduct."

I'd just taken a bite of taco, and I was forced to actually continue to chew and then swallow instead of staring at him openmouthed. "*He's* the one you're investigating? 'Splain, please?"

He wiped a strand of lettuce off his chin with the back of his hand. "Witness intimidation, improper disposition of drug seizure property, possible planting of drug evidence, not pursuing cases against major supporters. That sort of thing."

I felt a little mental click as a couple of pieces fit together. "The Galloways?"

"Exactly. After their restaurant was seized, it was auctioned. To Davis Sharp."

The damn lightbulb finally went off over my head. "Ohhhhh. That's Sharp's restaurant now!"

Ryan gave me a thin smile. "Correct. And Sharp bought it for a song. The judge who presided over the seizure and the plea deal concerning the son was . . ." He looked at me expectantly.

"Judge Roth," I breathed. "Who also happened to receive horking big campaign contributions from Davis Sharp, and had for the last ten years or so. Whoa. So he's dirty?"

"It appears so. We think that the entire drug bust and seizure was a frame-up, just so Davis Sharp could get his hands on that property." He sighed and scrubbed at his eyes. "We'd been working with the Galloways for several months now—trying to build a corruption case against the not-so-honorable Judge Roth. Unfortunately, they weren't as cooperative as we'd hoped."

"Why not? I would think that they'd want to see Roth taken down."

His face twisted in annoyance and frustration. "They did. But they also wanted significant financial restitution, and fairly soon. Sam was pretty ill, and the medical bills were crushing them. They weren't happy when we had to tell them that there was no guarantee that restitution would happen and, even if it did, it might take years. That sort of thing is completely out of our control."

I groaned. "So they resorted to blackmail."

His expression darkened. "That's our best guess."

I looked at him for several heartbeats. "Whoever killed them is also our essence-eater. But you're not convinced that it was Roth who pulled the trigger, are you?"

He shook his head. "Judge Roth isn't the only one who stood to lose if the corruption was exposed and not the only one in a position to be blackmailed. People who worked with him, campaign contributors, business associates... If we can ever get a break on this case, it's going to be a pretty massive shitstorm."

"Welcome to Louisiana politics," I muttered.

"It's a fucking spectator sport down here, isn't it?" Ryan took another bite of taco. "All right, let's keep going with the brainstorming. We also have the fact that Elena Sharp pressed charges twice against her husband for domestic violence and dropped them twice."

I had to grimace. That one I knew about. "Unfortunately, that's not all that uncommon. I can't count the number of times I've done the paperwork to put some jerk-off in jail, only to have the wife or girlfriend—or boyfriend—come down and bail said jerk-off out."

His mouth twisted. "All the time professing their undying love, right?"

"Something like that."

"Did Elena Sharp strike you as that type?"

"Not really. I mean, not the undying love part, at least. Unless it was undying love of the lifestyle that she didn't want to give up." I rolled my eyes. "To add to the fun, there's a rumor floating around that she was having an affair of her own—with our dear Judge Roth—and that Davis Sharp threw her out." I gave a shrug. "But my source was a Cardio Barbie in the locker room at the gym, so who knows how reliable the information was."

"Would that explain why she filed for divorce?" Ryan pointed out.

"I don't think so. She enjoyed being married to money. Why would she leave that to be Roth's mistress? She was afraid of something...or someone—so much so that she was willing to leave her comfy lifestyle."

"Maybe Davis wanted the divorce and had someone pressure her."

"Possible. Let's write it all down."

"I am, I am." He set the pen down after a moment and pushed the pad to me. "So. Connected?"

I looked down, then looked up. "I have no fucking idea. I can't read your writing."

He let out a snort. "Well, you've got three of the Roths connected."

"Carol and Brian, supposed murder–suicide—though I'm still not buying that scenario," I said, renewed annoyance flaring that I didn't have those cases anymore. I had very little faith that Pellini would push to find out who really killed them. "Brian's the son of the judge who is being investigated by the FBI for misconduct, and one of his main supporters, Davis Sharp, was found ass end up in the shower. Sharp happened to buy a piece of drug-seizure property for a song—property that was seized from the Galloways, who are also dead because they apparently tried to blackmail someone involved in the whole thing." I frowned down at the piece of paper. "So Harris Roth is connected to all of them, but why would he kill Carol and Brian? Or Davis Sharp? Even if he *was* boffing Elena, would that be worth murdering Sharp? I could possibly see him killing the Galloways if he was trying to cover shit up. But the others? And if it's him, *how* is he consuming essences? Or does he have something else doing it for him? And did he get that dog-thing to attack us?"

Ryan pulled the pad back to him. "Yeah, we're still missing a few pieces."

"A *few*?"

His mouth twitched in a smile. "Okay, a lot." He unwrapped another taco and started in on it. "Have you been able to find out anything about what could suck down essences like that?"

I shook my head, feeling another surge of annoyance that I'd screwed up my freebie questions from Rhyzkahl. "Still working on that. I'll be spending my free time in that damn library. And whoever it is, they're getting stronger, or at least better at it. Sam and Sara weren't already dead or dying when the killer pulled their essence out."

Ryan picked up spilled meat and cheese and stuffed it back into the taco. "Yeah, that's not encouraging news."

"More research for me," I said with a sigh.

"Well, be careful of that portal-thing."

I looked at the pile of empty wrappers in front of him.

I'd eaten three, and it looked like Ryan had torn through almost the rest of the dozen in the few minutes we'd been talking. "Good grief, Ryan," I said with a laugh. "Hungry?"

He grinned. "I'm storing up my strength, in case all of this turns out to be anywhere near as nasty as the last case I worked on with you."

"Ugh, don't even say that! I don't feel like dying again."

"Yeah, I'd probably have to pay for the funeral myself this time."

I laughed. "Take up a collection! All of my adoring fans."

"And your ex-boyfriends. And all of the coworkers you've been accused of sleeping with." He grinned. "Come on, I know you have the hots for Pellini and Boudreaux."

"I just ate. Don't do that to me."

He laughed. "I'm sure you have plenty of adoring ex-lovers. I'd have to hire security to keep them from throwing themselves onto the coffin in grief."

"Sad to say, I doubt you'll have to chase too many away," I replied with a mock sigh. "It's been far too long since I've had sex with a human."

The words were out of my mouth before I fully realized what I'd said. I fought to keep the teasing smile on my face, praying desperately that Ryan wouldn't understand the meaning beneath the words.

He slowly set the unfinished taco down and wiped his hands off, face going very still. I could see the thoughts ticking behind his eyes, putting together various comments and clues. Sweat stung my armpits, and a sick misery began to coil in my chest. *No, no, no. He's going to freak out.*

"A human?" he said, green-gold eyes lifting to mine, voice unbearably even.

I started to babble out a denial, some sort of retraction, but I knew it would sound lame and pathetic. Screw it. I was in this far. And what fucking business was it of his anyway? "The first time I encountered Rhyzkahl, I . . . uh . . ." Okay, maybe not so easy to say outright. At least not to Ryan.

His expression froze, his eyes going dark with either pain or fury. I couldn't tell. When he spoke his voice was so cold I thought it would crack. "You slept with him?"

I felt as if someone had dumped ice down my back. I'd been worried that he might have a guy-jealousy type of reaction, but this was something far more intense, as if he suddenly despised me. *Stop it,* I railed at myself. *Stop caring so much what he thinks.* It wasn't working. I couldn't help it. I did care. I couldn't bear the thought of him not liking me or respecting me anymore. "It's not how you think." I was trying to be calm, cool. I wasn't being very successful. "I mean, it's not like I summoned him and then immediately jumped his bones. I was scared to death at first. I thought he was going to destroy me!"

I swear he bared his teeth. "He *raped* you?"

"Holy shit! No. No, it was . . . it was totally consensual. No coercion or anything."

His face was like stone. "I don't get it. I don't get why you would have sex with a creature like that. I figured you for someone who had more self-respect than that."

I felt as if my breath had been robbed from me, and for several gaping seconds I could only struggle to regain the power of speech. "Self-respect?" I finally managed. "Who the fuck are you to be all self-righteous about this?"

"I just can't believe you fucked that thing!" he retorted, voice rough with what I could only assume was utter disdain. "Why . . . why would you do that?"

I stared at him, trying to control my anger and hurt and my ripping disappointment in him. I'd never imagined that he could be this judgmental, and I had the sick suspicion he was seeing me as someone who was so weak and needy that I *had* to find comfort from a demon lover.

"Because I'm *lonely!*" I exploded, standing and nearly tipping the stool over. "Because I've only ever had two boyfriends, and they were shitty in bed, and they never stayed very long anyway. I had this incredibly gorgeous guy wanting to kiss me and make love to me, and I *wanted* it. I don't have many friends. I mean, shit! I know he was just trying to get something from me, but y'know what? I wanted something from him too. I wanted to be touched and wanted and to feel—for a few fucking minutes—that I was sexy and desirable. And to feel—for a few fucking minutes—a way I knew I'd never felt before and would probably never feel again!" I stood there, chest heaving. *Shit. Shit.* How could I have said all that? How could he judge me like that?

His face twisted in what looked like a snarl, and his knuckles whitened as he balled his hands into fists. He abruptly stood and came around the end of the counter in two quick strides. I backed away in shock as he reached for me, my heart slamming in my chest as I came up against the sink. Was he really so angry that he would strike out at me? I couldn't believe it, but why else come at me like that?

But he froze as I retreated, his eyes haunted and his hand still extended toward me. I looked at him, wide-eyed, waiting to see what he was going to do.

We stood in that tableau for a breath, then he dropped his hand, suddenly looking tired and defeated. He was silent for several heartbeats, eyes on me as if desperately searching for something. Then he looked away. "I . . . should probably go now," he said, voice thick.

I swallowed, then gave a jerky nod. "Yes, I think that's a good idea." I managed to keep my voice from shaking, at least.

He turned to go but paused at the kitchen door, hand on the door frame, not looking back at me. "Thank you for helping out at the crime scene," he said, voice so low and rough I could barely hear him.

He continued out, and I heard the front door open and close. "You're welcome," I whispered. Then I gave in and sat on the floor of the kitchen and cried my heart out.

23

THE CHALK CRUMBLED IN MY HAND AS I COMPLETED
the last sigil in the circle on the basement floor. I sat back
on my heels and brushed the fragments away, careful not
to mar the diagram itself. I felt unspeakably calm. Or unspeakably empty. Either way, my hands didn't shake and
my focus was sharper than it had been since I'd come back
from the dead.

After Ryan left, I allowed myself to wallow in sobbing
misery for more than an hour, then drove home, feeling as
if something had let go. *I don't need his approval,* I'd
thought with a combination of anger and misery. Besides,
who the fuck was he to preach to me about the dangers of
dealing with demons?

I crawled into bed and slept like the dead for nearly
four hours, then woke just as the sun was dipping below
the tops of the trees that surrounded my house. I had
more than enough time to prepare for a summoning. It
wasn't a full moon, but that was the whole point.

I went through the protocols of the summoning carefully, but with a fluid ease that was gratifying. And when the time came to pull potency from the storage diagram, the power flowed into my control with a sweet and smooth surge, easily channeled into the ritual.

"*Rhyzkahl.*" His name filled the room as I held the portal open. I'd shaped this summoning as more of a call than a command—something that would normally have been wildly dangerous, but I was confident that Rhyzkahl would not seek retribution. Not when he'd already made it clear that he wanted further access to this sphere.

I felt the surge of power that indicated that something had come through the portal, and I invoked the bindings— more as a protection in the event that something other than Rhyzkahl had come through than for protection against the demonic lord. I knew too well that I didn't have the means to hold him.

The portal closed and Rhyzkahl straightened, a smile playing on his beautiful face as I released the bindings and wards. I didn't say anything, just stood beyond the edge of the diagram and waited. His eyes traveled over me and then—as expected—flicked to the storage diagram.

He let out a low laugh. "Very clever, dear one. Your moon is waning, and here you are with a demonic lord at your beck and call."

The last was a gibe, I knew, especially since I'd been punished before for assuming that I could get the lord to serve me. I inclined my head. "I have no right to expect you to be at my beck and call, my lord."

He stepped out of the diagram and over to me, putting a hand beneath my chin and tipping my head up. "You are more rested, I see."

"I would not wish to squander your gift, my lord."

He dropped his hand and laughed. "Please dispense with this obeisance, Kara. It does not suit you." He walked past me to the table in front of the cold fireplace, then turned to look back at me. "I am more pleased than you can know that you have discovered a way to circumvent the constraints of your dependence on the lunar cycle."

He hadn't expected this from me. It was nice to finally feel as if I'd impressed him, even a little.

I walked to him, slowly unbuttoning my shirt. "I am delighted to give you such pleasure." I stopped in front of him and let the shirt fall to the floor in a puddle of gray silk. A smile curved his lips as his eyes traveled over me.

"And this is the offering you have for me?"

I shook my head as I loosened the tie holding my silk pants up. They slipped to the floor and I kicked them aside. "Oh, no, my lord Rhyzkahl," I said as I stood naked before him. "This is not an offering for you. You still wish me to be your summoner, yes?" My heart pounded, and not entirely from lust. A deeply hidden part of me was aware that I was letting my hurt feelings rule my actions, but right now I didn't want to listen to it.

A flicker of something that might have been caution or confusion passed through his eyes in a fraction of a heartbeat, quickly shuttered, and I had to force myself not to feel a sense of triumph at his reaction. "I do," he said simply.

He pushed off the table and slid a hand through my hair to the nape of my neck, then pulled me to him. He tilted my head back and looked down at me, fingers tightening in my hair. "I do," he repeated in a low growl. "You are *mine*." His mouth came down on mine and his other hand dropped to my breast as he deepened the kiss with a near-savage intensity. I whimpered against him even as heat exploded through my body. *Yes. Need me. Want me.*

I managed to pull away from his kiss long enough to drag a breath in. "Prove it," I gasped in a half sob. *Please. Prove to me that* someone *wants me.*

Power flared hotly in his eyes, and his gaze locked on to mine for a bare instant before he lifted me and set me down on the heavy oak table. He pushed me to my back, his teeth bared in a silent snarl as he kept me pinned down with a hand on my upper chest. His other hand slid over my throat, pausing for a fraction of a second—just long enough for me to feel the weight of it—before moving down over my breasts and belly. My breath came in shallow pants as conflicting emotions clashed within me— desire, need, fear, shame.

"You wish me to pleasure you?" he asked, voice low and throbbing.

No. Yes. I squeezed my eyes shut as tears pricked them. What did I really want? I felt his hand between my legs, pushing my thighs apart. His fingers teased me, lightly pinching, and I sucked in breath as a shudder raced through my body.

"Or do you wish something other than pleasure?"

I swallowed harshly. "No," I whispered. No pain. I had enough of that.

He began to slowly stroke me. "Ah, but you are mine. It should not matter what you wish."

A slow warmth began in my belly, and I opened my eyes to look up at him. *Yes. Don't make me choose. Don't make me decide anything. Don't make me think about it.*

His mouth slowly curved into a smile, as if he'd scored a great and terrible victory. He lifted his hand from my chest, but I didn't move. He unlaced his breeches, and a heartbeat later I could feel him hard against me.

"I wish to fuck you," he said, surprising me with the bluntness of the statement. "I wish to fuck you until you scream with pleasure, and then I wish to fuck you some more." There was power in his voice—and a promise of things I could not even begin to imagine. He pressed into me and I moaned, both at the feel of him and at the intense eroticism of his words. He gripped my thighs and began to thrust. "I wish to fuck you until you scream my name and beg me for release, beg me for more, beg me for all I can do for you . . . and to you." He drove hard into me, hands clenched on my legs and mouth twisted in a snarl.

Yes. Do it. Do it all. Please! I arched my back as my climax built, breath coming in ragged sobs. His eyes glowed with potency as he continued to fuck me, never relenting, never easing. He wouldn't, I knew. Not until he was finished with me.

The thought alone was enough to tip me over the edge. The scream of pleasure that he sought ripped from my throat as he continued to thrust into me, perfectly matching the waves of my climax. Not until I was spent and limp on the table did he slow and stop.

I took several dragging breaths as he withdrew from me. He reached and brushed his fingers over my lips, then gave a soft laugh. "Such a beautiful scream, dear one. But I did not hear my name."

"Wait," I panted, "I—"

He didn't give me a chance to finish, seizing me by my wrist to yank me upright and wringing a shocked yelp from me. He lifted me effortlessly and carried me to the chair, then sat, holding me so that my back was to him. In the next breath he wrapped an arm around my neck and shoulders to pin me firmly against him. Somehow he'd rid himself of his clothing, and his skin was warm silk over steel against mine. I shuddered as he slid into me again, then moaned as his other hand slipped between my legs.

It felt like mere seconds before I was crying out and bucking in his hold. His arm was like a band of iron around me, and I clung to it desperately. "Beg for it, dearest," he whispered in silken command as he drove me higher.

"Please..." I could barely form the word.

"Ahhh...you can do better than that. Beg." His voice thrummed with power as his grip tightened and his pace quickened. "Beg for me to fuck you. Beg for release."

"Please..." My voice was little more than a keening whimper as I struggled against him. "Yes, please. I...I beg you. Please...all of it!"

"Now, scream for me," he hissed against my ear. "Scream my name. Scream for mercy."

I did. I screamed. I screamed his name as I thrashed in his arms. I screamed and begged and wept as he gave me everything I'd asked for and more.

24

I LAY ON THE THICK CARPET, CURLED AGAINST Rhyzkahl's chest as he gently stroked my hair. My body still hummed with the aftereffects of his attentions, even though some time had passed since he'd finished with me. *"Finished me" might be a better way to put it,* I thought wryly.

There was no doubt that Rhyzkahl was an absolutely exquisite lover. No human would ever be able to match his perception, his skill, and his restraint. *He's spoiling me for humans.* Not that I was overwhelmed with offers.

But that led to thoughts of Ryan. As much as the man had hurt my feelings and infuriated me with his judgmental crap, I still... *damn it*... I still cared about him, even if just as a friend. And if I was going to continue with the honesty, I had to admit to myself that this whole assignation with Rhyzkahl had been little more than a grudge fuck, my way of getting back at Ryan. *Great, so I said, "Nyah, nyah, I can too have sex with a demon. So there."* I sighed against Rhyzkahl's chest. *I'm so damn pathetic.*

"You are troubled, dear one," Rhyzkahl said, deep voice a rumble in my ear that was against his chest. "Were all my efforts for naught?"

I lifted my head, smiling despite myself. "Not for naught." Then I had to keep myself from laughing at what I'd said. "It was all very, um, erotic." I was getting a crick in my neck from looking at him from this position, so I propped myself up on my elbow beside him.

He reached out to stroke the curve of my breast. "I enjoy giving you what you desire."

"Whether I voice it or not?"

He smiled, potency shimmering behind his eyes. "I could do so much more for you. I could fulfill those desires that you have yet to admit to yourself, that you fear. You would be safe with me."

Gooseflesh skimmed over my body. I would be safe in most ways, this was true. But I could also see how this could be the thrall that Ryan had spoken of.

"But you are not yet ready," he continued, withdrawing his hand. "And allowing you to experience such too soon would be harmful." His eyes met mine, and the flare of power was unmistakable. "I will allow none to harm you."

I sat up. "You can't always protect me." I reached for my shirt. "Hell, something mundane could happen to me. I could get hit by a car or fall down the stairs or get shot by a suspect." I slid the silk on and began buttoning it. "And it's not all about the sex, y'know." No, sometimes it was just my feelings that got hurt.

"I could give you protection at all times, should you wish it."

I frowned at him. "What, have you by my side 24/7?"

He shook his head. "That is not what I had in mind,

nor is it feasible. I cannot neglect my own realm, else I will lose it."

That was an interesting tidbit and the first time I'd heard him make any sort of reference to the power struggles in his own world. "Then what?"

"I would assign one of my minions to be your protector."

I laughed. "That would make police work a bit difficult."

He merely shrugged. "I would emphasize the need for discretion."

Discretion? I had no idea how a demon could be discreet and still be effective. Obviously there was something I wasn't quite grasping. I grabbed my pants and pulled them on as I stood. Besides, a full-time protector could also be seen as a full-time chaperone.

"I'll be fine," I said. I looked down at him. He'd made no move to dress and was still lying on his side, regarding me. Damn, but he looked good.

"You have recently been hurt," he said. "It is why you sought comfort and distraction from me."

I opened my mouth to deny it, then abruptly realized that he wasn't speaking of a physical hurt. He'd sensed or read my confrontation with Ryan. I swallowed, suddenly not wanting to meet his eyes. "I . . . kinda had a . . . disagreement with a friend."

His lip curled, and I knew he was fully aware to whom I was referring. "He disapproves of me. How ironic."

Ironic? "What do you mean?"

"You might wonder how he knows enough to disapprove of my presence in your life."

I had no response for that, and in fact I probably stared at Rhyzkahl for a couple dozen heartbeats as my thoughts whirled in chaotic patterns. In one simple sentence, Rhyzkahl had managed to pinpoint all of my doubts and suspicions and fears about Ryan. Because I *did* wonder. Why did Ryan speak like someone with a great deal of familiarity with demonkind and demonic lords? Supposedly he'd only very recently encountered one, yet Kehlirik knew him and seemed to despise him. And did *Ryan* even know? *Maybe I'm better off without him.*

I almost did it. I almost asked Rhyzkahl to tell me what he knew about Ryan, but I stopped myself before opening my mouth. Yes, I wanted to know, but I realized that I wasn't so sure I wanted to hear it from Rhyzkahl.

Besides, there were other things I needed to know far more, and I simply couldn't waste this opportunity. "Can you answer a question for me?"

Now he sat up and began to pull on clothing. He dressed quickly, still not answering me. Finally, when he'd finished pulling his boots on, he stood and looked at me, lowering his head, eyes on me. "Is this a boon that you ask of me?"

Shit. He hadn't missed the fact that I had yet to agree to be "his" summoner. I took a deep breath. "At this time, yes." I had to hide my grimace. I would be indebted to him, but for now that was preferable to being bound more securely to him. *I guess the sex was a freebie.*

He folded his arms across his chest. I couldn't tell if he was pissed that I hadn't accepted his offer yet or pleased that I would now owe him one. "What is your question?"

"Something or someone is consuming essence. When it started, the essences were taken as the victims were dying, but now it seems as if the essences are being ripped out, killing the victims. Have you ever heard of someone being able to do that?"

He was silent and still for a number of heartbeats, eyes dark upon me. "We call those creatures who feed on essence *saarn*," he finally said. "Essence potency is addictive. One who has the ability to utilize it will quickly grow to depend on it, will crave it more."

"You mean it's going to get worse?"

"I cannot say. These creatures are rare," he continued, "no doubt because they are usually slain as soon as the ability is discovered."

I frowned. "But what is it? Is it a human doing this?"

"It is indeed possible," he replied, expression inscrutable.

"How?"

He lifted an eyebrow at me. "How is it that you are able to open a portal between our two worlds?"

That gave me pause. I'd been born with the ability and supposedly inherited it from my grandmother. "So it's an arcane skill that this person is born with?"

"In a manner of speaking," he said, sounding almost bored. "There are many humans with the ability to shape and manipulate potency. Some can open portals. Some can draw power from essence. A rare few are little more than parasites. You are all descended from the same source."

This was something I'd never heard before. I knew that there were other people with the ability to shape arcane power, even if they weren't able to open a portal, but I'd never heard this idea that every arcane practitioner shared some sort of great-great-grandpappy. *So what was that original source?* I wanted to ask him more about that, but I could already see that he was getting annoyed with the questions, and I wasn't sure how much more he would put up with. With regret, I wrenched my thoughts back to my original track.

"How is this person getting stronger?"

"Exposure to sufficient potency. Or perhaps consumption of another essence-eater." He lifted a shoulder in an elegant shrug. "There are any number of ways."

I shoved my fingers through my hair. "Okay, so how can I stop them?"

His eyes narrowed. "I dislike the thought of you pursuing one with this ability."

"Well, it's my job," I retorted. "And people are dying."

His mouth tightened. "Ah, yes, your duty to protect and serve." I could hear the sneer in his voice, his disdain not for what I did but for whom I chose to protect and serve. Then he inclined his head. "Yet I understand that this is a matter of honor for you."

"Yes. I swore an oath." Which was true, though I'd never really thought about it on this level. I'd been sworn in as an officer after graduating from the academy, and like everyone else I'd raised my right hand and done the I-state-your-name business and never thought twice about it, except that it was one of those things you had to do to be a cop. But for demonkind, an oath was serious, and honor was paramount.

But any hopes that he would be more inclined to help me due to it being a matter of honor were dashed when he turned away and strode toward the diagram. He was making a point. He had no need to be in the diagram to return to his own realm. Well, I guess now I knew whether he was pissed or pleased. But then again, it wasn't *his* matter of honor, it was mine.

"Rhyzkahl," I said, following him. "Please. How can I stop this killer?"

He spun to face me, lip curled in a snarl. "*You* can do nothing to stop this creature, save destroy it, and soon, before it grows too strong to be destroyed by any means that you possess."

I opened my mouth to ask *how* to track it down and destroy it, but he jerked his hand up to silence me. "I will answer no more questions for you until you agree to *my* terms," he growled. Then, with a shimmer of potency, he was gone.

25

It was a good thing that I'd slept so well before the summoning, because I sure as shit wasn't able to sleep after Rhyzkahl departed.

I stared at the ceiling in my bedroom, alternating between angst and anger at myself. Woo, boy, I sure showed Ryan, didn't I? I showed him that I could call the demonic lord. I showed him that I could sleep with whomever—or whatever—I wanted. Too bad I was left feeling like shit now.

Rhyzkahl was an excellent lover, there was no denying that. He knew all the right moves, could read my desires, gave me what I wanted when I wanted it—whether I knew it or not. He did all of the right "afterglow" things too, like holding me, stroking my hair, and murmuring sweet nothings.

But he didn't mean any of them. He was a demon, and anything he did for me was only part of some bigger plan.

Then, to really cap the night off, I'd managed to piss him off by not yet agreeing to be his summoner.

And why the *fuck* did I feel like I'd cheated on Ryan? That was the most insane part of it all. Ryan and I were most certainly not in anything remotely resembling a relationship. We'd never slept together, had never even come close to kissing. Was I feeling guilty only because Ryan had come out so vehemently against me having a relationship with Rhyzkahl? Though, again, that wasn't exactly a relationship either.

I sighed. Okay, so I really couldn't summon Rhyzkahl again unless I was willing to give him the commitment he wanted, but I had the storage diagram now. I could call any demon I wanted, whenever I wanted. I didn't need the help of the demonic lord.

So why did the thought of never calling him again leave me with an ache in my gut?

I was definitely the most screwed-up human in all existence.

My thoughts continued to churn and whirl in similar lines. I didn't remember falling asleep, but when my cell phone rang, I jerked out of something that was awfully similar to sleep.

I blinked away the scuzz in my eyes and managed to make out that it was the Beaulac dispatch number. I fumbled for the answer button. "Gillian here," I croaked. I glanced over at the clock. Five a.m. Gah. If I *had* slept, it wasn't for more than an hour or so.

"Detective Gillian, this is Corporal Powers in the radio room. Mandeville PD called. They found your business card at the condo of Elena Sharp."

I sat up. "Why were they at her condo? What happened?"

"She's dead. Apparent suicide. Want me to text you the contact info?"

"Yeah. Thanks," I said, trying to shake off the numb shock. Too convenient. Too much coincidence. It was all connected somehow. *Suicide, my ass,* I thought grimly.

ABOUT AN HOUR later I pulled into the parking lot of Elena Sharp's complex. The detective I'd spoken to, Robert Fourcade, had been fairly accommodating. And, after I'd given him a quick rundown of the case surrounding Elena's husband's death, he had agreed to allow me into the scene.

I pulled my badge out and showed it to the officer manning the door. "I'm Detective Gillian, from Beaulac PD. Detective Fourcade's expecting me."

The officer nodded as if he'd known I'd be showing up. "Right, you can go on in."

I stepped in, feeling a strange déjà vu, with crime scene superimposed over it. A couple of the officers inside gave me "who the hell is this" looks, but a burly detective with dark-red hair stepped my way.

"You must be Detective Gillian," he said, extending his hand. "I'm Rob Fourcade."

I shook his hand. "Call me Kara. Thanks for allowing me to come check out the scene."

He shrugged. "I got no problem with it, but there's nothing to indicate anything other than a suicide."

Yeah, well, I could see and feel things Detective Fourcade couldn't. I gave him an answering shrug and smiled. "But you understand why I wanted to check it out, especially since her husband was murdered."

"Paperwork. Loose ends. I know the drill." I could tell that he felt that I was wasting my time driving all the way down here. He jerked his head toward a back bedroom. "She's in there."

"I appreciate it." I headed down the hallway. I hadn't seen this part of the condo on my earlier visit. The walls were bare; the only decorative touch was an elegant vase with dried flowers sitting on a table against the wall.

The bedroom was more of the same. Solid, sturdy, and beautiful furniture that looked like it would last through an apocalypse. And lying across the expensive bedspread was Elena Sharp, quite clearly dead. I took in the sight of the pill bottles on the nightstand, then stepped closer to take a more thorough look at Elena.

I shuddered to a stop as I neared the bed and *felt* the body. I sucked in my breath, head spinning. The gaping lack of essence was so profound that I literally had to grab the bedpost to steady myself. This was far worse than Brian Roth and Davis Sharp. Worse even than the Galloways. I could feel the rending, the violence where this essence had been savagely ripped away while she was still alive. My fingers dug into the bedpost, and I fought to not puke.

"You all right?"

I hadn't realized that Fourcade had followed me into the bedroom. I straightened, taking deep breaths to try to regain something resembling composure. "Yeah, I'm ... just getting over some food poisoning."

He frowned and nodded, but I could see the faint derision in his eyes. He thought that I was squicking at the sight of a corpse. If he only knew how many corpses I'd seen in the past six months ...

"I don't want to rush you, but the coroner's office is here. As soon as you're done, they're going to bag her up."

"Sure," I said as I peered into the dead woman's face.

There was nothing to indicate that she'd died in the kind of arcane violence that I could feel. No look of horror etched into her features, no arcane sigils traced upon her body in blood, nothing else that would be there if this had been a scene in a movie.

"No forced entry," Fourcade continued, sounding a bit bored. "No signs of struggle. I guess this helps tie up your other case."

I looked at him blankly. "How?"

He waved a hand toward the pill bottles, and now I saw that there was a sheet of paper beneath them. "Note. Confession. It's why I called you," he said, as if explaining it to a three-year-old.

My jaw tightened, but I managed to keep my retort in check. I stepped over to the nightstand and read the note.

I cheated on my husband, then killed him. I couldn't take the shame of a divorce. Now I can't live without him, can't live with the guilt.

It was a decent little suicide note, but it totally rang false. "This isn't signed. It's just a printout."

"Half of all suicides don't even leave notes," he replied, mouth drawing down in annoyance. "You're gonna get hung up because she didn't dig out a pen and do it all nice and legal?"

"If you expect me to use this as a reason to close my other investigation, then, yes, I'm gonna get hung up," I snapped back, too on edge to censor myself. "Where's her computer?"

He opened his mouth, then closed it, face darkening. "How should I fucking know? Probably in one of the other bedrooms."

I walked past him to the hallway. I knew from my previous visit that there wasn't a computer in the sitting room. The door to the other bedroom was ajar and I pushed in, quickly scanning. "No computer in here," I called back over my shoulder. I heard a muffled noise that sounded like a growl, then the sound of opening and closing doors. I yanked gloves on and started opening drawers.

"Here," I heard after about half a minute. I returned to the hallway to see Fourcade holding up a laptop case, smug smile on his face. "One computer. Satisfied?"

I shrugged. "Halfway. Now, where's the printer?"

His red mustache was beginning to look pale in contrast to his florid face. "Maybe she wrote the fucking note and printed it out somewhere else."

How stubborn was the guy going to be? I knew that I shouldn't get into an argument with the detective about how to handle his own case, but I couldn't believe that he had zero interest at all that the case could be more than a suicide. A rational part of me tried to argue that toxicology testing would show whether or not it had been a suicide, since I seriously doubted that she had actually ingested the pills, but I wasn't interested in listening to the rational part at this moment. The past few days had been grueling and stressful, and I wasn't about to let this jackass do a slapdash job of investigating this scene.

"Look," I said, stepping toward him. "If she couldn't take the time to find a pen to sign her name, why the fuck would she take her laptop to someplace else that had a printer to print out a suicide note? All I'm asking you to do is to treat this like a homicide investigation until you know for a fact that it's *not.* I'm asking you to do your job."

The last sentence was one that I really should have internalized.

"Get off my fucking scene, Detective," he said through clenched teeth.

"Get surveillance video from the guard gate. See who came in," I pressed. Fuck it. I'd already completely pissed him off. "Check the prescriptions. Fucking investigate it!"

"Don't tell me how to do my fucking job. Get out!"

I took a step back to avoid the slight spray of spittle, abruptly realizing that everyone else in the condo had stopped working and was staring at us in the hallway. I scowled and squared my shoulders. "Fine." My gaze swept the others. "Don't any of you worry about this woman's murderer going free because this man was too damn lazy to put in a little legwork."

I left amid the openmouthed stares of Mandeville's finest.

26

MY ANGER AT MYSELF GREW AS THE DISTANCE FROM Mandeville increased. I'd been a jerk. An undisciplined, tactless jerk. There were a thousand ways I could have handled that whole situation differently, and any one of them would have been better and far more likely to result in Elena's death being investigated properly. It was possible— even probable—that Fourcade was a good detective. But faced with the antagonistic ravings of a detective from a neighboring jurisdiction, it was no shock that he'd become defensive. Then my reaction had been to embarrass him in front of his coworkers. I'd put him in a no-win situation and given him no way to save face. If he went and got those surveillance tapes now or checked the prescriptions—all the things that he would have most likely done on his own without prompting—he would look like an idiot who had to be told what to do.

I wanted to bang my head on the steering wheel, but since I was driving I decided that would probably be a bad idea. Instead, I settled for taking several deep breaths and focusing on the monotony of the drive to ease my stress. The drive from Mandeville to Beaulac was almost completely on back highways, and after about twenty minutes of pine trees and cow pastures I began to zone out, regaining a bit of the feeling of peace that I hadn't even realized I'd needed until it was gone.

Until a few months ago, my life had been fairly uncomplicated—before Rhyzkahl and Ryan, and before losing my aunt. I drummed my fingers absently on the worn steering wheel. There was a part of me that was glad my life was not uncomplicated anymore. The loss of my aunt gnawed at me, even though I had hope that it wasn't permanent, but I had to face the fact that I didn't *want* a staid and sensible life. I would never have become a cop if I did. I liked the action and the excitement, even though most of the time on the job was spent in long stretches of inaction. My field-training officer had told me that police work was ninety-five percent boredom and five percent sheer terror, but that five percent made it all worth it.

The sign for St. Long Parish flicked past as I approached the bridge over the Kreeger River. I'd wasted much of the day with the trip to Mandeville, but at least I could mentally cross Elena off as a suspect, even if I couldn't quite do so officially.

The loud bang on the right side of the car derailed my thoughts and sent my pulse racing. My hands tightened on the steering wheel convulsively as the car fought to swerve in the direction of the blown tire. Adrenaline dumped into my system as I felt the tires slide on the metal decking of the bridge. I steered into the skid, even though the retaining wall of the bridge loomed threateningly, and I managed to get the damn car straightened out and under control just shy of scraping the low concrete barrier.

I allowed myself a ragged breath of relief, then caught a movement in the rearview mirror, barely registering the large pickup truck coming up on me far too fast—

The truck slammed into the left rear corner of my car, spinning it, sending me jerking heavily against my seat belt, and knocking the breath out of me. I saw the retaining wall approach again, far closer and faster. I fought the steering wheel, and for a timeless instant I thought I'd regained control. Then the truck slammed into me again, and my stupid Taurus slid up the side with an agonizing shriek of metal on concrete, hovering on the lip for a heartbeat before tipping over the barrier.

The impact when the car hit the water jammed me against the seat belt again. I dimly felt something in my chest or shoulder give way, but the massive wave of adrenaline slamming through me didn't give me a chance to feel pain. Water sloshed threateningly against the windows as the car began to sink, and within three heartbeats the car had slipped under the surface.

I was shrieking inside, but within the car it was insanely quiet, save for the low creak of metal and plastic and the quickly rising sound of water rushing through the vents. *Stay calm! Stay calm!* I silently screamed at myself, teeth gritted together, breath hissing as I fought to undo the seat belt. My heart pounded as the water rose past my knees. *Stay calm, damn it!* That was the key to survival. Stay calm, wait for the water to fill the car and equalize the pressure, then get a door open.

I couldn't tell if the car was still descending or if I'd already hit bottom. I didn't know how deep the river was or what section of the river I'd landed in. For all I knew there was only a foot of water above the car. Or thirty. The seat belt finally came free and I gave a sobbing gasp of relief, then had to clutch wildly at the seats as the car began a lurching roll, coming to a disorienting stop belly up and nose down.

I stabbed at the down button for the window, but either the electronics had already gone or there was too much pressure from the water. The water continued to rush in, swirling angrily higher. I fought the urge to claw at the door, then took a deep breath as the water rose over my head. *Now* I could open the door. I grabbed the handle and shoved against the door with my shoulder, shuddering in relief as it pushed open.

But only a few inches. My relief shifted to horror as I tried again to shove the door open. *Something's blocking it. The car's wedged up against something.* I groped through the small gap, fingers brushing a rough wood surface. *It's a tree. Shitshitshit, the car's wedged up against a fucking submerged tree!* Hurricane Katrina had dumped thousands of trees into the waterways, and most still remained. I swallowed the fear that screamed at me to keep clawing at the door and clambered past the seat to get into the back. A pocket of air lingered there still, air that I gulped desperately, but it was shrinking quickly. My piece-of-shit car wasn't airtight by any stretch. I was shocked it wasn't already completely filled with water, considering how much it leaked when it rained.

I sucked in another breath and pushed myself down to try the passenger-side door, but even through the murky water I could see the dark shapes of the tree branches that kept both doors from opening more than a few inches.

I kicked back up to my pocket of air. My rising panic screamed at me to shoot the back windshield out, but a last remaining sliver of calm asserted itself. The car was upside down, my head was barely above water, and if I shot my gun—a Glock, which probably *would* shoot once—I'd most likely kill myself from the shock wave in the water, especially since I was carrying hollow points. But I still had other options. I yanked my gun out of my holster and took a deep breath, ducking under and bracing myself with my feet against the seats. I grabbed the gun around the butt and the barrel with both hands, then drove the end of the barrel into the rear windshield as hard as I could.

I felt the windshield give way on the third try, relief flooding me as the tempered shards of glass billowed away. I pushed up to the sliver of remaining air pocket, then took a last heaving breath and ducked under the water.

I tried to keep my eyes open, but it was pointless. I couldn't even see my hands through all of the silt in the water. I felt my way to the window and tried to worm my way out, but all I could feel was mud. My lungs began to burn from holding my breath, and I scrabbled frantically at the mud, trying to dig a way through. Horror flared through me again. This was the riverbed. There was no getting out that way.

My lungs screamed for breath, and I pushed up again to find the air pocket. Only about an inch of air remained, and I pressed my face against the carpet and sucked in one more breath. *The front windshield. Stay calm. You can get out that way.* I reached for my gun again, fingers fumbling on the empty holster as dread filled me. *Fucking shit!* I'd dropped it? Or maybe it hadn't been fully in the holster?

The pocket of air was gone now. Red haze began to

creep in on the edges of my vision. *I'm going to die,* I realized with a sick jolt. I'd faced certain death once before, but this time I didn't feel any calm acceptance. This time I felt terror and anger and everything else. I wanted to scream in rage, but I wasn't ready to give up that lungful of air just yet. The red burned across my vision, and then, without realizing it, I shifted into othersight.

I hung motionless in the water, shocked to my bones at the stunning wash of potency that swirled around me and the car. For a blinding instant I thought that the entire incident with the car going into the river had been an arcane attack, then I realized what I was seeing.

It was the *river.* The power of the raw element—a potency that I had never used before, never even been able to see before. I was accustomed to using the potency that formed the fabric of the planes, a power that felt sweet and hot and elegant. But this . . . this potency was raw and profound, and I could see how someone could be swept away in it.

I steeled myself and *pulled* at that potency.

It resisted me at first. It knew that I had no experience in drawing that sort of power—didn't deserve to hold it, to shape it. But I didn't want to shape it. I wasn't looking for anything elegant or pretty, not now when I had only seconds left. I pulled harder, and then it felt as if a dam burst. It came crashing in on me and I opened myself to it, feeling it rage into my control, *beyond* my control. I gathered it clumsily, as much as I could bear. The river shrieked through me, churning and foaming as I pulled.

And then I *pushed.* As hard as I could. Pushed the power away from me in a wave. I felt and heard metal and wood and plastic twisting and tearing. I could feel myself screaming, using that last breath, forcing it all out as the power surged around me, swirling into a vortex.

And then I could push no more. I had no more air, no more power. I floated in the water, completely spent and out of air, the ruins of the car swirling around me.

And then the *river* pushed. I felt it crush into me, forcing me up and up. I suddenly burst above the surface, as if the river had birthed me. I took a dragging gasp of air, catching a small wave and inhaling water as well. I coughed, struggling to tread water with limbs that had no strength. I could see the bridge and the bank, but I couldn't get my body to respond. *Too far. I don't have anything left to make it to the bank.* The current grabbed at me, pulling me toward the center. My arms felt like lead weights, dragging me back under. *Shit, so close.*

The water closed over my head again, but before I could sink any farther, I felt a hard yank at my hair. My head broke the surface and I let out a choked gasp of pain.

"I gotcha!" I heard a voice shout. "God damn it, I gotcha!" The grip on my hair quickly shifted to my arm and collar, and I was dragged over the hard metal edge of a boat, scraping my ribs and belly. I landed in a tumbled and ungainly heap against a tangle of fishing poles and empty beer cans, as I struggled for a full breath. "You all right?" the voice asked. "Was there anyone else in the car?"

I held up my hand, still coughing, trying to nod and shake my head all at the same time. I finally took an uneven breath. "No . . . no one else," I managed to choke out. "Just me." My eyes felt clogged with silt, and when I could finally breathe without agony, I focused on wiping them enough to look up at my savior.

Good ole boy was the first thing that popped to mind. He looked like he was in his sixties, dressed in stained jeans and a frayed white T-shirt. He had the deep leathery tan of someone who spent his days out in the sun and a wiry build with just a bit of flab around the midsection. He crouched next to me in the boat. "Y'sure no one else was in the car with you?" he asked again.

"Quite sure," I rasped. "I was by myself."

He relaxed visibly. "That's good. I saw the whole damn thing, saw the car go off the bridge. I was at the bend up there," he said, waving a hand in the general direction of upriver. "Got over here as fast as I could, but that car went under fast." He shook his head. "Good thing the river decided to spit you out," he said, giving me a grin.

I smiled weakly. *That's about what it felt like.*

He looked up toward the bridge, shading his eyes with a hand. "I heard a bang, then saw that truck just plow right into you. Next thing I knew, you was toppling right on over." He scowled, then pulled a cell phone out of a plastic bag in his tackle box. He glanced down at me. "You a cop?"

I nodded, feeling the effort of even that much movement. "Detective. Beaulac PD."

"Hunh. Make all sorts of enemies as a cop. I was a deputy with St. Tammany for more than thirty years. Retired now. Get to fish all I want." His eyes swept over the river, and I could see what I knew was plain old naked love. He dialed 911 and gave the dispatcher a brief rundown of the incident. He glanced down at me. "What's your name, darlin'?"

"Kara Gillian."

He relayed my name and told the dispatcher that he'd meet them at the landing by the bridge. A few minutes later, I felt the boat crunch up against sand, and he leaped deftly out and pulled it farther up. I stood as soon as I was marginally stable, though my legs were still insanely wobbly. But he grabbed my hand in his thick, calloused one and practically lifted me to the bank. I gave him a smile of thanks and then staggered two steps to a spot on the bank that was reasonably rock-free and sank to sit. *Holy crap, I'm not dead.* I looked back at the bridge, wanting to laugh and shiver at the same time. *Did someone want me dead, or was that an accident?* I hugged my arms around myself, then shifted into othersight and looked at where my car had gone in the water. The truck had hit me twice. Tough to believe that was an accident.

I could see none of the incredible potency of the river that had surrounded me before. Was it because I didn't need it anymore? No way to know, but I knew the river was just a river now. *I wonder if they'll be able to get my car out. And what they'll think of the damage to it.* I'd barely been able to make a blue glow in my hand back at my aunt's house, but just a few minutes ago I'd harnessed and controlled enough potency to rip a car into pieces.

And even that might not have been enough if the old fisherman hadn't been nearby.

I turned back to him. "Thank you," I said. "I don't even know your name."

He smiled, a nice, friendly, open smile. "Raimer. Hilery Raimer."

"I'll remember that name."

He nodded and looked back at the river. "Y'wanna hear somethin' strange? You're gonna think I'm crazy...."

"I'm the last person to call anyone crazy," I said with a weak grin.

He gave a small snort of laughter. "Funniest thing... 'bout five minutes before your car went into the river, I was anchored around the curve. Never woulda seen your car go in, and even if I'd heard it, I never woulda got here in time." He shook his head. "But I coulda sworn I heard a lady yelling at me." He glanced at me, uncertainty flickering across his face.

"Go on," I urged.

He shrugged, trying to play it off. "I dunno. I been out in the sun a long time. But I coulda sworn I heard some lady yell, 'Hey, old man, get your bony ass to the bridge. My knees hurt!'" He chuckled, shaking his head. "Not the kinda thing a guardian angel usually says, huh?"

I echoed his chuckle even as a chill walked down my spine. My knees?

Or my niece?

27

AS SOON AS I CHECKED MYSELF OUT OF THE ER, I HAD Jill take me over to the neuro center so I could check on my aunt. The fisherman's words seemed to echo through my head as I made a righteous scene, barging my way past the receptionist and nurses, holding my badge up and baring my teeth at anyone who even looked like they wanted to get in my way.

But when I made it up to her room, I got the shock of a lifetime.

"Where is she?" I whirled away from the sight of Tessa's empty and made bed to confront the nurse assistant who had followed me into the room. Cold misery threatened to sweep over me as my mind quickly ran down the possible reasons why Tessa wasn't in her bed.

"I've been trying to tell you!" the young woman panted. "She's been moved to another section." She bit her lip, hesitating.

The misery began to tighten my chest. "Where? Is she still alive?"

The nurse assistant gave me a nod that was clearly more emphatic than necessary. "She just needed to be given better care than she could receive here."

I gave her a hard look. "Is she on a ventilator now?" I'd tried to mentally prepare myself for this possibility, especially with how much her body had been declining, but it was still a harsh blow when the young woman sighed and nodded.

"Yes. It happened only a few hours ago. We tried to call you, but there was no answer."

"My phone got wet," I said numbly, in drastic understatement. "I need to see her."

"Of course," the woman murmured. "This way."

She led me to the third floor, a section of the hospital that *looked* like a hospital, with beeping monitors, and tubes, and a lingering absence of hope. She directed me to a room that held three other patients, each separated by a curtain.

I don't know how long I stood there, struggling to reconcile the knowledge that this was her body against the sight of the degrading form before me. The only part of her that was recognizable as being *Tessa* was the frizzy blond mop of her hair, and even that seemed to hang lank and lifeless against her skull.

I finally took the necessary number of steps forward to put me beside the bed and made myself pick up her limp hand, shivering in reaction to the feel of emptiness. *Come on, Tessa,* I thought toward her desperately. *I know you're out there somewhere. You need to come back. Time to come back now.*

Eventually I felt a gentle hand on my shoulder and I looked up, surprised to see Jill. Then I realized that she'd been with me the entire time, staying still and silent and giving me the time I needed.

"Come on, Kara," she said gently. "You need to go home. It's been a long day. She's going to be fine."

I looked up at her for several heartbeats, then nodded and slipped my hand from Tessa's. I knew I should feel encouraged by Mr. Raimer's comment, since hopefully that meant something was happening with Tessa, that maybe she was on her way back. But all I could feel was a desperate need to see some sort of improvement, a twitch of awareness. Anything but the fading body that surely wouldn't last much longer.

I walked out of the room, feeling weighed down and empty. I started down the corridor toward the elevator, then abruptly spun back and headed for the nurses' station.

"My aunt is *not* a DNR," I said to the nurse beyond the counter, nearly snarling. "Do you understand me? She does *not* have a Do Not Resuscitate order on her chart. If anything happens to her, you people will fucking do everything in your fucking power to keep her alive. You got that?" I could feel Jill's hand on my arm, but she wasn't pulling me away—most likely just making sure that I wasn't going to do anything more confrontational than snarl.

The nurse didn't seem particularly cowed by my vehemence. I could see in her eyes that she thought I was in denial and was being unrealistic, but fortunately—for her—she didn't give voice to any of that. "Yes, ma'am" was all she said.

I resisted the urge to repeat what I'd said, to tell her again that she needed to keep my aunt's body alive. It wouldn't make any difference, I realized. If my aunt's body coded, they would most likely go through the motions but wouldn't make any extraordinary efforts—a well-meaning but misguided attempt to spare me and my aunt a torturous wait for an inevitable end.

I looked at Jill. "I want to go home."

She nodded and led me away.

28

A POUNDING ON MY FRONT DOOR JERKED ME OUT OF the soundest sleep of my entire life. "You've got to be kidding me," I moaned as I yanked the pillow over my head. I needed sleep. I *deserved* sleep.

The pounding came again about three seconds later, and I lifted a corner of my pillow, a bleary glance at my clock showing me that it was nine in the morning. *Okay, so I've slept for twelve hours, but that doesn't mean I don't deserve even more sleep.* Especially after the heinous day I'd endured.

I sighed as the pounding came yet again. I knew who it was even without going to the door. There was only one person who would bother to drive out here just to yell at me. And I had no doubts that he would yell.

I grumbled an obscenity under my breath and hauled myself out of bed, groaning as every bruise, scrape, and pulled muscle announced its presence. I plodded to the front door and pulled it open without bothering to look through the peephole.

"*Your car went off a fucking bridge and you didn't even fucking call me?*"

I squinted at Ryan in the morning sun. A deep scowl etched his angular features, and a small vein stood out on his left temple. He didn't look as if he was about to lose his cool. He was *way* beyond that. "My phone got wet," I said. I'd thought about calling him. Briefly. But I hadn't wanted to expend the emotional energy that calling him might take, especially since our last conversation hadn't exactly ended on a pleasant note.

He made a strangled noise. "Your phone..." His hand tightened on his own phone, and for a brief crazy instant I thought he was going to squeeze it into a crumpled pile of metal and plastic. Then he glared at me again. "You couldn't find another phone to call me from? After your car went off a *fucking bridge?*"

Leaving him in the doorway, I groaned and started walking to the kitchen. "What are you, my father? I was a little occupied and a lot exhausted. The only real rest I had yesterday was the ambulance ride to the hospital."

He shut the door and followed me. "Were you hurt? How badly? Why did you need an ambulance?"

The level of stress in his voice surprised me and—I had to admit—sort of secretly pleased me. It was cool to know that anyone would worry about me like that—especially him, and especially after the other night.

I glanced back at him as I pulled the carafe out of the coffeemaker. "No, I wasn't hurt, except for a lot of bruising and a cracked rib." I dumped the remains of yesterday's coffee into the sink and began to wash the carafe out. "I submitted to the ambulance only because I knew I'd be able to lie down—which I would *not* have been able to do in the back of a state police vehicle." Since the accident had happened on a state highway, the state police had taken over the investigation. Unfortunately, that detail hadn't kept everyone with the barest trace of authority in Beaulac PD from descending on the ER to question me *ad nauseam* about what had happened.

"So you're all right?"

I gave him a nod, surprised at how tired he sounded. Maybe he'd been as upset about our fight as I had. Hearing that I'd almost died had to be pretty fucking awful, especially considering that our last words were less than pleasant. "Yeah. Car's toast. Lost my gun. And my notebook. And my phone." I gave a fatalistic shrug. "I'm still here, though." I hesitated a breath. "I'm sorry. I should have let you know I was all right."

He jerked his head in a nod of acceptance of my apology, then frowned, eyes on me as I shuffled around to make coffee. "What happened?"

"Still not really sure. I don't know if it was an accident or an attack." I got the coffee started and then leaned back against the counter, sighing. "I blew a tire and almost lost it. Then a big blue pickup rammed into me and I went over the side."

He sat down at the kitchen table, expression dark and troubled. "I don't like it."

"Well, I wasn't exactly liking it yesterday either. And I don't really much like it now, to be honest, since I hurt like hell."

Ryan glowered. "Let me guess: The doctors wanted to keep you overnight for observation, and you refused."

I gave him my best smart-ass sweet smile. "Such a smart boy you are. You're right. I couldn't stand it for another minute, and I had Jill take me home. I have a cracked rib and bruised sternum, and I'm on prophylactic antibiotics since I aspirated some water as well. I came home, stayed conscious long enough to change clothes, and then fell into bed." A shower was definitely high on my list of needs. I'd been too exhausted and depressed last night.

He slouched back in the chair. "Well, I'm glad you're all right," he said, tension beginning to clear from his face.

"Thanks," I said quietly. He met my eyes and gave me a smile that was rife with a number of emotions, foremost among them apology. I returned the smile. We were cool again. Or as cool as we could be with so many uncertainties and questions hanging between us. A pang went through me at the thought that we might never get past all that. There was so much about him that felt so very *right*—like the fact that he clearly gave a huge fuck whether I lived or died.

"Anyway," I continued, "I owe my life to a guy who was fishing on the river."

"He helped get you out?"

I gave him a brief synopsis of what happened after the car went into the river, though I left out the bit about the guy hearing someone telling him to go to the bridge. I didn't want to think about that too much, didn't dare get my hopes up too high, only to have them shattered if Tessa's body couldn't survive long enough.

I swallowed back the black mood that threatened, then opened the fridge and peered in doubtfully. I didn't have a whole lot to eat in the house. Grocery shopping hadn't been a huge priority lately. I glanced back at Ryan. "Did you bring donuts?"

He snorted. "No, sorry. I was more concerned with making sure you were all right."

I made a *hmmf*ing sound. "I'll be fine once I get coffee, a shower, and some food."

He stood. "Go shower. I'll make breakfast."

"You cook?" I asked, brightening.

"No, but I'll fake it," he said with a grin. He pulled the carafe out of the coffeemaker and poured a mug full, added a ridiculous amount of cream and sugar, then handed it to me. "This is how you like it, right? Like drinking a candy bar?"

I laughed and took the mug. "You definitely hang out with me too much."

The corners of his eyes crinkled. "Go shower. You stink."

I FELT BETTER after the hot shower, though a lovely pattern of bruising was beginning to show from where the seat belt had been. I dressed in jeans and a PD T-shirt and then came back out to the kitchen.

I laughed when I saw the white box on the kitchen table. "Did you drive code 3 to the donut shop?"

He glowered at me, but his eyes were dancing. "You don't have shit to eat in this house."

I snagged a chocolate donut out of the box, groaning softly when I realized they were still warm. "I seem to recall mentioning that. I've discovered that it's a great way to lose weight." I took a bite, savoring the rush of sugar and fat and everything else that was bad about a donut.

Ryan laughed. "Dear God, you look like you're having an orgasm."

"No, this is much better. Can you give me a ride to the PD? I need to check out a new vehicle. Jill said she'd come get me when I was ready, but since you're here, I'll impose on you instead."

"Sure thing. What about your gun and phone and everything else?"

I scowled. "Well, once I get the car, then I can go to the cell-phone place and get a new phone, and then go to the gun shop and buy a new gun." Beaulac PD didn't issue duty gear or guns. Officers were allowed to purchase their own as long as it was on the list of approved firearms. Nice in some ways. Not so nice in others.

He grimaced. "That'll get expensive."

I sighed. "I know." That was the not so nice part. I picked up the donuts. "I think it's going to be a whole-box kinda day."

I'D ONLY *THOUGHT* my old Taurus was a piece of shit. I was now the proud "owner" of an ancient Chevy Caprice, whitish, with the remains of old Beaulac PD decals clearly visible on the sides beneath a not-very-recent paint job. It stank to high heaven of cigarette smoke, the gas gauge was broken, and the foam steering-wheel cover was coming off in gritty little bits. *It's free,* I reminded myself. *No car loan, no gas bill, no insurance, no maintenance.*

After plunking down an uncomfortable amount of money at the gun shop and the cell-phone store, I headed back to my office. A pair of blow-up swimmies had been taped to my office door, along with a flyer for swimming lessons at the community pool. "Nice," I murmured with a smile. I pulled the swimmies off the door, my mood dimming at the sight of the note underneath telling me to report to my captain's office when I got in. *If I have to tell that damn story one more time...*

There was a stack of papers and a padded mailer in the in-box by my door, and I snagged them as I unlocked my office. I dumped the donuts and swimmies on the desk, then took a quick glance through the papers. It was all the information I'd requested in my subpoenas, and I skimmed quickly, finding nothing at all that contradicted Elena's statement to me concerning her financials.

Not that it mattered anymore.

I tore open the mailer to find a DVD within. It was labeled with the name of a local security company and a date and time stamp, and it wasn't until I dug through the envelope and found the accompanying note that I realized it was the surveillance video from the gate at Brian Roth's subdivision.

I pursed my lips as I looked down at the DVD. The Roth cases weren't mine anymore, so the proper procedure would be to hand it over to Pellini. *But will he even bother to look at it?* Sifting through surveillance video was tedious and boring, and I didn't exactly have the utmost confidence in Pellini's drive to find out what really happened.

I compromised. I fired up my computer and burned a copy of the DVD, stuck the copy in my bag, then stuffed the original back into the mailer and dropped it in Pellini's in-box. I even scrawled a brief note on a Post-it explaining what the DVD was and why I'd requested it. *Who knows. Maybe he'll actually go that extra mile.* I wasn't going to hold my breath, though.

Unfortunately, now I had to deal with my rank. After my previous captain, Robert Turnham, had been promoted to chief of police, a lieutenant from the patrol division had been tapped to become the captain over investigations—all of this happening in the time that I was "dead" and the first couple of weeks after that, before I returned to duty.

Captain Barry Weiss resembled a bulldog in darn near every possible way except for the fur. He was short and stocky and slightly bowlegged, with broad shoulders and a lower jaw that jutted out just enough to make the resemblance complete. I had met him a few times on scenes but so far had very little real face time with him.

I knocked on the frame of his open door. He looked up from his computer, peering at me over his glasses, then gave me a tight smile and waved me in.

"Hi, Kara, good to see you. I didn't think you'd be back so soon. You feeling all right?"

I nodded and sat in the chair in front of his desk. "Mostly bruises. I got lucky. Have state police found anything?"

He shook his head. "They collected some glass fragments at the scene, but it's a metal-grate bridge, so most of it probably went into the river. But I'll be sure to let you know if anything comes back. They're still trying to get the car out." He frowned. "Divers say it's a real mess."

I didn't say anything. They wouldn't believe any explanation I could give for the state of the car, so I figured it was safer not to offer any. And I didn't hold out a lot of hope for answers from the glass fragments. I already knew it was a blue Chevy pickup that had hit me, but in this area of rednecks and good old boys, that narrowed it down to, oh, say fifty thousand suspects, give or take ten thousand.

"Look, Kara," he said, leaning back in his chair and grimacing, "I hate to rag on you since you've just been through all that, but I got a call from Mandeville PD."

I winced. "Captain, I know I was out of line there. I'm sorry about that."

"Yeah, you were completely off base," he said with a scowl. "There's already a shitload of pressure to get this case closed, and now our only suspect in the Davis Sharp case is dead, by suicide, with a confession, right? So what's the damn issue? Let's get this case closed and get everyone off our backs."

"I'll tell you what the damn issue is, sir," I said, matching his scowl and forgetting to censor my words into a properly respectful tone. But I'd been through enough shit lately that I was pretty much beyond caring about tact and diplomacy. "Yes, Elena Sharp is dead, but she was never a strong suspect, and due to inconsistencies at the scene in Mandeville, I have *serious* doubts about whether or not she killed herself. To close the case now by naming her the killer is not only grossly unfair to both her and Davis Sharp, it will also allow whoever *did* kill them to go free."

He narrowed his eyes and made a *hmmf*ing sound. "Well...I can respect that. Do what you feel is right." Then he fixed me with a glare. "But if you ever act up like that on a scene again—especially with a cooperating agency—I'll suspend you so fast your goddamn little head will spin. Y'got me?"

I gave him the properly acquiescent nod he was expecting. "Yes, sir. It won't happen again." I knew I was damn lucky that he wasn't suspending me anyway.

He blew out his breath, once again reminding me of a bulldog. "One more thing. You've been recommended for an FBI task force dealing with white-collar crimes and other special circumstances." I thought for an instant he was going to roll his eyes, but he managed to restrain himself and limited it instead to merely a sour expression.

"Chief Turnham has already approved it. You'd be working with Special Agents Ryan Kristoff and Zachary Garner." He settled his glare onto me. "Don't think this will relieve you from having to take your share of cases in this jurisdiction, though."

"No, sir, of course not," I answered, caught more than a little off guard by the abrupt announcement of the recommendation. "Thank you for allowing me this opportunity."

He snorted. "Thank the chief, not me. I think it's bullshit." He shook his head, and I had to hide a smile at his stark honesty. "That's all." He waved a hand at me in dismissal, and I gladly took the opportunity to leave.

After departing my captain's office, I continued on out of the station. Technically, I was on medical leave for another day, which gave me a perfect opportunity to finally take care of the warding on Tessa's house and that damn portal. I headed to my aunt's house—stopping first at the Kwik-E Mart to buy Oreos and chocolate ice cream. The last twenty-four hours had been hell, and I needed all the chocolate and fat I could get my hands on right now.

I mentally reviewed the conversation with my captain as I drove. I definitely deserved the dressing-down I'd received over my behavior at Elena's condo, and even I could admit that the only reason that I hadn't been rewarded with unpaid days off was because of the accident. In that respect, I should probably be grateful to my attacker.

Of course, that was the only respect. I'd had to push my credit card dangerously close to its limit in order to replace my gun and holster as well as my phone, though I was holding out a ridiculous hope that the department insurance would cover some of it. Wouldn't *that* be a nice change of pace.

I climbed the steps of Tessa's house and did a quick othersight scan of the front-door area but didn't feel anything amiss this time. The aversions were still in place and apparently unaltered. I sighed and pushed in after unlocking the door, then headed to the kitchen and shoved the ice cream into the empty freezer. The piece of paper that had the names and lines and circles was still on the kitchen counter—our attempt to find some sort of connection between the murders. I folded the paper and stuffed it into my bag. After losing my notebook in the river, I knew I would need to start re-creating as much as I could remember.

I did a quick check of the library and the rest of the house, not sensing anything out of the ordinary, then locked the front door and headed upstairs to my aunt's summoning chamber. She had her chamber in her attic since there was no way in the world for her to have a basement where she lived. Basements in Louisiana were pretty damn rare, since the water table was so high. The only reason I was able to have one was because my house was situated on a hill. It was yet one more reason why I knew I would never sell that house.

Fortunately, the staircase to the attic was a real one and not a rickety pull-down ladder, since Tessa occasionally brought the demons she summoned down to her library. In theory, the attic could have been used as an additional bedroom, albeit a small one. I tugged the door open, making a face as a wave of warm air flowed over me. I flicked the air vent to the full open position, then stood in front of the vent for a few minutes as cooler air poured in.

Finally, when the temperature was bearable, I moved to the center of the room, pulling a piece of chalk out of my pocket. I sketched out a storage diagram, then sat back on my heels and channeled as much potency as I could scrape up into it—which wasn't much. But my idea was to continue to do this throughout the day—little bumps of potency that hopefully wouldn't wipe me out too much.

My plan for the rest of the day was to alternate between channeling potency, eating Oreos, and watching corny movies. Tessa had a huge number of DVDs, so after I came down from the attic, I settled myself in front of the TV and began to browse her collection. However, I quickly discovered that her taste in movies was similar to her taste in just about everything else—quirky, eccentric, eclectic. *The Killing Time. Metropolis. El Topo. The Heroic Trio. The Night of the Hunter. Jesus Christ Vampire Hunter. Dr. Horrible's Sing-Along Blog.* What the hell was that? I thumbed through, hand abruptly pausing on *Barbarians at the Gate.* I still hadn't looked at the video from the gate surveillance at Brian Roth's subdivision.

I retrieved the DVD from my bag and popped it into Tessa's player, then settled back with the Oreos and the remote. The screen was split into four sections—views from the main cameras at the entrance and the exit and then views from two lower cameras, designed to record the license plates of cars that came and went. The multiple cameras made viewing the video challenging, but after a few minutes I learned to ignore the license-plate views and focus on only the two main cameras. Good thing I had plenty of sugar in my system.

At the one-dozen-Oreos point, I saw a blue Prius exit the gates. I ran it back and checked the view that showed the license plate. Yep, that was Carol's; 6:30 p.m. Half an hour later on the video, I saw Brian's Ford F-150 enter. Well, that eliminated the outside possibility that Carol had killed Brian and then gone off to meet whomever she'd met, and it also helped clinch my theory that Brian hadn't been the one who killed her at the motel.

While my eyes glazed and my stomach protested the sheer number of Oreos that had been stuffed into it, I dutifully fast-forwarded through the next several hours of video, watching to see if the Prius returned or Brian's pickup left.

A flash of red caught my attention and I sat up, jamming my thumb down on the pause button. I slowly ran the video back, exhaling in astonishment as a familiar red Mercedes convertible came into view. "What the hell?"

I quickly checked the license plate view, then sighed. False alarm. Not Elena Sharp's after all.

But I kept the video paused on the view of the license plate. Frowning, I picked up my cell phone and dialed the Beaulac PD dispatcher.

"Detective Gillian here. Can you run a tag for me, please?"

After about a minute, I thanked the dispatcher and hung up. *Matching red Mercedes convertibles.* It wasn't Elena's car. It was her husband's.

I checked the time on the video: 11:30 p.m. I replayed the section several times, then ran it forward to find the point where the car exited the subdivision: 11:50 p.m.

I sat back, image of the red Mercedes frozen on Tessa's TV. I felt equally frozen. I'd wanted a connection between Brian Roth and Davis Sharp. Now I had it—but I still had to make sense out of it. Maybe Becky the Cardio Barbie was wrong, maybe it was Brian that Elena had been sleeping with, and not his father. *If so, maybe Davis found out that Brian and Elena were sleeping together, and went and killed Brian in revenge. That's fairly plausible.* But that didn't explain Carol's death.

I shook my head. I was getting ahead of myself. Just because Davis had been in that subdivision didn't mean he'd killed Brian. It didn't even mean he'd gone to Brian's house. *Stick with what you can determine for now,* I chided myself.

I hit the step button on the remote, taking the video forward one frame at a time. It was possible that it wasn't Davis driving the car.

No, a few frames later, the distinguished councilman was clearly visible in the driver's seat. *But there's someone with him,* I realized. Perhaps his wife? If he was confronting her lover, would he make her come along? Unfortunately, the angle of the camera made it impossible to see anything other than a dark shape in the passenger seat. I muttered several nasty words as I stepped the video back and forth, searching all views for any glimpse of the passenger. I knew it was a person because I could see movement, but that was the most information I could glean. I scowled. In the movies, the detective would simply take the video to the crime lab, and a high-tech computer would magically remove the glare and pixelation and windshield so that I could ID the passenger.

"Fucking real-world technology," I muttered.

29

DESPITE MY AWARENESS OF THE LIMITATIONS OF VIDEO
enhancement, I still intended to pass the DVD off to the
crime lab to see if anything at all could be done with it.
But in the meantime I had a summoning to prepare for, so
I returned to my original plan of channeling potency, eating junk food, and watching movies. By evening I had a
sugar high, the attic was pleasantly cool, and more important, my lovely little storage diagram had a day's potency
and was holding it perfectly. Moreover, I didn't feel overly
tired or drained. *Probably like the difference between
sprinting a mile and walking it with lots of rest stops.* I could
definitely get used to this.

I'd summoned in my aunt's chamber before but never
on my own. It felt strange to make my preparations and
sketch the diagram in here—almost as if I were trying on
her underwear. But I shoved my unease aside; I didn't
need distractions. I completed my usual preparations,
readied my implements, then stood at the edge of the diagram. Taking a deep breath, I pulled potency from the

storage diagram, relieved as the power flowed into my control with velvet ease—a thousand times easier than pulling it normally, even on a full moon. I quickly formed the protections and readied the bindings, giddily aware that I'd just increased my power as a summoner dramatically.

But right now I had to finish *this* summoning. I pulled the arcane power into place, forming the portal between the two worlds. I shaped it to the demon I desired, then finally spoke the name of the demon.

"Zhergalet."

Heartbeats later, a small squat creature that resembled a six-legged furry lizard crouched before me. Its body was only about three feet long, but it had a sinuous tail that was at least twice that length—though it was difficult to tell, since it never stayed still, winding and coiling constantly. It wore a bright green belt around its middle with small pouches hanging from it. Its pelt was a sleek dark blue that shimmered with a purplish iridescence, and its eyes were a brilliant gold, slitted just like a reptile's. I personally thought that the *faas* was absolutely gorgeous.

It snapped its head up and locked those gold eyes on me. "You summon in poor moon now not full you summon night need moon always full right?"

I hesitated half a heartbeat as I parsed the quick words and held the bindings carefully. Terms had not yet been negotiated, and I had to be careful not to give too much away yet. I gave a slow nod. "I normally summon on the full moon, yes."

Its tiny eyes darted around the chamber. "Tessa Pazhel before call me wards for me to make." I nodded again. That was why I'd called this particular demon. According to Kehlirik, this demon had placed all of the devastating wards in my aunt's house.

"I am Kara Gillian, the niece of Tessa Pazhel. I have summoned you here to serve me under terms that will honor us both."

It bared sharp teeth at me and cocked its head. It looked ferocious—and no doubt was—but I knew that the bared teeth were its own version of a smile. "Yes yes yes, offering you have?"

I picked up the canister of Café Du Monde coffee from the floor beside me, still keeping a firm mental grasp on the bindings. Nothing had been settled yet, and even a small creature like this could do considerable damage to my person. I'd shed enough blood already this year, thank you.

It gave a low warble and hopped forward. "Task you wish exchange for?"

I resisted the desire to squirm in embarrassment. "I require wards to be replaced throughout the house and in the library downstairs."

It blinked at me, then whipped its head around as if seeing its surroundings for the first time. It let out a low croon that was unmistakably sad. "Oohhhh . . . work gone. Pretty work all gone who make gone?"

I grimaced. "I, uh, summoned a *reyza* to remove the wards. I needed access to the house and library, and Tessa Pazhel is . . . indisposed."

To my surprise, the little demon straightened on its back four legs and puffed out its chest. "Yes yes! Take *reyza* to remove wards mine!" It hopped up and down, warbling. "Yes yes, agree to terms. Do work again. Pretty-work!"

Sheesh. I'd forgotten what a pain in the ass it was to listen to a *faas*. Sentence structure wasn't terribly important to them.

"Agreed," I said, and handed over the offering. The demon tucked it into one of the pouches at its belt, then waited for me to drop the bindings and protections.

I did so, then gestured toward the doorway, but it was already hopping in that direction. "I think the most important thing is to secure that portal in the library," I said as I followed it down the stairs.

It let out a horrified squawk and spun to face me, nearly causing me to lose my balance and tumble down the stairs. I grabbed at the railing as it glared at me. "Portal not *ward*?" it shrieked.

"Um, the *reyza* took down all the wards. I don't think he knew that the portal was there."

The demon bared its teeth, and this time there was no mistaking it for a smile. This was definitely an expression of menace, though I was fairly certain that it was not directed toward me. Fairly.

"*Reyza* know portal," it growled. "Feel it strong, know it. Uncovered to use or tell other use. Push through." It turned and bounded the rest of the way down the stairs and down the hall to the library before I could take a breath to ask it what the fuck it was talking about. I scurried after it, a not-good feeling settling into my gut.

I entered the library to see the demon crouching before the portal, spines on its back flared out and tipped with red. I stayed in the doorway. I'd never seen a *faas* that angry and upset before.

"What do you mean, push through? There were some creatures here earlier—"

It spun to face me. "Creatures kind? What like?"

"They were small"—I held my hands up, about six inches apart—"with wings and a stinger."

Zhergalet snorted. "*Hriss*. Pest. Came through self. Pushed not. Eat scrap feelings."

I pinched the bridge of my nose, feeling as if I was continually several steps behind the demon's thought processes. "Scrap feelings?"

It fluttered its hands. "Potency. Excess sucks up. Tired you become is all. Pest to swat. Worry little about *hriss*. Worry more if pushed big through portal."

I licked my lips. "You...would worry if something big was pushed through? How big? And pushed from where?"

"Big like me not me though. Demon push hard to do. Lower creature push not so hard."

"Big like...a dog?"

It cocked its head. "Dog what is?"

I held my hand a couple of feet off the ground to show the height. "Black, four legs, long face, mouth full of teeth, tail..." Okay, that could describe half the taxonomy of earth, but apparently the little demon understood my description. It hissed and shook its head.

"Bad bad. *Kzak*. Not come self through. Push only."

I was starting to get a headache from trying to understand it. "Okay, it's called a *kzak*. And it was pushed through. Why? From where?"

Zhergalet wagged its head. "*Kzak* sent damage cause. Hurt and kill. One dangerous some. Pack dangerous very."

"Wait. They're sent...to a specific target? Like an assassin?"

It nodded, hopping up and down. "Yes yes!"

A shiver of cold ran down my back. The dog thing had been sent. After me? Or after Ryan? "Kehlirik would definitely have known the portal was there?"

"*Reyza* know he would. Valuable knowledge. Take back status gain."

I scowled, feeling oddly betrayed even though I knew it was stupid to feel that way. Kehlirik had done precisely what I'd asked him to do—remove the wards. In the process he'd discovered the portal, and when he returned to the demon world he'd either used that information or sold it to the demon equivalent of the highest bidder. Then the portal had been used to send a *kzak* after... someone.

I wanted to sit down and hug my knees to my chest, but that wasn't a luxury I could afford at the moment. It had to be after Ryan. Had to be. Kehlirik didn't like Ryan, and maybe there were others who felt the same way. Besides, who in the demon realm could possibly want to hurt *me*? Rhyzkahl? I couldn't fathom any reason he would do so, especially since he'd stated often enough that he didn't want me to risk myself.

But what about some other demonic lord—one who knew that Rhyzkahl was trying to wear me down to get me to commit to being his summoner? Taking me out would cut Rhyzkahl off from this opportunity.

I gave in and slid down the wall and hugged my knees to my chest. Zhergalet merely continued to hop in place. "I do portal first. Cannot seal one day in. Take much time and many summonings to secure. But make pushes harder can do."

"Good, yeah." I waved a hand. "Do what you can. Make it hard for whoever it is to push shit through."

The little demon warbled and turned to its work. I knew that I should watch and see what I could learn about warding from the creature, but I was in serious need of comfort at the moment, and there was a pint of chocolate ice cream in my aunt's freezer calling my name.

30

I FINISHED THE ICE CREAM AND FELT A LITTLE BETTER—
and fatter—then distracted myself by going back to the
attic. The storage diagram I'd used for Zhergalet's summoning was intact and still had plenty of potency. Summoning the little demon hadn't taken much power at all,
and it didn't take long for me to channel enough to replace what I'd used, plus extra.

By the time Zhergalet had finished replacing the first
layer of protections on the portal and the house and had
been dismissed back to its own sphere, it was three a.m.
and I was fighting to stay awake. I had the unerring feeling
that the demon wasn't pleased to be redoing its work, and
I was also more than a bit dismayed to discover just how
much work it had been. My aunt had summoned the
demon four times to get what were considered adequate
protections in place. That had been near the end of last
year. However, Zhergalet revealed that she had summoned
it again a few months ago—shortly after my first encounter

with Rhyzkahl—and had asked it to beef up the protections considerably.

I sighed. I didn't have the energy to get upset about any of that right now.

I looked around the library. The current wards weren't much more effective than what I'd placed, though they were a damn sight higher quality. However, I'd learned that these were the arcane version of a base coat and were vitally necessary for creating strong protections, or so Zhergalet had stated. Repeatedly. Tomorrow—er, tonight I would summon the demon again and it could start building decent protections.

I'd also received a rambling and difficult-to-follow lecture in security, which was a sharp scolding at times, one that made me think hard about the security—or complete lack thereof—at my own house. *Okay, so I've been doing the equivalent of going shopping while leaving my bags on the front seat and my car unlocked.* Tessa had spoken of the need for security, but I'd never really taken it seriously. After all, I lived way out in the middle of nowhere and I was a cop.

In other words, after Zhergalet finishes Tessa's house, I have to get the demon to do mine.

But first, sleep.

MY CELL PHONE rang a few seconds after I curled up on the couch. At least it felt that way. But somehow, when I was able to blearily focus on the screen, it insisted that the time was one p.m.

"Kara Gillian here."

"You're not at the station. You're not at your house. You're not resting. You're pushing yourself too hard—"

"Shut up, Ryan," I growled. "You just woke me up, so piss off."

He chuckled. "Well, since you're not at your house, you must be at your aunt's."

"You really are too smart to be a fed. By the way, when were you going to tell me that I was on an FBI task force?"

"As soon as I got word that it had been approved. I'm assuming it's been approved since you're telling me about it."

"I guess so. My captain doesn't seem real happy about it, but he can kiss my ass."

He laughed. "Ah, I see you're in a pleasant mood today. Can I buy you lunch? Or, in your case, I suppose it would be breakfast?"

"I changed my mind. If you have to ask that, you're definitely *not* too smart to be a fed."

"Smart-ass. Meet me at the Lake o' Butter in half an hour?"

"Pick me up. My car's a piece of total shit."

"Your own damn fault for driving your other one into a river."

I growled something rude and hung up, but I was smiling.

I JUMPED INTO the shower and allowed the hot water to blast me for a blissful two minutes before I reluctantly shut it off. I toweled dry quickly and was just pulling on clean clothes when I heard Ryan's car in the driveway. Running my fingers through my wet hair, I headed to the door and opened it to see Ryan standing at the edge of the driveway with a slight frown creasing his forehead. "Is something different?"

"Yeah. Come on in while I find my shoes. I had the wards redone. At least partially."

He nodded, frown disappearing as he climbed the stairs. "Had them done? You summoned?"

"Yep." I shut the door behind him and headed to the bedroom. "Same demon my aunt used. They're not finished, though. It's gonna take a few go-rounds to get it done right, but it's still better than the crap I'd put up." I fished my shoes out from beneath the bed. "So please tell me that this task force is not really a white-collar-crimes task force, because I like you, but that financial shit bores me senseless."

Ryan laughed. "Well, I'm glad that the name of the task force is boring, because that's the point. Yes, we do our share of mundane investigations, but we also get called to anything 'not quite right.' I will admit that your background in White Collar did help with the approval on our end. Anyway, it's not a full-time gig, but now that we've pushed the various approvals through, it'll be easier to bring you on board for some of our unusual cases."

"All right, I can deal with that. Being on a task force sounded cool, but I didn't want to be pulled out of Violent Crimes entirely."

His eyes crinkled in amusement. "I'm so glad we could accommodate you. Now, hurry up and get your shoes on. Zack's holding a table for us."

ZACK WAS IN fact holding a table for us, but at nearly one-thirty in the afternoon it didn't much matter, since he was the only person in the place. "I hear that Ryan's convinced you to come to the dark side," he said with a teasing grin as I sat.

"Only occasionally," I corrected. "I'm not sure that y'all could handle my darkness full-time."

Zack snorted. "Some things are best left to the unknown. So, anything new going on?"

"Actually, yes." I leaned forward and lowered my voice, even though there wasn't anyone else nearby. "I summoned last night to get the wards at my aunt's house redone and found out some things in the process about that portal."

The two agents leaned forward in unison. "Spill," Ryan commanded.

"Well, first off, it looks like the *reyza* that I summoned to remove all the wards knew darn good and well that the portal was there. He would have realized it the second he made it into the library."

Ryan grimaced. "And he took that info back and either used it or sold it, right?"

"Most likely." I sighed. "I want to be pissed, but he didn't betray *me*. I mean, that's how their honor works. He did precisely what I asked him to do." I *was* still pissed, but I knew it wasn't going to do me any good, so I was trying to ignore it. "Anyway, that's just the beginning. Apparently it's some sort of connection between the spheres, but not one that large or higher-sentience creatures can get through. However, other creatures can be 'pushed' through from the other side."

"Like the psycho pixies?"

"No, those are some sort of pest and can make their way through on their own if the portal is open. Which, of course, it was. I was referring to something bigger. With teeth. And claws."

"The dog-thing," Zack breathed, sitting back.

I met his eyes and nodded. "It's called a *kzak*. And

Zhergalet seemed to think that it had been pushed through when the wards were down."

A series of expressions rippled over Zack's face, too quickly for me to get any sense of what he was thinking. I glanced at Ryan, but his expression was nothing but stony, brow lowered in a frown. "So the question is," Ryan finally said, "who or what pushed it through, and why."

The waitress came up at that point, and we paused our conversation long enough to order ridiculous amounts of unhealthy food.

"It went from that portal to the Ice House," I pointed out after the waitress had poured coffee and bustled off with our order. "Carl said that he'd fixed a broken window, so I'm guessing that it came through and busted out of the house. I think it's safe to assume that it was specifically sent after one of us." I paused, waiting to see if either of them would react or respond. Especially Ryan. Yet the baffled expression remained on his face. I looked at Zack. He didn't look baffled, at least, just quietly thoughtful. "Unless you think that the *busboy* was somehow the target of an arcane attack?" I said. I could feel myself getting frustrated and snarky, and I fought to control it.

After a couple of seconds with neither of them saying anything, I took a deep breath and continued. "It's . . . possible that it was after me. Rhyzkahl has asked me to be his summoner, which would increase his status and power. If an opposing lord wanted to thwart that, then the easiest way to do it would be to remove me." I shrugged lightly, though I sure as hell didn't feel in a light shrug kinda mood. I glanced at Ryan, nearly daring him to react negatively to the reminder that Rhyzkahl wanted me as his summoner, but he didn't react at all.

"Or it could be after me," Ryan said, voice low and

rough. "For whatever reason..." He trailed off, then lifted his eyes to mine. "Kara, I swear I'm not holding anything back from you. I honestly don't know."

I gave a short nod. Oddly, I believed him. I turned to Zack. "What about you?"

Zack blinked. "I wasn't there when it first attacked. It couldn't have been after me."

I narrowed my eyes. "No, but you sure as hell knew what Ryan was doing afterward."

A pained expression flickered on his face as he shook his head. "Only because I've seen him do it before, after other...odd encounters. We've worked together for several years now. There've been quite a few of those."

I sighed and slumped back in the chair. "Well, the portal should be sealed enough so that no more of them can be pushed through."

The waitress came back, sliding pancake-laden plates in front of each of us. Once again the conversation was suspended, this time because we were all too busy stuffing our faces.

"What about the psycho pixies?" Zack asked after a moment. "Those came through on their own?"

"Apparently so. They're called *hriss*, and I get the feeling they're like psychic arcane mosquitoes. Make you tired. Just one won't kill you, but a bunch of them could suck you pretty dry of potency."

Ryan's expression darkened. "Wait. Do they eat potency? Or life force?"

I opened my mouth, then shut it, mentally replaying Zhergalet's difficult-to-follow explanation. "You know, I think the demon *was* referring to essence."

"Maybe a herd of them is loose and sucking people dry?"

I pondered it, then shook my head. "No, that wouldn't explain the . . . rending. Plus, the *faas* seemed to think they were more annoying than anything." Then I frowned, an unpleasant thought occurring to me. "But I've learned that an essence-eater could become stronger by consuming another essence-eater . . ." I decided to leave out how I'd learned that.

"We were talking the other day about how the killer has changed," Ryan said. "First he was killing them and then sucking their essence up, and now he can kill them *by* ripping the essence out. Something changed."

My stomach spasmed painfully, and it wasn't because of too many pancakes. "You think that the killer got into my aunt's house, found the portal, and somehow got his soul-eating ability beefed up?"

He shrugged. "I'm just offering up a maybe."

I shoved my fingers through my hair. "Shit. I'll ask Zhergalet tonight." I opened my bag and pulled out the scrawled page with names and lines and circles. "In the meantime, I keep looking at how these murders are connected."

Zack peered at the page. "Looks like you have a lot of possibles and not a lot of probables."

"Yeah," I said with a sigh. "Tell me about it." I was beginning a deep and morose pondering of the situation when my cell phone rang. "Detective Gillian."

"Hi, Kara," a perky voice chirped. "This is Annie at the lab in Slidell."

It took me a couple of seconds to figure out what lab she was talking about. "Oh, oh, right, the DNA lab! Sorry. What's up?"

"I just wanted to give you a heads-up about your

request. I'll be writing my official report, but I figured you'd want to know that there was no match."

It took me a few more seconds to process that. "Wait, which case are we talking about?"

I could hear her shuffling paper. "Um, Carol Roth, homicide. And we had a reference sample for Brian Roth."

I felt like my thoughts were moving at half speed. "No match. So she did *not* have sex with Brian before she was killed?"

"Well, I can't tell you if there was penetration or not. Dr. Lanza would have to be the one to determine that. There wasn't any seminal fluid, so if she did, her partner was likely wearing a condom. But we tested some pubic hair that had been collected and the saliva that was swabbed. The pubic hair had a root, so we were able to do a comparison. It matched the saliva but didn't match your reference."

At least I'd been right about that much. *Brian was murdered to protect whoever Carol was having sex with.* Didn't help me much, though, except to confirm what I suspected.

I almost missed what Annie said next.

"Wait, back up," I said. "What?"

"I said that it was close. It wasn't a match, but it was pretty darn close."

"What does that mean?" My pulse quickened. I remembered just enough about DNA from college biology that I had a feeling I knew what it meant, but I wanted her to say it.

"Well, it's highly possible it was someone related to your boy."

I could almost feel my mouth hanging open. I wanted

connections, and here was a whopper of one. I said something that may or may not have been articulate, then closed my phone, gripping it tightly. A rictus of a grin stretched across my face as I felt the pieces click into place.

"Good news?" Ryan prompted.

"In a roundabout way. The DNA on Carol Roth didn't match Brian's."

He frowned. "And how is this good?"

"It was a partial match. There's a good chance it was someone related to him."

"Looks like Daddy Roth has been a bad boy," Zack murmured with a smile.

"*He* killed Carol," I said. "It may have been an accident, but he killed her."

Ryan held up a hand. "But do you think he was capable of killing his son? I know it's tough to know what goes on behind closed doors, but it sure seems like the two of them were close."

I lifted an eyebrow. "He wasn't so close that he had a problem screwing his son's wife." Excitement coiled within me as possibilities fell in line. "Plus, the surveillance video from Brian Roth's subdivision shows Davis Sharp's car entering at about eleven-thirty that night and leaving about twenty minutes later. There was someone with him too. What if it was Harris Roth? What if Harris panicked after he realized Carol was dead and called his buddy—who also happened to be his biggest political supporter?"

Ryan looked disbelieving. "I'm still having a hard time buying that Harris would be willing to murder his own son—or have him murdered—to cover this up. Screwing your daughter-in-law is one thing, but Roth looked pretty devastated at the funeral. I'm not sure he could have faked that."

I took a deep breath and forced myself to consider another possibility. "But what if Elena wasn't having an affair with Harris Roth? What if it was Brian instead? Then perhaps Davis killed Brian for screwing his wife?"

Zack raised an eyebrow. "A crime of passion . . . where he kept his cool enough to go ahead and stage it as a suicide to cover up Carol's murder?"

I grimaced. "Yeah, you're right. It doesn't fit. And Elena was attracted to 'powerful men.' Brian didn't really fit that bill." I dropped my eyes to the paper. "Harris Roth is the connection to all of them. I still think Davis Sharp was somehow involved in Brian's murder, but it doesn't make sense yet." Perhaps this was why Elena had been so afraid? Maybe she'd known who killed Brian. "But at least now we have something solid to work with," I continued. I looked at Ryan. "I figure we can get a warrant for a DNA sample to run a proper comparison, plus a subpoena for Harris Roth's cell-phone records."

"With the partial DNA match, I'd say you're right."

I nodded. I wanted badly to nail Harris Roth for everything—tie all of the murders up into one nice and neat case—but we didn't have enough proof yet. "I'll start typing," I said. *First, nail him on Carol's death. Then make him squeal on the rest.*

31

THE SUBPOENA FOR THE PHONE RECORDS AND THE warrant to request a buccal swab from Harris Roth didn't take long to type up, but it took me nearly as long to figure out what I was going to say to my sergeant. I dialed his number as I paced Tessa's sitting room, grimacing when Crawford answered on the second ring. This would have been a lot easier to do on his voice mail. *But it wouldn't have been the best,* my conscience reminded me.

"Sarge, it's Kara Gillian."

"What's up?"

I quickly explained the DNA results and my theory. Crawford gave a low whistle when I finished. "Damn, Kara. You sure don't think small, do you?"

I grimaced. "I know. But you gotta admit it makes sense."

"I can see where you're going with it, yes." He paused. "Kara, I hate to point this out, but the Carol Roth murder isn't your case anymore."

I could feel myself stiffening. "Sarge, I know, but the detail with the surveillance video and the—"

Crawford cut me off with a sharp laugh. "Don't sweat that shit. Fuck Pellini and Boudreaux. Lazy, useless fucks. I'll take care of any heat that comes down about you horning in on the case. Especially since it started out as yours. Easy enough to deal with."

I let my breath out, relieved. "Thanks, Cory."

"But, Kara," he continued, "if you're wrong about this, you're killing your career. Even a buccal-swab warrant is going to be a big slap in the face for a public figure of that stature. I'm not gonna tell you not to go ahead with this, but I want to be sure that *you're* sure."

"I'm sure," I said, trying to fill my voice with as much confidence as possible.

I heard him sigh gustily. "All right. I can meet you in about half an hour at—"

"Sarge," I interrupted him. "I...think it would be better if you, um, didn't come." I cringed at how that came out. But there was no easy way to put it. If Harris Roth could kill by ripping essence out, I didn't want to risk having someone there who had no way to defend himself or even know if he was in danger.

"I'm your sergeant, Detective Gillian," he reminded me, tone distinctly frosty.

I framed my words carefully. "Sarge, you once said that you'd seen a lot of shit in your career, and you were probably more willing than most to believe that some things defy explanation."

He was silent for several heartbeats. "And...this is one of those things that defy explanation?" I could hear the disbelief in his voice, but I thought I could also sense the barest edge of acceptance.

"It is, Sarge. I . . . I just need you to trust me." I rolled my eyes at myself. Holy crap, but that sounded lame, even to me. "Look," I said quickly before he could say anything else, "when all of this is over, I promise I'll give you as much explanation as you want." *If you really want it,* I thought. *And if everything works out.*

He fell silent again, but I could hear background noise, so I knew we hadn't been disconnected. "Is Agent Kristoff going with you?" he said finally.

My shoulders sagged in relief. "Yes, he is."

I heard him sigh again. "Fine. Keep me posted. I'll cover as well as I can if there are any questions."

He was hanging his own ass on the line for me as well, I knew. "Thanks, Sarge." I didn't add anything trite like *I won't let you down* or *you won't regret it.* There was too good a chance that either or both could happen.

"Be careful, Kara."

"I will."

I hung up, then clipped the phone back onto my belt, finding myself actually admiring Cory Crawford.

I JOGGED UP the steps of the courthouse while Ryan circled the block to avoid the trouble of finding a parking place. We'd left my car at my aunt's house. It was such a piece of crap that I was willing to use any excuse to get out of having to drive it. I flashed my badge at the security guard as I passed through the metal detector, ignoring the obnoxious beep. I glanced quickly at the schedule taped to the desk, pleased and relieved to see that the duty judge was again Judge Laurent. I'd experienced several moments of worry on the way over to the courthouse, running through improbable and not-so-improbable scenarios about judges refusing to sign the warrant for a fellow judge. I didn't think I'd have any problems with Judge Laurent.

His secretary was shutting her computer down as I entered the office. She looked up at me with an expression that clearly told me she wouldn't be happy with me if I made her stay past her usual quitting time.

I gave her my best winning smile. "I'm sorry to come in so late, but this should take only a second. Is Judge Laurent still here? I need a warrant for a buccal swab and a subpoena for phone records signed."

She sighed. "He's still here." She held out her hand for my folder.

"I really appreciate it," I said with what I hoped was enough fervor.

She just gave a brisk nod as she passed through the doors leading to the judge's office. A few minutes later she returned without the folder. "You can go on back," she said, holding the door open for me.

I nodded thanks as I passed by her. The look she gave me in return was narrow-eyed and measuring—no longer the bored resignation. *She must have glanced at it,* I realized. Oh, well. In less than an hour, everyone would know.

Judge Laurent didn't look worried or upset. He looked positively gleeful as I stepped into his office and shut the door behind me. "So, you're gonna nail that randy horndog to the wall for boffing his son's wife to death?" He cackled as he signed the warrant and subpoena in an overly large script, as if to be sure that no one could be mistaken about who had signed it.

"Well, sir, I don't have anything solid yet. That's why I need this DNA sample."

"Ha! You'll get it. That sonofabitch has nailed or tried

to nail every pretty girl in this city. Can't believe his wife puts up with it." He shook his head as he handed the folder back to me with the signed warrant. "Maybe she figures being married to a judge is worth dealing with all the women."

I accepted the folder from him, bemused. "I appreciate your time, sir. I'm hoping this works out the way I think it will."

He gave me a wide grin. "You just be sure to come back to me when you need the arrest warrant signed."

I couldn't help but chuckle. "Absolutely, sir."

I was still smiling as I let myself out, unsurprised to find that his secretary had left already. I pulled my cell phone out and dialed Ryan's number as I exited the courthouse.

"I have it," I said when he answered.

"I'm right around the corner. I'll pick you up in half a minute."

JUDGE HARRIS ROTH lived in Ruby Estates, about half a mile down the road from the Sharps. *Just a short walk for the judge to get some action,* I thought sourly as we drove past the sweeping staircase and ostentatious landscaping of the Sharp residence. Roth's house wasn't on the lakefront like Davis Sharp's, but he had a double lot that was still mostly woods in the back half. The house itself was large but didn't have the feel of plantation-wannabe that Sharp's did. The Roth house reminded me of an English country home—a two-story structure with stone exterior. I could see myself living in a place like this—lovely, tranquil, and quiet.

But not so tranquil right now. An ambulance with

lights flashing was just pulling out of the long driveway as we approached. Ryan and I exchanged a troubled look.

"Bad feeling," he stated.

"Ditto," I replied.

My bad feeling wasn't helped by the sight of another ambulance by the house.

"*Very* bad feeling," I said.

Ryan parked out of the way of the ambulance. We got out and jogged up the broad front steps. I had the strong impression I wasn't going to need the buccal swab warrant after all.

The door was wide open, so we walked right in. Inside, we could see paramedics clustered around a supine figure. A blond woman I didn't recognize stood off to the side, wringing her hands.

It was Harris Roth on the floor. Quite dead too, though I doubted that the paramedics had accepted the fact yet. But I could feel it.

"He's not the one," I said to Ryan in a low, rough voice. "Not unless he ripped his own essence out."

Ryan swore under his breath. I forced myself to step closer to the body so that I could approach the woman. "Ma'am? I'm Detective Gillian with Beaulac PD. Can you please tell me who you are and what's going on?"

The woman gulped and gave me a jerky nod. "I'm Connie Cavendish. I live across the street," she gestured with a fluttering hand in a direction toward the front door, "and I'm friends with Rachel. We sometimes walk together. Oh, my God, is he going to be okay?"

"The paramedics are working on him. He's going to be fine," I lied. I took her gently by the arm and steered her in the direction I figured the kitchen to be. Fortunately I'd guessed correctly, and a few seconds later I directed her into a chair at the kitchen table. "Ms. Cavendish, can you tell me what happened?"

Connie Cavendish twisted her hands together. "They... Rachel and Harris had a big fight. It's been so hard for them ever since Brian killed his wife and himself." She gulped and her eyes grew wide. "I mean, that's what everyone thought happened."

I fought the urge to shake her. "Yes, ma'am. What happened *here*? Where is Rachel Roth now?"

Connie took a shuddering breath. "I was in my house and I heard someone screaming. I looked out my door and Rachel was in the front yard, totally hysterical. So I ran to see what was wrong." She rubbed her arms, eyes still wide. "I couldn't understand her at first. Then finally I got that someone had called Harris to tell him that the police were on their way, about Carol." She paused to give Ryan and me an almost-accusing stare. I returned the look with a steely-eyed one of my own, and she dropped her gaze back to her hands in her lap. "Rachel heard it, heard the conversation. She said she and Harris got into a fight." Connie's lip quivered. "Rachel kept saying, 'He killed his own son to protect himself, he killed her and killed his son.'" Her shoulders shook, and she looked up at me with tears in her eyes. "What kind of monster would kill his own son?"

I was beginning to suspect what kind of monster, and I was fairly positive that it wasn't Harris Roth. "Where is Rachel now?"

"Oh, God. She was shrieking about him killing his son, then said that he'd collapsed, so I ran to the house and saw that he was on the floor. I... I guess he had a heart attack during the argument. I called 911. Poor Rachel was so hysterical. Full-blown panic attack. I didn't have any of my

Xanax with me, and I couldn't find any in her bathroom here." The woman looked utterly appalled and baffled that anyone *wouldn't* have a ready supply of Xanax in their house. "So I called 911 again and told them that they needed to send another ambulance. They left a few minutes ago with her."

I turned and hurried to the living room. Ryan stood beyond the kitchen, arms folded across his chest and a dark expression on his face. "It's Rachel?"

"Has to be. Hang on a sec." I moved over to where Harris lay on the floor. The paramedics had ceased their efforts to revive him, so I didn't feel too bad about pushing in and crouching by the body. I ignored the startled looks as I quickly rummaged through the dead man's pockets.

My hand closed on what I was looking for. "I'm with the PD. I'm just borrowing this," I explained to the staring paramedics, then I sprang to my feet and returned to Ryan. I jerked my head toward the front door, and together we ran back to his car. "Harris didn't kill his own son. *She* killed Brian, cleaning up her husband's mess after he screwed up and accidentally killed his girlfriend."

Ryan made a face. "He really was fucking his son's wife?"

I snorted. "From what I hear, he was fucking anything in a skirt." Another realization hit me. "Crap, including Laurent's secretary, I betcha."

Ryan gave me a questioning look as we climbed into his car.

"I know Laurent wouldn't have called and warned Roth. He hates him. Thought he was dirty and a lecherous slimeball."

"Sounds like a good judge of character."

"No kidding! And I know that my sergeant wouldn't

have called him, so the only other person who knew was Laurent's secretary. Who happens to be young, pretty, and ambitious."

Ryan glanced at the cell phone I'd retrieved from Harris's pocket. "Taking up thieving, are we?"

I shrugged and started scrolling through the call history. "A return on a subpoena for cell-phone records could take weeks. We don't have that much time."

"Then I heartily approve of your larceny. I take it we're heading to the hospital now?" he asked as he pulled out onto the road.

I nodded. "Yeah. But if Rachel Roth really had a panic attack, I'll eat my badge."

"It made an easy escape for her."

I tapped my fingers against my leg. "I wonder if she thinks she's in the clear now?" I looked over at Ryan. "We don't have a damn thing on her."

Ryan grimaced. "The DNA is going to show that Harris slept with Carol and, yes, he probably did accidentally kill her during rough sex." He shook his head. "It must have taken balls to call his wife and tell her what he'd done."

"Maybe it wasn't the first time she had to clean up after him." I fell silent as I continued to scroll through the swiped cell phone. We neared the front gate, and the sweeping staircase of Davis Sharp's house came into view just as I reached the records for the pertinent date. "He didn't!" I exclaimed, feeling a huge piece of the puzzle snap into place.

Ryan frowned at me. "What?"

I laughed. "Harris *didn't* have the balls to call his wife. My first theory was right—partly. He called Davis Sharp." I held up the phone in triumph. "But Davis must not have been alone."

Ryan's eyes narrowed. "Keep going."

"The Cardio Barbie was right. Elena and Harris were having an affair, and Davis found out and kicked her ass out." I took a breath to get my thoughts organized. Now everything was beginning to make sense. "The maid described the woman with Davis as having light hair. I assumed she meant blond, but now I think she meant highlighted—that brown/blond/ash look that Rachel has. So after Davis kicked Elena out, he then called Rachel up and told her about the affair..."

Ryan gave a snort of amusement. "Ah, the good old revenge fuck."

I grinned. "Exactly. And while they were busy revenge fucking, Harris was busy accidentally killing his daughter-in-law." I tapped the cell phone. "He calls Davis in a panic—"

"—and Rachel overhears and knows she needs to clean this mess up."

"Right," I said. "Rachel's smart and tough. She had no intention of divorcing Harris. She'd probably always put up with his affairs because she wanted the power and prestige of being married to a judge. It's been damn good for her business, that's for sure, and I'd bet anything that she was working up to running for judge herself fairly soon. If Harris went down for homicide—even negligent—it would drag her down as well."

"Tough bitch," Ryan commented.

"No shit! So Rachel had Davis drive her over to Brian's house." I paused, trying to fit it all together.

His frown returned. "She convinced Davis to kill Brian?"

I shook my head. "I still think Rachel did it. I don't

think Davis would have supported his buddy to that extent—especially after he'd found out about Harris and Elena. And it would have been easy for dear stepmom Rachel to get close enough to Brian to shoot him and make it look like a suicide." More pieces started to fall into place. "In fact, I don't think Davis had any idea that Rachel killed Brian until the next day, when it hit the news."

Ryan's mouth twisted. "At which time he proceeded to freak the fuck out."

"Exactly. He confronted Rachel about it and ended up dead. But before that, I think Davis called Elena and told her what happened. It's the only thing that would explain Elena's panic. And I'll bet you anything that if we check Davis's phone records, we can confirm it."

Ryan shook his head as he pulled onto the highway. "So why didn't Elena spill what she knew to the police? It would have saved her from being a suspect in her husband's murder."

I thought for a few seconds. "Elena was never a strong suspect, and she knew it. At first she was afraid that Rachel might have known that Davis had spilled the beans to her, but after I paid Elena a visit, I bet she realized that it would take only one phone call from her to finish Rachel off..."

"More blackmail," Ryan stated.

I gave a nod. "Yeah, that's what I think too. But I bet it wasn't for money."

Ryan flicked a questioning glance my way. I gave him a thin smile in return. "Elena Sharp *loved* being a society wife," I explained. "With Rachel's cooperation and assistance, Elena could return to Beaulac and play the tragic widow—"

"—and remarry as soon as she found a new sugar daddy."

Streets whizzed by as Ryan drove, a frown wrinkling his forehead. "So what is Rachel going to do now? We don't have any evidence to prove she killed Brian, so it's going to be assumed that Davis did it."

"Yeah, but you're forgetting one important detail."

He cocked an eyebrow at me.

"I'm a tenacious, stubborn bitch," I said. "We *can* prove that Harris killed Carol. Easy. DNA. I'll get the phone records to prove that Harris called Davis. And I'll find a way to prove that Rachel was in the car with Davis if I have to track down every piece of surveillance video in this city. And I'll grovel and apologize to Detective Fourcade in Mandeville and work with him to pin Elena's death on Rachel as well—surveillance, trace evidence in the condo, whatever it takes."

Ryan's expression turned grim. "She's going to know that we're figuring it out and that she can't walk away from all of this. It's blowing up in her face."

"Shit. It all makes sense now. Rachel did pro bono work at the neuro center and nursing homes, not out of the kindness of her heart but—"

"—to be near people whose essences she could slurp up," Ryan finished for me.

"And when she killed Brian, she couldn't pass up that juicy essence—"

"—and then she ran into one of those psycho pixies and got a lot stronger."

"Yes," I replied, "and stop finishing my sentences. It's starting to—"

"—get annoying?" His eyes flashed with humor.

"Smart-ass. She must have wondered why Tessa didn't have any essence, so she came to the house and she ran into a psycho pixie." I sobered quickly. If I hadn't taken all the wards down, she'd never have been able to get in. "And this means that she doesn't need any weapons to kill." A horrible thought struck me. "Oh, fuck. The ambulance—"

Ryan was dialing his cell phone before I could even finish the sentence. I listened, nerves on edge while he told the dispatcher that he needed a bolo—a be-on-the-lookout alert—on the subject that the ambulance had transported from Judge Roth's house, explaining that Rachel Roth was a murder suspect and considered to be extremely dangerous. I watched his face as he listened, seeing his eyes narrow.

Finally he hung up. "They can't raise the ambulance."

They're dead. A spasm of guilt twisted through me. I'd been too focused on Harris; I'd avoided seeing anything that could have allowed me to stop Rachel sooner.

"It's not your fault," Ryan cut into my thoughts.

"That's up for debate," I countered, worrying my lower lip. I could see the hospital a couple of blocks ahead. "Wait! Stop!" I pointed to a parking lot across from the hospital, where I could see an ambulance parked crookedly.

Ryan whipped the car over, somehow managing not to get clipped by the sedan behind him. He bounced over the curb and screeched to a stop beside the ambulance.

"You check the back!" I ordered. I jumped out of the car and ran around to the front of the ambulance, gut tightening as I saw the driver slumped in her seat belt. "Shit," I breathed, looking with sick dread at the dark-haired young woman and her open, staring brown eyes. I didn't need to check for a pulse. I could feel what had happened.

I stepped back as Ryan closed the back of the ambulance, face grim. *It was too easy for her. One was in the back with her, and then she reached through to the cab for the other one.* I was distantly aware that Ryan was on his cell phone again, calling it in to the dispatcher, but my attention was suddenly focused elsewhere as I realized where we were.

We were in front of the neuro center.

32

I STARTED TOWARD THE DOOR, BUT RYAN GRABBED MY arm to stop me. "Wait," he said. I looked back at him, a little surprised by the force in his grip. It wasn't painful, but it was solid, and it was pretty damn obvious that he wasn't going to let me go until he could say whatever he needed to say.

"Don't put me through thinking you're dead again," he said, voice low and just as strong as the grip on my arm.

I almost came back with something flippant—a smart-ass remark to lighten the mood—but the look in his eyes stilled that line of thought. I suddenly realized how terrible the aftermath of my death must have been for him. He'd seen me eviscerated, my chest and stomach sliced open by the claws of a demon. He'd watched me bleed out onto the white tile floor, and there'd been no reason to believe that he would ever see me alive again. And for nearly two weeks he had lived with the *knowledge* that I was dead.

I could see the naked emotion in his face. For this one instant he'd dropped his careful guard, letting me see that he *couldn't* lose me again, that he wouldn't be able to survive it a second time.

But as a friend losing a friend or as something more? I wished I could tell.

"I won't," I replied quietly. "I promise."

The tension in his eyes eased, even though we both knew that there was no way to ensure that such a promise would be kept. But I knew that it was more than that. He wanted me to promise that I wouldn't make the self-sacrifice that I'd been willing to make before.

I put my hand over his and squeezed briefly. "This bitch is going down. *That* I can promise."

He smiled, but I could see the flicker of unease in it. He knew I hadn't given him the promise he wanted, but at the same time he knew that it wasn't a promise I could give. Rachel wasn't as big a baddie as a demonic lord under the control of the Symbol Man, but I still had to stop her.

But he didn't say anything, just released my arm. There was an insane part of me that wanted to grab him and hold him and tell him what he wanted to hear, but there was no time and I had no idea what could be said.

We ran up to the front door together. I flashed my badge at the surprised receptionist without stopping or breaking stride, then bypassed the elevator for the stairs. I wanted to take the stairs two at a time, but I really wasn't in the best shape for advanced stair-running, plus my legs were a bit too short to make that anything other than agonizing. Luckily, my aunt was only on the third floor, so I didn't lose too much time. Ryan, the bastard, *did* take them two at a time, and then gave me what was clearly a smug grin when he reached the landing several seconds before I did.

I would have said something obnoxious to him, but

getting oxygen to my tortured lungs seemed a bit more important. I merely scowled and gasped for breath as I kept moving down the hall to my aunt's room.

Not that the running made any difference. I rounded the corner and careened into the open door of her room in classic cartoon fashion, complete with the screeching of my shoes on the tile. I expected to see some sort of dramatic tableau, with the role of the homicidal maniac being played by Rachel and the helpless hostage played by my comatose aunt.

Instead, I burst into the room to see Carl sitting by my aunt's bedside, quietly reading to her. He stopped midsentence and lifted his head to look at me, the barest trace of puzzlement crossing his features. I quickly scanned the rest of the room to make sure that Rachel wasn't hiding behind the door or anything else, but the curtains on all of the partitions had been pulled back, and I could see that the only people in the room were Carl, my aunt, and three definitely comatose patients.

"Busy room today," he said, setting the book down. "Is something wrong?"

Busy? "Who else has been in here?" I demanded, still panting. Damn, but I needed to get in better shape. "Has Rachel Roth been here?"

His brows drew together. "Yes. About ten minutes ago. Very strange."

"What was strange?" Ryan asked. He wasn't out of breath at all. I hated him.

Carl tilted his head. "She ran in here, much like you two, and seemed very surprised to see me. Then she told me that she was here to take Tessa downstairs for some tests. I asked her what tests, and she became very angry, then came up to me and grabbed my forearm." All of this was delivered in a calm, even recitation. "I had no idea what she was doing, but after a few seconds she let go, looking very puzzled and upset. Then she said, 'Forget it. I can go straight to the source.'" His thin shoulders lifted in a shrug.

"You didn't think to call the police or anything?" I demanded.

Carl lifted an eyebrow half a millimeter. "For what?"

He had a point. How was he to know that Rachel was a soul-sucking homicidal maniac? "She...couldn't kill you," I said, processing everything he'd said. "Must be something about how wards don't affect you."

Carl just shrugged again. "Well, she lit out of here. Would have been about ten minutes ago."

"The source?" Ryan murmured.

I let out a curse. "The portal. She's on her way to Tessa's house."

"Whatever that psycho pixie did to her before, she wants more," Ryan said, voice near a growl.

Shit. She could kill with a touch now. I didn't want to think about how much more powerful she could get. I whirled to leave, then looked back at Carl and stabbed a finger toward Tessa. "Protect her!"

He nodded gravely. "Absolutely."

A BLUE HONDA Civic was parked unevenly in Tessa's driveway when we pulled up, and I briefly wondered if Rachel had killed to get the car. On the way over, I'd called dispatch to modify the bolo on Rachel to warn officers off from attempting to apprehend her. I absolutely did *not* want anyone laying hands on her to try to arrest her.

Ryan and I approached the house, guns out and at the

ready. The window beside the front door was shattered, and the door was wide open. Obviously the aversion wards didn't have much effect on someone who was seriously determined to get in. *I hope the wards on the portal will be strong enough to keep her from getting another pixie-thing out.*

We made entry, one behind the other, covering the hallway and listening for any sounds. I motioned to the library and Ryan nodded. We could both hear movement within. *Please let those wards hold!*

I did a quick peek around the doorway, just enough to see Rachel standing in front of the portal, her back to us. The wards on the portal were still intact, to my intense relief.

"Don't move!" I commanded, covering her with my Glock. "Keep your hands where I can see them!" I stepped fully into the library, giving Ryan room to enter as well.

Rachel stiffened, but she kept her arms down by her sides. "You could tell, couldn't you?" Tension coiled in her voice, and her hands clutched into fists.

"Yes. I could feel it. I could feel what you did." I kept my gun steady on her, though my voice wasn't as stable. The memory of the gaping emptiness still left my stomach roiling. "You consumed their essence when you killed all those people."

"I didn't want to. I swear! I never wanted it to go so far." Her voice shook. "But I can't . . . can't stop. I mean, I *can*. I know I *can*. I just . . ." She trailed off, and I could see a shudder run through her.

Like she's jonesing for a fix. Shit. "How are you doing it?" I asked. I knew it was an innate ability—Rhyzkahl had revealed that much, though the thought that summoning demons and destroying essence might have similar roots was disturbing to me. But right now I was more interested in stalling until I could figure out what to do.

She let out a shaking laugh. "It used to be a little thing I could do. My grandfather died when I was five years old. They brought all of us kids into the room right after he'd drawn his last breath. Horrible to inflict that sort of experience on a kid that young anyway, but for me it was... providence."

"Because his essence had just been freed," I said.

I could hear her swallow. "Clinging by a thread to the empty shell. I could see it and feel it, and it felt so damn *good*. And when I threw myself at the essence, everyone thought I was throwing myself on his body in grief. By the time they lifted me off him, I'd pulled that essence into me." She turned her head to look at me, eyes haunted and dark. "You always remember your first time, right?"

"I've never consumed anyone's essence," I retorted. "I wouldn't know."

A tremulous smile crossed her face. "It was marvelous. Made me feel so good. I never forgot that feeling. When I got older, I did a lot of volunteer work in hospitals. But I never killed anyone. I always waited... until after it was over." She paused. "Then I got sick. Breast cancer. I was so scared and desperate, and I was seeing a client at a nursing home..."

"Why bother waiting for them to die, right?" I said.

"He was going to die anyway!" she snarled, but I could see the fear and guilt in her eyes. "It was simple enough to give him a fatal overdose of his heart medicine. And I got better. I... I figured it was like an organ donation. He died just a bit early, and my cancer was gone."

"But you kept doing pro bono work there," I countered. *That's it, keep talking.* I knew from experience that most people *wanted* to confess, wanted to tell someone, anyone, what they'd done. I was more than happy to oblige her. Maybe it would give me enough time to figure out a plan. "How many others have died before their time?"

"Only a few." Her voice was barely above a whisper. "Only ... when I couldn't bear the hunger anymore."

"But then you killed Brian," Ryan said, voice a growl.

She straightened her shoulders and shifted slowly to face us, keeping her hands where we could see them and her eyes on our guns. "Yes, but only because my dear departed husband was a fucking moron and a philandering asshole." The steel was back in her voice. This wasn't the addict speaking now. This was the scorned and vengeful wife. "I was willing to tolerate his indiscretions to a point, because being married to a judge was good for my career. But then he got stupid and killed Carol. He was screwing his *daughter-in-law*." Her voice dripped with disgust, and I had a hard time not sharing her sentiment toward Harris Roth. "Then he called Davis in a panic—"

"But you were with Davis, having a little revenge affair of your own," Ryan said.

"It was only fair," she said, shrugging. "But Davis turned out to be a pathetic whiner. Threatened to go to the police. Moron."

"But he'd told his wife everything," I pointed out.

"Another moron," she said with a derisive sneer. "You know what she wanted from me? She wanted to come back to Beaulac as if nothing had happened. Wanted me to make sure she'd still be 'accepted.' Useless bitch. She could have taken me down with one phone call, but she didn't have the balls."

I swallowed back a knot of anger. "But why kill Brian?"

I demanded. "He never hurt anyone. You couldn't figure out some other way to cover up Carol's death?"

Rachel's lip curled. "I wanted Harris to *suffer*. I knew that would kill him." Then her expression shifted to a sad and haunted smile. "Besides, Brian wouldn't have wanted to live anyway if he'd found out what they'd done."

"You have a healthy dose of crazy going on in there, lady," Ryan said.

The look she shot him was pure and glittering hate. "I'm not crazy. I did what I had to do. But..." She took a deep breath as if to steady herself. "But I didn't realize how much *better* it was to be right there at the very instant the essence was released, especially when it was...violent. None of it escaped me. I could take nearly all of it. God almighty, but it felt so good." Her eyes closed in remembered bliss. "I was so strong, felt so perfect. Then when Davis told me he was going to the police—"

"You took care of him too," I finished for her. "As well as the Galloways, when they were stupid enough to try to blackmail your husband."

She gave a small shrug. "That *was* pretty stupid of them."

"And Ron Burnside," Ryan said quietly, "the public defender who was going to run against Harris Roth. Did you take care of him too?"

Another shrug. "People die after surgery all the time. Such a tragedy." But I could see the satisfaction in her eyes.

My thoughts whirled in barely ordered chaos. *How are we going to stop her? Is there some way to reverse it? Strip her of the ability? We can't exactly stick her in handcuffs and put her in jail.*

"Why did you come here?" I asked. I was pretty sure I

knew the answer, but at this point I needed to get some hint or clue of what to do.

She shifted her gaze to me. "Your aunt. There was nothing there, but she was still alive. I knew she'd been injured during the incident with the Symbol Man, so I decided to find out what was so special about her." She tilted her head. "I drove past this house every day for two weeks, never quite able to get my nerve up to try to get in and look around."

The aversions and protections at work, I thought. *The good ones.*

"And then one day I just . . . felt like trying."

Yeah, that would have been when I had the damn things taken down. Idiot.

"Breaking in was fairly simple, especially since there was already a broken window in the back. I came in here and . . . there was something—a little Tinker Bell thing. It attacked me and stung me, but then I grabbed it." She shook her head. "I don't really remember what happened, but . . . God almighty, it was like consuming a dozen lives at once. I think I passed out . . . but when I came to, I was different. Stronger." Her voice dropped to a whisper. "Hungrier." A shudder racked her, and I could see a sheen of sweat on her forehead. "I don't want to have to kill anyone else. I swear. But I don't know how much longer I can control this." She flicked a glance at the warded portal. "It came out of that corner. I remember that. I figure if I can find another one of those things, then that could hold me for a while. Maybe I could just feed on those and not have to kill anyone else. But nothing's coming out." The look she gave me was one of desperate pleading. "You have to help me get another one of those things out. Please!"

I shook my head slowly. "Rachel, I can't do that. It would only make things worse. I'm sorry."

Her hands shook as she clenched and unclenched them. "No, you're not sorry. You *want* me to starve to death."

Would that work? Could she be weaned from this sort of addiction? "Let me figure out another way to help you."

"No! I don't have time for you to figure something out!" She licked dry lips. "If you won't help me, then I'll have to . . . to do something else. What? You think you can stop me?" She gave a laugh tinged with hysteria. "You can't shoot me."

"And what makes you say that?" Ryan asked calmly.

"You would shoot the poor distraught wife of a recently deceased judge, who came to see you only to find out more about her husband's crimes?" Her eyes glittered. "You don't have any proof that I killed anyone!" She took a step toward us.

"I don't fucking care," I snarled. "Take another step and I *will* shoot you." Better to risk losing my career than let her touch me.

She hesitated a second, breathing harshly, then shrugged. "Well, let's see how that goes then, shall we?" she said cryptically. I was still trying to figure out what she meant when she leaped toward us, hands outstretched.

I fired at the same time that Ryan did, my finger tightening spasmodically on the trigger. Spots of blood bloomed on the front of her shirt, but unlike in the movies, the shots didn't throw her dramatically across the room. Rachel stumbled forward as Ryan backed to the wall, and she grabbed his gun hand even as he pumped another round into her chest.

Ryan screamed—a sound I hoped to never hear again.

"Shoot me again and he dies!" Rachel rasped, clutching at Ryan's hand as he dropped his gun and went to his knees, his eyes wide and agony spasming across his face.

"No! Stop!" I shouted, fear for Ryan slamming through me. "Don't pull any more from him! I'll help you, I swear."

Her breath came raggedly, and she seized his hair with her other hand. "Drop your gun!" she ordered. Blood pumped from several places in her torso, but even as I watched I could see the blood flow slow and then—grotesquely—the holes close. Ryan shuddered, face graying, and I realized with horror that she'd pulled from him and somehow used his essence, his natural potency, to heal herself.

"Stop pulling from him!" I yelled again.

"Drop your gun," she ordered, "or I'll suck him dry!"

If I shoot her in the head, would that stop her? The thought flashed through my mind and I dismissed it just as quickly. I was several feet away from her, she was using Ryan as a shield, and while I was a decent enough marksman, I didn't trust my skill enough to be certain I wouldn't shoot Ryan in the head instead.

I slowly lowered the gun. "If you swear not to kill him or me, I'll . . . open another portal so you can get more of those pixie-things."

Her eyes narrowed in distrust. "How?"

"I have the ability to open a portal between this world and another. So did my aunt."

Her lips pulled back from her teeth. "Then do it!"

"I can't work with this one," I lied. "I have to create a new one. Swear you won't hurt either of us, and I'll open another one, just for you."

"He's really strong," she said, voice barely above a whisper. Her hand tightened on Ryan's arm and he gasped in pain. She actually licked her lips. "Never tasted anything like him before."

I could feel Ryan's essence pulsing erratically. "I can't open this portal," I said quickly, "but I can create another one. Up in the attic. It would take me only a moment... and it's much bigger and stronger." I dropped my voice. "But, if you kill him, I swear to you that I will call powers that you cannot even begin to comprehend, and you will be well and truly *fucked*."

Distrust, fear, and hunger flickered in her eyes, but she jerked her head in a nod. "Lead the way," she snapped, pulling Ryan to his feet. His breath rasped harshly, and his face was ashen. But he met my eyes and gave me a faint shake of his head. He thought I was giving in to her. Or maybe he suspected what I was planning to do.

"Try anything stupid and your boyfriend's a goner," she reminded me unnecessarily.

"He's not my damn boyfriend," I muttered as I turned and started down the hall toward the staircase. She followed, leading Ryan with the grip on his arm and his hair. He looked like shit, but there was still a murderous look in his eyes.

I opened the door to the attic and flipped on the lights. It was cool, bordering on cold, thanks to the AC vent that I'd left open. But more important, I had a diagram already sketched out, and the storage diagram beside it still brimmed with the potency I'd been siphoning into it for the past day.

Rachel exhaled softly as she entered the attic. "This is like that thing downstairs? It doesn't look the same at all."

I stepped to the edge of the diagram and picked up a

piece of chalk, then turned to look at her. "You're right. But comparing the portal downstairs to this one is like comparing a toy car to a Ferrari. You'll have access to much more power than you could ever get with the other." *Holy shit, I hope I don't fuck this up.* She had to be stopped, but I also wasn't about to let her loose to rampage through the demon realm.

But I knew she *could* be destroyed. Rhyzkahl had told me that much. I just didn't know how.

Her eyes nearly glowed with hunger as she looked upon the diagram.

"Kara . . . no, you can't do this," Ryan rasped, then he hissed in pain as Rachel squeezed her hand on his arm.

"Oh, yes, she can," Rachel replied with a low laugh. "Yes, this will do very nicely. Go ahead, do whatever you need to." She lifted her chin imperiously to me.

I will. "Stand back and don't touch any part of the diagram," I told her. "This will take a couple of minutes."

"Just get it done."

I didn't look at Ryan again. I wasn't sure if he knew exactly what I was planning to do, but I didn't want to see his reaction when he figured it out. I quickly lit the candles, sketched the needed changes into the sigils, then positioned myself at the edge of the diagram so that Rachel and Ryan were to my right. I lifted my arms and began the low chant, weaving the power into the summoning and allowing myself a brief twinge of pride at my ability to manipulate the stored potency. The runes and wards flared to life as I quickly worked through the required forms. I was taking some shortcuts, but it wouldn't matter with this summoning.

I knew I would be safe, especially with the offering I had ready.

The portal widened from a slit to a glowing vortex, and I could hear Rachel's triumphant laugh. *You won't be laughing for long, bitch.*

I spoke the demon's name, and a heartbeat later the portal went dark, the candles blowing out from a nonexistent wind.

"What happened?" I heard Rachel complaining. "Is it open? Is it done?"

My heart thudded painfully in my chest. I could sense *him* in the circle. I could hear Ryan's breath hissing through his teeth. He knew who I'd summoned. I lowered myself to one knee and bowed my head, clutching my hands into fists to keep them from shaking.

Blue light flared. Rachel gasped, and I knew I had mere heartbeats before she figured out that I'd duped her.

"My lord Rhyzkahl," I said, voice trembling despite my best effort to appear strong. "Save Ryan Kristoff and stop Rachel Roth, and I will serve you as your summoner."

33

I EXPECTED TO HEAR A SHOUT OF PROTEST FROM RYAN or some sort of noise from Rachel, but there was nothing but silence. After several heartbeats I lifted my head. Rhyzkahl stood before me, arms folded across his chest, face impassive. I risked a quick glance around, shocked to see a familiar white-marble hall and raised dais with the Mark of Rhyzkahl carved into it—a symbol that I knew all too well. I blinked in confusion and then looked back to the lord.

"No, we are not in my realm," he said, answering my unspoken question, voice low but thick with power. "This is merely an illusion that grants us time and privacy so that we can seal the terms properly." Now I understood. He hadn't actually frozen time or transported me elsewhere. This was no doubt like the dream sendings, where he manipulated the appearance of reality. And since this was no small thing that I was offering, Rhyzkahl obviously wanted to be absolutely certain that the agreement was a solid one.

I took a shaky breath, heart thudding. "The woman, Rachel Roth, is the creature I told you about. She can consume essence, and...and she's getting stronger. Much stronger. I think she consumed a *hriss* from the"—I hesitated, unsure whether to mention the portal, then realized that it was a bit late for that sort of worry at this point— "from the portal in my aunt's library." I thought I could see his eyes narrow, but I couldn't be sure. I swallowed harshly and forced myself to continue. "She came at us and we both shot her, but she got hold of Ryan and healed herself and is holding him hostage—sucking his essence out." Sweat stung my armpits despite the chill in the air. "She has killed a lot of people, and I don't know how to stop her, and—"

"And this creature you know as Ryan Kristoff is important to you," Rhyzkahl finished for me.

I struggled to work moisture into my mouth. I had the horrible feeling that I was about to burst into tears, which was really the last thing I needed to do when attempting to establish terms with a demonic lord. And, of course, the more I struggled to keep myself from thinking about crying, the more tears stung the backs of my eyelids.

"Yes, my lord. Wh-what manner of service would you have me offer you in exchange for your aid that would fulfill the bounds of honor?" Damn it, I *was* crying now. I could feel the treacherous tears snaking their way down my cheeks, and it took everything I had not to wipe them away.

"Stand up, Kara. Kneeling does not suit you."

I got awkwardly to my feet and then went ahead and swiped at the tears with the back of my hand. Rhyzkahl turned away from me and took the two steps to his throne, seating himself in a languorous manner. "This matter is more complicated than you can know," he said, looking thoughtful.

"Because of Ryan, right? He's not just an FBI agent?"

He gave no indication of denial or affirmation. "It is a complex matter. It is not so simple for me to interfere."

"Why?" I persisted. "Does someone want him dead? Is that why that *kzak* was pushed through the portal? To get him?"

His crystal-blue gaze speared me. "When did you encounter a *kzak*?"

"A week ago, I think. Was it after him?" *Or me?* I added silently.

His expression remained inscrutable. "I cannot answer that."

I scowled. I was definitely over the wanting-to-cry part. Now I was into the annoyed-at-being-in-the-dark part. "Can't or won't?"

"Let us get back to the matter at hand, shall we?" he said. He stood and strode to me, then cupped my chin in his hand and tilted it up so he could look down into my face. "You wish to have the threat this woman poses eliminated, and you wish Ryan Kristoff to be spared from this threat."

"Yes." I couldn't really nod with his hand under my chin.

"Yet you also wish to protect your world, your realm, from the chance that an arcane creature of my power would despoil it for his own gain."

"Yes."

He released my chin and took a step back, to my relief. He was a lot taller, and I was getting a crick in my neck. He clasped his hands behind his back and regarded me, a thoughtful expression on his face. "If this creature consumes Ryan Kristoff, there is little doubt that she would proceed to then destroy you." It didn't sound as if he was hoping for any sort of response, more as if he was working out a problem. I wished I had a clue as to what the problem was. I kept silent and waited for him to get to the damn point.

He was silent for several more heartbeats. "I have an interest in you and would prefer that you were not harmed by this creature." Then he nodded, as if satisfied with some internal debate. "You will summon me to your world no less than once every turning of the moon around your earth for the next three of your world's years. Upon being summoned, I will remain no longer than half of one day, unless additional terms are set at the time of the summoning. During that time in your world, I will do nothing with the intent of causing you harm or that acts against your own code of honor without your leave."

I quickly ran through what he'd said. Once a month for the next three years, for no more than half a day. "My code of honor includes obeying the judicial laws that apply to me. I would have you obey them to the same degree, unless I indicate otherwise."

He inclined his head. "Agreed. In return, I will remove the threat that this woman poses to you and to those you hold dear." I thought his lip curled in derision, but if so the expression was a brief one.

"And you will also agree," I said, straightening my shoulders, "on all subsequent summonings of your person, to answer no less than three questions that I ask of you, to the best of your ability."

A faint smile curved the corner of his mouth, as if

pleased at my temerity to bend the negotiation to my favor, even if only by a few millimeters. "One question."

"Two."

"Done. These are terms that I can and will abide by."

I let my breath out. "These are terms that I can and will abide by," I echoed. And, to my relief, they were.

"Give me your hand, Kara."

I extended my right hand, but he shook his head and reached for my left, turning it palm up. A knife abruptly appeared in his hand, a wicked and evil-looking artifact, with a blade that shimmered with an oily blue sheen and a handle covered in spikes that thrust between his fingers as he gripped it. The thought flashed through me that a careless grasp on that knife would be a painful experience. A dark-blue jewel capped the pommel with a dull light that seemed to flicker sluggishly from its depths.

A spasm of abject terror shot through me at the sight of the knife, for no reason that I could name. But before I could yank my hand back, Rhyzkahl tightened his hold and pulled my arm straight, then slid the knife across my forearm, perfectly following the thin scar on my arm from where I'd cut my own flesh to summon Kehlirik. A hideous wave of cold nausea swept through me at the touch of the blade, but it was gone as soon as the metal was no longer in contact with my flesh. I watched the blood well up from the shallow slice, then looked up at Rhyzkahl in time to see him make a similar slice on his own forearm. He took a step closer to me and pressed the two slices together. I expected to feel something—a shock or burning or something bizarre as the blood mingled—but all I could feel was the powerful aura of him that surrounded us both.

"And now the oath is bound in blood." He smiled and

kissed me—a light and strangely chaste kiss, especially compared to some of the deep and throbbing and heat-filled kisses he had laid on me before.

"I need to know something," I said after he stepped back. "I mean ... could you answer two questions for me now?"

He inclined his head ever so slightly in acquiescence.

"You said that the link you had with my dreams was broken when I died ... but ... do you still have *any* sort of link to me?"

For an instant I had the impression he wanted to laugh, but all he did was smile. "Perceptive and clever. In those last seconds before you perished, I forged a new and different link—one that I knew would survive your death."

The fucker. He hadn't lied to me before, but he sure hadn't told me the whole truth. But at least now I knew.

"Your second question?" he prompted. I had a feeling he knew what I was going to ask. I wasn't so sure I wanted to know the answer, but I knew I *needed* to know.

"What is a *kiraknikahl*?" I asked, voice cracking.

The demon's mouth curved in a hard smile. "A *kiraknikahl* is an oath-breaker."

A heartbeat later his throne room was gone and we were back in the attic, leaving me no chance to process the meaning of his answer. The knife was still in Rhyzkahl's hand, and even as I registered the change in the surroundings, he turned and seized Rachel, yanking her away from Ryan in a swift and fluid move. Before she could do more than widen her eyes in shock, Rhyzkahl had plunged the knife into Rachel's chest, directly into her heart.

She screamed and clutched at the knife, clawing at Rhyzkahl's hands as he held it buried to the evil hilt in her chest. Ryan sagged heavily to his knees, then looked up at

Rachel and Rhyzkahl. His eyes rested on the knife, widening in horror as he scrabbled weakly back, gaze locked on the blade.

Rachel screamed again—a sound a thousand times worse than the scream Ryan had made when she'd begun to steal his essence. Rhyzkahl slipped an arm around her waist, pulling her close to him in what could have been a loving embrace except for the knife he held buried in her chest. I could feel a malevolent coiling of potency filling the room, and I found myself drawing back from the two of them along with Ryan, not stopping until we were both up against the wall of the attic.

"No," I heard Ryan moan. "No. Not that." I tore my gaze away from Rhyzkahl to look at Ryan. A look of indescribable grief and horror filled his eyes. He suddenly turned to look at me, then his gaze dropped to my forearm, and, if anything, the grief and horror increased. "Kara. Kara, what did you *do*?"

I looked down at my forearm, expecting to see the line of blood, but instead I saw a swirl of potency where the cut had been. In the span of three heartbeats, the swirl coalesced to form an intricate mark on the inside of my forearm, as if tattooed there by arcane power. I knew the symbol well. The Mark of Rhyzkahl. I turned away from Ryan. I didn't need to hear his condemnation. "I did what I had to do."

The dark-blue gem in the knife's pommel suddenly flared, and Rachel sagged in Rhyzkahl's arms. He released her and stepped back, dropping her like a sack of flour. She collapsed into a heap, then, as we watched, her body shriveled and began to disintegrate until, a few heartbeats later, nothing remained but dust and clothing.

I could feel myself taking shallow gasps of breath. *Like*

a fucking vampire in sunlight. Oddly appropriate, though, I thought, in a corner of my mind that was trying to focus on something, anything, to keep from remembering the sound of that last tortured scream.

Rhyzkahl turned to me. He lifted the wicked knife in a mock salute, inclining his head to me. "As agreed," he said, with no elaboration, glancing briefly to Ryan and then back to me. I didn't need him to elaborate. He was informing me that he'd fulfilled this portion of the agreement.

I gulped and inclined my head to him. "As agreed," I echoed hoarsely.

He smiled brilliantly, then was gone.

Ryan slowly got to his feet, eyes on the tumbled pile of dust and clothing that was all that remained of Rachel Roth. I watched him warily for about a dozen heartbeats, but he made no move to turn to me or look at me.

"Are you all right?" I asked. He did look better. Whatever essence Rachel had drained from him had apparently gone back to him when Rhyzkahl destroyed her.

He nodded once without looking at me—a short, quick motion, the barest amount of necessary movement to give the required answer.

My throat tightened, and a feeling like cold lead settled into my stomach. A part of me had expected this sort of reaction, but that didn't make it feel any better. *He's alive. I've probably lost him, but at least he's alive.*

Lost him? I'd never had him. And now it was too late.

I wanted to say something else, but then I decided that I really didn't. I turned and headed out of the attic and down the stairs, all the time hoping to hear him call out to me, but when I reached the door there was still nothing but a calm ticking silence in the house.

I exited into dusky twilight in time to see a black Crown Victoria screech into the driveway behind Ryan's car. Zack ran toward the steps, stopping in his tracks when he saw me.

"Kara, I just heard the bolo—" He stopped, eyes on my forearm, face paling. I crossed my arms over my chest.

"Ryan's inside. He's fine—now. Rachel's been taken care of. I'm going home." I walked past him to my car, not looking back.

"Kara . . . ?" He sounded bewildered.

"Ryan's *fine*. I'm going *home*!" I repeated through clenched teeth, then I climbed into my car, slammed the door, and sped off.

34

IT TOOK SEVERAL DAYS TO CLEAN UP THE LOOSE ENDS
and complete the paperwork, but by the middle of the following week the cases were squared away. Carol Roth's
death had been ruled a negligent homicide, with Harris
Roth listed as the primary suspect. Arrest warrants had
been issued for Rachel Roth for the murders of Brian Roth
and Davis Sharp. I'd managed to scrape together enough
probable cause for warrants, though I knew there would
be no way to prove her guilt in court. It didn't matter. It
was all for the paper trail. It wasn't as if Rachel would ever
be found.

I didn't see Ryan in all that time. I'd driven by my aunt's
house the morning after the confrontation with Rachel,
prepared to keep driving if his car or Zack's car was there,
but the driveway was empty. And when I checked the
house, I found that everything had been cleaned and
locked up.

After that I went to the station and had a talk with my

sergeant. I started it out by asking him how much he wanted to know.

Sergeant Cory Crawford looked at me steadily and said, "Tell me whatever it is I need to know."

It worked for both of us.

For the official story, Sarge seemed content with one that ended up being close to the truth—minus the bit about Rachel sucking people's souls out. Harris screwed around, accidentally killed one of his paramours—who happened to be his daughter-in-law—and Rachel tried to cover it up by killing Brian and staging it as a suicide. Another loose end was tied up when the Roth house was searched and a dark blue pickup with damage to the right front bumper was found in the garage.

Sarge was also able to inform me that Judge Roth had been the one who'd asked to have me replaced with Pellini for the Brian and Carol Roth murders. "He probably knew that Pellini's a lazy fuck," he'd confided, "and figured there'd be less chance of the truth being discovered."

By the following Friday, the world in general had settled into something resembling normalcy. No one made any comment about the mark on my arm. Without othersight, the mark looked like a very faint, slightly shimmery henna marking, essentially invisible unless you knew it was there. I'd received some quiet congratulations from my rank on my handling of the various cases, but then it was as if they could sense that I didn't want to hear anything more about it, and the matter was left alone.

I put the last of the paperwork in my captain's box, more than glad to have it all done and behind me. I was the last one in the office; everyone else had been gone for hours. I locked the door to the silent bureau, then headed home—mostly because I couldn't think of anywhere else to go.

When I pulled into my driveway, Ryan's car was in front of my house. I parked my car next to his, a tired sensation of dread settling in my stomach. I wasn't in the mood for any sort of explanation, or justification, or confrontation.

I don't fucking care what he thinks at this point, I decided. Strangely, I almost believed it.

He wasn't in his car, but when I looked around I saw him sitting on the steps of my porch. I'd forgotten to turn the light on before I left, so he was almost hidden in the shadows.

I tugged the strap of my bag over my shoulder and walked up the steps. I was more than prepared to walk right past him if he started anything unpleasant.

"Kara, I need to talk to you," he said, voice low and rough.

I continued to the door and set my bag down, then flicked on the porch light switch. Ryan stood and came up the stairs to me, light from the bulb over the door catching the reddish glints in his hair. He opened his mouth to say something, then closed it, frowning. I started to ask him what he was going to say, but he spoke first.

"Kara, I . . ." He trailed off. I looked at him expectantly, trying not to prompt him in impatience and bracing myself for any number of things that he could be preparing to say.

"I appreciate you," he finally said, voice quiet.

My stomach did an odd flip and I got a lump in my throat. I'd had a boyfriend once tell me he loved me, and my only emotional reaction had been sort of a mental wince. This simple admission from Ryan made me feel a thousand times more special.

"Thanks." I didn't really know what else to say. Come to think of it, there wasn't much else that needed to be said, on either side. He'd pretty much nailed it with those three words—had taken care of all the fears and worry that I'd been nursing throughout the past several days. The relief that I hadn't saved him just to lose him was almost wrenching.

He exhaled softly, as if he was echoing my relief. "Now, give me your damn keys."

I blinked at him, then warily handed him my keys.

He took them from me and quickly unlocked the front door, then picked my bag up, grabbed my wrist with his other hand, and pulled me inside.

"Ryan, what the hell do you think you're doing?"

He kicked the front door closed and dropped my bag on the floor. Then he seized me by my shoulders so that I was facing him. At this point I was so stunned by his bizarre behavior that all I could do was stare at him.

"Kara Gillian, Summoner of Demons," Ryan said in a low but intense voice.

"Yeah, that would be me," I said with a scowl. "What the fuck is going on?"

"You're on the edge, foolish woman. You're spent and strained, and you look like you're on the verge of tears every other minute."

"Well, the past couple of months have sucked *major ass*, y'know?" I said, tears actually springing to my eyes. Then, before I even realized what was happening, I was bawling. Ryan pulled me close, wrapping an arm around me and holding my head against his chest. He didn't speak, didn't murmur anything comforting. All he did was hold me.

After a few minutes of me sobbing into his shirt, he shifted and lifted me in his arms, cradling my head against his shoulder as he walked to my bedroom. I'd never been carried like that before, the way the hero carries the damsel, and it made me cry harder. It wasn't a pretty crying either—it was full-body racking sobs, with a horribly snotty nose and my eyes swelling up. But Ryan just held me close, silent and *there*. He took me into the bedroom and laid me on the bed, shifting position smoothly to lie down beside me, pushing me to my side and wrapping his arms around me again from behind.

I cried like that, all wrapped up in him, until I fell asleep.

WHEN I WOKE up, I was alone in bed. I felt a brief stab of loss but, at the same time, relief. And then, when I came out to the kitchen and found a box of chocolate donuts on the table, I was even able to laugh.

My cell phone rang while I was making coffee to go with the donuts. I reached over and grabbed it, noting absently that it wasn't the usual ring tone.

"This is Kara Gillian," I said as I measured out the grounds.

"Ms. Gillian, this is Rebecca Stanford at Nord du Lac Neuro. Your aunt has woken up and she's asking for you."

I felt frozen in time for a thousand heartbeats, though it was surely far less. *It worked. She's back.* Finally a breathless laugh escaped me. "That's . . . amazing."

The other woman hesitated. "Um, yes. Though I do

want to prepare you; she may not be quite what you expect."

"What do you mean?"

"Sometimes after long comas, it takes a little while for the brain to work properly again. Patients will say things that don't seem to make much sense, and it can be quite shocking if you're not expecting it."

"What sort of things is she saying?"

I heard the other woman sigh. "She said, 'Tell my niece that if she thinks I won't flay her hide for serving a demonic lord, she's seriously deluded.'"

I burst out laughing. Tessa was definitely back.